WITCHING AFTER FORTY

VOLUME ONE

LIA DAVIS

L.A. BORUFF

Witching After Forty, Volume One

© Copyright 2020 Lia Davis & L.A. Boruff

Published by Davis Raynes Publishing

PO Box 224

Middleburg, FL 32050

DavisRaynesPublishing.com

Cover by Glowing Moon Designs

Formatting by Glowing Moon Designs

DavisRaynesPublishing.com

DEDICATION

Dedicated to Claire and Amanda. Our early morning heroes.

WITCHING AFTER FORTY SERIES

Witching After Forty follows the misadventures of Ava Harper – a forty-something necromancer with a light witchy side that you wouldn't expect from someone who can raise the dead. Join Ava as she learns how to start over after losing the love of her life, in this new paranormal women's fiction series with a touch of cozy mystery, magic, and a whole lot of mayhem.

A Ghoulish Midlife
Cookies for Satan (Christmas novella)
I'm With Cupid (Valentine novella)
A Cursed Midlife
Birthday Blunder (Olivia Novella)
A Girlfriend For Mr. Snoozerton (Novella)
A Haunting Midlife
An Animated Midlife
Feary Odd-Mother (Novella)
A Killer Midlife
A Grave Midlife

A Powerful Midlife (coming soon)
A Wedded Midlife (coming soon)
More to come

A GHOULISH MIDLIFE

WITCHING AFTER FORTY, BOOK ONE

CHAPTER ONE

The door of my Hyundai sedan closed far too softly. I glared at it, certain it was mocking me. Older car doors slammed much more satisfactorily. They were heavier and the extra weight echoed across the parking lot. Newer models, like my cobalt blue Dia here, weren't all about letting people know I had arrived. It was disappointing, really.

What else was I to expect? Not much was the same anymore. Even phones were less satisfying these days. Whoever heard about slamming a cell phone down in somebody's ear? Oh, sure, I could slam it, but then I'd have to buy a new phone.

Pfft. Whatever.

I was tempted to open the door and try again—really slam it, put some elbow grease into it. After nine hours on the road with only one short bathroom break, I'd seen enough of the inside of that car to last me a long time. Not to mention driving alone was making me talk to myself, and I wasn't that funny.

Stretching with my hands on my lower back, I scanned the

grocery store parking lot. There were exactly three cars, and the building was much, much smaller than I remembered. That was how things were when remembered from the perspective of youth, though. Everything seemed large during childhood. Although, it could've been a result of living for so long in a large city where the buildings were giant compared to that of a small town.

The last time I'd been in this particular small town was just last year for my Aunt Winnie's funeral. Why had so many of the people I loved died on me in the last five years? First Clay, then my favorite Aunt—two didn't seem like so much until the grief layered in.

With a heavy soul, I'd made the trip on my own then, too. I'd hated traveling without my husband, but he was gone now. A lump formed in my throat. I swallowed it and took a deep breath. It'd been five years since I lost the love of my life. Well, the first love of my life. The second had left me several weeks ago for a dorm, parties, and medical books.

Thinking of the little devil, I pulled out my phone and sent him a text. Wallie had insisted I message him the moment I arrived in Shipton Harbor. Nothing like having an overprotective son watching over me. Even if he was watching from Harvard University. I should have never taught him how to scry or that locating spell. I would never have any peace now.

Me: **I made it alive. I think. Unless I died and my ghost drove the rest of the way.**

Wallie: **Your ghost can text? That's impressive. Will you just haunt Aunt Winnie's house for the rest of eternity?**

Me: **That's the plan.**

Wallie: **Cool. I'll make sure to visit on holidays. If med school kills me, I'll be moving in.**

I laughed and replied: **Oh, no way. You find your own magical house to haunt.**

Wallie: **LOL. Love you.**

Me: **Love you too. I'll call you later.**

AFTER LOCKING the screen on my cell, I slipped it into my pocket and took another cleansing breath. The fresh scent of the ocean filled me. That was when I noticed the crisp, cool air that had wrapped around me like an old friend. I never used to like the cold, but for the last couple of years, I'd craved it. Hello, early hot flashes.

With a sigh, I headed inside the store, wishing Clay were walking beside me. I grabbed the cart while I organized my grocery list in my mind. Just as we had done once a week, every week, during our twenty years of marriage. Another ache formed in my chest, tightening it. I closed my eyes briefly and pushed away from the loneliness. Clay would've kicked my ass if he knew I was still grieving him this strongly. We'd promised each other long ago that if one survived the other, we wouldn't mourn. We would find the strength to move on and learn to live again.

I'd only agreed to the crazy-ass pact because I genuinely believed we'd die within months of each other at the ripe old age of one hundred and two. It never occurred to me we'd part ways at thirty-eight.

But a promise was a promise. I would try to keep it. That was why I'd returned to Shipton Harbor, to fix up the old house and put it on the market—hopefully, a quick sale. Then, I could go back home and decide what to do from there.

Here I was, but before I went to my family home, I needed a few things. The house was devoid of all foodstuffs, so I had to get enough to tide me over until I figured out how long I'd be in town, which depended on how much work the old Victorian needed.

There was no telling what sort of condition it would be in. After all, it'd been empty for a year with no magic to keep it alive. Aunt Winnie's magic had kept the beautiful three-story gothic building in tip-top shape. It also gave the house a personality that I loved. Without Winnie, it would be cold and normal. Normal was so overrated. And boring.

As I grabbed a buggy and headed around the produce department, picking up enough of my favorites for just a couple of days, I wished Aunt Winnie had left me enough money with the house to have a caretaker oversee the property. Instead, it had been boarded up for a year.

Regular houses didn't do well sitting empty. Magical houses usually died without a witch nourishing them.

As I looked at the apples, I fought my sadness. It could've been a lot worse. At least I still had my baby, Wallie. I focused on the mission—sell the house and make enough money to get back to what was left of my life. To the home my son grew up in. To Philadelphia.

That didn't mean it would be easy to sell the home that had been in my family for a couple of hundred years. If I was correct, the house had been built before the town even officially *became* a town. I'd never paid too much attention to the history of it or anything. Maybe I should've.

"Ava? Ava Howe?"

Cringing, I closed my eyes briefly and prayed to the goddess to give me strength. I knew that voice. It belonged to the absolute last person I wanted to run into tonight, or ever. I was grimy from the long trip, not to mention exhausted. I needed a sandwich and an enormous glass of wine. Maybe a whole bottle. Definitely, I'd deserve a bottle after facing my number one high school nemesis.

Turning, I plastered my best PTA-mom smile on my face. "Olivia Lockhart." I flipped my long brown hair over my shoulder and prayed I'd be able to extract myself as soon as possible, but high school was a long time ago. We were adults now. It would be fine.

"It's Lockhart-Thompson now." With one hand on the top of a little boy's blond head, she held out her other hand to show me a big ring. Geez, a huge ring.

Of course, I'd known she'd married Sam Thompson about five years before, just in time to have their son, Little Sammie.

Sam and I had been best friends for as long as I could remember, even after I moved away. We kept in touch.

"Of course. I'm not used to you with that name, though I'm thrilled my Sam has found the love of his life." I sincerely was happy for him. He and Olivia hadn't been friends in high school, and then afterward, Olivia had married and divorced. After her divorce, she and Sam ran into one another when Olivia was rear-ended, and Sam picked up the call.

He'd fallen hard. I'd been a bit dismayed that my best friend was in love with the biggest busybody Shipton Harbor High had ever seen, but who was I to pooh-pooh on his happiness?

Olivia, however, damn well knew my last name. I'd just seen her a year ago at Aunt Winnie's funeral. "I'm Ava Harper now. For the last twenty-odd years." I might've been widowed, but I'd kept Clay's name. I'd kept anything that had reminded me of him, even though he'd died five years ago. Right after Sam and Olivia got together, actually. That was a hard and dark time for me, but I somehow managed to be happy for my BFF. In return, Sam listened to me through the tears and then the anger of grief.

Olivia put her hand over mine on the handle of my cart. Her sympathy seeped into my hand, and to my surprise, it felt genuine. That was new. The last time we spoke, Olivia had wanted to burn me at the stake, or on a cross. Then again, that was right after she'd found out I was a witch.

She squeezed my hand. "Sam told me about your husband. I'm so sorry for your loss."

She'd said all this with less sincerity last year at the funeral. I ducked my head and gave the rote answer, the same one I'd given any time I went out in public and ran into someone who knew me before my world fell apart. "Thank you. It's been incredibly difficult."

"I can't imagine losing my Sam, but it's been five years now, hasn't it?" She raised her eyebrows. "Are you about ready to start playing the field again?"

The smile on my face froze. I extracted my hand from under hers and straightened my spine. "I'm here to sell the old homeplace and then get back to Philly. That's all."

Olivia's face fell again. "Oh, I hate that you're going to sell that beautiful old house. How long has it been in your family?"

Why were we having this conversation? Oh, right because Olivia was a busybody. Good to know some things never changed. Yay, me. Not.

"I was trying to figure that out in my head. When I find the records, I'll let you know." I winked at her and pushed my cart forward a few feet, but she didn't get the hint. So help me, if she didn't leave, I wouldn't be held responsible for my actions. How mad would Sam be if I turned his wife into a squirrel? I'm sure it would be worth the risk. Maybe. I shelved the thought for later. I didn't want to do it in front of Little Sammie, anyway.

"Well, I insist you come to have dinner with Sam and me very soon."

I kept going. "That sounds lovely, you can have Sam call me about it." I intentionally didn't invite Olivia to give me a call. I wasn't here to make friends, and I sure didn't trust Olivia. "I've got to run now."

After seeing Olivia and having to talk about Clay, I wanted to get the hell out of there. I *had* been feeling like I was ready to think about life after being widowed, but that wasn't at all something I wanted to discuss with Olivia Lockhart or anyone else from my childhood life in Shipton Harbor.

I sped around the store after that, snatching up anything I could quickly think of that I'd need for the next twenty-four hours or so. If I didn't remember it now, I'd figure out how to live without it.

The drive to the house took a good fifteen minutes. Shipton Harbor was a small town, but the house wasn't *in* the town. It was on a cliff overlooking the ocean on the outer edges of the city limits.

At the moment, that ocean was calm with medium-ish waves breaking. The scent of saltwater, sand, and sunshine swirled around me, welcoming me home. It was the only thing I missed about Shipton Harbor. Well, that and Winnie.

Maybe Sam.

Definitely not Olivia.

This beautiful, old, gothic Victorian stood tall against the blue sky with puffy white clouds. With the lights off—not because the electricity was cut off, but because no one was there—it looked sad and, well, dark. I stood beside my car and stared at the home I grew up in. So many emotions churned inside me. A voice from deep inside my mind said to keep the old place, and start a new life.

I wasn't sure I wanted to start over. I was forty-three for crying out loud. Where would I even begin?

Bracing myself, I grabbed my grocery bags and fished the house key out of my pocket. This was the big moment to find out how bad the house was inside. It'd been empty for the last year, since right after Aunt Winnie's funeral. I only had it and the water turned back on a few days ago, so at least I would have that. Probably.

My phone jingled my son's text tone in my pocket. My baby was keeping tabs on me. I couldn't help but smile. He was the one who came with me to Shipton Harbor and cleaned out the house last year. The perishables, anyway. It had been hard on both of us, him helping me in place of his father. He'd risen to the occasion. Wallie was a great kid. Now that he was settled in at college, I had no reason not to take care of this and get the house sold.

I'd been putting it off for too long, dreading the flood of emotions I was sure would overwhelm me at any moment.

On the other hand, those emotions could've been waiting to catch me off guard. Hit me when I wasn't expecting them. I needed to keep an eye on them. Keep them locked down tight.

The door creaked as if it was making the only sound the house had heard since the last time I closed it, or was it a sad kind of greeting? A cry for help? I couldn't tell.

I suppressed a shiver as I entered the open first floor. Everything was exactly as I'd left it. Furniture covered in sheets, boards on the windows, the whole shebang. The air was stale and smelled of dust, old magic, and salt.

Hurrying to the kitchen, I put the grocery bags on the dusty white tablecloth-covered kitchen table and flicked on the light. To my relief, it came on. It would be dark in a few short hours, and the last thing I wanted was no power. And that saved me a phone call to the electric company. They were lucky.

I opened the fridge and sniffed, then groaned while covering my nose. I'd scrubbed it before leaving it to be turned off, but it had still developed a smell. It was at least still clean. I had to get rid of the smell. I didn't have any herbs to mix up a spell, but I had picked up some baking soda while at the store. Thank the goddess for small things.

Unpacking my bags, I opened one of the boxes of baking

soda and put it in the back corner to start absorbing the smells. The freezer was next. I slid the second box in and remembered I forgot to buy a bag of ice. This old fridge didn't have an ice maker, so I was SOL for my Diet Cola for a while.

On that thought, I realized I might have to replace it to put the house on the market. I'd know for sure when the realtor came by. For now, I'd get the place ready for visitors.

Grabbing a towel out of the cabinet where they'd been all my life, I smelled it. It still had a faint scent of the homemade detergent Auntie used. She'd scented it with dried roses. Smiling, I dampened it and wiped out the cabinet my Yaya and Aunt Winnie had always used for dry goods, then put away the rest of the food.

With the kitchen settled, for the time being, I walked around the house before I went out to the car to unload the bags I'd brought with me.

Ah, but first, the boards needed to go. Drawing on my witchy side and not the *other* part of me that I refused to use, I used magic to remove the boards from the windows. The bright afternoon sun streamed in, lighting up each room so there was no need to turn the lights on as I went. The home was built with large windows in each room. I walked out of the kitchen toward the back porch and was surprised when a sense of dismay washed over me. Auntie had always kept an herb garden out here. It'd once been full of life and beauty.

Someone well in the past had converted the original porch of the house into a sunroom, then added another porch on the back of that at some point. Both the sunroom and the porch had been filled with a variety of herbs and flowers during Aunt Winnie's life.

Seeing it without all the little pots of greenery only drove home that I'd never see my Aunt Winnie again. She'd raised me, along with my grandmother, Yaya, and filled the hole that would've been there from losing my parents at such a young age.

My amazing parents were Beth and John Howe. I was five when dad died in a car accident while coming home from work. I didn't remember much about him, but the few memories I had were happy, and I cherished having that piece of him. We moved in here after that and became a house full of witches.

Mom's death had hit me hard. I was ten and she climbed a ladder to hang some holiday lights. A freak bolt of lightning had hit her. She was dead before she even fell off the ladder.

Shaking out of the memory, I backed into the kitchen, closing the door to the sunroom and my memories with it. I continued through the rest of the house to finish uncovering everything. Before heading upstairs, I grabbed my bags from Dia, my very tired car. One more thing I'd probably have to replace soon.

I lugged my bag of clothing up the stairs and into my old bedroom. Somehow, I couldn't bring myself to use Aunt Winnie's. All her things were still in there, for one thing, and it still smelled faintly like her verbena perfume. I wanted to keep it that way because it felt like she was still with me.

My old bed would do fine.

As I looked into Aunt Winnie's bedroom on my way to mine, a tinkling crash behind me made me jump nearly out of my skin. I whirled around to find one of the many, many knick-knacks had fallen off of the bureau lining one wall of the large hallway.

Glaring at the trinket, I wasn't sure what I expected it to do. A song and dance, maybe. If it did, I was getting back in Dia and hauling tail. Magical house that wasn't so magical anymore was one thing, but animated objects singing and dancing? No way. No how. My sanity couldn't take it.

I was sure it was probably from all the open windows and the vibrations of the house settling from having someone move around inside it after a year. What else could it be? No ghosts were around. I'd know. My other powers—that I would *not* think about—would've alerted me if that was the case.

I brushed it off and finished settling in for the night. It was nothing.

CHAPTER TWO

Twirling my finger in a circular motion, I pushed a small bit of magic into the air and smiled as tiny tornadoes whipped around the room, gathering up dust from the floor, shelves, and even off of the walls, and pulled it to the center of the room. Then, I conjured a larger tornado to collect the pile the smaller ones had created. I opened the door and ushered the larger cyclone out and all the dirt with it.

"Thank you kindly," I told the magic as it moved outside. The tornado made my hair twirl at the ends, acknowledging my thanks. Smiling, I moved from room to room, loving the feel and smell of the brisk fall air drifting in from the opened windows. I repeated the spell, dusting each room and evicting the grime from each window. Since I'd removed all the sheets earlier, this trip through the house was all about taking note of what needed to be done. I'd already noticed several repairs that were needed. Not to mention the furnishings were too obsolete for the buying market.

I loved the old, outdated Victorian.

So would the family that bought her.

As I went along, I conjured a notepad and pen and with a little magic animated them, so they'd follow me and make a list of things I needed to get at the store. I conjured another set to make notes of repairs needed.

All this drama, the sudden action of coming home and doing all this had been making me want to get my butt back in a chair. Something about being in this house and in Shipton woke up my muse. For the first time in five years, story ideas were buzzing in my head.

After the supply list was complete, I decided to get the office set up since it was clear that being home had ignited my creative juices. I hadn't written any significant number of words since I moved away. Then nothing since Clay died.

Must've been the salty air.

My office was exactly how I left it as if it were waiting on my return. I wasn't staying but that didn't mean I couldn't use it while I was here.

Once I cleared out the dust and laughed at the old type-writer, I set up my laptop and the few supplies I'd brought with me. Which included a million notebooks and my sticky notes stash. I may have a little notebook-hoarding problem.

It was well after the witching hour, and I realized I'd never made it to the store. Once I hit my office chair and turned on my laptop, the voices in my head chatted about all the adventures they were going on and words started flowing. The next thing I knew, it was pitch black outside and I had four chapters written on a book I hadn't even realized was in me.

Hot Damn.

Grinning, I sat back in my comfy chair and read back over what I'd written, surprised to find it as good as I'd hoped it would be as I'd typed. An abundance of pride and ambition filled me. I haven't written like that since before I met Clay. Even after we were married, I wrote and published, taking a break from it all to raise Wallie. I returned to it when he went to school because I didn't need to work. Clay made enough money, so we lived comfortably. My royalties were my mad money. Not that the money was mad, it was happy to be spent as much as I was to spend it.

However, it'd been a long time since I sat and wrote four effing chapters without my ADD kicking in. All in one sitting.

I stretched with my arms reaching for the high ceiling, a loud groan spilling from my lips, then I searched my office. There was something I was going to do but I'd been too involved in the new world I created to be bothered. A noise.

At some point during my amazing marathon writing sprint, something fell somewhere in the house. I'd been so into my story that I ignored it. Now that I was pulled out of the new imaginary world, I was curious as to what it was, if anything. All my life the house had a magic to it that made it alive, animated was what Winnie called it. It made noises often to get attention. However, there was no magic left in the house. I had all the windows open and none of them had screens, so it was either a random animal sneaking in or the wind knocking something over.

In the back of my mind, my subconscious brain was whispering that it was a bad idea. Things always ended badly for the lone female in the horror movies that went seeking out what made the unknown noise. Well, I wasn't just any lone female. I was Ava Harper, witch with a dark side. I wasn't afraid to use it.

Okay, that was a lie. I hated my necromancer powers. They didn't define me.

Plus, I wasn't in a horror movie. If I was, I would have been the first to die.

Deciding on taking my chances with the dangers that might or might not be waiting for me, I moved through the downstairs of the Victorian. My bare feet were silent as I checked each room. I didn't find anything that looked out of the ordinary.

Strange. I'd distinctly heard something break. Unless I was going insane, which could be the real reason my muse woke up.

That was highly possible.

Giving up on finding the source of the noise that I was beginning to think was a product of my overactive imagination, I crossed the large open living room set on getting back to the book I started. About halfway back to my office, a gray blur leaped at me from the stairs like some humongous furry bat. I screamed but managed to catch the large beast in both hands.

"Snoozles. Excuse me Mr. Snoozerton, you can't jump out at me like that. I'm old and could have a heart attack." I adjusted the twenty-pound, three-foot-long, Maine Coon in my arms to keep from dropping him. Seriously, the cat was the size of a large dog. Except for Great Danes. Snooze was more like a fluffy basset hound. Only he meowed and had claws.

"Snoozle, you can retract the claws." I bent over and lowered the monster to the ground. He looked up at me and let out a gruff meow. "I hear ya, Snooze." The poor cat had so many variations on his name it was a wonder he knew it at all.

Well, crap on a cracker. I didn't buy cat food. Turning back to the kitchen, I wondered where the grumpy old tomcat had been. Wallie and I had searched all over for Snooze with nothing to show for it. That crazy cat didn't want to be found.

I opened the cabinet with the canned food and pulled out the tuna while conjuring my grocery list to add Snooze's food. He was a special kitty and would only eat the most expensive food on the market, no thanks to Winnie for spoiling him.

Snooze purred loudly and rubbed against my legs. After draining the water from the tuna can, I emptied the contents onto a plate and lowered it to the ground. "Eat up, Mr. Snoozles."

My thanks were the growl-like sounds he made when he ate something he loved. It was a good thing I'd picked up tuna for myself. I laughed at the cat and left him to his meal. "I'm heading back to my office."

If I didn't tell him where I was going, he'd walk around the house meowing as loud as he could, even though he could just follow my scent.

Crazy cat.

As I walked past the front door, someone pounded on it loud enough to wake the dead in the next town over. Geesh. "It's the police. Open up." I cursed after I collected my heart off the floor and put it back in my chest. I might have screamed a little.

Marching over to the door, I jerked it open about to bless out whoever was trying to break down the door. I stopped short when I saw my best friend standing on the other side. His brown hair was in its usual unruly mess, which looked amazing on him. Dark blue eyes sparkled as he smiled at me.

As I took in his deputy uniform, I burst out laughing. I was correct that the knock sounded like it came from the police. "You didn't need to knock like you had a warrant for my arrest."

Sam Thompson, my best friend since the first grade, chuckled. "How do you know I don't?"

"I know. I've been too depressed to get into trouble." I meant it to be funny, but it came out pathetic.

Shaking his head, Sam's smile fell, and he stepped closer like he was going to hug me. I stepped back. I couldn't. I'd finally got my emotions under wraps. If I hugged him, the floodgates would open up. Instead, I held out my hand. "It's great seeing you again."

He took another step, forcing me backward. "Sam, don't you dare."

He leaped forward, grabbed my arm, and pulled me into him, hugging me tight. The feel of his arms around me cued the waterworks. Warm and secure. Sam was a great hugger. So had

Clay been. I gripped his shirt and buried my face into the center of his chest. "Jerk."

"It's good to have you home." The door clicked shut.

After a few minutes, I wrapped my arms around his back. "I miss him."

Sam sighed and framed my face as he leaned back. "I know."

"And I miss Aunt Winnie." I hiccupped a sob, only making him tighten his hold on me. Sam was the brother I never had. Always had been. We had this instant connection from the moment we saw each other in the first grade. "None of this was in the game plan."

He rested his cheek on the top of my head and held me and let me soak his uniform shirt. I wasn't sure how long we stood there. In true Sam fashion, he didn't tell me things that everyone else had told me. That things would be okay. Life goes on. Sam didn't say any of those things. He held me and let me pour out all the emotions that have been bottled up inside me.

When my tears finally stopped, I stepped out of Sam's embrace and wiped the tears from my face. "Not to mention, Wallie left me, too." I was a mess. It was all too much. Winnie's death triggered the grief from losing Clay, then Wallie going to school added to my loneliness.

I stared at the huge wet spot in Sam's shirt and frowned. "I'm sure the washer and dryer work. Maybe."

When I reached to touch his shirt, he took my hands and held them in his warm grasp. "I have a clean one in the car."

Of course, he did. That was Sam. Taking a deep breath, I waved him toward the kitchen. "Want coffee?"

"Sure. Olivia said she saw you at the store earlier today. Since I was in the neighborhood, I thought I'd check in with you. You know, since you called and let your bestie know you were here." His low chuckle made me smile.

"Just in the neighborhood, huh? You always keep clean shirts in your patrol car?"

He flashed the infamous smile that always got him out of trouble, or into trouble, depending on his mood.

After starting the coffee, I took out two cups and turned to study him. "That little guy of yours is way cuter in person."

Sam's face lit up. "He gets it from me." He winked then added, "He's a handful."

"They usually are at that age."

Sam glanced down at the large Maine coon stretched out on the floor as if seeing the humongous beast for the first time. "How is that cat still alive? Isn't he like a hundred?"

"No." How old was Snooze? Winnie got him as a baby when I was sixteen, and I'm forty-three. "Damn, that cat is twenty-seven years old."

I studied him for a long moment. Snooze didn't look any older than the last time I saw him, which was a picture Auntie sent me a few months before she passed. His coat was perfectly groomed and shiny. There were no signs of gray hairs or any other signs of aging like most elderly cats get.

It was a total mystery.

"Do you think that time you healed him after he fell from the top of the stairs did something to him?"

I jerked my attention back to Sam. We were in our senior year in high school and Snooze was a little over a year old and not as big as he was at the moment. Clay and I had just started dating a few weeks before. I tried to put that memory out of my mind because that was the day Clay found out I'm a witch with not-so-normal witchy powers.

Snooze had chased the three of us, Sam, Clay, and me, through the house, playing like we always had. The darn cat was a force and so energetic when he was in his younger years. Clay and I ran down the stairs and the crazy cat leaped off the top. The landing was rough, and I was sure he broke a lot of bones.

Shock and fear that I'd lost my pet flooded me, making me shake and my magic run wild in my veins. I hadn't had as much control over the necromancer part of myself as I wanted to believe. Not like I do now. I didn't think of what I was doing as I laid my hands on Snooze and pushed magic into him. All I'd thought about was how much I loved that cat and wanted him to live.

Shaking out of the memory, I frowned down at Snooze. "That would have only added a year to his life."

Surely I hadn't made him immortal. I wasn't sure that was possible.

Sam shrugged. "I've got nothing. Then again, I don't understand how a house can come to life either. I roll with it because your family is way cooler than mine."

A laugh escaped me. Sam had always told me that. He teased that it was the reason he was my best friend. To be cool. Only I wasn't the cool kid in school. Olivia made sure of that.

Speaking of the she-devil.

"So, Olivia."

Shaking his head, Sam pointed to the coffee pot that was sputtering the last drops of the rich liquid into the pot. "Olivia is not the same person she was in high school."

I poured the coffee and made a noise of disbelief. "She's not a busybody?"

"Yes, but not as bad." He took the cup I offered as I sat in the chair across from him. "Her first marriage was rough on her. It changed her."

For the first time in my life, I felt rage roll off my best friend. Sam was a gentle alpha male. Yes, he was protective over those he called family and would do what it took to keep them, me included, safe. He was also a compassionate, gentle, caring soul. The word hate wasn't in his vocabulary.

"What happened?"

He seemed to snap out of his rage-induced mood and held my stare for a long few seconds. "I'll let Olivia tell you when she's ready."

It took everything in me not to roll my eyes or groan aloud. I didn't want to be friends with Olivia. "I might not be in town long enough to get that story."

Once the coffee pot was empty, I realized it was morning. Sam and I had talked all night or was that all morning since it was after midnight when he stopped by. Now it was... 7:00 a.m. "Wow, I totally made you skip out on work."

Chuckling, Sam rose to his feet and stretched. "I told Drew I was stopping by."

"Drew?"

"The new sheriff." Sam's smile widened and his eyes sparked like they did when he had a plan. I was ignoring all the possible plans he would cook up that involved the new sheriff. I wasn't dating anyone. Ever. Again. Clay was it for me. Now it's me and Snooze.

"I'm sure I'll run into him sooner or later," I mumbled as I took our coffee cups to the sink. Out of habit, I rinsed them and went to open the dishwasher. Except Winnie didn't have a dishwasher.

Crap on a cracker.

I left the cups in the sink, deciding I'd deal with them later. "You're not in trouble for playing hooky at the witch's house?"

"Nope. He knew to call if I was needed. Not much happens in Shipton Harbor anyway." Sam leaned in and kissed my cheek. "I'll see you later."

I nodded and walked him to the door. It was true. The town was small and only recently became a tourist town, but still, nothing exciting ever happened here. It was easy to feel normal here.

"Have a great rest of your day." I waved to Sam as he got into his patrol car and drove off.

Closing the door, I scanned the living room, looking for something to do. I didn't sleep much, especially since Clay died. It didn't feel right going to bed without him.

Okay, Ava, you are being silly. It's been five years. It's time to move on.

Not forget. Just move on.

Besides, I promised Clay I would try.

I decided to call the realtor, Betty Knolls. Betty and Auntie were close friends and would most likely know right off what I needed to do to the house to get it on the market.

Now to remember where my phone was.

Ah, my office.

Sure enough, it was on top of the desk, face down. Picking it up, I dialed Betty's number. She answered on the first ring. At least I thought it was her until I heard the sultry voice on the other end of the connection. "Moonflower Realty."

Moonflower? I was sure I dialed the right number. "I'm calling for Betty Knolls."

There was a brief few moments of silence before I got a reply. "Betty is my mother. She retired a few weeks ago. By now she should be enjoying her beach house in Florida."

"Oh, wow. Good for her." I didn't know Betty very well, but I did know she was getting up there in years. "I'm Ava Harper. My aunt was Winnie Howe."

"Ah, yes. Betty left me some notes that you may return to sell off that gorgeous old Victorian." She paused then added, "Sorry, I'm Carmen Moonflower. I took over the company and am still getting organized. I hadn't expected you to call so early."

I hadn't either. "I haven't been to bed yet and thought I'd call before hitting the sack."

"Good thinking. That way I wouldn't come over and wake

you." Carmen paused again and I heard muffled talking in the background.

"Am I disturbing you?"

"Oh no, I just arrived at the office. Do you have a pen and paper handy?"

I nodded, realizing she can't see me. "Yes."

"As much as I do not want to see you sell the place, I understand." She let out a soft, sad sigh. "Here is the number of a contracting company owned by a friend that I recommend for all my clients. Just tell whoever answers that I sent you. They will know the name and are expecting you. Jude will know what the old house would need to be updated. Plus, he will keep the historical look to it so we could get the highest offer possible for it."

I wrote down the number and thanked her. Betty was a psychic and had always known what you needed whether you knew it or not. It didn't surprise me that her daughter seemed to also have the gift of sight.

After I hung up with Carmen, I called the contractor and made an appointment for tomorrow. I had too much to do today to deal with contractors. First was to try to get some sleep, then I had to get supplies and food.

I glanced at my computer and smiled, feeling accomplished. I got words, four chapters' worth, and scheduled the contractor to start work. Things were moving along. I hoped the repairs were minor and I wouldn't be stuck in town longer than I needed to be.

CHAPTER THREE

I went to bed with a big smile on my face, amazed at how good it felt to be writing again. A sense of accomplishment flowed through me. I'd have another book to send to my publisher in no time, and maybe then all my money problems would be less of an issue. If the creativity continued to flow, I was hoping to eliminate the financial strain altogether. This was the break I needed. The last of the insurance money went to the college, last month, to ensure Wallie was set, and it was either I got a book out or I got a job. There wasn't an alternative.

I might have to do both for a while. Before I considered a job, I needed to get the old Victorian on the market and then sold. See what type of timeline I'm working with.

Another amazing thing was that I slept for four uninterrupted hours. I haven't slept that well since before Clay died. Plus, I woke up with a smile on my face. That never happened because I wasn't a morning person. It took me at least an hour for my brain to wake up.

Not this morning. Even though it was late morning, swiftly approaching noon.

With my smile in place, I stood at the window, drinking my coffee, feeling more peaceful than I had since the love of my life left this earth.

This sea air was a miracle worker. I'd have to make a point to go on more beach vacations once the house was sold and I was back home in Philly.

Baby steps. I've told myself that for the last five years. That's what it had been—one baby step after another. *I can do this*.

Turning away from the window, I set my coffee cup down on the dresser on my way to the bathroom across the hall from my room. I was so looking forward to a semi-cool shower to recharge my senses and wake my ass up. One would think being in Maine in the fall that a hot shower would be better. *One* would understand if they had premenopausal hot flashes. Why did they call them flashes? I was hot all the time. There were no flashes. It was constant.

I turned the shower on and frowned. An awful groan coming from the pipes didn't sound very promising. Then rust-colored water spat and sputtered out of the shower head. The old pipes did *not* want to let me shower. Or bathe. Ugh.

Conjuring my magical list and pen, I added plumbing to my list of things I'd have to have fixed. The list I would be giving the contractor when he arrived tomorrow. My bank account was dwindling. Fixing this place up would clean it out if I even had enough, and then what?

Getting a job was looking like my reality for the next few months.

Giving up on the cool shower, I looked over my list of things I needed to get at the grocery and hardware store. I'd do as much of the repairs as I could myself.

Unfortunately, that wasn't much.

Nothing to do but dig into it. I washed the best I could in the sink. Not that I could fit inside the sink. The old sponge bath wasn't what I longed for, but it freshened me up enough to make the trip into town.

With my second cup of coffee in a travel mug, I started Dia and headed to town. On the way to the hardware store, I noticed a bookstore that hadn't been there the last time I was in town.

Who was I, an author of some success, to pass up a bookstore? Even before I became an author, I'd never passed up a bookstore. Pulling a U-turn at the next light, I backtracked to the land of fiction.

After parking Dia in a spot, I entered the store, inhaling the wonderful smell of books. There was nothing like it. It was almost better than chocolate. Almost. Looking around, I realized that I remembered the store now. Auntie brought me here once a week. While she went to the occult section, I disappeared into the various fiction sections. I read about every type of genre, and my tastes changed often. The storefront must've been updated since I was here last. That must have been why I hadn't recognized it.

"Hello?" I called out as I moved closer to the counter to my right.

"Come in." A thin man hurried out of the back. He looked familiar, but I couldn't place him. There was a friendly, warm energy that surrounded him. I couldn't help but smile. When he got up front and behind the counter, he stopped short while staring at me. "Oh," he breathed. "You're Ava Howe."

Well, I must've known him somehow. He sure seemed to know me. Could he be the same owner from when Auntie and I came all those years ago? No, he was much too young to have worked in the store over twenty-five years ago.

But he sure seemed to know me.

Then again, around here that didn't mean much. Small

town and all that jazz. Plus, the Howe family was infamous in this tiny town. He probably knew my family. Plastering a polite smile on my face, I held out my hand. "It's Ava Harper now. Nice to meet you."

"Oh, honey. We know each other. I was a year behind you at Shipton High. I'm Clint. Clint Homes." He shook my hand delicately as he continued to stare at me with wide eyes. "I have to say. I am the biggest fan of your books."

Oh, how nice. Someone who knew me more from my books than my family. Though if he went to high school at Shipton, he knew of my family, and possibly Clay, who had only gone there during our junior and senior years. "It's lovely to meet you again."

"Please, tell me you're moving back home." Before I could answer, he rushed around the counter. "Look here, look, I have a display here dedicated to local authors, of which you're the only one. You have your own special section here."

He dragged me to the first row of shelves and held out his hands. My trilogy of young adult novels was displayed proudly with a small, framed photo of my headshot and another frame with my official bio from my website printed out. "Wow," I breathed.

I was like a celebrity.

"I'm thrilled to have you here. Can I find you anything? What are you in town for? Are you moving back? Would you like some coffee?" He threw questions at me so fast I had to laugh. He was adorable and way too energetic for me. It was a good thing I had two cups of coffee.

Clint practically vibrated as I put my hand on his arm and squeezed. "Calm down." I laughed. "Coffee sounds wonderful. I'm in town to sell my family's house, and I'm starting to write again, so hopefully, you'll have more books to add to the shelf soon."

"You're writing?" He asked excitedly as he led me to the

little coffee pot I'd seen behind the counter. "Here." He pulled out a stool and we settled in behind the counter. I didn't know what had possessed me to say yes to coffee, except that Clint seemed genuinely interested in me, and I needed a friend and someone to talk to. It was nice.

"I'm so happy to hear you're writing." He fiddled with the coffee pot. "This will be ready in a jiffy."

"Well, my husband died five years ago."

He looked properly crestfallen. "I heard. I'm so sorry."

I ducked my head and became interested in my fingernails. Man, I needed a manicure, badly. "Thanks. I haven't been able to write a word since then, and before that, I was focused on being a wife and mom, but last night, the words flowed."

Clint straightened on his stool and clapped his hands together. "That's the best news."

I chuckled. "Yeah, for me, too. Lord knows I need the money."

Closing my eyes, I couldn't believe I said that. Was I so desperate for a friend that I spilled my failures to this stranger? Well, technically he wasn't a stranger. We went to school together, but still, we hadn't been friends. At least I didn't think so.

His jaw dropped. "You do?"

I nodded with a sigh. I've opened my big mouth and might as well finish telling him my life story. "Yeah. Insurance money's gone, and that house is going to suck up the last bit of what I've got. There is too much that needs to be done."

The smell of coffee filled the air as Clint studied me. "I don't know if you'd be interested, but I need some help around here. Business always picks up this time of year, and I've been wanting to reorganize. It would just be a couple of days a week, but if you want to, the job is yours."

Oh. That sounded perfect. I could write on days I didn't work here. Plus, working in a bookshop sounded like heaven.

"I'd love it, but I'm only going to be in town long enough to fix the house and get it sold."

He waved his hands and stood as the coffee pot beeped. "I'll take you as long as I can get you. I know we're going to be best friends."

He was right. However, I wasn't in town to make friends. I didn't need the attachments that I'd have to leave behind. A job would be great and working in the bookstore would be a dream.

"Well, if you're sure," I said uncertainly, then added, "Black coffee, please."

He handed me a cup and met my eye. "I'm positive."

We chatted for a while. He told me about his failed marriage, and I told him about my husband's death. It still hurt to talk about it, but I was able to get through it without crying. That was a good sign because it said that I was ready to move on—but not forget. I would never forget my Clay.

Before I knew it, it was nearly dinnertime. "I've got to run," I exclaimed. "I'll see you in a couple of days."

Things were looking up here in Shipton Harbor. Maybe the house repairs would go well, I'd write and work and go back to Philly with a book for the publisher and a renewed spirit. This was what I needed.

I made it through the hardware store fairly painlessly. Even paying wasn't as bad since I'd have a little bit of extra money coming in from helping Clint.

The grocery store was another story. I had to stock up. With the list of repairs I'd made, I'd end up staying in town for at least a couple of months. Longer than I'd hoped. I couldn't list the house until the repairs were done. I'd have to be here until it sold.

If I had the money, I could've hired someone to do the selling for me and come back to sign, but of course, I was broke. I'd have to see this through to the end. I hoped I wouldn't have to keep the old Victorian because I couldn't pay the mortgage on my house in Philly. No, I wouldn't think of that right now.

"Excuse me." A deep voice made the hairs on the back of my neck prickle as I looked for the particular brand of canned chili they used to sell here when I was a kid. It was probably too much to hope they'd still have that brand, but I was looking. I stepped backward and looked around, trying to get out of the man's way, even if his voice did send a shot of warmth to my soul, or were those the hot flashes?

But of course, I moved the wrong way and instead of giving him more room, I slammed right into him. His foot hit the back of mine and my knee went wonky. I lost my balance.

Down I went.

He hooked an arm around my waist to keep me from falling. They were large, strong arms that held onto me like a lifeline. Heat from those arms and the body they held me against challenged the best of my hot flashes. He smelled divine. Like clean mountains and spiced sage.

I closed my eyes, mortified, as he chuckled behind me, his lips much too close to my ears. I almost groaned at the sensations flooding my body. Peering upward, I discovered I was being held up by a policeman. He loosened his hold and I jerked away. The reality of what was happening came back to me as I smoothed my rumpled clothes and met his amused, beautifully handsome face. "I am so sorry."

I found it hard to stare into his unusual teal and blue eyes. At the same time, it was impossible to look away. He didn't have two different colored eyes. They were a mix of teal and dark blue. Teal being the dominant color. I'd never seen eyes like those before.

The corner of his sensual mouth lifted, and his silky voice flowed around me, caressing every inch of ignited flesh. "I didn't mean to startle you."

"Oh, you didn't. I was preoccupied and not paying attention." And I needed to not pay any more attention to the hottie in uniform standing way too close for my comfort.

Damn.

I hadn't noticed the way a man looked this intently since way before my husband died. This policeman had a chiseled jaw and high cheekbones. His short black hair made those incredible eyes stand out all the more.

"You must be Ava," he said.

My jaw dropped and I drew my brows together while shaking out of his spell. Even though he wasn't a witch, he had a power that surrounded him. I couldn't place what he was. "Am I really that infamous?"

He chuckled again, and the warm sound of his voice reached out to me again. I tried like hell to push the sensations away.

"No, I'm Andrew Walker. Drew. I work closely with your friend, Sam."

I closed my eyes briefly and sucked in a deep breath. *Stop being an idiot, Ava.* Why had this man thrown me off so much? Shipton Harbor had five thousand people. It wasn't like the police department was enormous. Sam was the deputy, so it made sense that this man, Drew, who was *in uniform* would know him. Gods, I was slow sometimes.

"Yes," I said. "I'm Ava, and I guess almost falling made me a dunce. Of course, you know Sam." I stuck my hand out and when he took it into his warm ones, his arms circled my hand and then twined up my arm. I pulled back quickly but not too fast so that I didn't seem rude. His energy seemed to cling to my skin in a sensual, non-threatening way. It was still unnerving.

As hot as this man was, my husband had been drop-dead gorgeous and had given me twenty years of wedded bliss. That was enough to last me the rest of my life. I didn't need to start something new and complicate my life. Especially since I wasn't staying.

"So sorry to have run you over." I moved toward my buggy, desperate to make my escape. It was hard to think with him there.

"No problem. It was the highlight of my day if we're being honest." He sort of half-winked at me, making my cheeks burn again.

No. Nope. I was in town for a few months and then back to Philly. Hot sheriff was not in my plans. No man was in my plans. Not now. Not ever. "I'll see you around Sheriff Walker."

"Drew," he called as I made a hasty escape.

Drew. Hell, no. He was not Drew and he was not hot. He was Sheriff Walker. Period.

Although, that might've been worse. I imagined myself in the situation I'd just endured, except much suaver and sexier, like I would've written it. Instead of yelling bye over my shoulder, I could've fluttered my eyelashes and told him goodbye in a sultry voice, emphasizing his title. *Officer* Walker.

Oh, no. No, no no. None of that.

Gods, I needed that cold shower now.

CHAPTER FOUR

B ang. Bang. Bang.
The sound of something hitting a solid object nonstop woke me from a dead sleep. I didn't get many nights of heavy sleep and I sure as Hades didn't like to be woken up from one.

I cracked one eye open and quickly squeezed it shut. It was bright. I needed to buy curtains for the windows. Especially my room. The cheap mini blinds were not cutting it.

The banging started again, followed by a whining sound.

"What is that?" I yelled. What time was it? Better yet, what day was it? Of course, no one was around to answer my questions. Not that anyone could hear me over that awful noise.

When the banging didn't stop, my brain fog cleared, and I realized what it was. I jerked straight up in my bed, blinking several times so my eyes adjusted to the sunlight streaming in through the open window.

Letting out a mixture of a groan and growl, I swung my feet over the side of the bed and grabbed my phone. It was Wednesday. I didn't bother paying attention to the time because I didn't care. It was morning and I didn't do mornings. Ever.

I'd met with the contractor, Jude Carter, two days ago about the repairs on the house, starting with the plumbing. I needed the upstairs shower working again. The downstairs bathroom was functioning, but it didn't have a shower because it was Winnie's oasis, as she liked to call it. I didn't like baths. There was no particular reason why I didn't like them, I just preferred showers.

Jude and I had planned for the construction crew to start today. I should've gotten up to greet them, but I'd forgotten they were coming today.

Grumbling under my breath, I tugged on some leggings, not paying attention to which pair I grabbed. I didn't care. There was no one down there I wanted to impress. Once dressed, I pulled my long brown hair up in a ponytail before heading downstairs. The noise on the ground floor was louder with all the windows still open and I was glad I didn't drink while writing last night. I'd be grumpier than normal from being woken up before I was ready.

A few guys moved around downstairs, making notes of things that needed to be fixed or updated. They didn't seem to notice me as I made my way to the kitchen. Once there, I turned on the coffee pot and wished I had some industrial-sized earplugs. Seriously, was all that noise necessary so early in the morning?

Glancing at the clock on the stove, I frowned and grumbled a little more. It was 10:00 am. Technically not early for normal people, but I wasn't normal. I was an author with my mojo back. Apparently, my mojo was a night owl. It was a good thing because so was I.

Mornings were overrated.

As soon as I had a cup of coffee in my hand, I slipped on

the flip-flops I kept at the kitchen door and ventured outside to say hello to the contractor. You know, be friendly and all.

"Morning." He called a greeting as he stood outside the cellar entrance. Lord, I didn't even know what all might be down in the cellar. I'd nearly forgotten it existed. Hopefully, nothing that would incriminate me or my family. Like bones of something or someone for whatever Aunt Winnie used for spells. Not that she used many bones for her spells, but it was Winnie I was talking about. Anything was possible, and nothing would surprise me.

"Need anything?" I walked off the back porch and peered down into the cellar, but nobody was screaming or running out with looks of terror, so it must not have been that bad. I made a mental note to check down there later tonight.

"Nope." He grinned as he inspected my neon green leggings. "We'll let you know if we do."

That grin turned into a smile that revealed two dimples as he met my gaze. His brown eyes were slightly darker than caramel candies. He was a cutie and young enough to be my son.

On that note...

"I'll be in my office if you need anything." I smiled and made my retreat, having satisfied my obligatory welcome and offer of help. Now it was time to go to work. I was trying to work out a schedule and manage my time better now that I have a book deadline. On my days off from the bookstore, which I start tomorrow, I'll work on my book during the daylight hours. I didn't need to stay up all night with the construction going on during the day.

But changing my routine was harder than it seemed.

When I entered the kitchen and spotted the bottles of water, my hospitable side got the better of me. I put the bottles in a cooler and covered them in ice, then dragged them onto the porch. There. Now they had plenty to drink if they needed it.

After topping off my coffee, I headed to my office. I was still feeling inspired by being back in Maine and my new prospects at the bookstore. It was a great feeling that I wasn't going to spend too much time thinking about.

I settled down at my desk to write, but my attention kept drifting out the window. I had the perfect view of their work truck and couldn't help but notice how young and fit several of the construction workers were. I spent more time watching them work and admiring the view. I had to stop myself from ogling before I was caught being a creeper. Plus, none of them set my insides on fire like a certain cop I ran into at the grocery store three days ago.

And I will not think about Officer Walker.

After lunch, during which I nearly convinced myself to make sandwiches for the entire crew, I sat back down to work. Oh, I offered to make lunch, but they politely declined. It was the mother in me to make sure everyone was taken care of. Maybe I'd get a pet to care for since my son abandoned me for higher learning.

On that thought, I searched my office for Snooze and found the large beast stretched out on top of the second desk Auntie used. He was on his back with his feet in the air, furry belly, and everything else exposed for all to see. The huge cat had no shame.

I was about to throw a paper ball at him when my cell phone started ringing. "Saved by the ringtone, Kitty Kat."

Snooze's reply was a loud snore that made me laugh.

Glancing down at the phone, I smiled when I saw the name, I answered with a cheery voice. "Hello, Uncle Wade."

My husband's uncle claimed me as his adopted daughter at my and Clay's wedding and had stood by me during the funeral. Plus, he came over frequently after Clay's death to make sure Wallie was taken care of and that I ate and didn't grieve myself into a grave right beside my husband. It was close at times. If it hadn't been for Wade and Wallie, I would have willed myself to die. Not to mention Sam, who called me every day for the first two years. Then cut back to every other day. I was annoyed, wanting to be left alone. Now, I was glad to have all my annoying family and friends.

"How's Maine?" His booming voice filled my office and warmed my heart.

"The same as it's always been. How are you?"

We chit-chatted for a few minutes about nothing and every-thing, mostly how he was hating retirement while enjoying sleeping in. "How is the house?"

I moaned, rolling my eyes. I realized he couldn't see the eye roll, so I had to use my words. "It needs so many repairs. Then when it's done, I'll list it. I might be here longer than I thought."

He must have heard my frustrations in my voice because he said, "Take advantage of your time there. Enjoy it like a vaca-tion. Plus, it's a great time to get back to your roots and find yourself. You must be happy to have Sam so close, right?"

I smiled. Wade knew Sam was close to both Clay and me, but mostly that Sam was like a brother to me. "Yeah, that's nice. Oh, I got a job at the bookstore in town, and I'm writing. There is that."

"See. Going home isn't all bad." He paused, then asked, "But how are you really doing?"

With a sigh, I sat back in my desk chair and decided to be honest. There was no use lying to him anyway. The man always knew. "Being in Shipton is bringing back memories I buried a long time ago. Part of me wants those memories to stay buried, but I'm okay, though my emotions are a bit wonky."

He chuckled. "Wonky is understandable. Want me to come help with the house?"

There was hope in his tone. Uncle Wade was a handy sort of man. He'd worked for a construction company for years, doing electrical work. I seriously considered his offer. It would be nice to have family close and free labor, but I couldn't pull him away from his home and his newly retired life. "If things get any more complicated, I might do that, but for now I've got it covered."

We talked about Wallie for a few minutes. He'd been checking in regularly via email and was so far loving being at college, as I'd known he would. By the time we disconnected, I felt full of love from the best non-dad I'd ever had. It also made me miss Clay.

Okay, none of that. Back to writing.

I got two sentences typed when something deeper in the house shattered, like glass breaking. It had happened a few times since I got back home, but I never found the source of the sounds. I had my suspicions that were solidified when I got downstairs and saw two of the workers nearly clutching each other in fear. Their eyes wide as they stared at the floor a few feet from them.

Nothing seemed amiss in the living room, though. "What's wrong?" I asked with a sinking feeling in my stomach. I opened my senses to see if there may be a ghost in the house. There wasn't one. At least that I could sense.

"A vase flew across the room and hit the wall," one of them said. He was one of the youngest on the crew, and I bet he hadn't been working for the company long.

I narrowed my eyes and looked around. "I don't see it."

The room was clean and fresh, the way I'd left it the other day when I'd used my magic to freshen it. "I'm sure it was the wind or something," I said, trying to convince them they'd lost their minds. "You both couldn't have seen something fly across the room that disappeared, could you?"

They laughed nervously and walked shoulder-to-shoulder to the door. Were they leaving? They couldn't leave. "Where are you going?"

"Leaving. We can't work anywhere where there's a ghost attacking us." They moved a little faster toward the door.

"Ghost? Did you see a ghost?"

They didn't answer and when I followed them, they almost ran outside. They were halfway to the truck by the time I got to the front porch. "Where is Jude?"

The worker who climbed into the driver's seat answered as he started the truck. "At the office." Then they left.

Damn it.

Heading to the kitchen, I put on a fresh pot of coffee, but something didn't feel right. Again, I stretched out my magic. Again, nothing ghostly or other was anywhere around. There was only one other option.

"You used to pull this shit when I was little," I whispered. "I thought all that died with Aunt Winnie." I looked around the kitchen and tried to quiet the unease.

When I was a kid, if I'd asked the house a question, it would've responded in some way. A cabinet would open and shut, or the light would flicker.

Nothing happened this time. More than likely, it was nothing more than the workers being superstitious. They'd probably grown up around here and heard the rumors about the house.

It wasn't like there'd been a real vase.

Just the noise. And their imaginations.

CHAPTER FIVE

"That's how it's done."

I met Clint's gleeful expression and smiled back at him as I closed the cash register drawer. "Easy peasy."

It was simple enough. After all, I did work as a cashier while in high school. Although the technology was more advanced now, the basics hadn't changed much.

Clint's gray eyes sparked with life. The man was easy to like, and I would've bet everyone in town loved him. It was a shame that I still didn't remember him from school.

"See, first days aren't as scary as they seem." He winked and moved around the counter, heading to the back of the store. We had a new shipment of books come in the day before. "If you need anything at all, yell for me."

I saluted his back. "Will do."

Satisfied that I could at least operate the cash register and take care of customers, he left me to it. He figured it would be faster for me to man the front and do some dusting than to try to teach me the sorting system right away. That would come over time when he wasn't so behind on getting the new books entered into the computer and ready for the shelves. I was happy to do whatever he wanted but unloading and organizing the books sounded like heaven. Especially if I got to touch each precious as I cataloged them. I hoped Clint taught me how to do it soon.

It was a slow morning, so I got everything behind the counter organized and dusted before my first customer came in. When the little bell over the door sounded, excitement filled me, then died almost as fast.

Of course, *of course* my first customer was Olivia. Great. Just what I needed.

"Ava!" Olivia squealed as soon as she walked through the door and saw it was me behind the counter. Super.

"Hey, Olivia, how are you?" I checked my watch as I stepped up to the counter across from her. The woman was too perky, and way too happy that I was back in town. Had she not had anyone else to torture since I left Shipton? "Where's Sammie?"

"He's at kindergarten. Can you believe he's old enough for school?" Olivia poked out her bottom lip and did a fake sniff.

I didn't bother to hold in my laugh. We weren't friends in high school and weren't nice to each other so why start now? Her sudden interest in me was suspicious. I kept feeling that if I let down my guard and accepted that she might have changed like Sam said, I'd be the one who got crapped on. However, I trusted Sam and loved him like a brother. He'd asked me to give her a chance, and I would try. I didn't think that meant talking to her all the time.

Now that she knew I was working at Imaginary Homes Bookstore, there was no stopping her from hanging out when I worked. That was fabulous. Not. Studying her for a long moment, I asked, "Do you work?"

She grinned and shook her head. "Nope. My settlement from my divorce helps me stay at home with Sammie and all the things I couldn't do with Jess and Devan." Sadness passed over her face, but it was gone in a flash as she smiled at me. "I know Sammie is my third child, but it wasn't any easier to send him off to school this year. It might've been a little harder. I miss that little guy during the day."

I understood about sending a child off to school for the first time. Wallie was in college, and I'd still cried when I had to leave him at his dorms. I'd cried ugly fat tears all the way home.

However, Sammie wasn't Olivia's first child. She had two others, Jess—short for Jessica—and Devan, from her first marriage who were in college. I didn't mention that she was a pro at this mother thing, even though it was on the tip of my tongue. A part of me wanted to tease her in a *friendly* way. What was that about?

I didn't understand the urge to be playful with her. We *weren't* friends. Plus, I was at work. It was so hard to be nice considering I didn't trust Olivia's bubbly, happy-to-see-me personality *at all*. I was halfway convinced Olivia had married Sam out of spite, or to piss me off.

That was how it had been when we were in school.

Olivia leaned against the counter and watched me for a long moment. Her gaze searched my neck and the surrounding area as if she thought she could see my witch mark. The most common area for the mark was on the neck or above the collar bone where it was easy to see or expose to other witches. Only those with magic in their blood could see the mark. Olivia had no magic. She was as human as they came.

It didn't matter whether or not she had the Sight. My mark was not on my neck. It was on the inside of my right forearm.

"Sooo," Olivia said, drawing out the small word as she gave up her search for my witch mark. I lifted a brow, waiting for her to continue. "Sammie's teacher, you remember her. Carrie Treehill, she was a couple of grades behind us?"

I nodded as if I had any recollection of this person. I didn't because I was terrible with names, and faces, sometimes. "Sure."

"Well, she left her husband, and everyone is saying he cheated on her. The jerk." Olivia pursed her lips, then widened her eyes and leaned in close. "I was thinking," she whispered. "If it's true, can we curse him? Because I really like Carrie."

We? Did she have a mouse in her pocket? I crossed my arms and glared at her. Olivia knew I was a witch. Well, she believed I was a witch like everyone else. No one but Sam and my family knew I was so much more. "First, cursing people brings you all kinds of bad mojo. Two, there is no *we*."

She deflated a bit. "Maybe curse is too strong of a word. We could do something, a spell maybe, that would make him feel sorry for being a cheating butt face." Olivia tapped her fingers on the glass countertop.

There she went with the *we* again. I didn't come back into town to cast spells on people. "That answer is no. I'm not that kind of a witch."

It was true. I wasn't. Not really. If I wanted to, and I really didn't, I could raise the dead, create undead creatures, and do other dark magic that gave witches a bad name in the first place. Necromancers were good like that.

My magic was stronger than the average necromancer. Plus, I also had witch magic. I was a magical hybrid, one of a kind. It was a secret I planned to take to my grave.

She gave me big eyes and a pouty lip. "Maybe just a little something? Like give him ED for a month?"

I snorted and then covered my mouth. The last thing I needed to do was encourage Olivia. "That is still doing harm."

Cheating wasn't a big enough offense for me to risk Karma visiting me. I wasn't about to say that out loud because Olivia would take it and run. No doubt she'd dig up more reasons to make the cheater pay.

A customer came in, nodded at us, and moved down one of the aisles of books. Olivia shrugged. "It was worth a shot. I guess I can wait for Karma to catch up with him."

Had she read my mind? "She will. Eventually."

Olivia's eyes widened. "Do you know Karma? Maybe you can call her?"

I tried so hard not to laugh and failed. "No, I don't know Karma. She might not be a person."

Glancing toward the bookshelves, Olivia tapped her fingers on the glass countertop and then checked her watch. "I need to go. It's my turn to bake cupcakes for the kids today. We should do lunch tomorrow."

I had a feeling that if I didn't have lunch with her, she wouldn't leave me alone. Then again, if I did, it was possible she still wouldn't leave me alone. It was a lose-lose situation. "Fine. Call me in the morning."

I didn't need to give her my number. She could get it from Sam's phone.

She let out a small squeal and clapped her hands. "I'll call you in the morning."

Before I could tell her not too early, she was gone.

Great. If she called my phone before the sun fully rose, I would seriously reconsider my no cursing-people policy.

The rest of the day was pretty steady and smooth. Customers came and went, many taking the time to chat about anything and anyone. Apparently, the hair salon wasn't the only place where the grapevine started. In my case, it ended because I wasn't about to repeat half of what was said. Most of it was ludicrous anyway.

Thankfully, I didn't recognize any more of my customers, and since they didn't seem to recognize me, I didn't offer up any personal information. The fewer people who knew I was here the better. I wasn't staying.

While the store was empty, I took the opportunity to take out a small bag of trash. Clint had mentioned the dumpster behind the building, and I remembered the layout from my high school days. In a town this small, there wasn't much to do but walk around—everywhere. Repeatedly.

The store wasn't huge, yet it wasn't tiny either. The front of the store was an open space with small round tables with comfy armchairs around them. There was a coffee station in the left-hand corner by the front door. The counter with the register was on the other side. Soft indie music drifted from the speakers mounted in the corners near the ceiling.

I breathed in the scents of coffee and books. This was my happy place. I couldn't have picked a better place to work if I'd tried. I'd have to turn one of the rooms in my home in Philly into a coffee bar-slash-library.

With the bag of trash in hand, I moved down one of the many aisles of books to the back of the store. As I passed the office, I stuck my head in and smiled at Clint. "I'm taking the trash out. Do you have any I can take?"

He looked up from his computer and smiled back. "Nope, mine's not full yet."

"Great." I pushed out the back door and felt magic in the air. Pausing outside the door, I scanned the area behind the strip mall. I didn't see anything, but there was no denying that someone was there, or had been there recently. Then a scent I'd never encountered but heard of hit me. A mixture of soil, rosemary, cedar, and a hint of sulfur. Those were a few of the ingredients to create a ghoul. Oh, no.

Surely there wasn't a ghoul in Shipton. That would mean a necromancer lived here. As far as I knew I was the only one. Since I didn't use my dark powers, ever, there shouldn't have been a ghoul around.

Shaking off what had to be my overactive imagination, I slung the bag of trash up into the dumpster shared by the bookstore, bakery, and hair salon. As I turned back toward the building, I saw it. Rather, I saw *him*.

Someone was lying behind the dumpster.

Without giving it a second thought, I grabbed onto my powers and probed him. *Those* powers. The ones I tried so hard to pretend weren't there, but I had to know. I had to check and see if the man was alive.

Damn it all to Hell. He most definitely wasn't alive. In fact, he was so dead there was nothing there for me to grab hold of whatsoever. If I'd practiced necromancy, been in touch with my powers, and if I hadn't locked them away years ago, I *still* wouldn't have been able to sense any life in this man. He'd been gone that long, and his soul had already moved on.

Only recent deaths still had enough life essence for a necromancer to tap into. Since I couldn't sense him at all, I guessed that he'd been dead for at least twelve hours.

I didn't have to physically touch him to know that. Shuddering, I closed my eyes. *Please let him disappear.*

No such luck. He was still there. At least, his body was. Damn.

With shaking hands, I pulled out my cell phone and dialed 911. "Clint!" I yelled. I couldn't take my gaze off the man's lower body. His upper body and head were hidden by the dumpster. I backed up and banged on the back door without taking my eyes off the dead feet. "Clint."

"911, what's your emergency?"

"Yeah, I found a body. Behind Imaginary Homes Bookstore, partially hidden by the dumpster." My voice was shaky with fear, but who could blame me? I hadn't seen a dead body since... Well, not like this, not since I was ten.

The door slammed behind me. "Holy shit," Clint whispered. "That's a damn dead body. Holy shit."

"No," I answered the operator's question, which I'd almost missed. "We won't touch anything. I haven't. I just threw a bag of trash in the dumpster. Clint inched forward and put his fingers on the man's leg. Checking for a pulse, I guessed.

"Back away and wait for the police to get there," she said.

I grabbed Clint's arm, and we shuffled to the front of the alley. He took a moment to walk around the building rather than touch the back door again and locked the front door before returning to me. "We're closed," he said in a nervous voice. "This is awful."

I wrapped my arms around my middle and nodded. Death was not my thing. It would only lead to pain and memories I didn't want to relive.

As soon as the police arrived, we tiptoed behind them back into the alley. It took them a while to catalog everything, but when they finally moved the dumpster, I caught a look at the guy's neck and gasped, slamming my hand over my mouth and backing away.

I knew what he was, and what was worse, I knew him. I'd just never realized that my aunt's old friend was a necromancer. I tried to keep from hyperventilating as I looked at the gray tattoo on his neck.

It looked the way my auntie's had. The way my Yaya's had, and the way mine had before I'd changed it. Witch marks were only visible to other witches, so I'd enlisted the help of Aunt Winnie. The tattoo was invisible to humans, thanks to her spell on the ink, but to other witches, it appeared green, like the Earth witches on my mother's side of the family. I got the other part of myself, the part I kept locked away, hidden, from Dad.

The police whirled around when they heard me, to see what I was gasping about. I had to think fast. Telling them that this poor dead guy was a necromancer wasn't an option. I had no idea which of them knew that I was a witch. Only Sam knew I was one as well, and he knew why I hated that power.

Probably none of the officers there had the first clue since I didn't recognize any of them. "Is Sam coming?" I whispered.

One of the officers walked closer. "He's on his way. Are you okay?"

"I just...I know the victim." A sob caught in my throat as the rest of the words froze there. He'd been killed. Necromancers were incredibly difficult to kill. I could see blood and what to me looked like a stab wound through his shirt. "How did he die?" I asked.

"Stabbed." He put a hand on my shoulder. "Are you sure you're okay?"

But how? Necromancers didn't just die when we were injured. The injury had to be incredibly bad. Either something fast and severe or so massive there was no recovery. "Stabbed where?" I asked.

"Directly in the heart."

Oh. That would do it if the knife was big enough and long enough.

But who would kill a necromancer? Who would know to stab in the right spot?

I knew the answer, but I didn't want to admit it to myself.

Likely only another necromancer or a *very* advanced magic user. We held our secrets close to our chests, and it wasn't common knowledge that we were hard to kill. Not common at all.

This whole debacle threw me back into the memory I tried so hard to repress.

The day I stopped using my necromancy magic was the single most traumatic day of my life.

My dad had been dead for five years. He was in a horrific car accident on the interstate involving a semi-truck driver falling asleep at the wheel. He'd been basically crushed, which explained how he'd died in a car wreck of all things. As a necromancer, a car wreck would've had to have been pretty significant to kill him.

And it was.

When he died, Mom mourned deeply and intently. Their love story was one for the ages, as she loved to tell me, but he'd died, and we came to live with Yaya and Aunt Winnie.

All I remember from those years was intense pain and great joy. Yaya and Auntie did everything in their power to help us through our grief, and once the worst of it passed, my childhood was pretty idyllic. They made sure we never felt the pain of not having a father figure, besides of course our grief of missing the man himself.

Christmas the year I turned ten was the day my life changed, and no matter how they tried after that, my life never turned idyllic again.

We were putting up lights on the side of the house. Winnie and Yaya had gone in to get another box of lights and Mom stood high up on the ladder. I held the bottom steady. Mom stayed still while we waited, not wanting to move that high up on the ladder without Winnie and Yaya out there to hold the ladder. Yaya was a strong enough witch that she would've slowed Mom down if she fell.

The next thing I knew, the ladder rattled, and it happened so fast I never could say why or how it happened. One second Mom was on the ladder, the next she was on the ground with her head bent at an unnatural angle.

Her eyes were wide and staring, and my magic whispered to me as I stared down at my mother, my best friend and biggest supporter. She was dead.

I screamed, unable to accept what I was seeing. Pain and torment filled my soul, and all I thought about was that I couldn't lose my mom like I lost my dad. Tears blurred my vision, and my breaths came in gasps of sobbing hiccups.

Mustering every bit of the shadow magic inside me, I

shoved it all into my mother's body as Winnie and Yaya ran from the house.

"Ava, no," Winnie cried.

But it was too late. My mother rose from the grass, her limbs jerking and popping.

"Mommy?" I whispered in horror. Backing away, tears streaming down my face, I immediately regretted what I'd done. I hadn't been trained in necromancy at all. I didn't know what I was doing. I'd thrown every ounce of power in me at my mother.

It had animated her, but it hadn't healed her.

Yaya yanked me behind her. "Ava you've got to pull it out."

Mom turned to us with her head still flopped all wrong. It must've broken significantly, because it hung from her shoulders by the skin, like nothing I'd ever seen before. "What's wrong with her?" I sobbed as I clung to Yaya's back.

Winnie put herself between Mom and me as well. "Honey, she was gone. Too far gone. You've animated her body, but your mother isn't in there. She's essentially a ghoul. You've got to pull the magic out of her." She spoke over her shoulder with her hands out, dark green smoke around them. She was ready to hit Mom with a spell, but I didn't know what good an Earth witch would be if I'd turned Mom into a ghoul.

Sobbing harder, I tried to yank on my power, but it was too hard. "I can't." I cried out. "I can't do it."

Yaya dropped to her knees and turned to face me. "Ava Calliope Howe. Grab a hold of your power inside your mother's body and yank as hard as you can."

I wiped my eyes and with my stomach heaving, I did as she said. I pulled so hard on my magic that when it snapped back into me, I flew backward with my gaze on my mother's body as it crumpled to the ground.

She was dead. My mother was dead, and I hadn't been able to save her.

For months, I had nightmares of my mother's body filled with demons and crawling out of the grave to scratch at my window.

From that day, I'd never used my necromancy power again. Well, except once. I had to save my Snoozles. I'd stamped it down. Until this week, when I reluctantly used it to see if that poor man was dead or alive, I'd pushed it away and ignored it.

CHAPTER SIX

Clint put his arm around me, pulling me out of the
memory. "Come on. Let's go over here and let them do
what they do."

I let him drag me away from the crime scene while my
stomach rolled with grief. I'd known William for years. All my
life now that I thought about it, but I'd never known he was a
necromancer. How had he hidden it?

I tried to think about the last time I'd seen him. At Aunt
Winnie's funeral. What had he been wearing?

I closed my eyes and leaned against the cool brick wall of
the bookstore around the corner of the alley and sucked in air,
trying to calm my racing heart.

He'd worn a suit, buttoned up with a necktie at the funeral.
I wouldn't have seen his mark then. Come to think of it,
William had worn suits often. He was a college professor and
had the tweed elbow patch thing down pat. He'd favored a
bowtie.

That was how I'd never seen his witch mark.

Holy shit. He'd been a necromancer.

Why hadn't they told me? If I'd known, maybe he could've helped me work through everything when Mom died.

But would I have listened? No, I wouldn't have. I was so horrified at what I'd done that it scared me from using my dark power. Training with someone wouldn't have changed my mind.

Just being around William's body was torture. I hated being around the freshly dead. Even though I knew there was nothing in William to resurrect, still, his corpse teased my powers. They wanted to animate his body; create a ghoul.

I'd done that once. Never, *ever* again.

Glancing over to the sheet-covered body, I hugged my waist. The Combs were good people. They were caring and everyone in town loved them. Now poor William was dead, but how? Why go after William?

"Ava."

Hearing Sam's voice took a huge weight off my shoulders. He'd help me get to the bottom of this. The truth, not whatever washed-out version we'd end up telling the police. If this murder was magically charged, we had to figure out how and why.

"Sam," I said in relief. He knew all about me, including what I really was. Even the people I'd grown up with who knew about magic and knew I was a witch didn't know my true nature. Sam did.

I grabbed his arm and pulled him farther around the front of the building. All of the looky-loos were crowded around the mouth of the alley. I belatedly realized Clint had been keeping them out of my hair.

Thank you, Clint.

"The body belongs to William Combs," I said in a hushed voice, looking around to make sure nobody was nearby. "He was a necromancer."

Sam's face paled. He knew the full extent of what that meant as well as I did. "I thought your kind—"

I shushed him and he continued with a lowered voice. "Your kind were super hard to kill, and that's what made your dad's death so strange?"

"We are." I crossed my arms and looked toward the crowd. "He was stabbed directly in the heart. That's one way to do it."

"Who could kill a necromancer?" he asked with one hand on his gun. He looked around like a gun would be any good against who-the-fuck-ever killed William.

"I have no idea. Another witch, maybe?" I shrugged and tried not to let the fear run all through me.

"Can you take something off of the body and do a tracking spell?" he asked.

I knew what he was asking. Necromancers could take a piece of the victim's flesh around the wound to see how he died. It was a tricky spell and took a lot of focus. "No. I've never been trained. Maybe William could've done it, but I'm not that person anymore."

"Bullshit," he muttered. "Remember, I knew you before your mom died. I know you're the most powerful necromancer anybody's ever seen."

I cut him a nasty glare. "I *could've been* the best, but that would've required years of training and intense focus to get to that point. That doesn't mean I can snap my fingers and do it." I pulled my sleeve down and wiped at my nose, not self-conscious about such a yucky act in front of Sam. "Besides, I don't think that prophecy is always true. I'm not that powerful of a witch in general."

If I were, I'd be able to bring my mom back and not as a soulless ghoul.

The prophecy I referred to was one that my Yaya and Auntie spoke of often. They seemed to think that I would grow into my powers and one day be one of the elite group of necromancers that possessed powers beyond raising the dead and creating undead creatures.

According to my necromancer half of my family, the first-born of the seventh generation of necromancers would be blessed with great powers. Supposedly, those powers included bringing back the dead, animating the undead so they were human, and a number of impossible abilities. All of which I'd never shown any signs of.

If I was this all-powerful seventh-generation necromancer, then would it have been hard for me to suppress the power for as long as I had? I thought that much power wouldn't want to be hidden away. Hence why I didn't believe in the stories passed down through my father's side of the family.

Because that was all the prophecy was—a story.

"Excuse me." A deliciously husky male voice pulled me from my thoughts and my personal conversation with my BFF.

Even through my shock and upset at William's death, I couldn't help but shiver at the timbre of the man's voice.

I lifted my gaze and spotted Sheriff Drew, who I hadn't realized was there. He must have just arrived.

When he started to walk over to us, my heart skipped a few beats. I admired how he filled out every inch of his uniform. Hot damn, he looked more like a stripper in a cop uniform than an actual cop. Had they ordered him a shirt a size too small? Because slow claps to whoever did that.

I bet it was that old secretary at the police department. She was a hundred if she was a day, and it seemed like she was always out on the front lawn of the police department with a menthol in one hand, talking to the officers, even when we were kids. I'd bet she was exactly the same nowadays. When I was young, she was always *inside* the police department smoking her menthols. Sam's dad had been an officer at the time, and Sam and I spent half our childhood at the precinct.

"Hello, Sheriff." As soon as my words left my mouth, he

smiled. Damn if the lift of his lips didn't make me weak in the knees.

However, his smile vanished almost as fast as it appeared. "I wish running into you wasn't at a crime scene."

Yes, too bad... Blinking, I studied him while slowly his aura drifted around me. For the life of me I couldn't figure out what it was about him that was *other*. I still couldn't pinpoint it. He wasn't a witch or a vampire. The fact that he was out in the sunlight confirmed the latter. Somehow, though, he wasn't totally human either.

"I'm assuming Sam got your statement." He flicked his gaze to Sam and then back to me.

"Yeah. My official and unofficial statement."

Sam nudged me with his elbow at my statement. He should know I don't have a filter on most days. I nudged him back.

Drew noticed our exchange, but he didn't comment. Clever man. "Ma'am, they tell me you discovered the body?"

Ma'am? Was he getting back at me for not calling him *Drew?*

Whatever. Calling him by his first name was too personal. We just met, briefly, in a freaking grocery store. We weren't at the stage of being personal.

I hadn't had a chance to ask Sam how much Drew knew about the supernatural, so instead of assuming he knew, I assumed he *didn't* know. Better to be safe than have to explain away my crazy. "I took out some trash and found him. I didn't move the body or look behind the dumpster, so I didn't realize it was someone I knew until they pulled the dumpster out."

Just then, a couple of paramedics wheeled a stretcher out of the alley with a deep black body bag on it. My heart broke for my friend. I wondered if anyone had called his wife.

"How did you know he was dead if you didn't see his face?" Drew asked with his pencil poised over his notebook.

Well, I couldn't say it was because I was a keeper of the undead, now could I?

Clint spoke up. He'd walked up with Drew. I was in such a daze I hadn't noticed. Geez. I needed to snap it together. "We checked his pulse on his ankle," he said. "Didn't touch him otherwise."

"William." A new voice interrupted us and sent ice straight to my heart. I knew that voice.

Drew hurried forward to intercept Penelope from launching herself at the body bag. "Ma'am, hold on." He put his hands on her shoulders, but it was too late. She'd gotten her hands on the zipper and yanked it back to see the body.

She stiffened and pulled back. "Oh, William," she whispered. Penelope Comb was a few years younger than my aunt Winnie. Mrs. Comb had silver hair; the color women nowadays pay big bucks to their hairdressers to duplicate. She was about three inches or so shorter than my five feet seven height.

I shuffled around everyone, so I was beside Penny. "Come on," I whispered as I wrapped an arm around her shoulders. I looked at Drew. "Is that sufficient for an identification?"

He nodded, drawing his brows together and closing off his emotions. I guessed because it kept him from getting too personal with the case. Still, he could show a little empathy.

She sobbed into her hands and turned into me. "That's my Willie."

"I know." I tightened my hold on her and urged her to come with me. "Let's go, Penny. I'll take you inside."

That was when she noticed me. We locked gazes and for a minute I got lost in her green eyes. Sorrow bubbled up inside me. "Ava." Then she started sobbing again.

CHAPTER SEVEN

We walked the long way around the building, passing Clips and Snips hair salon and Peachy Sweets bakery. I set our slow pace on purpose because I knew all too well what it was like to lose a husband unexpectedly.

Penny walked with her head on my shoulder. I felt the moisture spread into my T-shirt as she silently wept. My chest tightened, and a lump stuck in my throat, but no tears formed. Probably because they had dried up. I had no more tears to shed.

"Can I call someone for you?" I asked as soon as I got her in the car. I decided to take her home instead of inside the bookstore. If Sheriff Drew wanted to speak with Penny, then he'd have to go to her house.

She leaned over and clutched my hand. "You've got to avenge my husband's death, Ava. You've just got to."

Avenge sounded too close to revenge and not because they were rhyming words. I studied her closely as I spoke. "Penny, the police will catch the killer. If there's anything I can do to help, I will, but it'll be Sheriff Drew and his officers who will find William's killer."

"No, Ava the police can't stop magic. Not like you can." Her hands shook and she looked around the car wide-eyed as if she expected someone else to be in the car.

Her words slammed into my chest. I thought back to the smell of a ghoul when I exited the building.

"Was William killed by magic?" I asked, extracting my hand from hers. "Buckle your seat belt, please."

Once I was settled in the driver's seat and buckled myself in, I paused before starting Dia, waiting for Penny to answer my question. She didn't. She was in a daze, but it was clear she was in shock. Understandably so, but I couldn't help wondering if it was the grief of seeing her husband's body or was there something else?

It was almost like she had more information than she let on and was trying to gather her thoughts before spilling her secrets.

Leaving her to her thoughts, I started the car and drove out of the downtown district. I knew where they lived, not far from my Auntie's house, so I headed straight there.

Much like my mood, the day had taken a dark turn. Clouds blocked the sun and the wind picked up like the weather grieved the death of William.

The police can't stop magic.

Penny's words echoed in my head, and I *so* didn't want her to be right. Something deep inside me said she was. Great.

I hadn't been in town a solid week, and already magic was trying to suck me back in. I had to get clear of this murder, get the house sold, and get the hell out of Dodge.

"Okay, Penny, we're here. Who can I call for you?" I desperately didn't want to go inside with her, but what else could I do? I couldn't leave the poor woman here alone until someone else arrived.

"My daughter is on her way. I called her when the police called me, but she lives in the next town over. It'll be a few more minutes, at least. She was at work." She sat in the car and stared at her house in a daze. Her words were soft and almost robotic. "I can't imagine going inside and knowing he won't be there. That he'll never be there again. How is this possible?"

My vision blurred with unshed tears, and I tightened my grip on the steering wheel. Well, at least Crystal was coming. I couldn't make the sweet old lady go inside alone. I turned the engine off and palmed my keys. "Come on. I'll go in with you."

Penny sucked in a sudden, severe breath. She looked at me as if snapping out of her shock. Well, some of it, anyway. "Oh, you must come in. I need your help with something."

She unbuckled her seat belt and threw the car door open as a clap of thunder broke overhead. Ducking—I'd always been leery of storms—I hurried after Penny, curious to what had put pep in her step.

The Combs' home was a modest single-story, red brick home. The center of the roof rose to a point where the attic was. A small window in the center of the peak gave the illusion of having a second floor.

White shutters accented the windows. I've always loved their home. It was perfect for them and not at all what one would think a necromancer lived in. Then again, the old Victorian screamed that she was a witch's house and was proud of it.

Thinking about my family home, I frowned. I'd finally got the contractors to come back and work that morning. I hoped Old Vicky was behaving herself. On the heels of that thought, my phone dinged. Glancing down at it, I let out a sigh.

It was a text from Jude, the contractor. **House has locked us out. Call me when you will be here all day.**

That damn house. I'd never get it ready to go on the market

at this rate. I sent a reply. **I'll be home tomorrow. Don't come too early.**

I pocketed my phone as Penny unlocked the front door and scurried inside. The interior of the house was decorated in country chic, as it had been since I'd come over as a child with Auntie Winnie to practice magic with William.

I furrowed my brow. I didn't remember much about my time with William. He loved to tell me stories and would let me read from his volumes of magic books. At the time, I hadn't had a clue he was teaching me magic. Yaya and Auntie always made it schoolwork, which I hated, but not William. He put the fun in it.

"Penny?" I called to her as she disappeared deeper into the house. "Penny, why did I come over here as a child?"

"Why, to practice your necromancy, dear." She stuck her head out of the living room doorway. "You were supposed to come study with William after your thirteenth year, but your Aunt said you rejected your powers after your poor mother died."

That much was true. She'd asked me several times if I was ready to start studying and I'd told her in no uncertain terms that it was not going to happen. Eventually, she'd stopped trying.

"Come in here," Penny called. "There's someone I want you to meet."

I hurried down the hall and into the living room. I froze in the archway, not believing what I was seeing. Sitting on the couch, his hands folded in his lap, was something I'd never fully seen and never expected to see again in my life. I hoped not to, anyway.

He had pasty white skin with gray blotches in random spots. He had black, unkempt hair that covered his ears and across his forehead. Drab gray eyes watched me, and I swore there was some kind of recognition in his depths.

At least he was clean. His clothes looked new-ish and he didn't smell, other than like rosemary and fresh soil. The combination was oddly pleasant.

"Penny," I whispered, reaching out to her. I didn't know a whole lot about ghouls. "What is a ghoul doing sitting on your couch?" I asked.

She stepped forward, and the ghoul jumped up. My heart nearly burst in fear as he moved, but I held my ground. He bowed and scurried around the coffee table, through the two chairs on the other side, and out the door that led to the kitchen. "What is happening?" I squeaked.

"He's probably getting us some tea." She grabbed a tissue from a box on the coffee table and sat on the couch. "How is this happening? I feel like I'm losing my mind, truly I do."

I perched beside her, ready to take *the hell* off if that ghoul came creeping back in here, but I couldn't leave Penny with that thing. "Penny, I know you're hurting something awful, but you've got to tell me why a ghoul is making tea?"

"He was William's," she said. "He always kept a ghoul to do work around the house and tidy the yard and things."

I wanted to bang on my ears and make sure I'd heard her right. "You have a ghoul... *for housework?*"

"Well, of course. You would've if you'd trained up properly. I bet you've been washing dishes all these years by hand, haven't you?"

"No," I exclaimed. "I use a spell-like a normal person." A normal witch, anyway. Not a necromancer.

"Well, you've got to take him. Alfred has to be controlled by a necromancer or he'll get unruly."

It was getting ridiculously hard not to gape at Penny. "Your husband made a ghoul to do your housework and you named him Alfred?" Please tell me she was kidding. I looked around the living room. "Penny, is this a practical joke?"

She sat up straight. "Have you been taught nothing about

your heritage? Did your aunt and grandmother really let you refuse to the point of not knowing that ghouls are a part of life for necromancers?"

I pursed my lips at her. She was grieving something awful and didn't need me contradicting her or giving her any flak.

"Penny, I know nothing about controlling a ghoul. I can't take him with me. Your daughter can take care of him, can't she?"

She shook her head. "No, and I'm not sure how Alfred is still with us now that William is gone. I expected him to disintegrate or something. That's why I wasn't sure William was really gone because Alfred was still here."

Alfred walked back in. I studied him more. He walked with a slight limp and like his spine wasn't straight. The tray he carried as he advanced to us shook but only a little. Even with his jerky, unsteady moves, I was surprised he got around as well as he could.

I needed to do some research on ghouls.

My nerves were on extreme alert. I nearly ran from the room when he handed me my cup of tea. "I don't know how to control him."

"Why don't you tell him to do something and see what he does?" she asked, giving me a pointed, mom look. "William said he couldn't refuse an order from a necromancer, but then William made him."

"Sit down," I said timidly.

He sat. Immediately and without question.

"Do you understand me?" I asked.

Alfred nodded his head, unable to reply through the stitches on his mouth. Odd, I hadn't noticed them until that moment. Why would William sew his mouth shut?

I probably didn't want to know.

"Are you compelled to do as I ask?"

He nodded again.

I turned to Penny. "Okay, then, I'll find a way to release him from his flesh and that'll be that." I didn't have the first clue how I'd do such a thing, but I'd find a way.

Alfred jumped up off the couch and ran toward me, shaking his head vehemently. I squealed and backed into the couch. He grunted and groaned as he shook his head.

"Do you not want to be released?" I asked.

He shook his head.

"You want to live?"

He nodded.

"With me?"

Nod.

Fuck.

I looked at Penny. "What happens if I leave him?"

"He'll get unruly and eventually start killing."

Son of a bitch.

"Okay, then." Looks like I inherited a ghoul servant. What was I going to do?

Penny turned to me and took my hands. "Ava, listen to me. You've got to be careful. Alfred isn't just for dusting. He can fight. You're going to need him. What killed my William, it wasn't a random thing? It was a witch hunter."

I raised my eyebrows. "This isn't Salem three hundred years ago."

She sighed and clenched her fists. "Ava, witch hunters are very real. They're rare, but they exist. William believed that there was one, at least, witch hunter bent on eradicating all necromancers. William was killed by that witch hunter. I'm sure of it."

"Why wouldn't anyone have told me about this already?" I asked.

"The witch hunters are so rare. The hunting gene is passed down from father to son and mother to daughter. That's what the lore says. If a father only has daughters, the gene isn't passed. If a mother only has sons, they are human."

Interesting. Still, nothing I'd ever heard of. "Should I be worried?"

"Yes, that's what I'm trying to tell you."

Just then, the front door opened. I turned in panic, worried about who would be walking in, and see the ghoul standing in the living room, but it was William and Penny's daughter, Crystal.

"Crystal here was the only one of our children to inherit the necromancy gene, and it's very faint in her. That's why you must take Alfred." Penny pleaded. She didn't want the ghoul any more than I did.

I glanced at Alfred, who was still standing beside me as if waiting for me to direct him. Great.

As Crystal and Penny embraced and began to cry, I stood and motioned Alfred to follow me out of the room. "Well, we'll go. Please, call me later. If you figure out anything more about this witch hunter, let me know. I'll do some digging on my end."

Apparently, I had some homework to do in Ghoul 101 and an Introduction to Witch Hunters.

CHAPTER EIGHT

"Stay here." I eyed Alfred and thanked my lucky stars there weren't any lights in the diner's parking lot. No need for the locals to see an undead creature roaming the parking lot. Good grief, what had I gotten myself into? It wasn't like I could take him back to Philly with me.

"I'm getting some dinner." I reached for the door handle and paused while watching him. "Do not move."

This was unreal. By the time I'd actually managed to get out of Penny's house with Alfred, whom I still couldn't believe I was taking home, it had gotten pretty dark. It worked out for me since the last thing I wanted was for anyone to see Alfred. Not that there were a whole lot of people who lived around Auntie's house, but Alfred was pretty scary looking. I was still a little freaked out by him and he had to do what I said. So far, he had.

I paused again as I got out of the car, then looked back at the ghoul. "Um, do you eat?"

He looked at me with his dark eyes and shook his head. His

71

facial expression didn't change, but somehow, I knew he was sad. "You want to eat?"

Nod.

"But you can't?"

Nod.

"I'm sorry," I whispered. "Can you smell food?"

At least that was a head shake. He pointed to his eyes.

"You can see how good it looks."

Nod.

Well, that sucked a big one. "I'm sorry. If I can figure out a way to get you out of this existence without it meaning you dying, I will. I know nothing about ghouls."

He shrugged and turned to look out the front window.

With a light shudder, I slammed the car door shut, then pressed the lock button on the key fob twice. I didn't want to risk anyone accidentally opening the door. I probably should've taken him home first and then come back for food, but I was almost inside now.

I ordered my meal, a big greasy burger with extra fries, and sat at the counter while I waited. Every so often I glanced out at my car. Should I have cracked the windows? I knew ghouls were undead, but I didn't know if they needed to breathe. However, it was October in Maine, so Alfred didn't have to worry about heat stroke.

A feeling inched over me like inky fingers, something I'd never felt before. Even though I knew beyond a shadow of a doubt I'd never had this experience before; I also knew it meant another necromancer was nearby. His or her magic, even though it was somewhat contained, called out to me. A familiarity begging for my attention like an old friend I hadn't seen in forever.

Fear spiked through me as I tried to surreptitiously look around. Penny said a witch hunter was responsible for William's death, but I would cast out the idea that another necromancer could have also done it. When I glanced toward the diner door, *he* walked in. I knew what he was even before I noticed the gray witch mark on the side of his neck, telling me he was a necromancer.

His long, black hair hung down in his face, stringy and a little oily. Pale, slightly scarred skin made me think he had acne problems when he was younger. His face was dry, which didn't help hide the scars. Ugh. Poor guy. A little moisturizer would've helped that.

Dread danced on my spine, getting stronger and making me more nauseated as he got closer. The tall man's gaze was glued to my face. He knew what I was too.

Which raised a few questions. How had I not sensed William? Had he been able to block it somehow? Could I learn how and why?

He sat on the stool right beside me.

Of course. I worried if he could smell Alfred on me. According to Penny, it wasn't unusual for my kind to have ghouls.

I cleared my throat and started to slide out of my seat in the opposite direction, but he still had his gaze on me. "Owen," he said. "Owen Daniels."

A James Bond joke formed in my mind, and I quickly squashed it down before my mouth spoke the words out loud. No need to offend the man with dark powers. Besides, he knew how to use his powers. I didn't.

Damn. I realized that it might be a good idea to start learning, but I had no one I could trust to learn from.

Wait. I wasn't staying here. Once Old Vicky sold, I was out like last week's trash. Not that I was calling myself trash.

Owen Daniels felt dark, darker than any witch I'd ever met. I couldn't recall having been around another necromancer. We were a pretty rare breed, but other witches were dark as well, such as those who call themselves warlocks. I hated that I was a necromancer. Maybe because I'd kept it stamped down for so long, I hadn't sensed them and now I could, but why? I'd been using my power every time I told Alfred to do something. Maybe he listened to me because of what lurked beneath the surface.

Whatever, all my internal warning bells were going absolutely bonkers. He was so dark inside.

"Burger and fries," the server said and slid it across the counter to me.

I snatched up the Styrofoam container and practically sprinted out of the diner. As I pulled onto the road, I slowed and looked in the big windows in front of the diner. He was still at the counter.

Breathing a sigh of relief, I headed home. He wasn't following, and him being in town was a coincidence.

Or he was the murderer. Potayto, potahto.

"Okay, Alfred," I said as I parked in the circular driveway in front of the house. Timidly, I reached over and unbuckled his seatbelt. Poor thing acted like he'd never been in a car. He most likely hadn't. I had to help him buckle up when we left Penny's. Lifting my gaze, I found him staring at me as if waiting for me. I pointed to the house and said, "Inside."

He nodded and had no trouble opening his door. Maybe he was smarter than I thought. Then again, I hadn't a clue what I was doing.

Once we climbed the steps to the front porch, I unlocked the door while I balanced my food in one hand, then pushed the door open and cut on the lights. "Ground rules." I threw my keys in the bowl by the front door. "The house is being renovated. You *cannot* be seen by any of the contractors. It simply can't happen. Do you understand?"

Nod.

The workers were already threatening to stop all forward progress because the house was acting out. That was another

74

problem I didn't want to deal with. It annoyed me to no end the house would screw with the workers yet welcome me back home. No, when it was just me, Old Vicky was still and quiet.

That alone made me suspicious. Was it the house coming back to life, or did Auntie put a spell on it? I wouldn't put it past her to do something, anything, to keep me from selling the old place.

Focusing back on my other complication, I asked, "Okay, well, do you sleep?"

Shake.

"What do you do all night?"

After a brief moment of staring at me, he walked away. Um, 'kay. Quietly, I followed him into the living room where he turned in a circle. It seemed like he was looking for something. When he moved to the larger wall that still had the mount for the TV, he stopped and studied the wall.

Did he know the TV was there? I'd taken it out and given it to Wallie to use in his apartment.

Alfred darted from the room. I had to go into a light jog to catch up with him as he dashed up the stairs like he was on a mission.

I finally caught up with him in one of the guest rooms I'd shoved a bunch of Auntie's things into that I hadn't felt like dealing with. I was starting to see a pattern in my behavior. The "not wanting to deal with things" was a result of my grief.

It was going to do better, be better. It was a good thing my husband wasn't around to see me. He'd kick my butt into shape. Not literally. He'd most likely lock up my spell room.

I smiled at the idea. He hadn't been comfortable with magic, but he never told me I couldn't be who I was. I did that enough. However, the natural witch magic I got from my mother was something I enjoyed. It was pure and light. Not dark, like raising the dead and dealing with ghouls and other undead things.

Thinking of undead things, I entered the room and watched Alfred as he moved to the TV on top of the long dresser. He placed one hand on the television and met my stare.

"Oh," I said slowly. "You watch TV all night?"

Nod.

"Well, that's fine, you can still do that. Can you write?" I glanced around the room and figured it wouldn't hurt to make this room his.

He showed me his hands, drawing my attention back to him. The skin was tight and pale. As he tried to close them, he winced. They only closed so far. I wondered how he'd gotten along with his chores.

"You don't have to do chores here," I said. I was part witch and could perform spells better than most so cleaning wasn't an issue. Besides, I didn't like the idea of having a servant. Ghoul or not. "If I got you something you could type on, would you be able to?"

Nod.

Now we're talking. Well, virtually anyway.

"Okay, then great. Uh, well, it's late. I'm going to..." I stopped and stared because Snooze had just walked into the room.

The fat, gray cat looked up at Alfred, cocked his head, and then meowed louder than I'd ever heard the fool cat meow.

Then, Snooze *launched* himself at Alfred. He jumped into the ghoul's arms, and I panicked, expecting I'd have to break up a fight between my insane cat and the creepy undead guy. My heart leaped with him, and I thought the thing would get stuck in my throat for life.

But Snoozles, the little ass, rubbed his head all over Alfred's chin.

"He likes you," I breathed while willing my heart to slow to a normal pace.

Alfred closed his eyes and held Snoozles close, squeezing him without hurting the feline. Snooze reached up and batted at the string holding Alfred's lips together. I sincerely hoped he didn't unravel that string because there was no way I was sewing dead flesh back together.

Not tonight, Satan.

Drifting to the bed, I picked up one of the boxes and set it on the floor in the corner of the room by the window. When I turned to gather up some of the loose items spread out, Alfred was already doing it. He picked items up with care and placed them inside an empty box he found.

When I reached out for another box to move it off the bed, he tapped my hand. I looked up to see him shaking his head and pointing at himself. "You are not my servant. I'm perfectly capable..."

Alfred brushed my hands away, still shaking his head. The stubborn ghoul. "Okay, fine. Since you don't sleep, you can put these boxes in the room across the hall. I need to go through them and see what I want to keep and what I'm donating or trashing."

I had no idea what was in half the boxes I threw in here after the funeral. I wasn't in the condition to clean out the life of another loved one at the time.

Alfred seemed overly pleased with having something to do besides watching TV. I went over to the dresser and picked up the remote. It was a good thing it was a smart TV. Not much for watching the old boob tube, I didn't bother with getting cable. I had Netflix for when I was in the mood to watch something.

After I logged into the Wi-Fi, which I had made sure was at my disposal before coming to town, I set Alfred up with a profile on Netflix and handed him the remote. "There's no cable, but Netflix has enough shows to keep you occupied for a while." I paused as he took the remote and quickly figured out how to use it. "This is your room. You are free to roam the house. My room is at the end of the hall. I'm not a morning person so don't wake me before noon."

He nodded as he sat on the end of the bed and flipped through the movie choices. I wondered if I should put a parental block on his account. I shook my head. He had been a grown man when he died. Or was he created?

Damn, I needed to find out more about Alfred and his origin, but I'll deal with all of that tomorrow.

"I'm going to bed," I said. "Knock on my door if you need me and remember not to go downstairs when the workers are here."

After he nodded to let me know he heard me, I went downstairs to grab my dinner. I hadn't given Alfred a tour, but I'd had all I could take of this day. I grabbed a soda out of the fridge and took my food upstairs, then locked my bedroom door.

I dragged my dresser in front of it. The last thing I needed was some creepy ghoul coming into my bedroom in the night while I was sleeping.

Ugh.

Pulling out my phone, I sent Wallie a quick text. **Hey Wal Wal, love you bunches. If you have a spare minute in between your studies can you research if there's any true witch hunters out there?**

He must've had his phone right in his hand because he replied immediately. **Like Buffy?**

Rolling my eyes, I chuckled at my boy's sarcasm. **Non-fiction. Just if you can, sweetie.**

Sure, ILY.

I didn't have to look up what that acronym meant. I hated text-speak, but I used it sometimes to make my son happy. **ILY2**

CHAPTER NINE

After scarfing down my burger and fries, I sighed. No way I was going to bed anytime soon. My mind was running a marathon with all the crap that happened today.

My phone beeped, alerting me of an email.

Spam. As usual.

While I had my phone in my hand, I contemplated calling Sam. He could help me figure out what in the world to do with Alfred. The ghoul had said he didn't want to be released from his fleshy half-life, but I didn't know jack about ghouls. Was he a real person? Did he have a personality or a soul? I had no idea.

I pressed the buttons to call Sam and put it on speaker, then rethought my actions. If I talked on speaker, Alfred might hear things I didn't want him to. I wasn't sure how aware he was. He seemed able to answer questions, but did he have his memory?

So many questions.

"Hello?" Olivia chirped in my ear.

Ugh. She was the last person I wanted to talk to after the

day I had. "Hello, Olivia." Why was she answering Sam's cell? "Is Sam around?"

"No, he's on duty. He forwards his calls to me when he's working."

Lucky me. I wondered if she could hear my eyes rolling.

"Can I help you with something?"

Pretending to gag silently as she spoke, I shook my head. "No, I was hoping to run something past Sam." Then it occurred to me. Olivia was the town's busybody. If anyone knew who the new necro in town was, it would've been Olivia. "Actually, there is one thing. Have you seen a guy around town, tall, kind of greasy? He's got shoulder-length black hair and looks like a total creeper. He said his name was Owen Daniels."

Olivia went quiet. "I'll be there in five."

The line went dead. "Um," I said to the phone. "No?"

Shit! Why did Olivia have to attach herself to me like an unwanted ghoul? I already had one of those. I scrambled off the bed and shoved the dresser out of the way. "Alfred," I called as I yanked the door open.

I stopped short and found him standing on the other side with one of his weird hands raised. His facial expression couldn't change, but his eyes had widened. He looked surprised and more than that, I felt surprise coming off of him.

Damn this town. I didn't want to start divining the emotions of ghouls. "Were you about to knock?"

Nod.

"Did you need something?"

He stared back at me as if he didn't know how to express what he wanted. I didn't have time at the moment to play charades with a ghoul.

"Can it wait?"

Another nod.

"Well, you've got to go back to your bedroom and stay there. My friend Olivia is coming over and the last thing I need is her figuring out about you." I paused, frowning. "She's human. Even though she knows about witches, she doesn't know I'm a necromancer or about ghouls."

He nodded and backed away. He walked down the hall and straight into the room I gave him to stay.

I hurried after him and shut the door, then went downstairs so that Olivia wouldn't have any reason to come up here.

Five minutes later, the doorbell rang. I cracked the door open, but Olivia bustled in, chipper and smelling like lemon oven cleaner. "You saved me from a night of cleaning. My mom has Sammy since school is out for an in-service tomorrow, and Sam's at work. Now I don't feel guilty about not doing it."

She grinned like she won the lottery or something. Her long blonde hair was pulled up into a high ponytail. Her cheeks were a little flushed, but I couldn't tell if it was from cleaning or the excitement of bothering me. I was guessing it was the latter.

I almost crossed my eyes at the thought but caught myself. Be nice. This is Sam's wife and the mother of his beautiful little boy.

"Great. I'm so happy to help." I sighed and followed Olivia into my living room, noting how she scanned the room. She wasn't looking for something in particular because she'd never been inside the house before. I knew all too well the types of rumors that floated around about Old Vicky. Most of them were true.

"Okay, so the dish on Owen is that nobody knows who he is or why he's here. Everyone has noticed him, 'cause of course they did." She shuddered delicately. "He's so creepy. He looks half-dead himself."

She sat back and nodded her head decisively.

"That's it?" I asked. "That's all you know?"

She blinked at me several times. "Well, what else should I know? Besides, he bought an old lighthouse not far from here."

The lighthouse was interesting.

Shrugging, I tried to be nice. "I don't know, you just came over here to tell me you don't know anything?"

Olivia's grin almost made me smile back at her. "What, I can't want to spend time with my friend?"

I blinked a few times. How to answer her? "We're friends?" I kept my voice light. I wasn't trying to be a jerk, not really. It was hard to trust someone that spent her high school years making mine hell.

Maybe Olivia had changed like Sam said. It wasn't like I spent a lot of time around her since I left. In fact, I avoided her because I was still leery of her.

She responded with laughter. "That's what I like about you. Your sense of humor. Of course, we're friends, well on the way to being best friends."

Batting her eyes, she smiled again. I felt true joy coming off her as she spoke the words. Then she added, "Anyway, tell me about your son."

My first reaction was to tell her my son was none of her business. It was a knee-jerk response because of my trust issues, but Olivia was my best friend's wife, so it was highly possible that Sam had told her all about my business.

I tried to give her a few facts and get her on her way, but the next thing I knew we were at the kitchen table sipping on cups of tea and laughing about crazy things our kids did.

"I don't know how that boy made it to Harvard." I smiled as I downed the last of my tea. "At least not alive."

Olivia giggled. "I know what you mean. My two got more bruises walking through the house than anyone I know."

There was something in her tone that made me pay more attention to her aura. It had darkened slightly, but Olivia kept that smile in place.

Sam had mentioned that Olivia's first marriage was rough. I didn't ask for details, but I was curious as to what could make Olivia change her evil ways. I was afraid I didn't want to know.

Maybe she did deserve a second chance without me giving her a hard time. See, I can be nice and friendly.

"Sam said you lived in Philly."

I nodded and as I began telling Olivia about my home in Philly, a thump overhead made us both freeze and look at the ceiling.

That damn ghoul. What the hell was he doing up there? Watching TV wasn't that loud. Please, Universe, I hope he didn't lose a body part.

"What was that?" Olivia asked.

I masked my features and quickly said, "Either my cat or the house is misbehaving." Damn it, it was definitely Alfred. The room he was in was right over the kitchen.

Her jaw dropped and her eyes went wide. "The house... misbehaving?"

How was it she knew I was a witch but didn't know the house was magical? After all, it was one of the local legends. "Yeah, I think it's mad that I'm selling."

She giggled nervously. "The house is mad?"

I shrugged while hiding my smirk because it was way too much fun messing with her. Then I had a change of heart and filled her in on the truth about the magical old Victorian. "It's been in the family for a long time, and you know my family are all witches."

She eyed me carefully and nodded, so I continued. "My great, great, great grandparents built the house over a thousand years ago."

Maybe it hadn't been that long, but that was the story my mother told me, so I passed it on. Olivia lifted a brow while her lips twisted in a small smile. "A thousand years?"

"Yes, at least that is the story passed down to each generation. So that's how I'm telling it." I wrinkled my nose at her, making her laugh. It was a good thing we weren't drinking alcohol. "As I was saying. Way back when my great times four or five—I'm not sure—grandmother came over from Ireland, they settled here and built this house overlooking the ocean. It's said that spells were weaved into the wood as it was built, making the house magical. It would protect the witches who lived here."

Olivia stared at me with her mouth open and brows drawn together. Disbelief rolled off her in waves. "Are you serious?"

"Yeah. Now I'm sure it's only been a few hundred years. My mom told me that version of the story, so it's the one I told Wallie. He didn't believe me either, but the house was built by my ancestors and is magical to the point it acts alive. Although I thought it was Aunt Winnie's magic that kept it alive."

I told her about the house scaring off the construction crew. Olivia laughed so hard that I thought she would fall out of her chair.

We talked about nothing and everything for another hour, sharing laughs at other people's expenses. By the time I waved goodbye to Olivia from the front porch, I was no longer sure if she was annoying or if I appreciated that she'd come to distract me all evening. My mood had certainly lifted thanks to Olivia.

Damn it. I didn't need friends.

After closing the door and locking it, I sent out my senses to make sure the windows were all locked. Not that anyone would dare break into this house. Old Vicky wouldn't let them.

I stood in the center of the living room. It was where the heart of the house's magic was. "Vicky, you should be nice to the construction workers."

The floorboards under my feet shook. Her magic reached out, wrapping around me like a hug. The house didn't want new owners.

I sighed. "Look, I get it, but I can't maintain two houses and my life is in Philly."

The walls shook then, telling me she was not accepting that

answer. Ugh. "Okay, but you still need repairs done. I'll figure out something."

That seemed to satisfy the house because a low hum of pleasant magic swirled around me.

I hoped the old house would forgive me after I sold her. Maybe I could find a way to release the magic from the house. Then I wouldn't have to worry about it scaring off the buyers.

Sounded like a plan. I was totally adding it to my growing to-do list.

CHAPTER TEN

"Shut up," I yelled at my phone and threw the blanket over my head. It was way too damn early. I'd set my alarm for nine, but the sun was barely peeking over the horizon.

Finally, it stopped ringing, to my intense relief. I snuggled back into my pillow and dozed off almost instantly.

Seconds later, the shrill ringing filled the air again. Groaning, I reached out and pushed the answer button, then the speaker. "'Lo?"

"Good morning."

It was Olivia. For the love of everything unholy. Of course, it was Olivia. I needed to put a special ringtone on her phone number, so I'd know never to answer her call, but knowing her as well as I did, she'd just call from Sam's phone. I was doomed.

"Why are you up this early?" My voice was scratchy and deep, thick with sleep. Plus, I was thirsty. I had to pee. Damn it. Looked like I was getting up.

"I've been up for over an hour," she said in a sing-song voice.

The sounds of construction filtered through my door. They

were already here and working. "How do people function this early?" I whispered. "I feel like the dead." That was saying something coming from me.

"Well, I have so much news for you. I followed Owen last night and I think he's up to no good. After I left your place I passed by the diner, and guess what? He was there. I waited to see where he went, and he drove all over the dang place."

"Olivia. Does Sam know you followed this guy? It's dangerous." I couldn't help but imagine what could've happened to her. And Sam would have blamed me.

"We just won't tell him. How about that?" She sighed. "But no, I don't keep secrets from him. I'll tell him tonight."

"Good." I didn't love Olivia, but Sam did, and I loved Sam. For a relationship to stand the test of time, honesty was necessary. "I'm glad to hear you say you're not keeping secrets."

"Well, anyway, I'm here. I just pulled into your driveway. We're going to scope out Owen's lighthouse."

I scrambled out of bed and peered out my bedroom window. Sure enough, Olivia's red 4-Runner was behind the construction trucks. "Damn it, Olivia, it's too early to think right now," I muttered.

She laughed in response. "Hey, I have coffee."

"Okay," I said grudgingly. "You can come in. The door is open, the construction crew has a key."

I hurried through brushing my teeth and hair and dressed quickly. Before Olivia decided to come to find me, I stuck my head in Alfred's bedroom door. He sat on the bed with his hands on his knees and Snooze beside him, staring at his face. That cat was so weird. "Have you been like this all night?" I asked.

He shook his head.

"Did you come up when the construction crew got here?"

Nod.

"Okay, don't come downstairs while they're here, okay?"

Nod.

"Keep your door shut."

Nod.

I didn't know what else to say, so I shut the door and hurried downstairs.

Olivia sat at my kitchen table looking out the back door. Two coffees and a paper bag sat on the table. I nodded at Olivia, but she didn't even notice me. The bag was full of donuts. For the first time, I could've hugged Olivia.

I moaned and took out a cinnamon-covered cruller. "Thank you."

"Sure. Thanks for this." She nodded out the back door.

Two men were out there sawing something on a sawhorse. I didn't even know what the hell they were working on, but they'd already taken off their shirts.

She wasn't wrong. They were hot.

"The view is amazing." She sipped her coffee and gave me a rogue wink.

"Don't forget you're married." Did I really need to remind her?

She rolled her eyes. "Yeah, but I'm not dead. I love Sam, and I would never cheat on him. I mean have you seen him? He still rocks my world."

I held up a hand and made a face. "Okay, stop. Sam is like a brother to me. I don't want to hear about you two having sex, but you're right, this is a nice view."

We sat for a few minutes and ate. Eventually, the two men finished sawing whatever it was they were working on and took it back around to the front of the house.

From there the conversation turned a little serious. "I'm sorry," Olivia said.

"For what?" I grabbed another donut and looked at my new friend. My sleep haze was lifting thanks to the coffee and sugar.

"We weren't the best of friends in school. I wasn't the best person in school. I'm not that person anymore, and I'm sorry for the things I did that hurt you."

I brushed it off. "It's okay." I tried to make it seem like it wasn't a big deal, but it actually meant a lot that she'd apologized. I'd wanted to continue not liking her, but the more I was around her the more she grew on me.

I still didn't trust her, though, not fully. That would take some time and more donut deliveries.

"Wanna go see where Owen lives?" she asked.

I nodded. "I guess. I'm not working at the bookstore today. Might as well." I had a moment's concern over Alfred, but he had a TV and Snoozles. He'd be fine.

I followed Olivia out to her car, and she drove us down the coastal road to the old, abandoned lighthouse. It was only about a five-minute drive from my house. It wouldn't be difficult to walk, either. Hell, if someone wanted to get to my place from the lighthouse, they could've just walked up the beach for a while.

Not unnerving at all. Especially since the creepy necromancer bought the place.

Olivia parked at the edge of the lighthouse's parking lot. At one point, the old place had been renovated and turned into a restaurant and bookstore. That had gone under when I was a kid, and as far as I knew, it was abandoned. It was kind of dilapidated. Up until she died, Aunt Winnie mailed me all the local weekly newspapers every month so I could stay abreast of my hometown news. I'd never thought myself particularly attached to Shipton Harbor, but I'd read every single one of those papers, cover to cover. I'd read in the paper at some point that the lighthouse had been scheduled to be torn down, but the town's historical society kept blocking it.

In a sense, I was glad Owen bought it. I hope he kept it as a lighthouse.

We sat and watched the place for a few minutes. It didn't appear that anyone was home.

"Should we go walk around?" Olivia asked.

"I don't know." I realized we were both talking in hushed voices. "Why are we whispering?"

Olivia laughed. "In case the lighthouse fairies hear us?"

"Makes as much sense as any other explanation," I said. A smile tugged my lips. I was starting to see why Sam fell in love with Olivia. "Yeah, let's go poke around." We wouldn't go in, just walk around outside.

Olivia hit the unlock button on her door. "I'll leave it running. You know, just in case."

I had my hand on my doorknob when I saw someone. "Stop," I whisper-yelled. Olivia heard me and looked in the direction of my gaze. Another car had pulled up.

Olivia's car had darkly tinted windows. The only reason she didn't get tickets was because her husband was a cop, I was sure. "Duck," I whispered.

We crouched in the seat so that if anyone looked at the car, they wouldn't be able to tell if anyone was inside.

A tall slender woman dressed in a black thigh-length coat got out of the white Mercedes and walked inside the lighthouse, opening the door without hesitation, as if she owned the place. She didn't look like the type of person who'd hang out with someone like Owen. The woman was too...not classy, but there was no doubt she had money, or at least she dressed like she did. As soon as I saw her, bad feeling after bad feeling rolled over me. It was like nothing I'd ever felt before. Even from across the parking lot I picked up on her energy. There was a hint of power or magic that reminded me of what I picked up on Sheriff Drew when I first met him.

I still couldn't pinpoint what type of paranormal being he was.

"Who is that?" I asked.

Olivia looked at me with her head squished against the back of her car seat, her blonde hair ruffled and about as unkempt as I'd ever seen her. "I have no idea. I know everyone in this town, and I've never seen that woman before."

"I don't know who she is, but I know damn well she's up to no good," I said.

"How can you tell?" Olivia asked me in a scandalized tone.

I shrugged awkwardly with my body folded in half on the floorboard of the front seat. "I just know. Witch, remember?"

The back door opened and shut with a loud slam. "What are we looking at?"

We both screamed and whirled around, exposing ourselves if anyone looked through the front window of the car. Olivia's elbow landed on the car horn, and we all screamed this time. Me, Olivia, and Owen in the back seat.

"Get out!" I screamed at Owen.

At the same time, Olivia slammed her foot on the brake and threw it into drive. "We gotta get out of here," she screeched. Hitting the gas, she burned rubber getting us out of the parking lot.

The woman who had gone into the lighthouse came running out as Olivia made a U-turn in the middle of the parking lot.

"We're made," she yelled and floored it back onto the road and toward my house.

With Olivia's window tint and the erratic way she was driving, I couldn't get a good look at the woman's face, of course. Still no idea who she was.

I turned my attention to Owen, who was frantically trying to buckle up. "What are you doing in our car?"

He looked even paler than usual. "I was wondering why you were staking out my house." Brushing his hair out of his face, he leaned forward. "Can I ask where we're going?"

"Your house?" I asked, playing dumb. I didn't want him to

know we were there to spy on him. "You live by the lighthouse?"

"No," he said. "I live *in* the lighthouse. I moved to town recently."

"Turn around," I told Olivia. "Get him out of here."

She made another quick U-turn. "Do you know the woman that was at your house?" she asked as she pulled back onto the road.

He shook his head. "No, but you two were acting so strangely that I didn't have a chance to get a good look at her."

Olivia pulled back into the lighthouse parking lot, but the woman's car was gone. "Nice to meet you," Owen said. He hopped lightly out of the car and sauntered toward the lighthouse.

"What the hell?" I screeched. "Take me home please."

The entire five-minute drive back to my house, I chastised her for going after a man she didn't know. "All of this screaming and drama happened because you were too nosey, and you got me all nosey. Now, why don't you go home right this minute and tell Sam everything that happened. Maybe he can look into this Owen guy because I'm telling you, the guy is a witch."

"I will," she said with a grin. "Right away."

She stopped at the curb at the end of my driveway. Her eyes twinkled when she rolled her window down to say good-bye. "You gotta admit, that was fun."

I rolled my eyes and waved at her. Olivia was going to get me killed.

I didn't contradict her. It had been fun, dammit.

CHAPTER ELEVEN

The rest of Friday was uneventful, and I spent it going over everything that had happened the day before. I still haven't heard back from Wallie on the witch hunter research mission I sent him on. Then again, he was pretty busy with his classes.

Today was a new day. I got to sleep in without my phone ringing or the sounds of the workers. I'd just gotten settled on my novel and was making a good pace. I'd eaten breakfast, had a shower, and was sipping my second cup of coffee.

With no plans to go anywhere or do anything but write all day, I groaned in frustration when the doorbell rang. Somehow, I knew this meant I'd not be getting back to my writing, not anytime soon, anyway.

Besides, the house was freaking out the construction workers, despite our little talk a few nights ago. Old Vicky wasn't having any of this selling business. That was frustrating on a whole other level. I'd heard the workers talking about the house being haunted, even though I kept trying to blame things on Snoozles.

They weren't buying it.

The house wasn't the only thing clouding my thoughts. I had a dead friend, and speaking of, I needed to call Penny. Her poor husband had been killed, apparently, by a witch hunter, and I didn't have the first clue what that meant for me or my well-being. Not to mention creepy Owen.

Sighing, I hit save on my document and jogged down the stairs.

The construction crew had taken the weekend off. They'd offered to work for overtime pay, but I'd declined. I wasn't in *that* much of a rush to get back to Philly.

"Who is it?" I called through the door. I could only see someone's outline through the frosted glass.

"Sheriff Walker."

Oh. It was Drew. Sam's boss. Okay. Suddenly I was glad I'd showered. I hadn't put on makeup, but at least my hair was clean and hanging down my back instead of greasy and piled up on my head in a bun.

I unlocked and opened the door. "Please, come in. We're renovating, so excuse the mess."

A bump from the kitchen reminded me I hadn't warned Alfred to stay out of sight. Surely, he knew not to let the sheriff see him.

I indicated for Drew to sit on the sofa with his back to the kitchen, so if Alfred came into view, maybe Drew would miss it.

"What can I do for you, Sheriff?" I asked politely.

He grinned and I had to stop staring at his strong jaw. "Please, call me Drew. I'm here on official business, but unofficially."

I raised my eyebrows. "Okay."

"I'm going to jump straight to the point. I heard some rumors that have me concerned."

My stomach dropped. I had a bad feeling about where this was going. "Rumors?"

"They concern you, mainly. Also, I heard a few whispers about how William died that concern me." His eyes roamed the room before settling on me.

"The two sets of rumors brought you to me on official business?" I pursed my lips and crossed my arms.

"Well, in a way. I can't put these rumors into a report if you catch my drift. They're rather ludicrous."

I grunted but didn't answer because Alfred peeked out of the kitchen. I couldn't indicate he should hide without alerting Drew that someone was behind him.

Smiling, I waved my hand in front of my face. Drew stopped talking and gave me an odd look.

"Fly," I said sweetly.

He chuckled. "You see, if there's anything strange you should tell me or that I need to know, even if it seems ridiculous and fantastical, I need you to share it with me so I can work on bringing William's killer to justice."

"Well, I'm not sure what to say," I hedged. I wished Sam were here. If Drew was asking about these things, then he knew enough *to* ask, but what if he'd just found out somehow or heard some strange things? I couldn't very well tell him William had been a necromancer if all he'd heard was that some cult had been killing people in a similar matter.

"Why don't you tell me what you've heard, and I'll tell you if I know anything about it?" I suggested. I could come out and tell him I was a witch. That was a known fact in this town, but he was too much fun to play with.

A sharp bang from the kitchen made both of us jump and look toward the doorway. "Probably the cat." I launched from my seat and scurried around the sofa, but Drew jumped up too.

"Let me help," he said and rounded the other side of the sofa.

We reached the doorway at the same time and ended up jammed in the frame, shoulder-to-shoulder like we were on some stupid comedy show. "Excuse me," I grunted.

Drew looked up just then and saw the kitchen. I followed his gaze to see Alfred trying to pick up the teapot he'd dropped. The glass was all over the floor and he had a broom carefully clutched in his stiff hands. He'd stopped sweeping to stare at Drew and me fighting in the doorway.

A split second after Drew spotted Alfred, he dropped to the ground into a crouch and pulled a gun out of nowhere. I stumbled forward into the kitchen.

"Ava get down!" Drew yelled. "That's a ghoul."

The broom clattered to the floor and Alfred grunted behind me. Drew rolled forward, going past me as I threw out my hands and yelled. "Stop!" I screamed. "He's my ghoul."

Drew jumped up and backed toward me a few steps with his eyes and gun still trained on Alfred. "What are you talking about?" he asked with his brows drawn together to make them look like a unibrow.

I sighed in exasperation. "Put the gun away, Drew. If you know what a ghoul is, you know a bullet isn't going to do anything but make him mad."

As he slowly lowered the weapon, Snoozles jumped onto the kitchen table and stared at us with eyes that seemed to know far too much for a cat. He growled low in his throat, then jumped down and sat on his haunches in front of Alfred, who looked as frightened as it was possible for a ghoul to look.

What is it with Drew? That magic I felt when we met flowed from him, stronger. He was some sort of magical being. Maybe a shifter, like a rare one. He didn't feel like any of the ones I'd met before, but he could've been something unusual like a panda or something. Or a dragon. I'd never seen a dragon shifter, but they existed.

"I know you know more about William's death than you're

saying." He pointed at Alfred, who was slowly bending to pick up the broom again. "Especially now that I see you have a *ghoul*. If you don't tell me what's going on soon, I'm adding you to my short list of suspects."

I nodded. "Okay, yes. Come sit." I crowded him toward the living room again. Alfred out of Drew's sight seemed like a good idea.

He perched on the sofa but sat sideways so he could see both the kitchen doorway and the living room.

"I'm a witch," I confessed. I didn't know how much Drew knew about the supernatural, but I wasn't volunteering any more information than that.

"William was a necromancer. He had Alfred, and Penny asked me to take him. I've yet to figure out what I'm going to do with him, but for the moment he's my responsibility."

"Is there anything about his death you can tell me?"

"His widow thinks a witch hunter killed him." I watched his reaction to see if I could tell that he'd heard of witch hunters.

He blinked several times. "That lines up with what I heard."

"What did you hear?"

His face was impassive. "Just that there might be an active hunter in the area. Do you know of any witches moving into the area recently?"

"Besides me?"

We both laughed, and luckily he didn't repeat the question. I didn't want to tell him about Owen. Not yet. Not until I had a better read on the situation.

He stared at me, waiting for an answer to his question. I rolled my eyes. "I haven't been in town long enough to know who is new in town. I haven't even checked in with the local coven."

"Why is that?"

I worked my jaw and thought of all the ways I could write him into one of my books. I couldn't make up my mind if he'd be a hero or villain. "I don't plan to stay. My life is in Philly."

I frowned hearing those words leave my mouth sending an uneasy sensation through me. Because my life and my heart had died in Philly.

CHAPTER TWELVE

Sunday passed like a dream. I didn't leave home, which was amazing. No construction noises waking me or disturbing my writing. Alfred puttered around cleaning and tidying. I tried to stop him a few times, but he kept waving me off. I left him to it and chuckled every time he walked past my office because a few seconds later, Snooze would follow. The large gray Maine coon actually hopped happily along behind the ghoul. It was the craziest thing. I was beginning to think the cat liked Alfred more than me.

Even with them occasionally distracting me, I got a lot written. By the time I went to work on Monday, I'd knocked out three chapters and felt like a real author for the first time in years. Waltzing into the bookstore, I greeted Clint with a huge smile. "Morning," I chirped.

He arched an eyebrow at me. "What's got you all chipper? Did you get some?"

I burst out laughing. As if. "No, but my character did. That's close enough isn't it?"

The laptop clacked as he shut the lid. "That's not nearly close enough. We should find you a date."

"Oh, no. Thanks, but no thanks. My husband has been gone for five years, but I can't imagine opening myself up like that again." I put my purse under the counter and grabbed the coffee pot. "Thanks for the fresh pot."

As I poured my coffee, I realized that I spoke about Clay's death out loud without a crippling ache in my chest. That was a good thing, wasn't it?

"Pour me one, please," he requested as he set his travel mug on the counter.

"Sure." I brought the pot over and filled his mug. Our little coffee corner, as I liked to call it, was nice. It had a full display of regular and decaf coffee pots, sugar packets, and creamer. There was even a carafe with milk for those who like it in their coffee. The only thing the little corner of the shop was missing was pastries. "What's the plan today?" I asked as I replaced the pot at the station.

"Actually, I need to go get my haircut. I usually have to finagle an early or late appointment with my barber because we keep the same hours at our shops. Would you mind?"

I shook my head. "Of course not. I'm good with the register and if I have any questions, I can text you."

He beamed as I handed him the coffee. "You're a peach. I'm going to enjoy the experience, so don't expect me to rush back." As Clint slipped past me and grabbed his keys from under the counter, I waved at him.

"Don't think twice about this place. I gotchu."

He stopped at the door. "Don't hesitate if you actually need something though. I'm going to pretend I'm getting a haircut on the beach, but I'll be next door."

"Shoo," I called, waving my hand at him.

After he left, I started cleaning. For once in my life, I didn't mind it. At home, alone, I would've used magic to do the job quickly, but here in public, I dusted and wiped with my own two hands, like a regular person. Clint didn't have time to fuss with dusting while he did all the other things involved with running this place.

The front door had a bell on it, so when I finished around the counter, I grabbed the duster and started on the shelves. I'd hear someone if they came in.

They were kinda bad. I took a quick circle around the place, locked the front door for a second, and then twirled my finger in the middle of the room. Dust flew at me from all over the books, circling me as I twirled my finger.

Walking slowly so it didn't actually get on me, I headed for the back door. Lifting my finger, I directed the dust tornado to be higher and ducked under it. I still had to twirl my finger, but I leaned out the back door and looked both ways.

Nobody there. Good. I stepped back and pointed my twirling finger out the door, then tucked it against my palm once the dust was all outside the door.

It fell to the ground slowly, floating on the slight breeze in the alley.

"There," I said smugly and shut and locked the back door. I hurried back to the front and unlocked that door in time to see a woman walking from across the street.

She looked so familiar. I hurried around the counter and hopped on the stool before she saw me. "Hello," I called as she walked in.

The woman shot me a smile and walked toward the stacks. As soon as she turned around, I was sure. It was the same woman from the lighthouse. The woman at Owen's. Holy crap. The urge to text Olivia was strong, but if I did that, my crazy new partner in crime would rush over.

She gave off the same sort of feelings that Drew did. Now that I was closer to her, I felt it. A low hum of power that was magical but different from a witch. She must've been another shifter, but what the hell had she been doing at Owen's?

She browsed the stacks a little and then came up holding a paranormal romance.

"Will that be all?" I asked, trying my darndest to look like I hadn't seen her at Owen's.

"Yes, thank you." She gave me a polite but disinterested smile and paid with cash.

The second she turned to go out the door, I yanked my phone out of my purse and snapped a picture. I wished I'd thought of it sooner, so I could've gotten one of her front too, but I got her back and profile, so that would have to do. She walked out the door without noticing me snapping pics. I sent them to Olivia, who was apparently officially my new friend because I hadn't even considered calling anyone else to discuss this woman coming in.

"She just came into the store," I hissed into the mouthpiece.

"What? Who? Are you okay?" Olivia sounded sleepy.

"The woman from the lighthouse. She came into the store and bought a book about vampires and walked out."

Olivia gasped. "No, you're joking."

"No," I crowed. "I sent you her pictures."

"I got them. I don't recognize her at all, and I know everyone in town." Olivia sounded annoyed by that fact. It was laughable.

Just then I spotted Clint about to come in the front door. "Clint is back. I'll ask if she's ever been in before."

"Okay, see you later."

I hung up and pressed the app for my photos, bringing up the picture of the woman.

"How'd it go?" Clint asked as he came in the door. "I see you didn't manage to burn the place down while I was gone."

I laughed at the tease in his tone. "Well, I tried, but it wouldn't take."

He chuckled and put his keys up. "Anything happen?"

"We had a few customers; I dusted. That's about it."

He looked around. "Oh, wow." Scrunching his nose, he walked closer to the stacks. "There's no dust on the books." After disappearing through the stacks for a few moments, he poked his head back out. "You dusted them *all*?"

I shrugged. "I'm handy with a duster." Maybe I shouldn't have magicked the dust out of the entire store at once. It would've taken hours to do it by hand. Clint shrugged and came back to the counter. "Well, looks great."

"Let me ask you..." I held out my phone. "Have you ever seen this woman before?"

Clint took my phone and peered at it.

"There's a couple more," I said. "Swipe right."

He slid his finger across the screen and peered at the phone. "No, I don't recognize this woman. She's pretty though." He handed it back to me. "Why?"

I shrugged. "She came in and bought a book. She looked familiar.

He shook his head. "I don't think I've ever seen her in town before."

Clint let me take off a little while after that. By the time I slipped into the grocery store and got a few things and then made it home, all the construction trucks were gone from the driveway. Thank goodness. As much as I wanted them to be done, I was already tired of hearing the sounds of construction in the house.

Olivia's car was parked on the road in front of the house, though. I should've known she'd be here after seeing those pictures. I wasn't sure what we could do about the situation. It wasn't like the woman broke into my house.

I walked in the house to find Olivia sitting at the kitchen table sipping a cup of tea. Alfred walked over to the table with a plate of cookies. I froze in the doorway, shocked to see my ghoul serving my friend. "What's going on?" I whispered.

"Ava, why didn't you tell me you had such a lovely friend?" Olivia asked and gave me an exaggerated wink. "He's been ever so helpful since I came in."

Little Sammie came running in the back door. "Mom, you said he could play with me."

Alfred looked at me with his eyebrows raised.

"Alfred, do you *want* to go play with Sammie?"

Alfred nodded his head vigorously.

"Um, I mean, it's okay with me." The backyard was pretty secluded and led to a fence at the edge of the cliff that overlooked the ocean.

"Stay away from the fence, sweetie," Olivia called as Sammie ran out the back door with Alfred on his heels.

Snoozles came streaking out of the living room and followed them out. Crazy-ass cat.

I set my purse and bag of groceries on the kitchen table and walked over to the back door to look out at Sammie and Alfred playing tag with Snooze.

"You've been holding out on me," Olivia said. "*Where* can I get an Alfred?"

I gaped at my friend and watched her son play with my ghoul. Was she serious? Then a thought entered my mind. How much could one make selling ghouls? *Okay, stop right there, Ava Harper. You can't create and sell ghouls.* It was wrong. Besides, ghouls needed a necromancer to control them.

"You know Alfred is a ghoul, right?" I glanced at her, watching for her reaction.

She shrugged. "Of course."

"You're not surprised to see one in my house."

A frown dimmed her features, but it vanished almost as fast as it appeared. "Sam told me you are more than a witch."

Her tone was low as if she wasn't sure I'd approve of Sam

sharing my secret. They were married, so Sam would tell his wife things. Since no one was knocking on my door with a lynch mob, I assumed Olivia hadn't shared it with anyone. "What did he tell you?"

"You are a necromancer." She peered out the window watching Sammie run around the yard with a ghoul. "I wasn't sure if he was teasing me or not, but when we walked in, Alfred was descending the stairs. I knew he wasn't alive. I mean look at him. That was when I realized Sam wasn't joking. Did you create Alfred?"

I shook my head. "I inherited him."

"Ah, from William."

When I jerked my gaze to her, she laughed. "I've known the Combs for a long time. Penny babysat for me when the asshole went on his weekly 'business meetings.'" She used air quotes as she spoke. "I knew William was a necromancer. Is that why he was killed?"

I sighed. "Penny thinks so."

Sammie's squeal of excitement drew my attention back out the window. "Maybe I can glamour Alfred to look like a dog," I said weakly.

We both burst out laughing. How was my life this crazy now?

CHAPTER THIRTEEN

A knock at the front door pulled me from watching Alfred play with Sammie. Who in Hades is knocking at my door? "Watch them," I hissed at Olivia. "Let me go see who in the hell is here now."

I rushed through the house and peeked out the glass on the front door to see Owen standing on my front porch. My heart lurched, getting stuck in my throat. After taking a deep breath, I opened the door a crack and peered out at him. A gasp escaped me as I took in his condition. "Shit, what happened to you?"

I opened the door wider to get a better look at him. He looked like he'd had the shit beat out of him. There was bruising and swelling on the side of his face. His hair was more of a mess than his usually oily look. His shirt was torn at the sleeve.

"Can I please come in? I need to sit." He looked like he was about to fall over. His aura was dim like he was in a lot of pain and exhausted.

"Come in," I said. "Better than you collapsing on my porch."

Owen staggered forward. I threw his arm over my shoulders before he fell over. "What happened to you?" I asked again.

We struggled toward the couch. "Olivia," I called. "Come help."

She ran into the room and gasped. "Oh, no." Rushing forward, she helped me lay Owen out on the sofa. His black hair splayed over my pillows.

When he settled down, he let out a shaky breath. I let him relax before saying, "Let me heal you, then you can tell us how this happened."

Owen and Olivia both gave me crazy looks. "Heal me?" Owen asked with his brows drawn together. *Yeah, I know. Not many witches can heal.*

I nodded, grinning at him. I wasn't sure if my grin was helping to ease his mind or not. Right then he was staring at me like I was about to do the impossible. Maybe I was. "I haven't done it since I was a kid so bear with me."

He continued to stare at me with wide eyes but didn't stop me. I took that as his permission to use my magic on him.

I thought back to when I'd healed Snooze all those years ago. Then, I was shocked and panicked that I'd lost my beloved kitty. In my panic, I hadn't realized the cat had died and I brought him back to life. That was a fact I never pointed out to Sam. My best friend thought I healed the cat.

Owen wasn't dead. He was injured and I couldn't let him bleed out in my house.

I gathered my magic and energy into the center of my body then directed that light and energy to my hands. I like to think my healing powers had nothing to do with my necromancer half, but I'd be lying to myself. It was the ghoul making and raising the dead part of the power I refused to practice. Healing injuries was different. It was positive and light.

When my hands started to glow with bright blue light, I lowered them to Owen's chest. My magic flowed into his core, fueling his magic to speed his healing abilities.

My light faded and I sat back, proud that I did it without harming anyone. Owen sucked in a shaky breath and looked at himself. Flexing his hands and chuckling in disbelief, he sat up slowly as I moved to sit on the chair across from him.

"Better?" I asked.

"Yeah, but..." He shot Olivia a guarded glance, unsure.

I quickly glanced at her as well to see if she was still upright. She knew I was a witch but seeing how much power I had, was different than knowing. Focusing back on Owen, I said with a sigh, "You can speak freely in front of her. She knows what I am."

"I've never heard of a necromancer being able to heal like that," he said with a voice full of wonder. "I mean I guess it's possible, but that should take a lot of power."

Laughing, I looked at Olivia, who watched our exchange with fascination. "Well, that's silly."

"No, seriously. Witches can make poultices and potions to speed healing and give a little energy to cushion the pain. Necromancers raise the dead, but the creatures that come back are undead, but to heal injuries on the living? Not supposed to be possible. There's a rumor of an ancient line of necromancers that can heal, but they supposedly died off like a hundred years ago."

I shrugged, not liking the suspicion on his tone. My family legend was that we were one of those ancient lines that Owen had mentioned. I was a seventh-generation necromancer, which was supposed to make me the most powerful dead-raiser on earth. I didn't believe any of it, and I wasn't going to volunteer that information to Owen. Especially since I didn't know him.

"Maybe you're not as worldly as you think. I haven't done it since I was a kid, anyway." I sure didn't want to get into that, though. I changed the subject quickly. "What happened to you?"

"After you left me at the lighthouse, I went in to find a woman inside. I assumed it was the one you mentioned. She attacked me and tied me up. I've been there ever since, waiting to die."

Olivia and I stared at Owen in shock. My heart raced and fury began to build. That woman was in the store today. Acting like any other normal person and not the psycho she was turning out to be. Definitely not like she was holding anyone prisoner. "All this time?"

He nodded. "I'm starving by the way. If you've got something."

"Yeah." I rushed into the kitchen and grabbed a bag of chips and a bottle of water. I considered calling Alfred in to cook dinner, but I wasn't sure I wanted Owen to see him yet.

"Oh, thanks." Owen took the bag and ripped it open before shoving a handful of chips into his mouth. "So," he said through his full mouth. "She's been trying to get information out of me about Ava. She's obsessed with you. All she did was grill me about you and your dad."

Dread slammed into me, sending flames of fire through my veins. My voice shook as I asked, "What about my father?"

"She thinks he's alive. That you're hiding him."

I chuckled like a crazy person. "Well, jokes on her because he's dead. Why would she think you'd have this information?"

He shrugged. "I never met your dad but I'm a necromancer. Maybe that was why. Like we have a hotline or a club or something. I never got her name, but she was definitely a hunter. She could've killed me."

A hunter. Like a witch hunter, I guessed.

"How did she keep you from using your magic?" None of what he was saying made any sense.

He rolled his eyes. "A sigil. I walked right into it, too. Rookie move."

Well, then I was more than a rookie, because I didn't have a clue what sigil would bind his power, but I didn't want Owen to know that.

"That's why she's here. She's after you and your dad. Why? I have no idea." He took a drink of water, then leaned forward with his arms resting on the tops of his thighs. "You probably have a lot of questions about who I am."

"You can say that." My tone was flat when I spoke. I glanced at Olivia and crossed my eyes, making her snicker.

Owen saw the exchange because his lips twitched. "I've only been in Shipton Harbor for about six months. The moment I arrived, I felt the magic in the air. Several witches lived in the area but had no idea there were other necromancers. Your and your father's magic still lingers in this house, mixed with the centuries of witches living here. I assume it's been in the family a while?"

I nodded, finding it interesting that he could sense the magic so easily. Then again, I might be able to if I didn't suppress half my power. "My ancestors built this house, and it hasn't been owned by any other family."

"That makes sense. Most active houses are like that. It's how they become animated and do not do well when the family leaves it." Owen paused.

His words settled in the back of my mind. The old house wasn't dealing well with me wanting to sell it. That made me wonder if the house would continue to chase others off.

"In fact," Owen continued. "The magic from the house spills out into the town. I pull from that power to aid my own spells. William did the same."

That was news to me. Had William used the power from the house to create Alfred?

Just then Sammie came bursting through the back door at top speed. "Mommy," he wailed. "I hurt my knee."

Owen and I watched as Olivia scooped Sammie up in her arms, but then scurrying behind him came Alfred with Snooze hot on his heels.

Alfred saw our visitor and froze in place, his eyes bouncing from me to Owen.

Owen's gasp reminded me that he didn't know about Alfred. Whoops. "You have a ghoul?" he whispered. "I mean of course you would, you're a necromancer, but I've never seen one like this."

Like what? I so desperately wanted to know about ghouls and if Alfred was average for a ghoul or not. Owen's statement told me that Alfred was not average. He was more, maybe. "I'm surprising you left and right today, aren't I?" I chuckled, then turned to Alfred. "All right, Alfie?"

The ghoul stopped short and if a creature with limited facial movement could look shocked, Alfred looked shocked. He grunted.

Shrugging, I smiled at him. "I can't have a nickname for you? You're growing on me."

He gave a stiff shrug as Snooze jumped up on the back of the chair and jumped for Alfred, reaching for his string with his front claws. Alfred stepped to the side and Snooze landed hard on the ground.

"Ghouls are only that animated when they're resurrected by an incredibly powerful necromancer. Where did you get this one?"

"He was William's."

Owen swung his gaze to me in shock. "I knew William. He wasn't powerful enough to do this."

I shrugged. "That's all I know. His wife said I had to take him, or he'd get unruly."

Owen nodded. "Unruly is right. This is insane."

Tell me about it. My life had become insane in the short time I'd been in town. I couldn't wait to see what other insanities were waiting for me.

CHAPTER FOURTEEN

"Well, Alfred is neither here nor there. So as far as anyone who is not in this house, he doesn't exist." I didn't need the whole town knowing about my double life. I quickly changed the subject back to the mysterious woman. "The vibe I got off of that woman that kidnapped you was extremely similar to the same feelings I get when I'm around the sheriff."

Olivia's jaw dropped. "What are you talking about?"

"At first I thought he was some type of shifter." I looked at Owen for confirmation. "Different species feel different to you, too, right?"

He nodded and crammed more chips into his mouth. "Oh, yeah for sure."

Thank goodness it wasn't just me. "I can *feel* the difference between a human and a witch. Different witches give off different... vibes. I don't know a better word for it. Maybe energy is a better way to explain it, but, for example, I recognized Owen as a necromancer the moment he walked into the diner the other night."

Olivia nodded, understanding. "Okay, so if this strange woman is a hunter, then Drew must be as well?"

I nodded. "That's certainly how it seems."

Disappointment and worry filled me at that assessment. Why were there hunters in Shipton? Were they working together to take down witches?

Just when you think you've found a nice guy, he turns out to be a hunter.

Olivia sat Sammie on his feet and pulled her phone out of her back pocket. "I've got to get Sam over here. He might know something about Drew."

That was a good idea. Sam would give us the deets on the *good sheriff* while keeping our secrets.

Standing, I motioned to Owen's empty chip bag. "I'll make you something more substantial than chips." I walked into the kitchen and pulled out ingredients for a simple spaghetti. Easy and fast and would feed a bunch of people.

Alfred came in when the doorbell rang and shooed me out. "I don't mind cooking," I said, glancing at him. "Olivia can let Sam in."

He shook his head and waved his hand at me. I'd gotten so used to him that I didn't think twice when he grabbed my arm and pulled me away from the stove.

"Fine." I laughed and wiped my hands on the dish towel. "Thank you, Alfred."

He gave me a light push toward the living room.

"Hey, Sam," I said as I entered the living room. "Dinner will be ready soon."

Olivia plopped on the couch beside her husband, but he barely acknowledged my presence. He was staring at Owen, who had moved to one of the chairs across from the couch.

"Tell us about Drew," Olivia said.

"Who is he?" Sam nodded toward Owen.

"Sorry," I said. "Introductions. Owen, this is my oldest

friend, Sam, and Olivia's husband. Sam, this is Owen, he's another Necromancer, but we need to know about Drew."

Sam didn't look like he felt much like talking. "Why?"

"I was attacked by someone supernatural. I'm fairly certain she was a hunter."

"A hunter?" Sam looked pretty skeptical. Not that I blamed him. I'd known about all this witchy stuff all my life, and this sounded pretty crazy.

"Someone that takes out witches. Thinks we're evil," I explained.

Sam nodded. "Okay. Didn't know that was a thing."

"Yeah, me neither. Would've been nice to have known years ago." I sighed and turned when Sam sat straight upright and looked over my shoulder into the kitchen.

Alfred was putting plates on the kitchen table.

Sam screamed and jumped up, pulling his gun, and firing before I could move.

"Sam, no," I screamed. He was a great shot, I wasn't worried about any of us being hurt, but I also didn't know what a gunshot would do to Alfred. "Put down the gun," I screamed as the sound of the gunshot echoed in my ears, ringing and pounding inside my head.

Sam holstered his weapon. "I think I hit it," he whispered. "There's some sort of zombie in your kitchen."

"Samuel Nathaniel Thompson," Olivia slapped her husband on the arm. Then she did it two more times. I could feel the fear rolling from her. "What have you done? Our son is here."

Just then, Sammie exited the bathroom that was on the opposite side of the living room from the kitchen, eyes wide. Olivia rushed over and scooped him up. All the while glaring at her husband.

I glared at Sam too. He should know better. "One, I don't

know where your common sense went. Two, that is not a zombie. Three, this is my freaking house."

I launched myself out of my chair and rounded it, heading into the kitchen to check on Alfred. He was cowering in the corner, apparently unhurt, but in the middle of the kitchen floor, twitching, laid Snooze.

My heart stopped for a few brief moments while my eyes teared up.

"Snoozles," I cried, dropping to my knees.

He looked at me and meowed piteously. As I reached my hands forward to try to heal him, he shivered and jumped up, leaving a small puddle of blood on the floor.

What the hell?

Sitting on his haunches, Snooze licked his front paw, beginning to clean the blood off of it. I leaned forward and picked him up carefully, not wanting to injure him further.

I laid him on my lap and searched his abdomen.

Then I searched it again.

"There's no injury," I whispered. "He's not hurt."

From the corner of the room, Alfred made noises like he was trying to tell me something while pointing at Snooze. Had the crazy cat jumped in front of the bullet to save a ghoul?

But why?

I pushed the thoughts aside, making a mental note to think about it later. At this rate I needed notes for my mental notes.

I did a final check of Snooze, feeling his little body for any cuts or anything, I felt a lump in his stomach. He purred as I blew on his fur, trying to get it to part so I could see his skin.

Before my very eyes, his skin split open, and a bullet popped out.

Then, the skin knit back together. Snooze wiggled and climbed out of my lap as I stared in shock. "Did anyone else see that?" I whispered.

Surely, I wasn't going insane.

"I did," Olivia said. "That cat just expelled a bullet."

Thank the gods.

"Is it a ghoul?" Owen asked. "Sometimes if you raise a ghoul right after it dies, like immediately after, it looks pretty normal."

I gaped at him as Snooze shook his tail and began to lick his midsection. It made sense, and deep down I knew that. However, it didn't work with my mother so why would it work for Snooze?

Somehow, I didn't think Snooze was a ghoul. It was possible. Ghouls wouldn't die from a gunshot. They were undead, after all.

I told Owen about when I thought I healed Snooze when I was a kid. At least that was what I was calling it. The cat had stopped breathing and his heart stopped. So technically he died. As I told the story I realized that Owen was right about raising the dead and looking normal. Not sure why I didn't think about it before that moment. Maybe I was in denial about using my necromancer powers to bring Snooze back to life, but that didn't make sense either. "He was a kitten then. Smaller. Well, just over a year old. He's bigger now than he was. Plus, he *has* aged. He couldn't be a ghoul."

Had I turned my cat immortal? How was that even possible?

We cleaned the blood as I kept glancing at Snooze, shocked that he healed from a fatal bullet wound.

When Snooze jumped on the table and tried to get after Alfred's string again, I knew he was fine.

"Sam," I said once everything was clean. "Come eat and I'll tell you all about Alfred."

Owen stood in the doorway nervously, dry washing his hands. "Can I join you?" he asked.

I walked over to the older man and touched his hand. "Not only can you join us, but you're staying with me. You can't go back to the lighthouse, and I know that woman knows where we are, but we'll be stronger in numbers."

He threw his arms around me. "Thank you, Ava. You're a good person."

I didn't know about a good person, but I tried to do the right thing. Aunt Winnie and Yaya would've had it no other way.

Feeling better about doing one good deed, I stared at Sam until he shifted uncomfortably in his chair across from me.

He hung his head. "I'm sorry, Ava. I freaked out. William's murder has me stressed. When was the last time our small town had a murder? Not in my lifetime."

I reached over the table and covered his hand. He turned it over and squeezed mine in return. Spearing a quick glance at Olivia, I watched for a hint of jealousy. Although she stared at Sam and my linked hands, she wasn't jealous. Maybe she had changed. I have a feeling Sam is the reason. Well, part of it.

"Sam, it's not okay to shoot in the house, but I forgive you this one time."

Olivia shook her head. "I'm still mad."

Sam let go of my hand and wrapped an arm around his wife, kissing her on the corner of her mouth. He whispered something that made Olivia's cheeks color. I *so* didn't want to know what he said.

Little Sammie chose that moment to spill his drink. The red fruit juice flowed over the table and right into Sam's lap. I snorted and pointed at Sam, "Karma has your number."

Just then, Alfred rushed over with a towel to clean the table and floor. He eyed Sam the whole time.

"What is his deal?" Sam asked, pointing to the ghoul.

"Alfred, this is my best friend, Sam." Alfred grunted and dropped a clean towel in Sam's lap before leaving the room. I laughed. I was beginning to like Alfred more and more. "I inherited Alfred from William."

Owen and I filled Sam in on the witch hunter and our theories that William was killed by magic and that we didn't know why.

Sam said, "You know that you are a possible target now. I'll look into the mysterious woman. Does Clint have video surveillance in the store?"

Frowning, I shook my head. "No, just the standard alarm on the doors and windows."

"Don't investigate this on your own." Sam glanced at me and then at Olivia. He apparently knew us better than anyone.

I gave him a sweet smile. "Why would I do that?"

If that crazy lady thought she was going to come at me, she was certifiably insane, and she deserved to be taught a lesson on why coming to my hometown and killing my dear old friend and beating up Owen wasn't something I'd let go easily.

If it meant unlocking powers that scared the shit out of me to protect my town, I would.

CHAPTER FIFTEEN

It was bright and early the next morning. Seriously bright. Every curtain in every downstairs window was pulled back to allow the sun to stream in. I was tempted to put on some shades.

Alfred had just set a plate of eggs and sausage in front of me at the table when the doorbell rang. I sighed and started to get up, but Owen held up a hand. "The least I can do is answer the door."

I smiled and settled back down. The construction crew was due soon, so Alfred would have to get upstairs and out of view, but it wasn't even six yet. Why was anyone out and about at this hour?

For that matter, why was I up?

Oh, yeah. The smell of coffee lured me from my slumber.

"Alfred," I muttered. "We gotta teach you to sleep in."

He huffed a little air through his nose. Clearly, he disagreed with me about early mornings. Only I would get a ghoul who is a morning person.

Olivia rushed into the room. "They called Sam into work super early," she said in a shrill voice. "They found a body."

My blood ran cold. My mouth hung open for a few moments before I asked, "Not another one?" What the hell was going on? "Before I came back to Shipton Harbor, the town had seen like one murder in its entire existence? Now we've had how many in the two weeks I've been home?"

"This is number two," Owen said. "I was almost three."

"Is it supernatural?" I asked.

Olivia shrugged. "How would we know?"

That was a good point. Sam wouldn't know how to tell, and if Drew knew, he wasn't telling. None of us were sure yet what in the world Drew was.

Alfred set another plate at the table and pointed to Olivia. She gave him a pleasant smile and dug in. "Thanks, Alfred."

"Where's Sammie?" I asked.

"Oh, on the way home last night Sam's mom called and asked for him to come stay, so we dropped him off. It's so nice having the grandparents close."

I nodded. That would've been nice for me when Wallie was little, but Clay had insisted we live in Philadelphia, near his family. His uncle was the next best thing.

I loved my husband with all my heart, but I wouldn't have let Wallie stay with his mother for a whole night for all the money in the world. Or free babysitters.

Clay got his dislike for magic from his mother. She thought people with powers were the devil. So, no, I wouldn't let Wallie stay with her for long periods. I once caught her pouring Holy Water over my son's head after the first time he showed signs of using magic. That was the last time she kept him for more than a few hours. Even then it was because I had no choice.

I was lucky in that Uncle Wade was Clay's father's brother and thought Clay's mom was crazy. Wade and I bonded over that.

Sam called a few minutes later. Olivia jumped when her phone rang, making me laugh. After answering it, she relayed the information to us. "The coroner has loaded the body up. It was pretty bloated, but it looks like it was Betty Knolls."

I gasped. Betty was my aunt's friend and the town's realtor. How in the world was that possible? Olivia put her hand over the phone mouthpiece. "What?"

"Betty was supposed to be my realtor. She was friends with Aunt Winnie, but when I got to town and called her, her daughter told me she retired and moved to Florida. She was a witch, not a necromancer. I guess that kills our theory that if she's a hunter she's after necromancers."

"Uh..." Olivia shook her head. "Betty didn't have a daughter. Just a son." She returned her attention back to Sam on the phone. "Can you get us in to check and see if it's a supernatural death?" A few seconds later, she hung up. "Let's go."

Thank you, Sam.

I ran upstairs to change clothes and do something with my hair. It looked a mess, so I slapped on a ball cap that said *I Smell Children*, a nod to my favorite witchy Halloween movie, and headed for the stairs.

When I went back downstairs, I found Alfred cleaning up after breakfast. "You better get upstairs when you're done and lock yourself in the bedroom. The construction crew will be here any minute."

Alfred nodded.

"Okay, I'll see you in a bit." I jogged outside to find Olivia behind the steering wheel of her 4-Runner and Owen in the backseat.

"I guess you're with us now?" I asked.

He grinned at me. "That okay?"

I shrugged. "I guess." He was nice enough. I kind of felt guilty for judging him based on his appearance. Besides, he could verify if Betty was killed by magic. I wasn't a hundred percent sure what to look for.

Olivia drove us straight to the hospital and circled around to pull into a small alcove. "This is where they take deliveries, but the morgue is right down the hall," she said. "Makes it easier and more discreet to load and unload bodies without the public seeing."

Nodding, I unclipped my seatbelt and got out, noting Sam holding the hospital door open for us. "We need to hurry. I haven't been able to think up an excuse for why you're here."

"We won't be here long. Owen and I will be able to tell if it was death by magic. Then we'll leave." I slid past Sam and entered the hallway that led to the morgue.

We came to a sliding glass door that opened automatically. I didn't want to be here. The last time I was in a morgue was to ID Clay's body. The cold white tiled walls and the stainless-steel tables were too clinical for how I remembered Betty.

As I crossed the room to the wall of drawers where the bodies were stored, I hugged my waist, thankful that there weren't bodies out in the open. I'd seen my fair share in the last week.

Sam pulled open a silver door and rolled a body out on the big silver slab, like on TV. I recoiled in horror. Owen waved his hand and the smell disappeared, but there wasn't anything he could do about the sight. The body was bloated like someone had inflated it with air. From what I understood, corpses dumped in the ocean would fill with the body's natural gasses. What I hadn't expected was her flesh torn back in places. Other spots of her skin had holes in it like the scavengers of the ocean had been nibbling at her.

Sam stared at Owen in shock. "That's a handy trick."

Owen shrugged. "I do what I can. Not my first dead body."

But through the repulsion and their conversation, I looked at Betty. It was a sad day, indeed.

"Well, she was killed with magic," Owen said as he peered at her witch sigil.

I didn't see it at first. Then I found it at the base of her throat on the left side. My insides froze from dread and anger.

"How can you tell?" Olivia asked.

"You can't see her witch mark, but Ava, look here." He pointed to her sigil. "It's jet black."

I shuttered. "I figured that had something to do with death."

He grimaced. "Only magical murder, usually. It's possible to get it for other reasons, like if a spell she did went wrong, but that doesn't happen often. The most likely culprit is that she was blasted with a spell or energy ball or something."

My vision narrowed, and my mind ricocheted back to my childhood. To the day my mother died.

When it was all said and done, her witch sigil had been black. I hadn't known it meant anything, and neither had my aunt or grandmother, apparently. If they had, they took it to their own graves.

My mother had been killed by magical means. I fisted my hands into the sides of my shirt because I was still hugging my waist. My mom's death wasn't an accident.

"Ava?" Owen asked. "Are you okay?"

I shook off my shock and logged the information away. I had no way of knowing who had caused the bolt of lightning to hit my mother, but now I knew it hadn't been a freak accident. Until I figured out more, I wasn't about to tell anyone.

"Yep, just a little overwhelmed with this." I indicated Betty's body.

"I'd say based on the darkness around her mouth, though, that this was a ghoul attack." Owen pointed to black streaks around Betty's lips. "That's where they suck out the soul."

Olivia and Sam looked at me.

"Alfred?" Sam whispered. "I've never in my life seen another ghoul."

I shook my head. "I don't think it could be."

"I agree with Ava," Olivia said. "He's wonderful with Sammie."

Sam gaped at her. "You let our son play with a ghoul?"

Olivia shrugged. "They were within our sight, and they had fun."

Sam glowered and cut his wife a scathing look. "Well, at the very least, we need to question him, pronto."

"Why don't we ask Betty?" Owen asked. "She could tell us."

I looked at him in horror. "Like, ask her who killed her?"

He raised his eyebrows. "We *are* necromancers."

I waved my hands. "By all means."

He rolled up his long, black sleeves. "I'm not as strong as you are, but I think I can manage this." Leaning forward, he put his fingers on Betty's shoulders. "Betty," he whispered. "Who killed you?"

A squelching sound came from her mouth. Olivia stumbled backward, gagging. "Oh, no," she said. "I'm not here for this."

"Try again," I whispered.

Owen touched her shoulder again. "Betty, tell us who killed you."

Her mouth opened but didn't move other than that. She gurgled. Oh, ew, ew, ew.

"Who killed you?" he repeated.

Betty said something without moving her lips. "Harmon?" I asked.

"Marlin," Sam said. "That sounded like Marlin."

"Try one more time, please, we hate to bother you, but it's important." Owen focused on Betty's bloated face, and we all leaned in close.

"Carmen!" she nearly shouted. Water and other fluids shot

out of her mouth and splashed me in the cheek. I'd been leaning the closest.

Olivia ran for the corner and gagged as I frantically tried to wipe the liquid off my cheek.

"That was definitely Carmen," Owen said.

Sam nodded as he rubbed Olivia's back. "I agree."

"Should we at least talk to Alfred?" Sam asked.

I shrugged. "I don't see how it would help, but we can question him."

"Question who?" Drew asked from behind us. We all jumped and whirled around almost as one person to find Drew standing there looking at us with his eyebrows raised.

Oh, fuck me sideways. How much had he heard?

Sam and I exchanged a look. My brain worked overtime to come up with something to say, but all I could think of when I saw Drew filling the doorway of the morgue was, he was a hunter.

"Sammie," Sam said. "To make sure he didn't eat the, uh..."

"Nickel," I said at a near-shout. "I'm missing a nickel, and we think Sammie ate it."

Drew lifted his brows, looking extremely skeptical. His gaze roamed to Olivia and Owen. "You're all standing around a murder victim discussing whether or not Sam's kid swallowed a coin?"

All four of us nodded with wide eyes, fooling nobody, least of all Drew. Man, we were all busted.

"Sure," he said. "Whatever you say." He glanced toward the door behind him. "I'm going to pretend all of you are here for some legitimate reason because I've got this poor woman's son out here ready to identify her body."

I gasped and put my hand over my mouth. That poor boy and here we were standing over her body like a bunch of lookie-loos. I was going to Hades for this.

Looking around the room, I spotted a set of double doors. "Through there," I hissed, motioning everyone in that direction.

We all hurried into the second part of the morgue and into the corner. I looked around and realized the room had a dead body in it, out on a table, halfway covered by a drape. "Oh, no," I whispered. "How disrespectful."

I hated being in there. Sam peered through the little square hole in the door. "He's walking over to the body," he said in a low whisper that we could barely hear.

Oh, great. A play-by-play. Sam was almost as bad as Olivia. I snorted then slapped my hand over my face. "I need a drink after this," I whispered.

Olivia nodded and mouthed, *me too.*

"Connor," Drew's voice drifted from the other room. "You have to give a yes or no answer. You don't have to stay in here, I understand how difficult this is."

Connor's voice came through the doors next. "Yes. That's my mother."

"Okay, son, wait for me in the hall. I'll close this up and we'll go to the station to fill out a little paperwork." Drew's voice was soft, but I heard the fury brewing in it. There was also compassion that I hadn't expected from a witch hunter. Then again, I didn't know anything about them. Other than what Owen said.

Sam opened the door and motioned for us to follow when the coast was clear, and we tiptoed toward the outer door. We looked like a damn group of cartoon characters tiptoeing around like this.

Connor's voice made us stop short at the door. Sam peeked through the little square and ducked quickly back down. "He's just outside the door," he mouthed and pointed.

"We were estranged," he said.

Drew made a murmuring sound of understanding.

"But she was my mother. I can't believe she's gone. I can't imagine who would hurt her."

"Do you have any other family?" Drew asked.

Connor let out a little sob. "No. It was always me and mom. No family left at all, not that I know of."

I widened my eyes at Olivia. She mouthed at me, "Told you so."

Sam peeked out again, then cracked the door open and reached one hand out. Drew stuck his head in. "What?" he hissed.

"Don't leave yet. Tell him you forgot something," Sam whispered.

Drew's head disappeared, and his footsteps faded down the hall toward the outside door. The footsteps loudened and Drew burst back into the room. "What?" he asked, looking aggravated.

"My realtor," I said in a quiet voice. "She told me she was taking over as my realtor because Betty was out of town. She also said she's Betty's daughter."

Drew's jaw dropped. "That is some relevant information."

I threw my hands up. "I know. That's why we called you back." Even though we weren't sure what in the world he was.

"Does this realtor who isn't Betty's daughter have a name?"

"Carmen Moonflower." She had to be the woman who attacked Owen. I was sure of it now.

He nodded at Sam. "Meet me at the station. After we do this paperwork, we'll pay Ms. Moonflower a visit."

I told Sam everything I knew, which was bupkis, and he left me, Olivia, and Owen looking at each other in total confusion.

"Now what?" I whispered.

CHAPTER SIXTEEN

"Now," Owen began. "Now we go home and talk to Alfred. If he's not the ghoul that did this, maybe he can help in some way."

"I don't see how," I muttered and headed toward the door.

When we reached the car, Olivia's phone beeped. "Shoot," she whispered. "I've got to stop and get Sammie. And I'll stop whispering now."

I giggled because this whole day has been insane. "That's fine with me. I like having him around. He's a cutie."

She grinned at me. "You're such a good friend. I didn't want to have to give up on our murder-solving fun."

I shrugged. Friends now. Enemies before. Yet, I didn't want her to have to leave, either, and she wanted Sammie around anyway.

She ran into her mother's place and was back about fifteen minutes later with Sammie clinging to her hip. After she buckled him into his car seat beside Owen, he stared at the older man with wide eyes. "Who are you?" Sammie asked.

"Owen, I'm a friend of your mommy's."

"Your hair is dirty."

I tried not to laugh as Olivia gasped. "Sammie, that's not nice."

"It's okay, he's little." Owen said but didn't provide an explanation. I was a little disappointed because I wondered if he just had extremely oily hair. I heard him take a shower last night, so I know he was clean. Poor man.

I was starting to feel bad about thinking he was dirty.

When we pulled into my driveway, the contractors were about to pull out. They stopped and rolled down their windows. "What's going on?" I asked. "It's awfully early."

"We're taking off early for today," Jude, the foreman said. "That house..." He shook his head. "You'll be lucky if I convince my guys to come back tomorrow."

Ugh. What now? "Thanks," I muttered absently as I stared at the house. "I can't even begin to know what to do about the house who hates the construction crew."

Owen asked, "Did you try talking with the house?"

"Yes. Obviously, that didn't help."

As we stepped out of Olivia's car, another vehicle pulled up behind us. As soon as I saw my old black sedan, the one I'd passed down to my son, my heart leaped with joy.

"Wallie!" I cried and raced to the car.

He jumped from the driver's seat and gave me a big hug, picking my feet up off the ground because he was a lot taller than me. "Hey, Mom. Missed you."

When he sat me on my feet, I framed his face. He had my green eyes and his father's jet-black hair. Wallie also got his height and lean muscular build from Clay as well.

I was nearly in tears, not realizing just how much I missed my son. "I missed you so much, Wal Wal." I squeezed him tight. "But what in the world are you doing here?"

He eyed the other people who got out of Olivia's car. "It's about what you asked me to research," he said in a quiet voice. "Maybe we should go for some privacy."

"About the witch hunters?" I asked.

He nodded and widened his eyes, then glanced around to see who else could have heard us.

"It's okay, they know all about it. Come on in, sweetheart." I took his hand and walked him into the house as Owen and Olivia followed, Olivia carrying Sammie. "The one thing about Shipton Harbor, it's too small of a town for someone to have secrets."

I glanced at Wallie and noted how he nodded but was still unsure.

"Alfred," I called up the stairs. "The construction crew is gone early." I turned to Wallie, smiling. My baby boy was home. "You'll love Alfred. He's a hoot."

Wallie frowned and glanced at Olivia, then asked, "You're Sam's wife?"

"Yep." Olivia grinned and indicated to Sammie on her hip. "This is little Sammie."

Wallie smiled at Sammie. "Hi, little man."

The ghoul in question walked stiffly down the stairs. I was learning his facial expressions, though at first, it had seemed like he didn't have any, on account of his stiff face. He was astonished to see Wallie there. I also felt a small amount of anxiety rolling from him. I couldn't blame him after being shot at by my BFF.

"Alfred, this is my son, Wallie. Wallie, this is my ghoul, Alfred." I watched my son carefully for his reaction. What I saw was confusion and fear.

"Mom, what's a ghoul?" Wallie glanced from Alfred to me and back again. His nose crinkled.

"The long story short is that a local necromancer died, and

Alfred was his. Alfred doesn't want to be freed from his fleshy prison, and ghouls need someone controlling them at all times, so now Alfred belongs to me." I shrugged. "That's all I know about them."

Wallie gaped as Alfred shook his hand vigorously.

I grinned at them. "He's happy to see you, Wallie."

Alfred nodded.

Wallie shook himself out of his stupor at meeting Alfred and turned back to me. "Anyway, Mom, I enlisted the help of my roommate. We figured out in the first few days that we both know about all this stuff. He doesn't have any magic, but his stepmom is a witch, so he knows about it."

I raised my eyebrows. "A lucky coincidence in a roommate."

He nodded. "Yeah, but he's a computer genius, right? I asked him to help me look into this witch-hunter business. He got some good information."

I ushered him into the living room. "Well, come, sit, tell me about it."

He stretched out in one of the chairs while the rest of us settled around him. I noticed Alfred heading toward the kitchen, probably going to make us something to eat or drink. I wished I could explain to him that he didn't have to keep doing this. I felt bad that he always did things without me asking.

Owen noticed where my attention had gone and said, "It's a ghoul's job to provide services to their handler."

Nodding, I sighed. "I guess." We still needed to talk with Alfred about Betty's death, but I wasn't sure how at the moment. Besides, Wallie had dirt on the hunters.

"Anyway, we found some websites that seemed a little more legit than the ones that were basically Buffy fan sites. Dustin hacked into one and found it had a whole private network behind it. Super protected with multiple firewalls and other stuff that I don't really understand but Dustin does. We hit the mother lode." The grin on Wallie's face made me proud. If med school didn't pan out, he'd most likely go into private investigating or something.

He pulled a bunch of papers out of his bag and handed them to me. "The gist of what we printed off was that the Walker family has been hunting for years."

Olivia and I both gasped. "Did you say Walker?" she asked. She leaned over and snatched the papers from my hand, scanning them and rifling through them.

"Yeah, there's even a family tree in there." He looked at Olivia, then leaned forward. "Why?"

"That's the local sheriff's last name, and we've gotten some other type vibes off of him." I pointed to Owen and then myself as I spoke.

Wallie nodded. "Well, check the page with the tree. It seems this thing doesn't pass down to every kid, and they only have the family member with the gift on the tree."

Olivia shook the papers. "Here it is."

"There's something else," Wallie said. "I'm having some crazy powers out of the blue."

Owen spoke up for the first time. "You didn't have powers before?"

Wallie gave him a weird look. "I did, but they were pretty low-key. Basic witch stuff. This is bigger. Like, I can heal super-fast, and I don't need an actual spell to achieve what I want. I think about it and will it so."

Okay, that wasn't normal necromancer powers so maybe he wasn't one after all. I had hoped it would skip him altogether and he just got the witch half of my family.

"Then," Wallie added, lowering his voice. "We went to a party that was near a cemetery and I felt the dead."

Crap. That was necromancer magic. "I was sure hoping that you would be spared those powers."

I sank in my chair as Alfred entered with a tray of coffee

and snacks. When he sat it on the coffee table, I said, "Thanks. Can you hold off on making dinner? We want to talk to you about something."

Alfred looked unsure as he scanned the faces of everyone in the room before he took a seat on the floor next to Sammie, who was playing a game on his mom's phone.

"When you started using your necro powers again, it must've jump-started his," Owen said.

"How can that be? We'd have to be connected in some way." For the first time in my life, I wish I trained more when I was younger, but I was so scared of my powers that it was hard to focus on how they could be controlled.

While Olivia was still reading through the papers, I thought of a way we could get Alfred to answer our questions.

"Here he is." Olivia moved to sit beside me and shoved the papers under my nose. "He's on their tree, one of the last on here. Along with a woman named Carmen that appears to be his first cousin."

I stared at the paper in shock.

Holy crap on a cracker. They could be working together to kill off necromancers and witches. That meant my life and Wallie's were in danger.

Turning to Olivia, I was about to tell her to go home and not come here, since she was human and now in danger by default. Was it too late?

Olivia flipped through more pages and gasped. "Moon-flower is also here. Isn't that Carmen's last name?"

Alfred sat up straight and made muffled sounds like he was trying to talk while waving his arms in the air. Fear darkened his aura and reached out to me.

"What is it?" I asked.

Owen then asked, "Do you know Carmen?"

Alfred nodded vigorously and made the sounds again.

"Are you scared of her?"

Nodding got faster.

I glanced at Owen who frowned and asked, "Did you kill Betty Knolls?"

Alfred's eyes widened and he shook his head. Then started making S sounds.

"Carmen." Dread slammed into my chest when he nodded, confirming what I already guessed.

Snooze trotted into the room and went after Alfred's string, harder this time. Olivia shooed him away and he growled at her. "Hey. Don't growl at me, psycho cat."

Snooze twitched his tale and walked about halfway to the kitchen and lay down in the middle of the floor, watching us.

I rolled my eyes at the cat. He was so weird.

Focusing back on Alfred, I asked, "Are you sure?"

Nod.

Damn, Drew and Sam went to talk to a killer. Drew could be working with her and taking out Sam.

I dug into my pocket and sent Sam a text. **You coming over for dinner?**

I didn't want to say anything about Knowing Carmen is the killer in case Drew was right next to him when he checked the message.

Sure, since my wife and kid are there. lol

Okay, he was joking so either he wasn't at Carmen's, or she hadn't tried to kill him yet. I risked asking, **Everything good on your end?**

Yep. Wrapping it up. Be on my way in a few.

When I looked up, I met Olivia's stare. She was still sitting next to me and saw the text. "I don't like any of this."

"Neither do I." I directed my next question to Wallie. "How long are you staying?"

"As long as you'd like me to. I don't have classes tomorrow, so I can stay through Sunday."

Alfred jumped up and went to the kitchen, most likely to

start dinner. Good because all this talk about killers and death was making me hungry.

CHAPTER SEVENTEEN

"Wow, here's irony for you." Olivia held a single sheet of paper. "The first witch hunter was born here in Shipton. Guess what?"

Owen and I stared at her, waiting for her to continue. Wallie sat in the chair with her head back and eyes closed. He wasn't asleep because he wasn't snoring. Olivia finally rolled her eyes. "You're not going to guess?"

When I waved my hand to continue, she let out a sigh. "The first witch hunter was half-witch, half-human. Apparently, being half-human dulls their powers enough the baby never gained the mark of a witch, but she had enough magic in her veins that she was stronger and faster than a human."

"And the ability to cast spells so they could hunt down other witches." Yeah, I could totally see the irony in that. "But why hunt your own kind?"

Olivia shrugged. "It says here that a witch fell in love with a human. The human hated witches, so she hid her powers and lied, saying she was human. They married and had a baby. When that baby showed signs of having magic, the husband was so enraged at his wife's betrayal that he killed her. Then he raised the baby to hate witches and to use her magic to hunt them."

Alfred tapped the wall to get our attention. Dinner was done. I hadn't even noticed the delicious aromas coming from the kitchen. We'd been so engrossed in the witch hunter story.

Glancing at the table, I noticed all the food. My stomach rumbled to life. "Oh, let's go eat."

As we walked through the living room, my doorbell rang. "You all go ahead, I'll get it."

I opened the door after making sure Alfred was out of sight, and Sam walked in without waiting for an invitation. Then again, he was my BFF and this house had always been a second home for him. When I was about to close the door, Drew slipped inside. I frowned at him but said nothing. Sam didn't yet know about Drew and what we'd learned. We hadn't called him to fill him in yet.

"Um, hello," I said as Drew barged in. "Please, do come in."

"Thanks. Are those burgers I smell?" Sam grinned. Drew nodded politely to me and followed Sam.

I snorted. "Yes, but I don't know if it's a good idea for you to..." My voice trailed off as he walked down the hall, ignoring me.

Drew followed but stopped at the door to the kitchen and turned around, as if just registering my words. "Wait, you didn't want me here?"

I gaped at him. "Well, it's not that I don't, but you've got some explaining to do."

He looked toward the people in the living room and then back at me. "What do you mean? We came here to tell you about Carmen. That's why we're here."

"We know you're a hunter," Olivia said from the kitchen.

Drew's facial features didn't change, and I wonder if he even heard what Olivia said. Something was off with those two.

I cut through the living room into the kitchen before them. "Everyone sit."

My table, though large, was suddenly very full. Drew and Sam sat, and Sam looked at us all with wide eyes. "What's up?"

"My son, Wallie." I pointed at him for Drew's benefit. "Found out about the hunters, and that Drew is descended from a long line of hunters that also includes Carmen."

Sam frowned at the sheriff while Drew shook his head, his forehead creasing. "I'm not, and I don't know Carmen. I hadn't met her before tonight. Her explanation was perfectly reasonable."

"Yes," Sam said. "Perfectly reasonable."

See? Weird. We had a witness and documented proof that Carmen is a witch hunter and had a motive to kill William and Betty. Sam and Drew just sat there, like we were all wrong.

I thought not.

Olivia and I exchanged a glance. "What did she say?"

Drew didn't blink as Alfred handed him a plate with a burger and bun. He just started piling on condiments. "She is her step-daughter."

"Did you confirm this with Connor?" I asked

Olivia was looking at Sam. "Sam?"

They both shook their heads as Alfred handed Sam a plate and he started fixing it.

"No," Drew said. "It was perfectly reasonable."

"Yes, perfectly reasonable," Sam echoed.

Olivia looked at me with her eyebrows raised.

Owen stood. "Sam, may I look at your eyes?" he asked

"Sure," Sam said jovially.

Owen peered close at Sam. "They've been spelled. Should be easy enough to break."

"How?" I asked.

He grinned. "This is fun. You've never broken a glamour?"

Drew and Sam kept eating, obliviously happy as I snorted.

"I didn't even know this was a glamour. I thought glamours were for changing the appearance of things."

"It can change the appearance of someone's mind, too, so to speak," he said. "Anyway, let some magic pool in your hands." He nodded at Wallie. "Want to try?"

Wallie grinned big and nodded. "Hell, yeah."

"Okay, Wallie, you stand beside Sam, and Ava beside Drew." We moved around the table and positioned ourselves. I let my magic pool in my hand. My hands glowed as magic arched between my fingers.

Olivia gasped. "It's so pretty."

"Magic, when visible, tends to come out the witch's favorite color. Mine is bright, hot pink."

Wallie grinned. "Mine's green." The magic pooling in his hands was forest green.

I smiled at a memory of my mother. "So was your grand-mother's."

"Okay, let the magic build in your hand. Not an energy ball. More like an energy pancake. Swirl it around." Owen demonstrated, and shocker, his magic was dark gray. The guy was so weird.

"When you've got as much as you can hold without it spilling over, ask them to look at you, then slap their face as hard as you can."

Olivia gasped and Wallie grinned. I stopped short. "Wait," I yelled. "Just wait."

Owen and Wallie looked at me, disappointed. "What?" Wallie asked.

"Sam has been my best friend all my life," I said. "You're not slapping him like that."

Owen's chair scraped as he scooted back. "I don't know of another way to get them out of this glamour."

"No, this is fine," I said and stood. "But if *anyone*," I glanced at my new friend, "sorry, Olivia, not even you. If anyone gets to slap Sam, it's me." I shooed Wally out of the way. "You go slap the sheriff."

Olivia's face broke into a huge grin, and she burst out laughing. "Hang on, one sec." She pulled her phone out of her pocket. "Okay, do it."

I let the magic pool in my hand again and looked at Sam. "Sammy?"

He glanced at me and once I was this close to him, I could tell his eyes weren't right. "Yes?"

"Remember in middle school? When we were doing the talent show?"

He smiled. "Yeah, we had a lot of fun."

"You remember how you got scared and left me on the stage all alone and I had to sing the duet myself? Both parts?"

His bland smile didn't change. He just kept nodding. "Yeah."

"This is for that." I hauled back and slapped him as hard as I could.

Wallie smacked the sheriff at the same. Their heads jerked and Sam stood, grabbing my wrist. We locked gazes and I could see that his eyes were clearing. The glamour, vanishing. After a few moments he drew his brows together and frowned. "Did you just slap me?"

I smiled and relaxed while moving my hands so our palms pressed together. "Do you feel better?"

"Better from what?" Sam stepped back from me and lowered into his seat.

"What the hell is going on?" Drew asked.

Taking my seat again, I gave him a half-hearted smile. "Ah, now that you're yourselves again, we can try this again." I turned toward the food and began building my burger. "Drew, we know you're descended from a family of hunters and that Carmen is your cousin."

Drew's jaw dropped. "Holy shit. I didn't even recognize her."

After several seconds, he confessed that his family were witch hunters, but he was not. He didn't have anything to do with that life. "I hated that life and could never see why my family hated witches so. As far as I know witches had never threatened us or harmed us. I didn't see the justice in hunting them like animals. That's not who I am."

While Drew spoke, I did a simple truth spell. I didn't care if it made me out as mistrusting. I didn't know Drew or his intentions.

But he was telling the truth. He didn't hunt witches, but could he hunt down a family member that was a hunter?

"Okay, well, we need to find out about Carmen," I said. "Drew, can you get any information on her?"

I thought of his words about not liking the family business. If I hadn't done the truth spell, I'd call bullshit, but he was truthful. He didn't want to be a hunter. That didn't mean he didn't use the magic that flowed through his veins.

"Yeah, sure, let me just call my mom." He left the dinner table and pulled his phone out of his pocket.

I met Olivia's gaze as we ate quickly and quietly, all of us straining to hear what he said, but he spoke too softly. Darn it.

Several minutes later, he returned, taking his seat across from me. "I had no idea Carmen was in town or hunting, first of all. It's not like I keep up with distant relatives. Most of them think of me as an outcast."

He shook his head and finished his burger before continuing. "Hunters can see witch marks, and I saw William's. So yes, I knew he was a necromancer. I figured his killer was a hunter, but I didn't know for sure or even who. As far as I knew I was the only hunter in the area."

"But you're not a hunter," I pointed out with a raised brow and a flat tone.

He pressed his lips into a thin line and worked his jaw. "Exactly. It wasn't me."

I sniffed. "Me neither."

After a few minutes of staring at each other, he said, "I'm sorry for not coming clean about that sooner. It might've gotten us answers before now."

"Yeah, and maybe Betty would be alive," I said darkly.

He shook his head. "No. The coroner says Betty died a couple days before William but was probably in some sort of cold storage for a while before the body was dumped."

I shuddered at the thought of sweet Betty stuffed into a deep freezer. "Poor Betty," I whispered. "Maybe she recognized Carmen for what she was." Betty had told us who had killed her, but the decomposition was too far gone to get more than that.

"Yes, that's my guess. Most witch hunters leave regular, run of the mill witches alone, but Mom said Carmen went rogue a long time ago. She's after necromancers."

"Why?" I asked.

"Mom says Carmen's father was killed when she was a teenager by a necromancer. Carmen has been angry since then." Drew wiped his face. "I can't believe she spelled me. She's so far gone she's *using* magic, and hunters are supposed to be against it. Not using it."

"That means she'll come after us now." I looked at Wallie, who was most likely starting to show necromancer powers, too. "You're in danger. I want you to go back to school, right now. Let us deal with this woman."

He snorted. "Not a chance, Mom. I'm not leaving you."

"But how do we deal with this?" I asked.

Drew sighed. "I can pretend to still be under her spell."

"Me too," Sam agreed.

Okay, that might work as long as the guys could pull it off.

We sat around the dinner table and discussed one option after another for how that could be to our benefit.

In the end, we decided we had to draw her out. If we could get her somewhere with all of us around her, we could subdue her. Get her to confess her crimes. Drew would arrest her for William's and Betty's murders. It was the only thing we could think of.

Once we had a plan worked out, Drew stood and moved to the living room to call Carmen to set the trap. The rest of us sat as quietly as we could so we didn't make the crazy rogue hunter suspicious.

Sammie sat in his seat next to his mom making clicking noises with his mouth while playing on his tablet. I considered putting a magical circle around him to muffle his noises.

In less time than I thought it would take, Drew returned but didn't sit. "She's agreed to meet me there in about an hour. I'm heading there now."

Everyone else jumped into motion. When I started cleaning off the table, Alfred appeared and pushed me aside. I laughed softly and let him have at it.

I entered the living room and found Olivia and Sam discussing something in a hushed argument kind of way. Moving to stand beside them, I asked, "What's up?"

Olivia huffed. "My parents are out of town."

I glanced at Sammie who was sitting next to Wallie chatting away. "Wallie can watch him. Alfred is here. The house won't let Carmen or anyone with ill intent come inside."

As if agreeing with me the walls of the living room vibrated and a knock sounded on the ceiling above our heads. Olivia gasped and stared at me wide-eyed. "Was that the house?"

Laughing, I nodded. "Yeah. Do you now see why the construction crew gets scared off?"

"We should set up cameras just so we can see their reaction

when the house acts out." Olivia started to giggle, which made me laugh more.

"I love it, but later. Right now, we have a rogue hunter to take down."

It took some time, but I finally got Wallie to promise to stay here with Alfred and Sammie. He couldn't argue too much with me since I told him that his job is more important because he was keeping the kid and the ghoul safe. Which meant Wallie would stay safely at home as well. Plus, Wallie could protect Sammie and control Alfred. At least Alfred would follow Wal's directions because my son was a necromancer.

I turned to Sam and Olivia. "Ready?" I asked in a low voice with my stomach churning. Now that we were putting the plan into motion and fast, I was starting to have doubts.

Olivia looked like she was about to come apart at the seams. Not because she was scared, but excited. I made one more attempt to get her to stay. "Olivia, your kid has only two parents. Both of you shouldn't go. Carmen has already killed two people that we know of. Think about staying behind."

Wallie grunted. "I only have one parent."

I sighed. "I kind of have to go, Wal. I'm the necromancer."

Not that I wanted to. I definitely didn't want to, but Carmen had to be stopped. I had powers. They might need me. Hopefully, Drew and Sam would be able to handle it on their own, but if not, Owen and I would be there.

Wallie settled down with Sammy on the couch. Alfred hovered by the stairs, and I could tell he was concerned. There was nothing I could do to ease his mind.

"See you soon," I said brightly.

At the last second, Wallie ran over, right before I shut the door. He pulled me into a big hug. "Love you, Mom. Be careful."

I looked my boy deep in his eyes. "I will. I promise."

CHAPTER EIGHTEEN

The quiet morgue wasn't any less creepy now that it was dark. It was a *lot* creepier. I shivered as we crept down the cinderblock-lined hallway and through the glass sliding doors of the morgue.

Drew was already inside. I stopped briefly to admire how handsome he looked in his uniform. You had to appreciate the tight pants and shirt that practically hugged his lean muscles. He lifted his gaze in my direction, and I jolted into motion while averting my eyes elsewhere. I was busted for checking him out.

Now that I knew he wasn't out to kill me, I felt pretty guilt free and a little less crazy while ogling him. I couldn't help it. The man was hot.

Drew didn't take his eyes off me as he addressed everyone in the room. "If we're doing this, and you guys here..." He looked at Olivia, then swung his gaze to Sam. "You let her come?"

Sam threw up his hands in exasperation. "I don't control that woman. I'd like to see you try."

I coughed in my hand to hide my laugh. No one was fooled though. Olivia and I exchanged a glance, then burst into nervous laughter. Like either of them could control a woman.

Drew rolled his admittedly handsome eyes and held out his hands. "All of you except Sam in the other room. Stay quiet. We'll try to cuff her and take her quietly. Hopefully, we won't need any of your magic."

"That would be nice," Owen said. "But I doubt it." He leveled as stare on Drew. "Were you trained? As a hunter?"

Drew nodded, his features turning dark for a moment. "Yeah. I was trained."

"Good. Sam wasn't, and Sam is human. Hunters do have a little extra *something* in their blood that makes them stronger, healthier. Sam doesn't. You'll have to protect him."

Sam bristled, but Owen shook his head. "I mean no offense, but you're human and she's not. We're just in the next room, ready with binding spells. Remember the panic word."

"Snooze," Sam said. "We know."

Owen turned and held the door open for Olivia and me. We stood just inside the room and listened. When Carmen arrived and the doors clanged, all three of us jumped, even Owen, who seemed nearly nonreactive.

"Carmen, thank you for coming in." Drew's voice filtered through the door strong and clear. "We just need you to provide a positive identification. Your brother was unable to do it."

"Of course, it's no problem," she replied. The room was quiet for a moment. The sound of shuffling feet made my heart lurch into overdrive. I took a chance and peeked through the little window.

Drew had his gun out, pointed at Carmen. She had Sam in a grip in front of her with a knife to his neck. "Sleepy!" Drew yelled, then cursed. "Uh, Tired, Dozer."

I burst through the door with my hands out, Owen and

Olivia on my heels. "Good try. Snooze," I hissed at Drew as we inched forward. "Carmen," I said louder. "Let him go. He's human."

"This blade is cursed," she said in a low, melodic voice. "One touch to his neck and he's dead."

My pulse quickened and my insides burned with fear for my best friend's life. If only I could knock her out with my power without harming or killing Sam, but I wasn't confident that I could.

She grinned, more like bared her teeth. "Now, all I want is your father, Ava. Give him to me and this will be over."

"He's dead, Carmen. He died a long time ago." I tried to keep my voice soothing but couldn't stop a bit of a tremor. "I'm sorry. I wish he were alive, too, though for *very* different reasons than you."

She snarled and pushed the blade of the knife to Sam's throat. We all flinched, and Drew lunged forward, but froze again when nothing happened. "What the fuck?" Carmen yelled. "Why isn't it working? It should kill anything magical with a touch, except necromancers. They require a little more zing."

Sam sighed. "Thank goodness." With a yell, he elbowed Carmen in the chest.

She flew backward and slammed into the table holding the poor, bloated, abused body of Betty Knolls.

Betty's body slid off the table with a sickening squelch. She slammed on the floor, liquid spreading out in all directions. Including under Carmen's feet.

I stopped and watched in awe as Sam scrambled away from her. She danced, trying to get her balance, sliding in the goo that was part Betty, part ocean water.

A giggle slid up my throat, the sort of giggle that made me feel like I was going to take a one-way train straight to Hell for laughing, but Betty was long gone and watching Carmen glide and skid over that goop hit me funny. Maybe it was the stress of the situation. I just couldn't help it.

Olivia hissed as Carmen got her balance. "I'm so glad you laughed," she said. "Because I was about to lose it."

Owen shot us a glance. "Those kinds of blades don't work on humans," he explained as Carmen held the knife out, pointed at us, and stood in a defensive position.

"Okay, so don't get near the blade," I said. "On it!" Olivia yelled. She rushed forward as I yelled.

"Olivia, no." I threw out my magic, trying to throw up a shield around Olivia, but nothing happened. I kept trying to no avail. My magic wasn't working.

Carmen jerked back and looked at Olivia in amused confusion as my new best friend tried to slap at her. Carmen grabbed Olivia's wrists, somehow maneuvered them into one hand, and then turned her around to press the blade to her throat. "You forgot that it's still a sharp knife," Carmen said. She raised her hand to plunge it into Olivia's throat, but Sam and Drew moved. Sam blocked her hand, and the knife flew out of it, and Drew jerked Olivia out of Carmen's arms.

Carmen dropped to the floor, then surged back upward with a scream. Both Drew and Olivia went flying. Sam didn't go as far. He slammed into Carmen from behind, and somehow, she had the knife again. We all tried to get to her, but Sam was holding his own, avoiding the knife and getting some blows in. They fought around the room, crashing into cabinets, and knocking over tables, and got closer to Olivia.

Olivia saw an opportunity and grabbed Carmen's wrist. She leaned forward with a shrill shriek and bit her wrist.

Carmen jerked away from both of them, dropping the knife and retreating. "Olivia, get the knife out of here," I yelled. "It's stopping my magic."

It had to be. That was the only thing that could be crippling my powers. Olivia darted out the door into the hallway. My magic flooded back into me with a rush.

"Carmen, you can't stop my magic now. It's time to give up."

Carmen looked around with wide eyes, assessing the situation. Olivia darted back into the room, stopping *right* in front of Carmen. Carmen wrapped her arms around Olivia's throat and squeezed.

"No," I screamed, but it was drowned in everyone else's screams.

My magic exploded out of me like a bomb. I sent it all out, all the power I could muster. My necromancer power opened up and I welcomed the flow of dark magic in my veins. If there were any dead bodies in this morgue, I wanted their help.

Betty sat up with a squelch, scaring Carmen and causing her to drop Olivia. Sam rushed forward and grabbed her arms, pulling her out of danger. I kept up the flow of magic, somehow, I'd managed to press Carmen into the wall and hold her there, so I didn't stop.

As Sam pulled Olivia into the back room, the body we'd seen earlier in the day lurched through the doorway and into the room. "Get her!" I yelled. "Sam, stay in there with Olivia. Owen, get Drew out."

Carmen held out her hand, and that damn knife materialized in it. Having it in the room was like a punch to the gut of my magic, but it didn't stop, thankfully. It did weaken, though. As Carmen fought against it, she swung the knife out and sliced Betty.

Betty's body shuddered, then erupted into a shower of dust, all the liquid and squelching, swollen mass disappearing.

The corpse from the back room shuffled forward, faster than I would've expected.

As the corpse fought Carmen, I noticed something out the window on the door to the hallway. Blinking, I split my focus between keeping my magic going, and scooting over to see who was walking down the hall.

When I saw them more clearly, I gasped and nearly let my magic go. Carmen waving that knife around made it harder for me to keep hold, but I managed it, barely, and backed up.

Skeletons streamed through the door, all of them totally decomposed. There was no flesh left on any of them, though several had hair.

Carmen screamed and lunged at the corpse from the back part of the morgue and managed to cut him with the knife. The skeletons kept coming. They rushed toward her. Every time she touched one with that knife it disintegrated, but more kept coming through the door.

And more. "Where are they coming from?" I whispered.

"There's an old graveyard across the street," Drew said. "It's got to be there."

I thought I told Owen to get him out of there. I studied Drew and shook my head. No, the stubborn man wouldn't leave. It wasn't worth arguing over right then.

A cemetery. Great. Just my luck. The skeletons swarmed and through the mass of bones, I saw them get the knife away. They picked her up, screaming, and walked her through the doors. I let my magic go then, but it was done. They weren't stopping.

A new kind of fear rose inside me.

"Can you stop them?" Owen asked.

I breathed deeply and pulled on my energy, but it was no good. "No."

Sam and Olivia came out of the back room, Olivia conscious again. "Are you good to follow them?" I asked.

Olivia nodded with one hand on her head. "Hell, yes. I've got to see this."

"Try again to stop them," Drew said. "Don't let them kill her. I can put her in jail, put her away for the rest of her life."

"I'm trying," I said. Lifting my hands, I let my magic flow from my palms. "I command you to stop."

It didn't work. What was I doing wrong?

Thank goodness for the darkness. We followed them across the street. They walked through the wrought iron gates of the old graveyard and several of them stopped. They faced us at the gates and wouldn't move. I tried to stop them, to inanimate them, but they stood firm.

Carmen's screams intensified, over the hill and out of sight and then they stopped. Silence filled the air.

The skeletons in front of us stepped to the side, allowing us to enter.

Drew, Owen, Sam, Olivia, and I rushed into the graveyard. "Split up," I cried. "Find her."

We pulled out our phones and flashlights, searching all around the headstones, but after an hour, we gave up. The skeletons milled about, some of them standing around, some following us. A few sat on headstones and looked around.

"She's gone," I whispered. "They took her."

CHAPTER NINETEEN

"We have to send these skeletons back to their graves," Owen said, turning to me. "They can't stay here."

I shrugged and looked at the closest one, leaning against a headstone. He was missing his left arm. Gathering my energy and magic, I focused on him. "Go," I whispered.

He stood and stumbled forward, then without warning, exploded. I cried out and fell back against Owen.

"Maybe a bit too much," he said.

Drew took my hand and helped me upright. "You okay?"

I stared into his teal eyes that had specks of blue in them. Something passed between us that I couldn't explain. A sensation or energy flowed between us, teasing each of our auras. The urge to reach out and touch him was strong.

"Okay." Owen pointed to another skeleton. His voice breaking whatever trance I fell into. "Try again, this time not so hard."

I focused on another bony dude. I wasn't sure how I knew it was a guy, but it was. "Go back," I whispered, letting a trickle of power go toward it.

My magic hit him in the leg, and his left leg bones disappeared entirely. He fell over against a headstone and the rest of him broke apart. Bones went everywhere and a cat screeched and hauled ass out from behind one of the headstones, making Olivia and me jump.

Owen snorted. I turned to see Sam and Olivia bent over with silent giggles as Olivia clutched her head.

"Thanks a lot, my friends," I said sarcastically. "Even though you're super mean, come here. I'll heal your head."

Sam helped Olivia limp forward so I could put my hand on her head. Healing her was easy and in a few seconds, she sighed in relief. "Much better."

"Why was that so easy?" I asked. "Why can't I do that with the skeletons?"

Owen cocked his head. "Why don't you?"

He took my hand and walked me to the cemetery gates. "Look at the whole graveyard. Heal the skeletons. Not fully. Just heal their state. Their proper state is in the ground, at rest. Heal them to that state."

I shrugged. Worth a try.

Usually, I placed my hands on people when I healed them, so this would be tricky. The skeletons didn't need actual healing. The last thing we needed was a bunch of undead beings roaming the town. What they needed was to go back to their resting places. To sleep once more.

A thought formed in my mind, and I closed my eyes while lifting my hands in the air. My power flowed out in all directions, and I could feel it touch each skeleton as it went. I felt their confusion and their need to obey me. "Time to go back to sleep. You served me well tonight."

One by one, I sensed the skeletons moving to their graves. When everything was nice and quiet, with no signs of bones, we walked back to Olivia's car, exhausted. "Back to my place?"

Olivia nodded. "Yeah, but I'm not driving. I'm too tired."

Sam took the keys. I climbed in the back seat beside Owen and stared out the window in a bit of a stupor. We made it to my house quickly, and by then I was beyond bone weary and didn't even notice Drew had followed us in his squad car until he put his hand on the small of my back.

I was too tired to jump in surprise. "I think I used too much magic," I whispered.

The next thing I knew, I was up in Drew's arms with my arms around his neck. Even exhausted, I couldn't help but feel a thrill of excitement. He was carrying me inside. Who does that any more?

Was there anything hotter, ever, anywhere?

No. There was not.

Drew got me inside and set me gently on the sofa as Wallie ran in. "What's wrong?" he cried. "Is she hurt?"

"No, Wal, I'm okay. Just exhausted. I used too much magic; I think."

Drew pulled a blanket off of the chair and wrapped it around me. "Are you sure nothing hurts?"

"I'm fine." I smiled at him. "Thank you."

He sat at my feet. "Carmen is gone," he told Wallie. Alfred hovered in the doorway, and I could've sworn he was relieved when he heard the news.

"Where?" Wallie asked.

"The skeletons took her," Olivia said brightly, then giggled.

Wallie gaped at us. "The what now?"

"It's a long story," Drew said. "If Ava is sure she's okay, I'm going to go home and let you lot fill him in."

I caught his hand as he got up. "Thank you," I whispered.

He touched his forehead where a hat would be, as if he'd forgotten he wasn't wearing one. He gave my hand a gentle squeeze before letting it go. "Yes, ma'am."

A bit of a western or maybe southern accent slipped out and holy shit. He got about ten times hotter. Did he grow up in the south? Visions of him riding a horse in a cowboy hat flitted through my head and I wanted everyone to go home so I could spend some time upstairs.

Alone.

"I'll walk you out," I said, unwinding the blanket from around me.

Drew said goodbye to the rest of the crowd, and I stepped out onto the porch with him. "Thanks again," I whispered.

When he took my hand, my energy recuperated quickly. Drew stepped close. "You were pretty amazing tonight," he said. "You're untrained?"

I nodded. "I just wanted you all to be safe."

As he leaned closer, I stared at his lips. Was he going to kiss me?

Just before his lips met mine, the porch light flickered. I looked at the door in surprise to see Alfred peeking through the curtain.

"I should go," Drew said, chuckling. "I'll talk to you soon, okay?"

"Sure, yeah."

I watched him walk down my porch steps and sighed. What a man.

CHAPTER TWENTY

I slept like the dead, which was saying a lot after what we went through last night. Olivia and Sam went home with a sleepy Sammie, and Owen settled into my Aunt Winnie's old bedroom, which he'd chosen as his. I didn't mind. He was cool.

Someone yelled up the stairs as I brushed my teeth. "Hey!"

I didn't recognize the voice. Rushing out of my room in my nightgown, I looked downstairs in confusion.

"Yeah?" I asked through my mouth full of toothpaste.

"We quit!" the construction foreman yelled back. "I don't know what kind of Halloween bullshit you've got going on, but we saw the man dressed up like a zombie in your upstairs window. Enough is enough. We'll send our bill; you're not stiffing us on this after playing all these practical jokes on us."

I gaped at him as he threw up his arms and walked away. Hurrying back to the bathroom, I rinsed out my mouth and got to my front window in time to see the men throw their last few tools in the back of one of the trucks, then they all peeled the hell out of there.

"Shit."

"I can help," Owen said. "I know how to do construction with magic. I can show you. I need a place to stay on a more permanent basis since the lighthouse was so damaged, and you need training."

I turned to see him leaning against my door frame. "I haven't decided to stay."

"Oh, come on. After what we went through together here, me, you, those cops, and that crazy woman? You're going to walk away from this?"

Chuckling, I looked at my torn-up yard. The big bulky construction trucks had done a number on it. I thought about the front living room that was still pretty much torn up, and the fact that only one bathroom worked in the house.

Unless I could find a construction crew that specialized in magical houses, how else would I get it fixed?

"Ava," Owen said softly. "I've never in my life seen anyone animate that many corpses. It just made you tired. It would've killed me to try. I've also never met a necromancer that can heal. Your line is supposed to be extinct."

I sank onto the bed. "You know rumor has it I'm a seventh-generation necromancer to the Howe family."

"Ah." Owen stuffed his hands in his pockets and watched me. "That answers that. The Howe bloodline is extraordinarily strong. Your powers will only grow stronger. Especially now that you opened them up like you did last night."

Frowning, I lifted my gaze to his. "I guess I'm hanging around for a while, aren't I?"

"You need to let me train you." He sat beside me. "Wallie will need it as well."

"Yeah, I suppose that's true. Okay, Owen, looks like we're roommates."

He grinned. "Great. Let's go make a list of what we need to fix this house."

We got busy doing that, and I checked in with the bookstore. Clint was happy to take me on a more permanent basis, thankfully.

Two days later, I walked out of the downstairs bathroom, covered in plaster, my hair in a big, messy, slightly greasy bun. Owen and I had made serious progress in there today.

I grabbed a carton of ice cream and a spoon and ate straight out of the container as I leaned against the kitchen cabinets.

"Come in," I called when someone rang the doorbell. "Ah, shit." I dropped a blob of chocolate ice cream on my white shirt. I wasn't expecting anyone, but it was almost definitely Olivia. She loved to pop in. I wiped off my shirt, then threw the rag in the sink, turning to find Drew standing in the kitchen.

Super.

Damn it.

I squeaked and ran into the laundry room. After a quick glamour to make me look like a normal human, not too fancy, but definitely not covered in plaster and ice cream, I walked back out.

He burst out laughing. "You know I saw you before, right?"

"No, you didn't, so there." I gestured toward the table. "Have a seat. What can I do for you?"

"I came to update you. Nobody can find hide nor hair of Carmen."

We figured that much, but I nodded anyway. "That's good, I guess. I hate that it resulted in her death, but she had to be stopped."

"I agree, though I would've rather put her in jail. The other thing was that some citizens complained about seeing the skeletons." The corners of his lips twitch.

I gaped at him. "No." I hadn't even thought about that.

"Yes. Since Halloween is next weekend, they thought it was some sort of skit and wanted to find out who put it on, so they could complain that they hadn't had a chance to buy tickets." He chuckled then, making me smile.

My dismay turned to humor, and I sat down and laughed. "Next time I'll do an event invite on social media."

Drew laughed with me. "Great idea." He studied me for a moment. "Go out to dinner with me?"

My giggles caught in my throat and before I could overthink it, I replied. "Okay."

He nodded once. "I'll text you." With that, he stood. "I gotta get back to work."

I scrambled out of my seat and followed him far enough to watch him walk down the hall with his tight butt in his tight uniform pants.

"Bye," he called.

I finger waved, and as soon as the door closed, let my glamour go. Owen poked his head out of the bathroom door. "Was someone here?"

Walking over to the island, I grabbed the ice cream and ate a huge spoonful. "Mmhmm."

I said yes to dinner. With the hottie sheriff. When I wasn't even sure if I was staying in Maine.

What had I gotten myself into?

COOKIES FOR SATAN

WITCHING AFTER FORTY BOOK 2

1

VOODOO ANGEL

"Move it a little to the left." I tilted my head like it would give me a better viewpoint of the large evergreen tree. "No. Come forward a half a step. Then to the right... That's it!"

Sam, my BFF since we were in diapers, scowled at me. "That is where I had it in the first place," he said through his teeth. He clenched his fists and his arm muscles contracted as he shifted it again, turning it.

I waved my hand while giving him a scowl of my own. "It's really not."

Maybe it was, but I wasn't about to admit it. "Rotate it? Please. I think that side might be better." I crossed my arms and studied it as Sam glared at me. "You know how important this is to me."

Flexing again, he turned the larger-than-him tree around. "I do know how important this is to you. So, keep telling me, I'll keep moving it, but would it kill you for once to notice how much I've been working out?"

He waggled his brows and gave me a cocky grin. Was that

why he volunteered for putting the tree in just the right spot under my direction? Of course, it was.

"Uuuuugh." I went boneless and collapsed on the couch in mock disgust. Of course, I noticed how toned he'd gotten since the last time I saw him before I moved back to Shipton Harbor. But I sure as hell wasn't going to tell him that. "Does this work on Olivia? I mean, she's your wife. She *has* to pretend you're hot. You do know that?"

Crickets chirped as he stared at me. I hid my smile as he said, "Look, Ava, I get that we're best friends and like siblings and have been all our lives, but you don't have to be hurtful."

Olivia chuckled beside me on the couch. "It does *not* work."

With a snort, Sam glared at his wife. "Liar."

I twirled my finger. "Just turn the tree, muscle boy." It had to be perfect so that it could be seen from the street, which was down below the house. I wanted tasteful and noticeable décor, without going over the top. A tree through the window was a must.

This was the first Christmas I'd looked forward to celebrating since Clay, my beloved, deceased husband, left this earth to find a new adventure without me. We were married for twenty-one years. He'd been dead for five. Just wanted to make sure that was clear.

I hadn't been sure I'd decorate the house this year, but my newfound family, which included Alfred, my ghoul-butler-slash-friend-slash... he's sort of a pet? And Snoozle, my immortal, very large Maine coon cat, as well as Owen, my needed-a-place-to-live necromancer and sort-of trainer, and Olivia, Sam's wife—good lord, they're a mouthful—all insisted that I at least put a tree up. They didn't say I had to decorate. That was on them.

But believe me, if they decorated the house, they were also taking that shit down in January.

Not that Snooze could put ornaments on the spruce-fir. He was more likely to knock the thing over trying to climb it.

And not that they'd decorate correctly. I would probably end up redoing everything, anyway. I wasn't normally super anal-retentive, but hey. It was Christmas. It had to be perfect this year.

The sound of wild animals trampling down the stairs made me turn to investigate. Of course, there were no wild beasts in my house. Just a mini version of Sam running ahead of Alfred, who carried a large box of holiday decorations from the attic. Owen walked slower behind the ghoul with a smaller box in his arms.

Sammie rushed through the room and stopped to stare up at me. I looked back with one brow raised. I tried to keep a straight face but failed miserably when he cracked a snaggle-toothed smile. The kid was too stinkin' cute.

After a moment, Sammie folded his little arms over his chest and mean mugged me. "You gonna do magic?" He loved it when I did little tricks for him.

A giggle drew my attention to the brat's mother, Olivia, sitting on the sofa doing her best impression of a project supervisor. Of course, Olivia had told her son I could do magic, prompting months of him cutesy-ing his way into me coming up with more and more small magic tricks. I just hoped my new best frenemy didn't tell the five-year-old that I could raise the dead.

Focusing on Sammie, I said, "Maybe. I thought you wanted to decorate the tree."

Sammie pressed his lips together. "Why not both?"

Chuckling, I waved my finger at the box of decorations that Alfred had carried down earlier, before running up to grab the rest of the holiday loot, and made the lights wrap themselves around the tree and plug themselves in while Sammie cheered and clapped.

"Why couldn't you do that with the tree itself?" Sam exclaimed.

With a shrug and a grin, I pulled out my phone. "My way was more fun."

Ignoring Sam's low growl, I checked my messages. My son, Wallie, was supposed to come home for the holiday break, but he was running late. He was in college at Harvard University studying to be a doctor. Wallie was a bright kid and could do anything he set his mind to. I'd used a huge chunk of Clay's life insurance to pay for the first four years of Wallie's higher learning in advance. The less the kid had in loans, the better off he would be.

A weather alert came up on my phone that it would snow later in the evening. Frowning, I went back to the messaging app. Wallie was driving up from Massachusetts. I tried not to worry, but I was his mom. It was part of the job.

On that note, I sent him a text. **Are you here yet?**

I didn't worry about him texting and driving. He was bringing a girl friend with him so she would reply to my text. My Wallie was a responsible driver. And he knew I'd kill him and cut off all financial help if I caught him texting and driving. **About an hour away**.

That was not my Wallie who replied. The lack of sarcasm was my main clue.

Tell Dr. Wallie to drive carefully. It's supposed to snow later tonight. Call me if you run into trouble.

Wallie's female companion replied with, **Will do.**

Great. His friend, who happened to be a girl, was going to think I was an insane, nagging mom.

I wasn't. I was a cool mom. I raised the dead and was the master of a ghoul. And possibly had turned my cat into one by accident. Oops.

"Texting Wallie again?" Olivia asked as I sat back on the sofa.

"Yeah." I sat the phone on the arm of the couch. "I wish I knew more about this friend he is bringing. He wouldn't even tell me her name."

"Really? Why?"

Sam snorted and answered for me. "Because Ava would dig up information on the poor girl and text Wallie nonstop about things she found."

I huffed and crossed my arms. "Not true."

Sam mimicked my pose. "Really? What did Aunt Winnie do when you started dating Clay?"

Umm. Yeah. Aunt Winnie drove me crazy with the stuff she supposedly dug up on Clay. Half the crap, I swore she made up.

Sam added, "I just hope the poor girl is magical in some way so she can fire back with all the overprotective witchy games your kind plays."

I stuck my tongue out at him and stood. As if on cue, Snooze trotted into the living room from the kitchen, licking his lips. Did ghoul kitties *need* to eat? Or was the fat cat just addicted to food?

Alfred glanced at the cat as he set his box down in front of me.

"Thank you, Alfred." I bent down to open the box while Owen set his down next to it. Meeting Little Sammie's gleeful gaze, I asked, "Which is it, little man? Magic, or are you going to decorate the tree?"

He pressed his lips together and tapped his chin. I laughed so hard at the cuteness that I had to clutch my side.

Smirking, the little monster put his hands on his hips. "Both. You use magic for the area I can't reach."

Smartie pants. That's what he was. "You got it." I scooted forward. "You tell me what to do and when okay?"

"Wait!" Sammie held out his hands as if to stop all motion in the room. "I want to put the star on top."

"Err." Did I have a star? Yaya used to put a voodoo doll on top as a joke. The thought made me snort out a laugh. Then tears formed and rolled down my cheeks as I remembered this Christmas, in this house, would be without Yaya, who died when I was nineteen, or Aunt Winnie. She died last year, and I'd moved back here a few months ago to sell the house. But then, I ended up falling in love with my family home again and decided to stay. Plus, I had a menagerie of misfits here, all counting on me.

"Ava." Sam touched my shoulder, his voice soft with concern.

I waved him off. "I'm good, I'm fine. This is part of the grief process." I sniffed and stood up. "Remember the voodoo doll?"

He burst out laughing. "Is it in there?"

Rifling through the smaller box, I shrugged. "I don't know. We'll find out, I guess."

Olivia sat up straight. "Share the inside joke with the rest of the room."

Instead of telling her, I dug through the boxes until I found the doll.

Holding it up for all to see, like one of Bob Barker's ladies on the Price is Right, I explained. "So, this thing was Yaya's favorite Christmas decoration. She liked to use it as the star on the tree." I smiled thinking about my Yaya. She'd been gone for over twenty-four years now. Way, way too long.

Olivia giggled. "She put that on top of the tree?"

Nodding, I smiled through the tears. Even after all these years, it hurt to think about her, albeit in a better way now than it had in years past. "Yaya was my mother's mom and also an earth witch. I think she did it to annoy the coven. Yaya loved and accepted my dad, but the coven shunned him for being a necromancer. It was a different time back then."

The latter didn't matter to me. Some of the same witches were still part of the coven that had voted to not allow dad, or later me, into their sacred club. Hence the reason I wasn't going to pay them any visits.

"That would do it," Olivia said. "I'm sorry I never got the chance to meet her."

Olivia and I hadn't liked each other when I lived in Shipton Harbor before. We'd been enemies, of a sort. I couldn't stand her, was what it had boiled down to.

But she'd changed dramatically since then. "Me, too. She would've loved you." The new Olivia, anyway. She probably would've hexed the old Olivia. I'd considered it many times myself.

Maybe that was why Yaya had gotten along with Dad so well. They both had a dark streak mixed in with their magic.

Handing the doll to Sammie, I smiled at the thought of Yaya hexing Olivia. Maybe some itching spell. "The doll goes on top this year. In honor of Yaya, Aunt Winnie, Mom, and Dad."

This Christmas was going to be different and memorable. I couldn't wait to start making memories with my newfound family.

2

IT'S MY PARTY AND I'LL
SUMMON IF I WANT TO

"Hello?" Wallie's voice interrupted my decorating. My heart lurched with excitement while the rest of me softened with relief that my only child made it home alive.

I hated the thought of having to use my powers to bring him back to life. But I would've.

I'd been floating ornaments to the higher branches with one hand while Sammie decorated the lower ones. In my other hand, I held a glass of wine Sam and Olivia had passed to me and Owen to enjoy while we decorated.

"Come in, honey," I called, settling the last ornament, and stopping the flow of magic. I didn't know anything about this girl Wallie was bringing home and how much she did or didn't know about magic and our world. It was better to wait because I didn't need people giving my baby shit for being a witch. Alfred had been warned to make himself scarce until we knew more about her. I did a quick scan to be sure the ghoul was out of sight.

"Mom," Wallie said excitedly. "I want you to meet my girl-friend, Michelle."

Ah, so it was girlfriend now. On the phone, he'd said friend. Probably to stop me from going into overprotective mode and researching her family history. Yeah, I know. But really, I wasn't as bad as Sam said.

I wasn't. Not much, anyway.

Smiling at Michelle, I checked her over without being weird. At least, I hoped it wasn't weird. Hey, she was dating my son. What could I say?

Michelle had a natural beauty to her that radiated out from inside. Her chestnut brown hair had streaks of blonde through it and was in two braids that framed her round face. A dusting of freckles went across her nose and topped her cheeks. And she had the brightest blue eyes I'd ever seen. She stood about three inches shorter than me with modest curves. Adorable as all get out.

She stuck out her hand with a bright smile. "It's really cool to meet you, Mrs. Harper. I've never met a necromancer in person."

"Oh, so you know?" I asked, raising my eyebrows at Wallie. Why was he telling people about my secret?

"Sorry, Mom, yeah. Michelle is a witch." Wallie lifted a shoulder as he helped Michelle out of her coat.

She beamed at him and pulled her arms out of the sleeves of the coat, then turned her adorable smile to me. Despite myself, I already liked her.

Once her coat was off, I saw her witch's mark above her right collarbone. The pentagram glowed blue, indicating she was an elemental witch. Wallie, Owen, and I were the only ones who could see the mark. Humans without magic couldn't see the mark of a witch, or necromancer in my case. But I'd had my mark tattooed over with magical ink that disguised me as a garden witch.

"My specialty is water," she said, confirming my guess about being an elemental. Her focus shifted from me to look around the room. She waved her arms around. "This house is amazing!"

She inhaled and closed her eyes briefly as if sensing the magic that lived inside the walls and foundation of the house. Owen had said when I first met him that he could feel the power and admitted to using it on occasion. So, it made sense that Michelle could feel it too.

"We've had many different types of witches in the family over the years," I said. "I remember my Yaya saying the water witches always loved it here because of the ocean being just by the cliff."

Michelle's eyes widened at the idea. She beamed at Wallie. "Show me?"

He grinned and ducked his head. "Sure. The sun should be going down at any time now. It's a wonderful view."

I pushed them toward the back door. "Go on, you can catch up with me later. Oh, here." I waved my hand and created a bubble of warmth around them. "That'll keep you comfy for the sunset."

Wallie waved his hand around at the invisible heat. "Cool. You've got to teach me."

I winked at Owen. He'd just taught me the trick the week before. "Sure," I said brightly. "You got it."

I'd been training with Owen over the last month to learn to control my necromancer powers. We would need to teach Wallie soon too. I regretted not being able to teach him as he grew up. I was just so set on not ever using my dark magic that I'd neglected my duty as a magical mother to my son. Besides, Clay's mother had thought I was the devil incarnate and that I'd passed on my evilness to Wallie.

Shaking out of the thoughts of that old hag, I turned in time to see Sam put an ornament on the tree, in exactly the wrong spot. I waved my hand and directed it to a more appropriate section to make it more symmetrical. His son was a better ornament hanger.

My best friend jerked his gaze to me and pressed his lips together in a thin line. He was trying to be offended but I saw the humor in his depths. My BFF knew me too well, and I knew damn well he had put the ornament in the wrong spot on purpose.

Little Sammie was busy putting all the soft and less breakable ornaments we'd laid out for him on a few branches right together at the bottom. It was too cute to move.

I'd do it tomorrow.

"I really want this Christmas to be super special," I said, not sure what else I could do to make it different.

Olivia jumped up. "Let's do something big," she suggested. "Like a big party." Her face lit up with the idea. "The renovations are done. Let's throw a party." She clasped her hands together.

"I don't know. What if the house misbehaves?" I asked. "It doesn't like people."

"That's not true," Sam said. "It didn't like the contractors because it thought you were going to sell it."

Which, originally, I *was* going to sell it. But since I'd chosen to stay, it seemed to settle into a happy magical house. I cocked my head at Sam. "How do you know?"

He shrugged. "I don't know. I get a feeling. It was angry before, but now it's happy." He squinted and then closed his eyes while breathing deep. "Also, the house is a boy."

"Is that true?" I asked the room. "Are you a boy?"

Nothing. "Why won't it talk to me?" I asked. "It's *my* house!"

A random creaking sound from upstairs had all of us freezing and looking up. Except for Sammie. He kept hanging ornaments.

Shuffling on the floor upstairs made me cock my head. "Oh,

it's Alfred. Not the house." Of course not. It wouldn't talk to me when I wanted it to. Not that it said actual words, but it did things to let you know what it meant.

"House, if you could give me a sign, something to show you'd be cool with a party?" I breathed deep and tried to listen. Nothing. Crazy house.

"He says his name is Winston," Sam said.

Sure. The house spoke to Sam. I was skeptical because out of all the stories of the house being alive, I'd never heard anyone talk about the damn thing speaking out loud—or otherwise.

Olivia and I stared at him for a long while before Olivia asked, "Honey, how many glasses of wine have you had?"

He shrugged, holding up his glass and peering at the wine. "A... a few."

This whole thing could be Sam getting back at me for the tree placement. But I played along just in case he was serious. "Winston?" I asked, tilting my head slightly. "Is that right?"

Nothing. Again.

I threw my hands up. "Whatever, okay. Winston, Vicky, Geraldo, whoever you are, we're having a Christmas party here, and we're inviting a *lot* of people. Are you going to be quiet?"

Sam sighed and leaned back on the sofa. He hummed while Olivia and I rolled our eyes at each other.

"Winston says he'll behave." The smug smile on Sam's face made me want to give him a purple nurple like I had when we were kids.

Olivia leaned into her husband and whispered, "If you can still do that when you're sober, I will bang you so hard."

Sam's eyes flew open and a wicked smile formed. I *still* couldn't tell if he was BS-ing us or not.

"Bang," Sammie said. "Bang, bang!"

A laugh shot out of my mouth then I slammed a hand over my mouth, turning away from the five-year-old.

"Yes, honey." Olivia stared at her son with wide eyes. "Bang

183

is the sound an explosion makes. Or a door shutting really hard."

Sam coughed to hide his laugh as Sammie yelled. "Bang!"

"Damn it," Olivia whispered.

"Damn it!" Sammie yelled.

"Okay!" I waved my hand and Sammie's mouth clamped shut. Then I put on my best straight-mom-face. "No potty words in my house, little man. You're old enough to know better."

His eyes widened and he patted at his mouth. I released the spell. "You agree?"

Sammie nodded and pointed at Olivia. "But Mommy said it."

I gave Olivia a pointed look for Sammie's sake, then looked back at the mini version of Sam. "Well, Aunt Ava says no."

"Yes, ma'am," Sammie whispered, ducking his head, and poking out his lower lip. Great, the five-year-old guilt trip. It was a good thing I was still as immune to it as I was when raising Wallie.

"Can you move in with us?" Olivia asked.

I shook my head and wrinkled my nose at her. "No. You'll learn how to do that." She had older kids, too. I was fairly sure Sammie, as her later in life baby, had it a lot easier than her older kids had.

She giggled.

"Party!" Sam yelled. Big Sam, not his mini-me. "What kind of party?"

Was he not sitting here a few minutes ago when we discussed this? What other kinds of party would one have close to Christmas? *Wait. Don't answer that because I don't want to know.*

Kinky.

I glared at Sam, figuring I should start cutting him off on the wine soon. He really cut loose on his days off from being a deputy sheriff. "Just a really cool Christmas party. Nothing special, food and songs and maybe like a game of dirty Santa."

"What's dirty Santa?" Sam rolled his head and sat up so he could drink his wine.

Alfred shuffled into the room from the kitchen before I could answer Sam. The ghoul's presence made me think about the noise I heard a few minutes ago. "Hey, Alfie, were you upstairs a few moments ago?"

Alfred shook his head. He didn't speak because his mouth was sewn shut, and I wasn't sure if the string was holding his jaw on or not, so I left it. We'd figure it out one day. Right then Alfred seemed content with the way he was.

I looked around for the fat immortal cat and found Snooze lying stretched across the open doorway between the living room and kitchen. Guarding the realm of food, no doubt.

I let out a heavy dramatic sigh and glanced up at the ceiling. If no one was upstairs, then the house was trying to communicate, and I didn't acknowledge it. The house was so touchy. "Oh, damn, Winston. I had no idea."

Sam chuckled. "Told you. Now, what is dirty Santa?"

"Every person brings a silly or funny or cheap and weird gift and you exchange them," I explained. "In a nutshell. Oh, and you can steal other people's gifts."

He nodded. "That sounds fun."

Wallie and Michelle walked in from the hall that led to the backdoor. "You were right," Michelle said excitedly. "That was a gorgeous sunset."

I couldn't help but smile back at her and nod. Damn it! I did like her.

"What's going on?" Wallie asked with his brows drawn. "It feels serious in here."

That was my boy. He got his suspicious nature from me. "We're going to have a big community party for Christmas," I announced, then opened my arms wide. "Right here at the house."

Wallie nodded while yawning. "Sounds fun. I'll do the music." He grabbed Michelle's hand and pulled her toward the door. "We're tired, so we're going to get our bags from the car, then hit the hay."

My smile froze on my face as I realized my son was staying in the same room as his girlfriend tonight. I wasn't ready for that. Oh, gross.

I bit back a big yack.

"Uh, Wallie, uh, we remodeled your Yaya's room for you," I said in the tiniest voice that had *ever* come out of my mouth.

"Cool, Mom, thanks." He ducked his head and pulled Michelle out the door.

I thought about having Alfred help them with their bags and do a little spying. But Michelle hadn't noticed the ghoul yet, and I wasn't sure how she would react. I'd wait until the morning to do the ghoulish intros.

A scream went off inside my head as I watched my little boy, who wasn't so little anymore, and Michelle run outside. Olivia and Sam stared at me. There was a tremble in my voice as I said, "They're sleeping together."

"What did you think, they were going to play pinochle?" Olivia asked.

"I didn't think, I didn't!" I moaned and slumped forward, but then jerked upright again when Wallie and Michelle came in again, their bags in their arms.

"Goodnight, sweetie!" I plastered a smile on my face. "Sleep well, Michelle."

Wallie waved and said goodnight to Sam and Olivia, then they headed upstairs. When they were about halfway up, I ran toward the staircase. "Remember the walls are thin!" I ducked behind the living room wall.

Their footsteps paused, then Wallie groaned. "Oh, gross. She thinks we're going to do it here."

Michelle gasped. "I'd never."

I knew they were only saying it for my benefit, but I chose to believe it and collapsed in the armchair beside the Christmas tree in relief.

Alfred tiptoed out of the hallway behind the stairs and looked at me. "It's safe, Alfie. We'll introduce you to Michelle tomorrow."

He nodded and shuffled to the kitchen.

"I have the best idea. The best. Oh, my gosh." Olivia jumped to her feet and clapped. Excitement flowed from her in waves. It was a little frightening.

"For our party, let's summon... Wait for it." She sucked in a deep breath and fluttered her hands. "The *real* Santa."

3

NOT TODAY, SATAN

E arly in the morning, well, early for me because I forgot Wallie liked to wake up with the damn roosters, I sat at my small, round kitchen table working on my second cup of coffee. I'd asked Alfred to not come out of his room until I was ready for him to meet Michelle.

Even though I heard the kids up, because that was what woke me, I hadn't gathered the courage to knock on their door. Good grief, my baby boy was having sex. Not at the moment but in general. He had. He did. *Someone, please send wine.*

A tapping sound drew my attention to the ceiling over my head. Alfred was wondering when he could come down. His bedroom was right over the kitchen. I picked up my phone to text Wallie—because it was now normal to text my kid while he was in the same house instead of yelling for him—just as my son and his girlfriend entered the kitchen.

So, playing it cool, I instead sent Alfred a message. **Come down in five minutes**.

I'd gotten Alfred a tablet a few weeks ago so he could ask me for things and surf the internet. I was still undecided if it

189

was a good idea or not, but it made communication with him easier.

However, he refused to tell me if it was okay to remove the string. Snooze seemed to think so because the crazy cat kept trying to pull on the string that hung from one side of the ghoul's mouth.

Michelle sat across from me and beamed. "Morning."

I frowned. "Don't tell me you're a morning person." Maybe I liked her less.

I had too many of those in my life, I didn't need another.

Michelle laughed. "Not usually. Being here so close to the ocean and meeting you has me wired."

Wallie came to the table with coffee for Michelle and himself. His girlfriend turned her full wattage smile toward him, "Thanks, sweets."

Sweets. She had already started with the pet names. This was serious. "So how long have you two been dating?"

Wallie looked uncomfortable and didn't want to answer me. Michelle glanced at him and rolled her eyes. "We met a couple of weeks after school started. We didn't want to say anything to parental units until we were sure it was working."

"I knew when I met her." Wallie's words settled deep inside me and warmed my soul. Okay, fine. I liked her. Ugh. Damn it.

The knowing-that-you-met-The-One feeling was something I knew well. I'd felt it with Clay the moment our eyes locked.

And again, with a certain sheriff, whom I will not name at the moment. I was sure if I mentioned his name out loud, he'd show up. I owed him a date, but I wasn't sure I was totally ready for it. The One or not, I was a widow. That held weight.

Pushing away all thoughts of the hottie sheriff, I covered Wallie's hand. "I knew when I met your dad."

Witches really didn't have fated mates or anything. It was

more of a magical connection. Once acknowledged, it was hard to break away from the attraction. Hence why I hadn't really acknowledged the connection to the sheriff fully.

I heard Alfred descending the stairs. Focusing on Michelle, I asked, "Have you ever seen a ghoul?"

She froze with her cup to her lips, then a grin formed. "You have a ghoul? I knew it!"

A few moments later Snooze pranced into the kitchen and headed straight to his food bowl. The three of us watched the cat. Michelle said, "I've never seen a cat that big before."

"He's a Maine Coon," I said and took a drink of my coffee.

Wallie added, "He's also immortal."

Michelle glanced between us with her mouth open. "Seriously? How?"

I pointed at myself and shrugged. "Untrained necromancer who thought she was healing him. Instead, I brought him back to life. I'm still not sure if he is a ghoul or some other type of undead immortal."

Wallie laughed. "We just go with the flow of weirdness around here."

I gave him a cross-eyed look and called out to Alfred who was hovering outside of the kitchen, out of sight. "It's okay to come in and meet Michelle, Alfred."

I watched Michelle with interest as the ghoul entered the kitchen. He moved closer to me, and I didn't blame him. Sam had shot at him and Sheriff Drew pointed his gun at Alfred when they met him. The ghoul was a little leery about meeting new people. Lucky for him, Michelle didn't have a gun.

"Wow." Michelle stood and walked around the table to Alfred.

Okay, I hadn't expected her to approach him right off. Then again Sammie had done the same thing. That kid *loved* the ghoul.

Most people thought he was a zombie. In a way, he did look

kind of like one, only he didn't have flesh missing in places and he didn't eat brains or living things. Or anything.

Alfred had grey, pasty skin that had a dried-out look to it. His eyes were a little milky and unclear, but he swore he saw just as well as everyone else.

"Hello. My name is Michelle." She held out her hand to him.

Alfred glanced at it then at me. When I nodded, he shook her hand and did a little bow.

"Alfred doesn't talk but he understands everything we say to him." I glanced up at my ghoul and smiled. "What's for breakfast?"

He handed me his tablet, which I hadn't noticed until that moment. I read over the choices and handed it back to him. "Make enough for Olivia. She's supposed to stop by so we can talk more about her idea to summon Santa Claus."

I couldn't believe I'd agreed to that. What if old Saint Nick was too busy? Would he be pissed that we summoned him like a demon to attend our little party?

"Summon Santa?" Michelle sank into her chair and stared at me.

"It was Olivia's idea. But it *would* be cool if he agreed to come to the party." I shrugged and picked up my coffee cup and realized it was empty. Instantly, Alfred was there to take it from me. He grunted, which was his way of asking if I wanted more. "Yes, please."

A knock sounded on the door. I started to stand when Owen yelled from the living room. "I'll get it."

It was great to have roommates that cooked and answered doors for you.

Olivia's chipper voice flowed into the kitchen moments before she did. She took a seat next to me and nodded to the kids. "Morning."

"Morning," I said.

Alfred sat a cup of coffee in front of both of us before he went back to preparing breakfast.

Olivia didn't waste any time directing the conversation to summoning Santa. "So, did you think about it? Can it be done?"

"We need five to make it work," Owen said. He held out his hands and ticked us off on his fingers. "Me and you, Wallie and Michelle. Know any other witches?"

I hummed, thinking of how many other witches I knew. I really didn't want to go to the coven. "Does it have to be a witch?"

"Me! I'll do it!" Olivia jumped up and down in her seat. "Sammie is with Sam's parents and I've got nothing else going on."

I exchanged a look with Owen. He shrugged, which I took as it didn't matter if Olivia wasn't a witch. "Okay. But you do exactly what we tell you to do. I don't know how you'll react to the magic running through you. Once it starts, you can't back out and break the circle."

She nodded eagerly. The original plan had been to send her upstairs to hang with Alfred and Snooze while we got the conjuring part of everything done.

We'd planned our whole party for a week before Christmas, and it was all going down tomorrow night. Which meant we needed to summon Santa today.

But Owen was right. It really would work better with five.

About ten minutes later, the five of us were inside the ritual room in the attic. It was a large open space with bookshelves that lined the walls and an enormous pentagram carved into the center of the wood floor. "Okay, so everyone at a different point on the pentagram. We're summoning a saint, so this shouldn't be a big deal. He's not literally running around taking toys to children. He's a conduit for good, and if we're lucky, he'll want to hang with us and bless the party and maybe the town."

Owen nodded. "Yes, I've heard of this being done. It's supposed to bring great fortune upon those who come into contact with Saint Nick."

That made me relax a little more.

"Are you guys still trying to convince yourselves this is a good idea?" Wallie asked with a chuckle.

I shook my head. "No, I'm pretty happy with this."

Michelle nodded. "Great, because I am *dying* to meet Saint Nick. I can't wait to tell my mom!"

Owen winked at me. "You're the strongest. You lead."

Great. I hated being the leader. Taking a deep breath, I stepped to the east and the focal point of the pentagram. We had an amethyst crystal at each point as well as a circle of candles around each stone. Amethyst was used for balancing magic and to help power the spell. "Okay everyone, light your candles at the same time."

I squatted down and used my long grill lighter. "North," I said, pausing to make sure everyone lit theirs at approximately the same time. "South," I said next. "East, and finally, West."

When they were all lit, I knew it had worked because the flames all burned far higher and brighter than they ever could have under normal circumstances.

The rune for the jolly old elf was drawn in every corner of the pentagram, under the crystals. *"With the guidance of the Universe and the powers that be, I call upon Saint Nicholas to hear my words, feel my calling. Santa Claus, I summon you."*

Clapping my hands together, I focused my power on the center of the pentagram, which we'd left empty, and gasped, nearly staggering backward when a blinding flash of light filled the room. I sucked in a deep breath and rubbed my eyes, but it was like a camera flash had gone off, putting spots in front of my eyes.

"Well, hello." A sexy, male, British voice. Okay. Saint Nick was British. I rubbed at my eyes and then blinked rapidly, trying to clear the burn spot from my vision. "I've had my eye on you, Ava. Though I have to say I was highly surprised to feel myself being tugged to your little ensemble here."

Squinting, I began to make out the profile of a man. He was tall and broad, but his face wouldn't come into focus. "Sorry," I mumbled. "I didn't expect the flash."

After a couple more seconds of clearing my eyes, they focused on the man.

And he looked nothing like I expected. "Whoa," I whispered. "You look different from the legends."

He spun in a circle. Broad shoulders, narrow hips, and an ass I could've bounced a quarter off of.

I turned my head to exchange a glance with Olivia, but she wasn't there. "Er, where are my friends?"

"Downstairs, tucked into bed asleep," he said as he picked a nonexistent lint ball from his expensive-looking black suit.

I narrowed my gaze on his face. "Why?"

"Because they needed a nap. And I needed to figure out why you summoned me earth-side."

Walking in a circle around the pentagram, I made sure not to disturb the chalk line. "You have the power to send my friends to bed? Even from the pentagram?" My warning bells should've been going off, but somehow, I didn't sense danger even though something wasn't right. Uncertainty settled in the pit of my soul. This was not Santa.

"Of course I do." Nick straightened his suit and looked mildly offended. "I *am* Satan, after all."

I halted my progress as the man who called himself Satan nudged the edge of my pentagram with his toe. "You did the summoning part perfectly, but you didn't put the trap part in. You know I can walk right out of this, right?"

To prove his point, he walked across the ritual room and

unbuttoned his suit jacket as he settled himself down into a wingback chair in the corner.

Holy Christmas balls. "No, no. I conjured Saint Nick. Santa. Kris Kringle."

His big grin did something to me, deep inside. Something naughty. Oh, hell no.

Oh, and judging by the look on his face, he knew exactly what it did to me deep down.

I need an adult!

"Santa, Satan. This happens all the time. Funnily enough, it's not the names that are the problem, even if they are similar. Old Nick's sigil is really similar to my own. Do one squiggle in the wrong direction and hello Jolly Old Saint King of Hell."

I squeaked and backed away, covering my mouth. This was so wrong on so many levels. "Sorry, so sorry. Didn't mean to bother you, sir, if you don't mind you can just go back to where you're supposed to be right now."

He moaned. "This is such a boring time of year in Hell. People get all regretful and repentant around the holidays. My business goes way down."

"I wanted Santa," I said weakly.

The devil lifted his brow and gave me a crooked grin that sent shivers down my spine. I needed to get rid of this evil demon *pronto*. Toot suite. He stood again, and when he spoke, he inched closer to me with his voice low and seductive. "I could be your Santa. Our names are close enough."

Not even close. "I can see it now. You, in a red suit with your pitchfork. Not happening. Not today, Satan."

His sexy, leerish grin morphed into a wide smile. "Oh, Ava. I like you." He spun in a circle and his suit changed in a whiff of smoke and became a traditional Santa suit, complete with hat... Except it fit him like a glove. It was like strip-club Santa.

But somehow classy. Oh, Lord. This was not happening.

The coven was going to love this one. Yaya was probably laughing her ass off in the afterlife.

"Don't you think I could pull it off? I've never wanted kids, not sure if I even like them. But they are the future for us all. They are young and can be molded into—"

I held up a hand, stopping him from finishing that sentence. "You will not be molding any of them into little demons."

He laughed; the sound echoed through my house. "Ava, my dear, most children are little demons."

Laughing humorlessly, I continued backing away, ignoring my raging libido. "What do I have to do to get you to go back to Hell?"

"That's not happening. Not today, Witch." He winked. "But I do like you. When we meet again, please, call me Luci." With a tap on the side of his nose like the real freaking Santa, he disappeared.

I moaned and turned toward the stairs, screaming. "Olivia! Wake up! Owen, Wallie, Michelle! We just conjured the *devil*!"

4

IT'S ALL FUN AND GAMES
UNTIL SOMEBODY CONJURES
SATAN

My lungs burned and my heart felt like it was going to jump out of my chest as I sprinted down the stairs. "Okay," I puffed. "I'm starting an exercise regimen as soon as the holidays are over."

I burst into my Yaya's old room and ran to the bed. Wallie and Michelle lay on top of the blankets, serenely asleep. They were cuddled into each other, looking cute as ever. But I needed them awake. I shook Wallie. "Wal, wake up." Nothing. Panic filled me, and I shook him harder. "Wake up, Wallace Harper, you wake up right this instant!" I yelled as I shook his shoulders.

He moaned and blinked several times. "What? Who... when, what happened?"

I smirked. He was worse than me when someone woke him. It always took me a little bit to realize where I was. As he oriented himself, I rushed around to the other side of the bed and grabbed Michelle's shoulders. "We conjured Satan, *wake up!*"

The moment her eyelids fluttered open; I ran for the door. "Owen!" I screamed. "Olivia!"

I didn't know what bedroom Olivia was in since she didn't live here, but Owen had taken to using the one that had been my mother's. After we remodeled it, and I had cleaned out all the personal things, preserving some of the items for Wallie and distributing others around the house, it hadn't bothered me to let him use it as his own. Alfie had taken the only remaining guest room, so I had to let Owen have Winnie's or Mom's.

Winnie's was still too fresh. Too painful. That's why it went to Wallie.

Owen had decorated it with a lot of black. I burst into his room to find him lying the same way, serene, on his back. Since he was in bed alone, he was in the center and looked calmer and more peaceful than I'd ever seen him.

"Wake up!" I screeched. So much for serenity.

Owen sat bolt upright. "What?" His black hair was plastered to the back of his head like he'd been asleep for hours instead of minutes.

"Santa is Satan!" I screamed. "Santa is Satan! Gotta find Olivia, come on!" I scurried out of the room and as Michelle and Wallie watched on from the far side of the hall with shocked expressions on their faces, I slammed into the door to my bedroom, across the hall from Owen's. The door hit the wall and I sagged in relief. Thankfully, Olivia was asleep on my bed.

"Wake up!" I jumped onto the bed and shook my friend. "Up, up, up!"

She screamed in my face as I screamed in her face, which startled me, so I screamed more, making her scream louder and start to fight me.

"Stop screaming!" Owen screamed.

"Why *is* everyone screaming?" Michelle asked.

"Santa was Satan!" I fell back to rest on my haunches in the middle of the bed and clenched my fists. "We have to find Santaaaaaa!" I sucked in a deep breath. "I mean Satan." My chest heaved. "Why are you all so calm?"

"Take a long, deep breath," Owen said. "And explain."

"Okay." I sucked in a breath and used it to tell the whole story. "The summoning worked. And when he appeared, he made you four disappear. But he didn't hurt you, so that's good. So, so." I sucked in another breath and tried to quiet my mind and get the conversation straight. It was a futile effort. "Um. He said that the sigil for his name and the sigil for Saint Nick's names are really close. It's not a Satan-Santa thing, even though their names are so similar."

Everyone stared at me in shock.

"What do we do?" I cried.

"We have to go find him," Owen said. "And send him back. Where would he have gone?"

I looked at my friends and family, at a loss. "Our party is tomorrow. We have a hundred or more people invited here, and we haven't even begun decorating. And now we have to go find *Satan?*"

This was a mess. A hot one and then some considering an evil archangel that looked better than most GQ models was running loose in my small town. It was all my fault!

My cell phone rang downstairs. With the way this day was going, I ran to catch it, flying downs the stairs in record time. Picking it up, I frowned to see it was my boss, from the bookstore. "Hey, Clint! What's up?"

"There's a gorgeous man in a tight-fitting Santa suit in here, and he says he knows you," he whispered. "And he helped himself to a cup of coffee."

I squeezed my eyes shut. Visions of Clint checking out the devil filled my mind. "Clint, that is a bad man. Let him take anything he wants. He's a bad, bad man. Don't make him mad."

"Ava," Clint hissed. "I've never seen a more attractive man in my entire life!"

I pulled back and looked down at my phone, confused. "Clint, aren't you straight?"

"I am. Yep, yeah. Straight as a pin. So why do I want to jump his bones?" he hissed.

I sighed. "I know. He's pretty charismatic. So, listen, just give him what he wants and get him out of the store, okay?"

Wait. We needed to find Luci in order to convince him to go back to Hell. "On second thought, keep him there. I'll be right there."

"Okay but hurry up!"

He hung up, and I turned to my friends. "We gotta get to the bookstore right now!"

Together, the four of us rushed to the door at once. Olivia tried to go out at the same time I did, and we got stuck in the door frame. We backed up and tried again. She giggled, and I rolled my eyes. Turning to the side, I pushed her out the door. "Dummy, we can both fit."

She left a trail of giggles as she dug her keys out of her front jeans pocket. My car was blocked in by Wallie's car, so we all sprinted for Olivia's Four-Runner. "Put Sammie's booster seat out into the yard!" she yelled.

I threw myself into the front passenger seat while Wallie flung the booster seat like a frisbee.

"Geez!" Olivia began backing up before everyone was fully in. "I said put it in the yard, not throw it like a damn football."

"Hey!" Owen yelled, jerking his door shut. "Let me get my seatbelt on."

Olivia careened onto the road and laughed gleefully. "I can't wait to meet Satan!"

"Olivia!" I grabbed her arm. "This isn't happy-fun time. This is serious."

As her phone began to ring, she fished it out of her pocket and handed it to me. "That's Sam, see what he's got to say."

What he's got to say, like we were just having a normal day. Gods, I hoped this wasn't the beginning of normal days for me.

"Sam, you're on speaker," I said. "What's up?"

"Why did I get a call about a sexy man in a Santa suit stealing a sub from Knuckle Sandwiches?" Sam's voice sounded concerned and serious. But I noticed there wasn't an ounce of surprise in his tone. Like I don't do crazy shit all the time.

"Why do you think we'd know anything about that?" Wallie asked defensively.

I pressed my lips together to keep a laugh in. That was my boy!

"Because I know damn well you crazy women were going to conjure up Jolly Ol' Saint Nick."

Yeah, he had us there.

"Hey," Olivia and I said at the same time.

"It went wrong, didn't it?" Sam asked with a sigh.

I thought about continuing with the defense strategy Wallie started, but I didn't have time to play around. Lucifer walking around town was serious. "Yes," I said sullenly. "We conjured Satan."

The line was silent. For a moment I thought my BFF had hung up. Then he said in a flat tone, "Satan? As in... Satan?"

"Yes. Lucifer. He wants to be called Luci. Or had he meant for only me to call him Luci?"

Olivia pulled up in front of the bookstore and illegally parked. I guessed she could do that; she was married to the deputy. I wasn't technically, maybe soon, dating the sheriff. I didn't have time to think about that either.

Olivia took her phone from me. "Gotta go, honey, we're going to try to get him back in the bottle!"

"Wait," Sam cried. "What bott—"

Olivia dropped her phone down in her purse and grinned. "I'm sure he'll catch up to us soon."

He sure would. I bet he and Drew were already on their way and most likely tracked Olivia's GPS on her phone.

We hurried in the bookstore with Owen, Wallie, and Michelle on our tails to find Clint comforting a woman behind the counter. Oh no, what had the devil done? Satan, not Clint. "What happened?"

The woman, I now recognized as Carrie Treehill, Sammie's kindergarten teacher, fanned herself with a magazine.

"Carrie?" Olivia said. "What's wrong?"

The woman jumped off the stool. "Olivia, thank goodness."

"Carrie, this is my best friend Ava." Olivia gestured to me, then to the others in our little Satan lynch mob. "And our friend Owen, and Ava's son Wallie, and Wallie's girlfriend Michelle."

Carrie blinked and nodded at everyone, with an expression on her face that clearly said she'd instantly forgotten our names.

"What happened?" I asked again.

"The uh, *Santa* that we talked about, did something to her." Clint put his hand on Carrie's back.

I leaned forward. "What did he do?"

Carrie's eyes darted around. "Olivia, could I talk to you alone?"

"Of course." Olivia glanced at me and asked, "Do you mind if Ava comes?"

Carrie shrugged. "That would be fine."

"You can use the office," Clint said.

"We'll be right back." I led the way into the office and perched on the side of the desk so that Carrie and Olivia could have the chairs.

"So, what happened?" Olivia prompted. I felt like a parrot on repeat trying to get information from Carrie.

"I was just browsing for books, and this man, this gorgeous, lickable, *edible* man walked by. I stared at him. Couldn't help it." Carrie paused and her cheeks turned red as if she was flushed just thinking about the devil man. I could totally see why. Luci was as hot as...well, sin.

Carrie took a breath and continued. "So, I rounded the stacks to see him again, and all of a sudden he was right on top of me."

"Yeah?" I asked, my heart skipping a few beats. If he hurt pure, sweet Carrie, I was going to curse him. That was if I *could* curse the devil. "Then what?"

"Then, he put his hand on my forearm." She reached over and grabbed my arm just above my wrist. "Like this."

"What did he say?" Come on! The suspense was killing me.

"He said, 'Beautiful day. Beautiful woman.' And then he smiled and I..." Her eyes widened and she shivered and lowered her voice to a whisper. "I had an orgasm."

Olivia and I gaped at each other. Then Olivia fell out of the chair laughing. I ignored her while focusing on Carrie. "An... orgasm? As in, the big O?"

She nodded vehemently. "An orgasm! A shaking, crying out, wet panties, weak knees orgasm. My insides clenched over and over, and my mouth went totally dry, which always happens when I come at home with my little vibrating pal."

Wow, that was TMI. I'd never be able to look at her the same again. Pure, my ass. Nodding, I held up my hand. "Mine does too. Interesting. I'd like to read the science behind that."

I really didn't know what else to say. Carrie really seemed distressed about the whole thing.

"Who cares about the science, she just got insta-shagged by Sat—" Olivia broke off and coughed delicately. "Santa."

"We gotta find him," I said softly, trying to hold back the laugh bubbling up inside me. It wasn't funny. Okay, it was, but poor Carrie would go the rest of her life comparing sex to the instant orgasm Lucifer gave her. "Are you okay, Carrie?"

She nodded. "I'm fine. Go, do what you need to do, but girls, if he does it to you." Her eyes rolled up in her head and she sighed. "Enjoy."

5

I SAW MOMMY KISSING SATAN CLAWS

The doorbell rang just as I put my pearl earrings in. Before coming up to get ready, I'd been thrilled at how amazing the house looked. I was proud of how everyone had pulled together to get everything ready for the party.

We'd spent hours searching Shipton Harbor for Satan, with no luck. When the devil didn't want to be found, he wasn't found.

Dread sank in my gut. I knew the damn demon would show up at the party. That worried me mostly because I wasn't sure what he planned to do once he arrived.

The doorbell rang.

"They're here," I called, running from my room in my bright red ballet flats. "Alfie, time to go to bed!" Alfred stuck his head out of his bedroom and nodded at me while giving me a thumbs up. "Is Snooze in there with you?" I asked.

Nod.

"Okay, have a good night, you two!"

Wallie and Michelle were already downstairs putting the finishing touches on the décor in the back sunroom. The scents of sugar cookies, cinnamon, and spices filled the air. The railing of the staircase was wrapped in green garland and white lights.

Multicolored lights framed the windows and draped across the arches that lead to the kitchen and the hallway that leads to the bathroom and the sunroom. My large tree sat against the far wall, in front of the big bay window. Gifts I'd gotten for Wallie, Michelle, and the rest of my new extended family sat under the tree. Stockings with each of our names on them hung over the fireplace.

This was going to be a great Christmas. As long as Luci didn't show up.

"I got it," I called as I hurried down the stairs. Throwing open the door, I grinned big to find Olivia, Sam, and Sammie dressed in their holiday finest. "Come in! Welcome to Christmas!"

More people waited behind them, and the next thing I knew, I was in a greeting line that didn't look like it was ever going to end. Where had all these people parked? I hadn't considered parking. Oh, my goodness.

Even though my house was huge, I cast a spell so that the front porch, sunroom, and backyard were warm. It was like a bubble of warmth surrounding the place so that my guests could be comfortable no matter where they went. I just hoped they didn't ask where the heaters were.

People I hadn't seen in years, that I definitely hadn't invited, people that Yaya knew, and Aunt Winnie, even people I vaguely remembered from my father's funeral, all poured through the doors, handing me hostess gifts of more wine than could ever be used in a year, and dish towels, and cute little knick-knacks and bric-a-brac.

"Who are all these people?" I hissed over my shoulder. I didn't even know who was there at this point. Wallie and Michelle, Sam and Olivia, and Owen had been trading off standing behind me and taking the gifts.

It was Olivia who answered. "They all want to see the house. Everyone's been curious about this place since like... forever."

And when the line died down, leaving my home full of conversation and laughter, Sam leaned forward. "Winston is happy. He loves having all these people here."

"Are you drunk?" I whispered over my shoulder as my boss walked up the sidewalk. "Hey, Clint!"

"He's behind me," he hissed, hurrying forward on his tiptoes. "The Santa!"

Clint scurried into the house as Sam and I gaped at the last person coming up the walk.

It was him. "What are you doing here!" I squeaked. Sam and I rushed out the door, and he slammed it shut behind us.

"Am I not invited to the party that seemed to have been an open invitation?" he asked and flashed a brilliant knee-weakening smile. "I brought gifts." He slung a sack forward that I hadn't seen in the dark. "For the little demons."

Sam stepped forward and used his best big-time cop voice. "I'm going to have to ask you to come with me, sir, uh, Satan."

"Okay, okay, but if you let me come in, I promise I'll be on my best behavior. Please, though, call me Luci. And look, I've got a present for you." Luci reached into his sack and brought out a wrapped gift. "Just for you, Samuel Wallace Thompson."

Sam took it uncertainly. "Um, thank you."

"Go ahead," Luci said. "Open it." He bounced on his toes. Was he excited?

Of course he was.

Sam looked at me with wide eyes. "How does he know my name?"

I shrugged. "He's the devil. I mean, he brought you a gift. Might as well open it."

Ripping the paper off of the small box, he opened it to find... I peered over his shoulder. "Is that a hot wheel?"

Sam gasped and pulled the car out of the box. "This is a 1977 White Z-Whiz," he said.

"Ohhh." I grabbed his hand and brought the little car closer in the light. "I remember when you asked Santa for this. It was the last year we believed, and when you didn't get it, we swore not to believe in Santa anymore."

"It was too expensive for Santa, is what my parents said. It was rare even back then." Sam looked up at Luci with a face full of awe. "How'd you know?"

Luci grinned. "It's a gift." He looked at me. "I've got something for you, too."

Umm. I wasn't sure about his gifts. I didn't need an orgasm when I had guests to entertain. Although it *had* been a while... Nope. Not going there.

Reaching into the bag, he pulled out a box that was definitely a little too big to have been in that sack. The red velvety bag didn't look like it had much in it.

I stepped closer to peer into the bag, but he moved it out of my line of sight.

I eyed the package Luci held out to me but didn't take it. "I should go in, to my party."

"Open it, Ava," he said.

I sighed and took the package, then opened it and gasped. My heart melted while the rest of me was in shock. It was an original Gameboy, new in package. "How?" I whispered.

Sam's jaw dropped. "No shit."

We stared at each other. I knew he remembered that Christmas, too. "Aunt Winnie and mom didn't like video games," I said. "So, I asked Santa for this Gameboy. And he didn't bring it."

"Well, there you go." Luci winked. "I'd leave it in the box if I were you. It's pretty valuable like that."

He whisked past a shocked Sam and me and went inside.

"Does he have something like this for everyone?" I asked, meeting my BFF's gaze.

"I hope not, or else all these people who don't know jack shit about magic are going to have huge questions."

Eek. He was right. I didn't want to have to whip up memory spells or come up with excuses.

Luci stuck his head back out the door. "Don't worry. The rest of the gifts are for the kids. And your hot wife."

After Luci darted back inside, Sam rushed in and headed straight for Olivia. I laughed and shook my head. Who knew Satan had a heart? I certainly hadn't. Still, Luci was devious, and I needed to keep an eye—or two or six—on him.

By the time people began to leave, we'd made a huge dent in all that gifted wine that was brought, and all the kids were beyond excited about their gifts. Luci had been a hit.

Toward the end of the night, someone rang the doorbell. "Excuse me," I said to the people crowded around my kitchen table.

When I answered the door, Drew stood on the other side in his uniform. He had worked so Sam could have off to attend the party. I'd been disappointed that he wouldn't be here. Seeing him on my front porch in his uniform warmed my insides. His large arms tested the strength of the threads of his shirt. I let my eyes roam over his broad shoulders, muscular chest, and trim waist. The man *had* to work out to look so yummy.

Sheriff Andrew Walker was a couple of years older than me and born to a family of witch hunters—a magical group of humans who hated witches and dedicated their lives to hunting and killing them. According to Drew, he had no interest in killing anyone unless they deserved it. Being a witch didn't make someone bad or evil. I agreed with him.

"Hey," I said, not able to stop the smile that spread across my face. "I wondered if you'd make it."

"Sorry, I let everyone else off duty tonight so they could come to the party. We've been slow, and I wanted to give you my gift." He raked his gaze over me, and I lost focus for a few minutes.

I stepped out on the porch and closed the door. He knew about my powers, and that I was a necromancer, so it wasn't a surprise that he didn't ask how the porch was warm.

"Oh my gosh. I didn't get you anything."

The door opened behind me and a red-suited arm with a white-gloved hand stuck a small gift out. "Except for this," I said, snatching the gift away from Luci's hand.

The door slammed as Drew gave me a quizzical look. "I forgot about this," I lied lamely.

Drew held out a small bag with a bit of tissue paper sticking out of the top. "You first."

My insides fluttered, and I felt like a teen with her crush. I'd say the first crush, but my first crush had died five years ago, after twenty-one years of wedded bliss.

"Okay, thanks." I pulled the tissue paper out of the top and peered down in the bag under the front porch light and gasped.

It was a glass figurine. I pulled it out and began to laugh. "It's a reaper!" Clutching it close, I beamed at Drew. "It's perfect. Thank you so much."

He leaned forward and pressed a soft kiss on my lips. I was so surprised by the kiss that I didn't have time to react before he stepped back. Good thing because we might have gone at it right here on the front porch. I wasn't interested in being the party's entertainment.

"Okay, open yours," I said when he pulled back.

I was just as curious about what it was as he was. I hope Luci hadn't given him something cursed. He unwrapped the small box and inside was a ring.

Oh, come on. A ring? No!

"Oh, it's got a blue stripe," he said. "This is really cool."

Really cool. Okay, yeah. A blue line ring.

He pulled it from the package. "Oh, it's silicone! That means I can wear it on duty."

"I don't want you to think it's a romance thing," I said in a small voice. "I just thought of you when I saw it." Especially considering I saw it for the first time when he opened it. Luci was going to pay for that. Somehow.

The radio on his shoulder squawked. "I gotta go," he said. "But this was amazing. Thank you."

"Thank you, too." I looked at my reaper. "It's going on my bedside table."

His grin widened. "I like that."

He sort of saluted me then hurried down my walk. The door opened behind me and someone yanked me back inside.

"What did you get him?" Olivia hissed. "What did he get you?"

I explained what happened, and we squealed for a moment in the living room doorway before Sam called her away to talk to someone.

"Excuse me," Luci said.

"Thank you for that gift," I said. "That was pretty cool, although at first I was super freaked out about it being a ring."

He winked. "I knew it would work out." Then, he looked up. "Oh, look. Mistletoe."

Of all the... "No, I didn't hang that. I intentionally didn't do mistletoe."

Luci gave me a mischievous grin. "I happen to have a few tricks up my sleeves."

"Well, this isn't happening," I declared.

He gave me pouty lips. "Oh, come on. It's tradition."

"Fine, a small one, but it doesn't involve, like, my soul or a deal or anything. I've seen that movie. No strings."

His face softened, and he put his hands on my cheeks, then bent forward and pressed a firm kiss to my forehead. "I really like you," he whispered.

Turning to the room, Luci raised his hands. "Hello, everyone! My name is Luci, and I think I've been able to meet each of you through the course of the night. I've been making up my mind about something and I'm thrilled to say I have decided."

I tugged on his suit jacket. "Decided what?" I asked in a near panic.

"I bought the vacant house next door. I'm moving to Shipton Harbor!"

I gaped at the devil. Olivia walked up behind me. "There is no vacant house next door," she whispered. "It's undeveloped land."

At least it had been that morning. After sharing a panicked look with each other, we rushed past Luci to look out the living room window, which was pointless in the dark.

But when we got there, we were shocked to see an enormous, gothic home with beautiful lighting highlighting the many turrets and porches.

I turned back to see the gathered townspeople congratulating Luci.

Sighing, I plopped down on the couch. "Welcome to the neighborhood."

Lucifer Morningstar was now my neighbor and would be staying in town. I wasn't sure for how long, but it couldn't be good to have the devil living in my town.

Well, my goal to have a memorable Christmas was achieved. Just not as I'd planned. At least I hadn't accidentally raised the dead and no one had died.

A Christmas miracle.

READ AN EXCERPT FROM
BITTEN IN THE MIDLIFE

Bitten in the Midlife is the first in a new spin off series featuring Hailey Whitfield, whom you met in this book. The new series is titled, Fanged After Forty and we hope you love Hailey and her friends as much as Ava's.

Get your copy of Bitten in the Midlife Here

Here is the first chapter of Bitten in the Midlife.

Chapter 1

The day had finally come, and I could hardly contain my excitement.

I never knew starting over at the not-so-ripe age of forty would be so freeing. It was like a huge weight lifted off my whole body. And I was *free*!

I didn't have to look at my ex-fiancé's face anymore. Nor

did I have to watch him openly flirt with all the other nurses. I didn't have to watch him move on happily with the tramp he cheated on me with.

Jerk.

He was a lot more than a jerk, but I was *not* thinking about him anymore. Plus, karma always got back at people who deserved her wrath. And I was starting my new life in a new city, in my new-to-me house.

The best part of this move was that my best friend since we were in diapers was my neighbor.

We were celebrating this glorious day together with champagne on my front porch, ogling the movers as they unloaded the truck and carried all of my things into the house.

It was a great way to celebrate on a Monday.

See? All Mondays weren't bad.

Another thing that made this move better for my sanity was that I was closer to my two older brothers. One I adored and loved, Luke. The other was the eldest of the five of us, and... the poor guy wasn't everyone's favorite. We all loved him, but we wouldn't walk out in front of a bus to save him. Oliver was just...Oliver. He was a hard person to figure out. Oh, calm down. We'd save him. We might just shove him out of the way extra hard.

Pushing away thoughts of family and ex-jerkface, I went back to supervising the movers. It was a tough job, but someone had to do it.

"What about that one?" Kendra asked.

I hid my smile behind the crystal flute she had brought with her.

My bestie had taken the day off to celebrate with me. She was a lawyer and had just won a big case, so that gave us double the reasons to celebrate.

Good times!

I watched mister tall, dark, and delicious with rippling abs, a luscious tush I could've bounced a quarter off of and one of those cute little man buns carry a large box toward us.

He was young enough to call me mama but still legal. Maybe being a cougar wasn't such a bad idea. Just as long as he left before the sun was up. I had no plans to wake up beside another man, ever.

Did you hear me? *Ever.*

It would give my eldest brother Oliver something else to turn his nose up at and lecture me about why it wasn't a good idea to date a man young enough to be my son.

At least Luke would support a fling with the hot moving man. On second thought, Luke supported orgies and any manner of sexual escapades. That was a little too many hands, arms, legs, and bodies for me.

No, thank you. Although... maybe... Nope.

As the cutie with the man bun walked past, he batted a pair of lashes that looked like someone had dipped them chocolate, and I glanced down at his pants, totally by accident.

No, really. I didn't mean to.

But oh, my. His pants fit like they'd been painted on. Molded to every move of his body, but also like they were begging to be torn off. It'd been a while since I'd had a back to rake my fingers down.

Kendra, my bestie for as long as I could remember, cocked a dark brow, then shrugged. "I have socks older than he is."

I snorted, then giggled. It was probably the champagne, but who cared. "I didn't say I wanted to marry him."

God forbid. One bite of that sour apple was enough for me, and even if spitting out that second bite wasn't my choice, I was over the whole idea. Kendra had it right. Her love 'em and leave 'em lifestyle was my inspiration from now on. New start, new motto.

Broken hearts were a young woman's game, and I wasn't young enough to be willing to risk another. No way, buddy.

"Since when is a little bump and grind enough for you?" Skeptical was Kendra's middle name, while a smile flirted with her lips. The skeptical part sure helped in her budding law career as her last name was Justice, after all. Literally.

Kendra didn't trust easily, which was why she'd stayed single after her divorce almost fifteen years ago.

I shrugged and watched a mover lean against a dolly full of boxes while he rode the truck gate to the ground. Shirtless, muscular, and blond were apparently my new turn-on. Who knew I had a type? "Being left at the altar was eye-opening and threw my entire life in a new direction," I mumbled.

And this direction's sheen of sweat, when combined with the champagne, put thoughts into my head. Fun thoughts. Sexy thoughts. Thoughts a newly single woman with no prospects had no business having. Or maybe every business having them.

The best part was I didn't have to wake up next to anyone or answer to anyone. Ever. Again.

"Have you found a job yet?" It figured Kendra would change the subject to something more serious. What a way to snap me back to reality.

She was such a buzzkill sometimes.

"No, but I put in applications and sent out resumes to hospitals within fifty miles and every doctor's office in the greater Chestnut Hill-Philadelphia area. I also found an agency that offers private nursing. I'm thinking of checking it out." At this point, I had to take what I could get. My life savings had gone into the sanity-saving move.

Kendra nodded. Her approval wasn't essential, but the validation was nice. "Have you met the neighbors yet?"

She knew I'd come to tour the house and talk to the previous owner about a week ago. Kendra had been on some witch's retreat.

Pointing to the house on the other side of mine, she said, "Sara lives there with her 2.5 kids and a husband that is never home. She's nice but on the snobbish side. She is one hundred percent human, like you. But don't tell her anything you don't want the whole neighborhood to know."

Kendra had connections with the neighborhood I didn't yet. There were two reasons for those connections. One, she was a witch. Two, she'd lived in this neighborhood for the past fifteen years. She'd moved right after her divorce to start a new life with her kids. Of course, now she had a great relationship with her ex. They made better friends than lovers, as it had turned out.

It had been the same years ago for me and my ex-husband, Howard Jefferies. Our divorce had been messy and painful, mostly because I hadn't wanted to admit we'd fallen out of love with each other. I was bitter for a long time before we'd finally become friends.

"No. I've been here a couple of times, but always during the day when people are working, I suppose." I hadn't met a single soul besides the previous owner, Ava Harper, who was also a witch, and her extended family that had been with her.

Kendra hid her smile with another drink. "The neighbors across the street are," she leaned closer to me and lowered her voice, "*weird*."

"Yeah?" I glanced at the house across the street. "How so?"

It was a large three-story, modern brick home with a balcony that wrapped around the top floor. I wondered if the top floor was one large room or a separate apartment or living space.

Black shutters accented the windows, which appeared to be blacked out. The front door was crimson with black gothic-looking embellishments. There was a front porch on the ground level that was half the length of the front of the house. The lawn was perfectly manicured with lush green grass and expertly trimmed bushes.

"You know, weird." Kendra cocked an eyebrow. "*My* kind of weird."

Maybe she'd had too much to drink, or I had because I wasn't following whatever it was she hinted at. Then it hit me. Oh! *Her* kind of weird. "You mean like...." I lowered my voice to a whisper as I looked around to make sure there wasn't anyone in earshot. "Witches?"

She shook her head, and I grinned. A guessing game. Awesome. I so sucked at those.

I kept my voice low enough so only the two of us could hear. "You said there's more than witches out there. Is it one of the others?"

This time, she tapped the left side of her nose and smiled. Kendra so loved her dramatics.

"Werewolves?"

"No."

"Werepanthers?"

"Nope."

"Bears?" I paused for another negative reply then ran through a list. "Dragons? Lions? Cats of any kind?"

"No, no, and no." She kept her brow cocked and her smirk in place. She loved torturing me with these crazy guess games.

"Llama, dog, sock puppet?"

She burst out laughing at the latter, drawing glances from the movers. We laughed together like old times. God, I'd missed her so much. Being around Kendra was soothing after everything I'd been through.

"If we were playing the hot-cold game, I would say you were getting hot, but you're very cold." That helped so much. Not. Cryptic hints were her thing. "Brr." She ran her hands over her arms and faked a shiver. Then cackled like the witch she was.

"Zombie? Something in the abominable category?" Now I was reaching into the tundra. While Philly was cold in the winter, anything of the snow critter variety wouldn't stand a chance in a Pennsylvania summer.

"Warmer with zombie, a little too cold with the snowman."

My tone dropped to reflect my almost boredom. "Ghoul? Ghost? Alien?" She was losing me.

"Oh, come on!" She stood to her full height and leaned against the rail on the porch to stare at me. "You're dancing right around it." She let her tongue slip over her canine.

Oh, snap! No way.

"Vampire?" I whispered that one, too, because somewhere I'd read vamps could hear every pin drop in a five-mile radius. Then again, that article was on the internet, and you couldn't trust anything on the web. At least I didn't.

I stared at the house again after her wink, indicating that I guessed right. Finally. Now, the gothic embellishments and blacked-out windows made a little more sense. However, the home looked normal at the same time.

"Wow." Were they friendly vampires?

"Yeah." She nodded with her lips pursed.

We both shifted to look at the truck, then as one of my boxes went crashing to the ground and the sound of breaking glass tinkled through the air.

I groaned inwardly and hoped it wasn't something valuable in that box. The movers would be getting a bill for it if it was.

Later, after the hotties had left and the sun began to set, Kendra started unpacking the kitchen while I worked in the living room. Thank goodness they'd put the boxes in the rooms they belonged in, thanks to my OCD in labeling each one.

I was knee-deep in opened boxes and bubble wrap when the doorbell rang. "I'll get it," I called to Kendra in the kitchen.

Not waiting for her to answer, I swung the door open and froze.

The most exquisite man I'd ever seen stood in the doorway. Hellooooo handsome.

This guy was...tall. Well, taller than my five-one height, but then, most people were. He towered over me with a lean, more athletic than muscular form. His deep amber eyes reminded me of a sunset while his pale skin said he didn't spend much time in the sun. Light hair, something in the blond to strawberry variety, brushed the tops of shoulders. Shiny, clean, and begging for my fingers to run through the strands.

Smiling as if he could read my mind, Strawberry Man handed me a basket strongly scented by blueberry muffins. The smell made my mouth water. Or was that him? Maybe he was Blueberry Man. Oh, geez. I hadn't even said a word yet. Had I?

"These are for you." He nodded toward the basket, looking a little uncomfortable.

Oh, yes, they were. His large hand brushed mine as I grabbed it, and I sucked in a short, quick breath. At some point, I'd become awkward. And ridiculous.

And I remembered I hadn't brushed my hair all day since the movers arrived. Damn.

The porch was smaller with him standing on it, somehow it had shrunk, and I couldn't draw in a breath around him. Dramatic, yes, but so true. Or maybe he was too hot, and all the oxygen had evaporated in his presence. Either way, I found it hard to breathe and think.

"Th-th-thank you." I was like a nervous teenager who'd just met her very first pretty boy. I chuckled, hiccupped, and would've fallen out the door if not for the frame I'd somehow managed to catch my shirt on.

He nodded and tilted his head, smiling. Damn if my knees didn't go weak. "No problem. If you need anything at all, I'm Jax, and I live right over there." He pointed to the house across the street. And the back view of his head made my heart pitter-patter and my belly rumble as much as the front.

"You're the...." I didn't know if he, if they, were loud and proud with their creatures of the night status, and I didn't want to take the chance of outing Kendra for telling me. Unfortunately, I thought of it a second *after* I started speaking. "Neighbor."

His grin hit me like sunshine poking through the clouds on a rainy day. Ironic, since vampire meant allergic to the sun in a deathly kind of way.

"Yeah."

I didn't know if I should invite him in. What if there was a Mrs. Vampire? The last thing I needed was to become a jealous vampire wife's main course.

Like the queen of the dorks, I held up the basket, gave it a sniff, then hiccupped again. "Thanks for the goodies."

As I spoke, I wished again I'd taken a moment to brush my hair or put on a clean shirt before I answered the door. Vampire or not, this guy deserved a neighbor who combed her hair.

Get your copy of Bitten in the Midlife Here

I'M WITH CUPID

WITCHING AFTER FORTY BOOK 3

CHAPTER ONE

"You look ridiculous," I said to the mirror while glaring at it like I could somehow magically change how it made me look. It was totally the mirror's fault that nothing I tried was working.

With a moany scream of frustration, I wiped off my eye makeup. Again.

I'd watched makeup tutorial after makeup tutorial and every time I ended up looking perfect on one side and like a damn raccoon on the other. If it was Halloween or a witch's ball, the two-faced makeup job would've worked.

But it wasn't Halloween, nor was I going to a witch's ball. Only coven members were invited to those, anyway. Those prudish, magical busy-bodies didn't want their precious coven tainted with the dark magic of a necromancer.

What the eff ever.

And I was running out of time. Just like the white rabbit, I had a date.

At least I had started doing my eyes before the rest of my makeup. Thanks to one gorgeous English man and his tutorials, now I didn't have to redo my base every time I screwed up my eyes.

Again.

Ugh. What was wrong with me? I'd put on war paint a countless number of times before my husband died and a handful since. Why couldn't I do it now?

It was the fact I was going out on a date with sex poured into human skin, Sheriff Drew Walker. Just thinking his name made my girly parts tingly.

Holy crap in Hades, I was doomed.

"I'm here!" Olivia's voice drifting up from downstairs made me sigh in relief. It was about dang time.

Stepping out of the bathroom, I yelled, "Thank goodness, Liv, I need you!"

I rushed back into the bathroom as she stomped up the stairs. A few seconds ticked by and she didn't show, as if she'd gotten distracted on her very short trip down the hallway. She *was* easily distracted.

Seriously, Liv, what the Hades? I threw my makeup wipe into the sink, then walked through my bedroom and into the hallway. My jaw hung open as I stared, not believing what I was witnessing.

"Who's a good boy?" She scratched Snoozle's jaw while he purred and twitched his long, fluffy tail happily. "Who's Auntie Livvy's sweet immortal kitty?" She made kissy and num-num-num sounds until I cleared my throat.

"Think you could give me some attention like that? You are my best friend. Snoozle already has a best friend." I crossed my arms and frowned. My huge grey Maine coon cat, who I accidentally made immortal when I was seventeen, hadn't had anything to do with me since Alfred came to live with us. Unless he was hungry and Alfie wasn't around, which was almost never.

I continued to stare at Olivia until she grinned at me and gave Mr. Snoozleton one last scratch. "You look ridiculous."

"That's why I called you. Help me." I tightened my robe and glared at my best friend.

I smiled at the fact that I was calling Olivia my best friend. We hadn't always been friendly to one another. In high school we were always at each other, playing pranks and mean girl stuff on each other. And I couldn't remember why.

A door down the hall opened, and Alfred, my ghoul, shuffled out. He grunted and walked toward us. I'd sort of inherited him from a friend who'd been murdered last year. I'd solved his murder and taken down his killer, but doing so had unlocked my necromancer powers, which I'd been trying to suppress all of my life.

And as the only necromancer in the vicinity, I got custody of the ghoul.

Alfred had become more than my responsibility. He'd become part of my growing family. And Snooze decided upon first sight that Alfred was his new BFF. And the forever part of BFF was literal since they were both immortal.

Bending, Alfred picked up Snoozer and glared at the old, grumpy cat when he tried to bat at the strings that kept Alfred's mouth sewn shut.

I'd tried several times to convince Alfred to let me remove the strings, but he wouldn't allow it. And he'd refused to tell me why.

Snooze never would stop trying, though.

They went down the stairs, and Olivia giggled and grabbed my arm. "Come on, then."

I sat at my vanity with my face pointed upward and patiently waited for Olivia to fix the damage I'd done.

"Ava, you're forty-three years old. You've done your own makeup for what, thirty-three years?" She sighed in exasperation.

"Thirty. Yaya wouldn't let me wear makeup until I was thirteen." Not that I wore it often. I really didn't think I needed much of the stuff. But this was a first date. It was a big deal!

Olivia brushed something on my eyelids while we talked. "I remember," she said in a slow voice that told me she was focusing on my lids. "We used to make fun of you for being the only one not wearing makeup."

I didn't respond. It was the first time she'd really fully referred to the fact that we used to be enemies, and she used to torment me. She was a different person now, who loved and supported me.

She sighed "I've never told anyone. I had to hide behind the bushes when I got off the bus and carefully and completely wipe off the makeup every day before I went home."

Wow. I'd never known that. "Why?"

"My mother had to be at work before I caught the bus for school. So I could sneak and put her makeup on every morning, as I used my allowance to slowly buy my own." She chuckled. "My mother was a firm believer in baby wipes. She kept a pack in every room for quick cleanups. Said they were cheaper and faster than other options."

"You do the same thing," I said, moving my jaw as little as possible.

"I do. But that's how I got my makeup off every day. I'd take a handful of baby wipes in a baggie in my backpack. She, to this day, thinks I began applying makeup when I turned sixteen. I had to let her show me how."

I giggled. "Then why did you give me such a hard time?"

"Because I was weak." She sighed and the brush moved away from my eyelids.

I risked a peek. She'd perched on the end of the armchair beside my vanity. "I've never apologized to you for how rotten I was through high school. Having children of my own opened my eyes." She put her hand on my knee. "And I'm sorry."

Leaning forward, I took her hands. "It's forgiven. I know you're not the same person."

She wrapped her arms around me. "Neither are you, you know. You were painfully shy. I know now you were dealing with some major grief no child should deal with."

My heart pounded with the memory of my mother being struck by lightning.

Olivia sucked in a deep breath. "Your eyes are done. Just apply your mascara, you know I don't do that. I'm not trying to blind you today."

Giggling, I turned to do as she said, but the doorbell rang.

"Are you expecting anyone?" Olivia asked. "It's not time for Drew."

I carefully layered the black goop onto my eyelashes. "No, but Owen is downstairs. He'll answer it."

Olivia stood and tapped my curling iron. "Ah," she hissed. "It's ready."

"No, hang on, I've got this one." Pointing my finger at the mirror, I twirled it and focused. "I've been practicing this."

My hair curled into perfect beachy waves as I applied just the right amount of magic. "If I twirl too fast or too slow, the curls either look like corkscrews or they don't take. Just the right amount of magic, and..." I spread my hands, and my chestnut brown hair lay on my shoulders in perfect waves.

Too bad I only had mascara on one eye. "I wish I could get a spell for makeup to work as well."

"Ava!" Owen called from downstairs. "It's for you!"

I exchanged a glance with Olivia, then hurried out of my room and down the stairs. It couldn't be Drew already. He didn't seem like the type of man to be this early.

Owen, a necromancer who had moved into town not long before I came back, held the front door open. Owen stayed here with me—and Snooze and Alfred, and occasionally my son Wallie when he came home from college—teaching me how to

231

use the powers that I'd suppressed for so long. I'd had a darn hard time controlling them.

"Who is it?" I asked.

Owen shook his head. "Uh, see for yourself. I don't even know how to explain this."

Furrowing my brows, I rushed to the door and looked on the porch and saw... the most unexplainable sight.

"What?" I gasped.

A skeleton stood on my front porch. Fully... skeletonized. No flesh whatsoever.

"Hello."

I had to pick my jaw up off the wooden porch planks. He spoke. No vocal cords. Hell, he had no *neck*, yet he spoke.

"Hi," I whispered. Stepping back beside Owen, I tilted my head toward him without taking my eyes off of the skeleton. "How is this possible?"

"Uh, it's not. I've never heard of a skeleton speaking. So, this is all on you, the ultra-powerful necromancer." Owen pressed his lips together to hide his smile.

Nodding, accepting the fact that since I was—supposedly— more powerful than all the other necromancers, I stepped forward again. "How can I help you?"

His jawbone moved, teeth clacking as he spoke. "You raised me during your last training session."

As I fought for words, Owen leaned forward, peering at the skeleton. "The one in the woods on the other side of Luci's place?" he asked.

The skeleton nodded, purposefully moving his skull up and down on his vertebrae. "That's the one."

This was not happening. Not tonight.

Movement past Mr. Bones caught my attention, and I gasped. My heart slammed against my chest. "Shit," I whispered. "Get in here!"

Shoving Owen behind me, I reached out and grabbed the

dry, surprisingly smooth hand of the skeleton and yanked him inside, praying he wouldn't fall apart, considering he didn't have any tendons to hold him together.

My prayers were not answered. The skeleton stumbled as I jerked him forward and all I could do was watch in horror as he hit the floor hard enough for his skull to pop off of his shoulders and bounce across the living room.

"Oh," Olivia whispered. "No."

I gasped and then pressed my lips together to hold in my laugh as the skeleton's body began to look around for his head.

"To your right," Owen said. I glanced quickly at him to see he had a look on his face similar to my own.

Just trying to hold in the laughter.

Mr. Bones army crawled across the floor, chasing after the head. If I laughed, it would only prove that I was finally cracking—going totally insane.

When the poor schmuck found his head, he just plopped it on his shoulders and jumped to his feet as if it happened all the time. Surprisingly, it stayed put and no more body parts clattered to the floor.

"Is that going to fall off again?" I asked.

He grinned at me and it was the freakiest thing I'd ever seen. There were no words to describe the full teeth and bone smile. He didn't have muscles and skin to pull lips up in a smile, yet I knew he was grinning. "As long as I don't fall that hard again."

He had hit the floor pretty hard.

"How can you even see to walk?" I whispered as he passed by me, but that had been a question I'd asked myself ever since the first time I'd animated a cemetery full of skeletons to help me kill an evil witch. But they could see or at least had known where they were going and what they were doing. Now, I added a talking skeleton to my long list titled, What the Everloving Fudge?

Remembering the patrol SUV coming up the road before the skeleton lost his head, I slammed the door shut, turned, and then screeched as I rushed to the stairs. "Olivia, he's here!"

"I'm right behind you," she said in a wispy voice. I lifted my gaze to find her still staring at the skeleton in shock.

"You!" I barked, pointing at Mr. Bones. "What's your name?"

"Lawrence, but you can call me Larry," he said.

"Fine, Larry, go find Alfred and Snoozle. Probably in the kitchen. *Stay* in there with them until I'm out the door. I do *not* have time for this."

Sprinting up the stairs, I returned to my vanity and applied my mascara with shaking hands. "Are you okay?" Olivia asked. There was a giggle in her words like she was about to lose it any moment.

Why did insane crap always happen to me? Ghouls, skeletons, haunted houses.

I nodded, which smeared my mascara all over the side of my eye because I didn't move my hand away before nodding.

The doorbell rang as I licked a Q-tip and tried to dab the mascara away.

It didn't work.

With the thinnest thread of magic, I tried again. It worked this time. Thank goodness.

"What are you wearing?" Olivia asked. "I'll grab it."

"Black dress in the closet," I said as my date's voice drifted up the stairs. Owen had answered the door.

Butterflies fluttered in my belly. Not literally, it was a feeling that now I thought about it, was nothing like actual butterflies. It was more like gas or the need to lock myself in the bathroom.

I rushed through applying lipstick, stopping just long enough to make sure I didn't have any on my teeth, then threw off my robe and let Olivia help me into the dress.

"Okay," I said, looking around the room. "You grab my black strappy heels. Oh, and my wrap."

She ran back to the closet. Meanwhile, I filled a small, silver purse with a compact, my phone, some cash, ID, and my lipstick.

I stilled and stared at the door.

"What's wrong?" Olivia asked.

"What if he lied about not being a witch hunter? I mean, he is one, because it's like being a witch. It doesn't go away because you quit practicing. But what if he is hunting again and this is a trap?" Drew came from a long line of witch hunters. He'd told us he'd renounced the family business.

Olivia lost it. She laughed so hard she had to cross her legs to keep from peeing herself. When she came up for air, she said, "Stop. This is Drew we're talking about. Plus, he's crazy about you."

"He'd have to be to get involved with me." I sighed and met her gaze. "I live with an immortal cat, a ghoul, and a necromancer I just met months ago. And now a skeleton followed me home! No sane person would sign up for that."

Olivia laughed again. At least she had a little more control over it this time. "Take what you get and don't pitch a fit. Drew is hot. You'll have a wonderful time."

Two minutes later, I walked down the stairs as if I hadn't just rushed through the most panicked pre-date preparations since I was sixteen and getting ready for my first date with my now-dead husband. Also, the only man I'd ever dated.

Until tonight.

But Olivia was right. I shouldn't question it. Just roll with the craziness.

Because that was my life now.

CHAPTER TWO

"You look beautiful." Drew ran his gaze over me as I descended the stairs and his teal eyes crinkled in the corner. There were sparks of desire in those depths that made me want to cancel the dinner and go straight to dessert.

"Thank you. I'm so glad we're finally doing this," I whispered. Giddiness bubbled inside me. Oh great, I was the shy, insecure sixteen-year-old again.

He held out his arm. "Me, too. More than I can say."

Heat pooled in my belly as I came to a stop inches from him. Every time we'd tried to go on a date, something crazy happened. He'd first asked me to go on a date with him after the skeletons I raised took the evil witch hunter, Carmen, to Hell or wherever they took her. That was nearly two months ago, but that whole week had been a disaster.

Then we tried a few days before Christmas, which was another disaster. I'd tried to summon Santa for the open-invitation party I'd thrown for the town. Instead, I'd summoned Satan, and had to deal with that.

I was still dealing with that. I'd finally come clean to Drew with what I did after he confronted me about the new magical being who'd made Shipton Harbor his new residence—aka Satan, aka Luci, aka my neighbor whom I was trying to figure how to send back to Hell. I doubted the skeletons would take him.

So all I could do was deal with the situation and keep an eye on the devil to make sure he didn't kill anyone. At least until I found the right spell or ritual to get rid of him for good.

I hadn't been successful thus far.

As we walked out of my front door, I glanced to the left, to what used to be a large, open field, but now was a gigantic manor house that Lucifer built in a matter of minutes during our Christmas Eve party.

The whole town seemed perfectly complacent and willing to accept the fact that the home had come out of nowhere. I suspected Luci did some kind of mind fiddling on them.

Turning, I made a show of locking the door. My entire menagerie had come to the foyer to see me off, all out of Drew's sight, thankfully. I grimaced at my unusual family. Part of them, anyway. A human, a necromancer, a ghoul, an undead cat, and now, and hopefully not for long, a talking skeleton.

My life was a slapstick comedy show, and I wouldn't have it any other way. Except maybe to bring my husband back, but it was far too late for that. He died five years ago and tonight, I was walking out the door for my first date since.

No pressure.

"So, what's the plan?" I asked. "You've been pretty hush-hush about our date."

Drew opened the passenger door on his SUV to let me slide in. "I'm going to be honest. I worried so much about making the perfect date, I didn't make reservations in time."

He looked so worried about not having the date lined up just right that I had to laugh.

"It's okay. We could go for fast food," I suggested. "I don't mind."

With a scoff, he turned on the truck. "No, I managed to get reservations, but that's all I've got. Dinner at the Ocean Tale on the coast."

"That sounds lovely." In a bold move for me, I reached over and touched his arm. "You didn't have to put so much pressure on yourself."

He slowed the SUV at the end of my driveway and turned his arm over to clasp my hand. "You're gracious," he whispered.

Gracious, ha. More like my life was insane and this was the most normal thing I'd done in ages. With Drew, it wasn't likely I'd be raising the dead or dealing with unruly ghouls. At least I hoped the hell not. In the last few months, I'd learned a lot from Owen about how to control my powers. No need for a repeat of the cemetery incident. I was getting better. Not perfect, but better.

"I'm just happy to finally be doing this," I said, suddenly uncomfortable holding hands. The ghost—not literally—of my dead husband sat between us, a heavy burden to take with me on this date. My chest tightened, and I wondered if Clay would have approved of Drew.

Maybe I wasn't ready for this after all. It'd been five years, sure, but was there a time limit on grief? I didn't think there was.

"You've had a crazy couple of months, haven't you?" he asked. Drew asked, not my dead husband, who wasn't actually there. "With the murders, then that Christmas party."

I grimaced. "My life is certainly *different*, that's for sure."

He glanced at me, only taking his eyes off the road for a moment. "Is that a bad thing?"

I thought about his question. "No, I don't think it is. Wallie is happy at college, and I've got a new little family here. People who need me. I'm finally learning to use my powers and control them."

Drew grinned while looking out at the road in the waning light. "Family isn't always blood."

"What about yours?" I asked. "What is your family like? I mean, I know they're hunters and all, but there's a reason you're not with them."

He was quiet for a few seconds before answering. "I haven't talked to my father and brother in years. Mom, even though she's a hunter, she understands why I don't want that life. We talk every few months or so."

"Why not more often?"

He looked at me out of the corner of his eyes and frowned. "Every time we talk, she tries to get me to apologize to my father."

"For what?"

"Rejecting my heritage." His tone was dry and held a hint of anger. "She's still a hunter, after all. I guess she thought I was going through a stage and would *get over it*, as she would say."

Oh great, another mother-in-law that was going to hate me. And I had no idea where the mother-in-law title came from. Holy crap. It was our first date. "She's going to love it that you're dating a necromancer."

He laughed. It started as a chuckle that went into a full-blown laugh out loud that made me giggle. I was being serious and had no idea why he found my comment so funny.

"I should tell her on our next call." He turned his head to me and brought my hand to his lips. "If you're worried that I care about what my mother thinks of who I date, don't. My family could go to Hell."

"Maybe we should introduce them to Luci." The words escaped my lips before I could reign them in. A big laugh, something akin to a guffaw escaped my lips next.

Drew smirked in response. "Don't tempt me."

I glanced toward the road in time to see a flash of tan fur blur by. I gasped and pointed. "Watch out!"

Drew slammed on the breaks, sending the SUV skidding sideways. When the vehicle stopped, it faced the woods with the lights illuminating the underbrush. Directly in front of us a ferret panted and looked around. It was tan and a lot larger than most I'd ever seen. The little guy was missing the top of its ear and had bald spots in patches like it'd been in fights.

And then, to my utter shock, the damn ferret flipped us off. At least that was what it looked like as he held his paw out with one middle toe extended upwards.

"Did he just flip us the bird?" Drew asked, squinting at the animal.

I nodded and whispered, "I think so."

He chuckled again and we exchanged a glance. "Never a dull moment with you."

"Hey! I didn't have anything to do with that ferret." I glanced back out the windshield, but the animal was gone.

"Are you okay?"

Focusing back on Drew, I giggled. "Yeah. Let's get to the restaurant before something else decides to jump out in front of us and start cursing at us."

He threw the car into drive and we talked about the ferret on the way. Before long, we pulled into the parking lot of the restaurant. Drew turned off the engine and grinned. "Wait there."

He hurried out of the driver's seat and around the front of the SUV to open my door. "Ma'am."

I took his hand and smiled. Of course, I didn't *need* the assist, but it was nice to have it. He was old fashioned and so sexy.

Once we entered the restaurant, the maître d' took us to a table at the back, in front of a large window that overlooked the ocean as the sun set on the water. It was beautiful and romantic.

"A bottle of your finest champagne," Drew said. "Since it's a special occasion."

I chanced a touch of his hand again. "You don't have to do that."

"Of course he does!"

The voice that interrupted what I was sure was about to be a sweet retort from Drew made my back tense, and a tickle of fear went up my spine. Oh no. *Not today, Satan!*

Luci had come to dinner. Yay, us. Not! Why couldn't I have one night without chaos?

Turning in my seat, I sucked in a deep breath and looked up at the devil and his date. "Carrie," I gasped. "What are you doing here?"

Gods, if Luci compelled her, I was going to kill him.

My best friend's son's kindergarten teacher stood on the arm of Lucifer and beamed down at me. "Luci here invited me out for Valentine's day. It's so fun running into you guys."

Drew and I exchanged a glance. I gave him my best apologetic look.

Yeah. Fun. That was one word for it.

CHAPTER THREE

L uci spread his arms and grinned cheekily. "Just call me
Cupid," he said in a booming voice.

And we all knew what cupid rhymed with.

Narrowing my eyes, I leaned forward and spoke through
my teeth. "You better not be wearing a diaper."

Wickedness crept into his dark gaze and one side of his
mouth lifted in a devilish smirk. In the next moment, his black
suit disappeared to be replaced with nothing but a large white
diaper. He had tiny pink wings at his back and a bow in one
hand. It would've looked completely ridiculous, instead of just
mostly ridiculous, except he had the body of a Greek god.

He did the classic baby cupid pose right before changing
back to normal. Well, normal for Lucifer. On the best day, he
was half insane.

I sat with my mouth open because no words would form to
express my shock. I scanned the restaurant and to my relief, no
one seemed to notice. No one except Drew, who looked ready
to bolt for the door or maybe shoot Luci. With Drew, it was a
fifty-fifty chance either way. And Carrie had her hand over her

mouth like she was trying not to laugh loud enough to draw attention.

I was about to tell him to go away and ask Carrie to hang out. It would ruin our first date, but at least we'd save the poor innocent Kindergarten teacher from the lecherous Lucifer.

But Luci's laughter cut me off as he pulled out the chair beside me. "You don't mind if we join you, right?" Not waiting for an answer, he ushered Carrie into the seat. She smiled at me, and I couldn't tell if it was forced or not. I didn't know her well enough.

"Actually," Drew said, rising halfway out of his chair, but Luci walked around the table and clapped him on the back.

"There's a good man," Luci said. "We appreciate the invitation."

Annoyance flowed through me, making my magic tingle to life. No, I couldn't zap Satan in public. It might not have been a great idea in private, either, but I probably would've risked it.

Drew's comment was more of a protest than an invitation but Drew clamped his jaw shut and sat back down, shooting me an apologetic look.

Lucifer sat in the chair beside Drew, across from Carrie. "What are your plans for after dinner?" Luci said. "Going necking?" He winked at me and nudged Drew as he waggled his eyebrows.

Carrie giggled behind her napkin, but Drew was saved from answering by the return of the waitress with the bottle of champagne.

Luci looked up, sitting closer to her than Drew, and smiled. "Hello, my dear."

The server's gaze caught on Luci's face, and his effect on her was immediate. "Hey," she breathed. Her shoulders slumped as her entire body relaxed. He'd caught her in his... sway? I didn't know what it was, but it was potent.

My eyes rolled so hard that I thought they'd get stuck in the back of my head. I conjured my notepad where I kept my to-do lists, then turned to the page that had Luci written on top. Ignoring the devil, who peered across the table to see what I wrote, I made a note to create anti-compelling charms to pass out to the townspeople.

Luci tapped my notepad with the tip of his finger. "You've got quite the list going there."

I glared at Lucifer and pointed to the number one item that I'd written in a heavy black marker. "I will be the one to send you back to Hell. Might not be today or tomorrow. But I'll figure out how."

A spark of pride and intrigue lit up his dark depths. "I love your dedication." He practically purred at me. I was pretty sure he was trying to get me all hypnotized like the server, but I was made of sterner stuff, so I stuck my tongue out at him.

He laughed, seemingly delighted before he turned to the waitress and said, "The dinner will be on the house tonight. It's the least the restaurant can do for the fine gentleman who protects the streets of our town." He motioned to Drew, who glared.

"That's not necessary."

She didn't seem to hear Drew. "Of *course,*" she said in a hushed tone. "On the house."

Maybe I needed to move the anti-compelling charms up to the number one spot. At least until I figured out how to send him back to the underworld. Maybe I could find a reaper...

"We'll need another place setting," Luci continued, gesturing to the empty space in front of Carrie and himself. "And glasses for champagne."

The server, whose name tag read Skye, squeaked and scurried away.

Lucifer straightened his tie and beamed at Carrie. "My dear, is champagne good for you? I can request something different."

She shook her head. "No, that sounds great." Lowering her lashes, it was like she couldn't look at Lucifer for too long at once. I didn't blame her. The demon was a walking, orgasm-inducing entity possessing a human form.

It was a good thing that I seemed to be immune to his charms.

The server returned, followed by a fellow in an apron, carrying silverware, two more menus, and two more champagne glasses. Skye set glasses of ice water in front of Luci and Carrie.

"Allow me to pour?" she asked, holding the bottle out for Luci to inspect.

He pursed his lips and peered down at the bottle. "Excellent."

As he turned his gaze toward me and Carrie, smiling, Skye began to pour.

"I'm quite looking forward to this evening," Luci said. "I've got a few things up my sleeve to make this a most enjoyable experience."

"Uh," Drew said.

"Yes, don't worry Drew, it's all on me tonight. I've been scheming up a good plan."

"No, it's just the champagne."

We all looked at him, but he was pointedly looking at the glass in front of Lucifer. I swung my gaze down to see the server had been pouring champagne non-stop as she stared at Luci. It was now puddled all over the table and in danger of running off into Lucifer's lap.

"Oh," she cried and jerked the champagne bottle up. "I'm so sorry!"

Lucifer grabbed his silverware and unwrapped the napkin in time to stop the flow of champagne onto his undoubtedly expensive suit.

"Allow me," Lucifer said as Skye tried to take the napkin and clean up the spill.

He set the pristine black cloth over the champagne, and when he wiped once, the table underneath was bone dry.

Skye gaped as Luci handed her the damp napkin. "Those things never absorb spills. That's incredible."

He winked and gently took the bottle from her hands. "I think you'll find that one to be particularly absorbent. I'll finish this if you'll give us a moment to browse your menu."

Nodding, the poor girl scurried away with a totally confused expression on her face.

Lucifer watched her go with a speculative look on his face. "I'll be sure to leave her a good tip. It's overwhelming to be around me sometimes."

Luci was sure of himself, that was for sure.

Drew caught my attention and widened his eyes. I wasn't sure what he was trying to tell me, but I didn't get it. I wasn't about to try to get out of this night with Luci and risk pissing off the devil, who so far seemed awfully fond of me. At least, until I figured out how to get him home. His home. Hell. Not mine.

Would it be rude to just get up and leave? What would Luci do if I offended him? I wasn't sure I really wanted to find out. And I didn't feel comfortable leaving Carrie alone with the devil, either.

"We're going to go powder our noses," I said, smiling at Luci and Drew. "Excuse us."

Taking my sort of friend's hand, I weaved through the tables to the bathroom.

As soon as Carrie shut the bathroom door behind us, I whirled on her. "What are you doing here? With him?"

She arched a perfectly trimmed eyebrow at me. "Luci? Whatever do you mean?" Moving to the mirror, she inspected her makeup and opened her purse.

A sinking feeling that he had her under his spell churned in my gut. How could I warn her off of him without telling her the blatant truth? "Listen, Carrie, he's not a very good person. I know a few things about the man and—"

Carrie sighed and seemed to drop her pretense. "I know," she said urgently. "I know about it all. The witch stuff. I know who Luci really is." She sighed and hung her head. "But what was I supposed to say when he asked me out for Valentine's Day? No?" She laughed and turned, leaning against the counter. "Besides, you didn't feel the orgasm he gave me with one touch before Christmas. At the bookstore? Best orgasm of my life. Imagine what he could actually do," she lowered her voice. "You know. In *bed*."

Glancing past the orgasm stuff, I knew she was right. She couldn't have said anything but yes to his invitation. "You know?" I hadn't had any idea she was a witch. "What kind of witch are you?"

"I'm not. My many-times great grandfather was a sprite, or so the family legend says. We can see witch marks, but the power that many of my ancestors had is long gone."

I pulled out my compact so I didn't have to look her in the eye and let her see my shock. "A sprite," I whispered. "They don't exist." Sprite, part of the Fae, were nothing more than bedtime stories told by witch mothers to get their children to sleep. They were said to be troublesome and chaotic.

"They do," she said. "But they outlawed human-Fae matings many centuries ago and virtually disappeared from this world. They mostly live in Faerie now, but occasionally visit. They love popping in to scare me when I'm relaxed." She rolled her eyes. "They're sweet but mischievous."

There was still so much about the world I didn't know. Hell, my Yaya hadn't believed in fairies at all. "Okay, so you know. So, now what?"

"Now, we go have a lovely dinner and hope that Luci loses interest in me pretty quickly. After giving me another of those orgasms, hopefully." She laughed weakly. "Or else you'll have to help me banish the devil."

She was right. There was nothing left to do but make the best of the evening. "Okay, but if you're in over your head, I can arrange for a call to get you out of this." Olivia would've been happy to do the emergency call thing, and I knew she had Carrie's number since Carrie was Olivia's son's teacher.

"No, so far so good. And he seems to be a gentleman. I can't be sure, of course, but I think he's got a code. He won't hurt me." She laughed. "Unless I deserve to be hurt, but I don't think that's the case. The kids haven't driven me quite that crazy."

I looped my arm through hers and chuckled with her as we walked back to the table where Drew and Lucifer seemed to have broken the ice.

They both jumped up to pull out our chairs as we walked up to the table. "Ladies," Drew said. "Luci here was just telling me he's looking for a cleaning service for that gigantic house of his."

"Oh, I know a lovely woman," Carrie said. "She cleans the school as well."

Skye returned to the table and Luci opened his menu. "Silly us, we haven't even looked at the menu."

We all got down to the business of ordering, and as soon as Skye wrote it all down and walked away, menus in hand, Luci leaned into the table with a twinkle in his eyes. "I think I have just the ticket for this night."

He snapped his fingers, and I had a horrible feeling of falling. It only lasted for a split second before I jerked as if I'd sat down hard.

And we were in a totally different restaurant. Delicious-looking food already sat on the table in front of us, chicken covered in a delectable sauce for me, steak for Luci and Drew, and some sort of pasta for Carrie. "Where are we?" Drew asked in a deep, rumbling voice full of threat.

"Paris," Luci said. "Ready for a lovely night of sightseeing, and then I'll take you both home, all the better for your trip."

Drew looked at me with his eyebrows raised. It was ludicrous, obscene to think we could possibly be in France, but then, I'd always wanted to see the Louvre. And the Eiffel Tower. "It sounds great," I whispered. "And you did want this to be a night to remember."

Drew's apprehension broke and he grinned. "Okay. I'm game."

We ate, but no matter how much we sipped the champagne, the glass never ran short. And even though I ate until I wanted to unbutton my pants, I never depleted the delicious chicken or broccoli on the side.

"This seems like a waste," Carrie said.

Luci nodded and tutted his tongue. "You're right." With another snap of his fingers, the food disappeared. "Now it's in doggie bags in your refrigerators. The leftovers won't auto replenish, however."

Smiling, I met Carrie's gaze and found her looking excited as well.

"Well," Luci said, standing and straightening his tie. "Shall we?"

CHAPTER FOUR

My heart pounded with anticipation. Getting to sightsee in Paris with Drew was an unexpected delight, one I couldn't pretend to be upset about. Sure, it was risky, parading around with the devil. But it wasn't like I'd promised him my soul or something nuts like that.

Besides, I was a necromancer. If that wasn't the definition of dark arts, I didn't know what was. I'd tried for a *very* long time to deny my nature, but it had become impossible, so now I embraced it and had taken major steps to learn how to control my necromancer side.

Thus the skeleton waiting for me at home. Ugh. I would not think of the creepy walking, talking bone bag who wanted me to find his murderer. Not today. It was Valentine's Day, and I was on a date with the sexy sheriff.

Lucifer put his hands on the double doors leading out of the restaurant. I couldn't see past the frosted glass windows to the city outside, but in a moment of pure anticipation, I grabbed Drew's hand and grinned cheekily. "I'm so excited," I whispered.

Drew squeezed back. "I have to admit, so am I. I've always wanted to go to France."

Luci opened the doors with a flourish and stepped outside with his arms spread. "Welcome to Paris," he crowed.

Following him out, I looked around, ready to face a new city for the night. But all there was out the door was a parking lot and behind that, a bunch of trees. "This is Paris?" Carrie asked. "I thought it would be brighter."

Luci walked out into the parking lot and turned in a slow circle. "This isn't right."

Drew leaned in. "Something is wonky."

Yeah. It'd been wonky since Luci sat at our table. But it was interesting that the devil actually got something wrong. Now I had ammo to fire at Luci when he annoyed me, in the form of, "like that time you took us to Paris, in the woods?"

And I wasn't afraid to use that ammo. Well, maybe a little. But I *would* use it.

Suddenly, Lucifer slapped himself on the forehead. "Oh, I'm sorry. I'm not so used to being topside."

He snapped his fingers, and suddenly we stood on a cobblestone street with three or four-story buildings surrounding us. The place was lit up with old-fashioned street lights, and at the end of the alley, people walked back and forth, all kinds of people.

"This is more like it," Carrie said.

"Where were we before?" I asked.

"Paris, Tennessee, I believe," Luci said. He straightened his jacket and adjusted his button at his wrist as we giggled. "Shall we?"

Carrie and Lucifer took hands and walked toward the people and the crowd.

Turning to Drew, still holding his hand, I swung my arm. "Shall we?"

Hurrying behind Lucifer and Carrie, we broke into the

crowd and the splendor and might of Paris opened up before us.

Cars sped by on a street paved like any in America. I never knew France also drove on the right. The side streets were cobbled with people walking all over the place. Carts with vendors, restaurants with their tables out on the sidewalk, so many overlapping sights and sounds.

I sucked in a deep breath, expecting to smell bread. What else should Paris smell like besides bread? Maybe assorted pastries or roast chicken.

Instead, my olfactory senses were assaulted with a much less pleasant smell. "Is that urine?" I asked in surprise.

Lucifer sighed and nodded his head. "Unfortunate, isn't it? Parisians love dogs, and the city hasn't done the best job of providing public toilets." He winked at Carrie. "Mind your step, but once we're inside the Louvre, the smell disappears."

"How far is it?" I asked.

Lucifer gestured to the right. "Walk this way, please, my dear."

People moved out of our way as we continued on the sidewalk, instinctively avoiding the devil and his entourage. "On the right, you'll find the Arc de Triomphe du Carrousel. From there we can stroll through the Place du Carrousel and make our way to the Pyramide du Louvre, and finally on to the Louvre Museum.

Laughing, we hurried forward, staring up at the gigantic archway of the Arc de Triomphe. It took a while to walk from there to the museum, but under the night lights everything sparkled, and I soon stopped noticing the awful smell.

When we got to the gates of the museum, I sighed in dismay. "It's closed." Why hadn't I realized the time difference? It was getting pretty late here in Paris.

But Luci tapped his nose.

Drew put his arm around my shoulders. "I don't think anything is closed to Lucifer, Ava."

With a laugh, I leaned into him. "I think you may be right."

The doors to the museum opened as if invisible guards stood at attention to let us in. "Haters," Luci said, "Will tell you to skip the Louvre. It's too expensive, too many people. But it is my favorite place in old Paris." He turned in a circle on the marble floors as statues and works of art looked on. "The biggest and brightest throughout history, showcased here in one sixty-thousand square meter place." He winked at Carrie before swinging his arm around Drew. "And it's only us here. Even the guards have decided to take a sudden nap after turning off the security systems." He skipped forward, dragging Drew with him.

Carrie and I followed at a near run. I felt like a child going on a big outing for the first time.

"Where to first?" Luci asked. "The Code of Hammurabi? How about Napoleon's apartments? This was his palace, you know."

Blushing, I ducked my head. "Is it too cliche to say the Mona Lisa?"

Lucifer stopped walking and turned to face me. "Not cliche at all, my dear. The Mona Lisa is my all-time favorite work of art." He closed his eyes and clutched his chest as we walked. I kept having to move my gaze from Luci to the glorious sights inside the museum. I couldn't believe we were actually here.

"Leonardo was one of my favorite humans to ever grace this Earth," Lucifer said. "He was inspired." Shaking his hands, he whirled in place and sort of skip walked. "The world burned brighter when he walked in the room."

"So, you knew him personally?" Drew asked.

Lucifer slung his arm around Drew again. "I knew him. Oh, I knew him. We were friends, confidantes. Brothers." He sighed. "Such a shame he's not with me now."

I raised my eyebrows. "In Hell?"

Lucifer scoffed. "No, here, literally, to explain his artistry to you."

I wondered where Leonardo's spirit was, but I wasn't going to ask out of fear that Luci would raise the famous artist from the dead or something. I didn't think I could handle that at the moment.

"However, you are in luck because I know all about the histories of each item here." He waved us to follow and stopped at The Venus de Milo, an ancient Greek statue. "This glorious statue was made during my brief but successful sculpting period. It's a shame about her arms. I was particularly proud of her fingers. Delicate work, that."

The devil sculpted? I didn't think so. As I arched my brow and was about to question him, Carrie said, "Um no. It was initially attributed to the sculptor Praxiteles, but based on an inscription that was on its plinth, the statue is now thought to be the work of Alexandros of Antioch."

Lucifer's lips twitched before he replied with, "Who do you think Alexandros of Antioch was?" He bent into a flourishing bow. "At your service."

Carrie and I shared a glance. She shook her head like she didn't believe him. Just then Drew touched my lower back and leaned in until his lips touched my ear. I suppressed a moan at the feel of him so close. His words were barely a whisper. "I think Luci is full shit."

A laugh burst from me, earning me a glare from the devil. I glared back until he straightened his jacket and led us to the next exhibit. Then I whispered back to Drew, "I think you're right. But let's play along. This could get interesting."

We moved through the museum at a leisurely pace until we stopped in front of the Mona Lisa. Excitement filled me as I studied the painting. There was something about seeing it in person that made the trip to Paris complete. Like I had to see it, or I really hadn't been there.

"This," Luci said proudly while waving his hands in front of the painting like he was auditioning to be Vanna White's replacement when she retired. He turned to face us with the Mona Lisa illuminated behind him. "Is me."

We stared at him blankly. I asked in my best skeptical tone, "What?"

"It's me! da Vinci painted me. As a woman!" He smiled wide like he was proud and excited to share this unknown, most likely a lie, secret.

Carrie started giggling, then laughed. "Maybe Leonardo told you that, but I read the painting is of the Italian noble-woman Lisa Gherardini, the wife of Francesco del Giocondo."

Luci waved her off. "He couldn't go around telling people he painted the devil, now could he?"

He had a point there. However, I doubted da Vinci painted Satan at all. I peered closer at the painting then Luci, then the painting.

"It's so much smaller than I expected." I gave him a signifi-cant look. "Alluding to something?"

He snorted and blustered as Carrie giggled behind her hand and Drew sounded like he was choking on his own spit. I ignored them and looked closer.

The whole thing was maybe two feet high. I'd expected it to be like four or five feet tall. I peered closer, squinting. With nobody else here, I was able to get within a few feet of the iconic painting. Quickly, and feeling like I was being *quite* the rebel, I ducked under the little wooden fence and nearly pressed my nose onto the glass in front of the painting. There was a resemblance around the eyes, and maybe if Luci's jawline was softened and... No. No way. Lucifer was far too masculine. Too ruggedly handsome. "Whatever helps you sleep at night," I said and moved on from the painting. Whatever the truth, I'd never look at it the same again.

After a little while of drifting around the museum, I stopped at the Psyche Revived by Cupid's Kiss sculpture.

Luci wedged himself between Drew and me, ignoring the growl from the sheriff. "I saved the best for last since it's Valentine's Day." He indicated the large sculpture. " Once upon a time, I *was* Cupid, and I woke Psyche." He sighed, a sound of remembrance. "Sweet moment."

We fell quiet, and I glanced at Carrie. She shook her head, silently laughing. Then Luci said, "Of course from my kiss, she woke and became the first vampire. I didn't know what the outcome would be at the time, but que será, será." He winced and shrugged.

I rolled my eyes, making Carrie laugh harder. "Even I know that Cupid is Eros, the Greek god of Love. Psyche is his wife. You are not the god of love."

Luci straightened his spine and lifted his chin. "God of Love, Angel of Desire. Semantics." Grabbing Carrie's hand, he twirled her into his arms and moved from side to side in a dance to music only he could hear. Then, he announced that it was time to leave.

It was my turn to giggle. The poor devil had gotten tired of us correcting his warped knowledge of history.

We walked out of the museum into the cold night air, laughing, thrilled with all we'd just seen. It was late, but I was wired, ready to take on the world.

"One more thing," Luci said. "Thanks to the time difference, it's nearly dawn."

I gasped. "We've been here that long? That makes it what, almost two at home?"

Drew checked his watch. "Sounds about right, yeah. My watch updated the time automatically."

Lucifer snapped his fingers and we were instantly outfitted

with cold-weather gear, hats and mittens, and gloves. Good thing, too, because the night air was surprisingly brisk. "Now, on to the last part of our perfect Valentine night," Lucifer said. He snapped his fingers again and without warning, we appeared at the top of the Eiffel tower.

The sudden difference in altitude took my breath. As I staggered backward, lightheaded and gasping, strong arms wrapped around me from behind. "Shh," Drew said in my ear.

My body flipped from being unsteady to a raging inferno as Drew's arms wrapped around my stomach, just below my breasts.

"This is incredible," Carrie whispered. I peeked around to see her being held similarly by Luci.

And then, I looked past her. The sun had just begun to peek over the horizon, bathing the city in a pink glow of warmth and promise. "Whoa," I whispered, echoing Carrie's sentiment. "Amazing."

We weren't just on the top level of the tower. We were on the extreme top, the small tower where the radio antennas were set up. On the relatively small platform, two blankets waited, suspiciously unbothered by the buffeting wind.

On the same vein, in the winter clothing, I was perfectly comfortable, even though the February temperatures combined with the wind should've left me half frozen.

Drew sat on one of the blankets and patted the spot beside him. With a big grin, I lowered myself and snuggled close as he wrapped his arm around me.

The sun topped the horizon, and I leaned my head on Drew's shoulder. "Beautiful," he whispered.

"I agree."

"Oh, I was talking about you," Drew whispered in my ear. "The sunrise pales by comparison."

Oh, smooth.

CHAPTER FIVE

"Well," Lucifer said with a sigh. "I suppose that's the perfect end to our night."

I nodded with my head still on Drew's shoulder. "That was pretty perfect."

"Back to reality, my loves," Luci said. He stood and offered his hand to Carrie, and Drew did the same, but I was already halfway to my feet.

I'd had enough snuggling for one day. I still hadn't reconciled being with Drew to my feelings of grief and betrayal for my husband.

That was a therapy appointment for another day.

"Could you drop us back at the restaurant we started at?" Drew asked. "I'd like to get my SUV."

"Sure," Lucifer said brightly. He took my hand and bowed, pulling it to his lips in a grand gesture. When my skin tingled from the almost touch of his mouth, he looked up at me and winked. "See you soon."

With a rush of air, Luci and Carrie disappeared, as did the

spectacular views. We sat inside Drew's SUV in the dark, six hours earlier, back in Maine. If Drew felt anything like me, his head was reeling and stomach churning.

"Wow," he whispered.

Yep. He felt like me.

"I can't begin to describe how crazy that was," I said. My eyes had suddenly gone scratchy, ready for bed. "But I'm exhausted now. Like, bone tired."

Drew chuckled. "I am, too. I think I've got enough juice to get us home, though."

We were quiet on the drive. Halfway there, he put his hand on the seat between us, palm up. I laid mine in his and sighed, my feelings an enormous mix of happiness, guilt, and just plain sleepiness. The ride was a comfortable quiet though. Nice. I still wasn't sure about him, but I reflected on the amazing sights I'd seen during the night.

When he pulled into my driveway and parked, my heart raced with nervousness, chasing away all signs of exhaustion.

I hadn't planned to do this, but now that it was time to say goodbye, I didn't want to. "Would you like to come in?" I asked in a soft voice, then met Drew's gaze.

He blinked his teal eyes. "I would love that."

My household was still sound asleep, so we moved quietly into the house. I led Drew to the living room and took his coat, the same one Luci had conjured. "Wait here," I said in a soft voice. "Wine?"

Drew nodded. "Yes, that sounds nice."

I moved through the kitchen quickly, opening the bottle and grabbing two glasses.

When I returned to the living room, Drew took the bottle and poured. "To us," he whispered.

Smiling, I sipped the red wine and waved my hand so a fire sprang up in the fireplace.

"After all we've seen tonight," Drew whispered, "That still amazes me."

I couldn't help feeling smug. I'd been a witch all my life, but even still, I liked showing it off when I could.

Drew leaned forward and captured my lips, and I was suddenly so glad I'd shaved my legs. I hadn't planned on things to get steamy, but to be safe, I'd gone over them. Then lotioned them. Twice.

"Excuse me?" A hesitant voice interrupted us. "Is this a bad time to ask about my murder?"

Oh for the love of the undead!

Drew squawk-yelled, a startled, manly type roar, and before I knew it, he'd pulled his gun and shot.

Where the hell had he been hiding that thing?

The skeleton, Larry, ducked. He moved so fast that his head rolled off his shoulders. *Again.* Oh hell, I wasn't picking that up.

Luckily, Larry's body rushed over and scooped up the skull and put it where it belonged, faster this time than the first. Then he held out his hands, waving them. "Stop shooting!"

I barely heard him through the ringing in my ears from being so close to the gun when it fired.

Still waving his arms, Larry looked with his empty eye sockets down at his ribs. "You nicked me!" His bones clinked together as he patted himself. "I think I'm okay, though," he said, sounding relieved.

"How is he... real?" Drew asked in a shaky voice. Thunderous footsteps on the upper level told me that the gunshot had woken Owen. Great. An audience.

"Uh, well, I'm not totally sure. He says he needs me to help solve his murder." I walked past Larry and peered at the pretty white trim around the door. "You shot my door frame," I muttered.

Turning to find Drew standing close to Larry and studying his face, I had to giggle. "You cops have got to stop shooting undead things in my house. They're par for the course."

Drew still had a tight grip on his gun as if not sure about the skeleton. Then out of nowhere, Snooze leaped for Drew and knocked the gun out of his hand. When the cat landed on his feet in front of the gun, he turned and snarled at Drew, then sat with his butt squarely over the trigger. Like, literally, his butt-hole was touching Drew's gun.

I gaped at my cat. Oh no, I couldn't handle it if Snooze had adopted Larry, too. My house was going to run out of bedrooms soon!

With a sigh of exasperation, I pointed at Larry. "Get upstairs right now. I'm too tired to deal with all this tonight." Turning, I moved my finger from Larry to point at the stairs, where Owen stood in a ratty blue robe, gaping at us. "Take Snooze with you and find Alfred and *stay* there."

Larry hung his head and shuffled past me while motioning to the cat to follow. Then, the two of them went up the stairs like a couple of errant children. I didn't know what Snoozy's deal was, nor did I care at the moment.

After Drew picked his gun up and placed it in the holster inside his jacket, he turned to me with an apologetic look. He was too cute to stay mad at. Then again, I wasn't the type of person to hold a grudge for long.

"You have to fix my trim," I said as I eased closer to him.

He nodded, his lips lifting in a smile. "I will. Next weekend. We'll make a day of it."

I raised a brow. "It's going to take all day to fix the trim?"

"No, but I figured we could go hang out the rest of the day."

He really was sexy. Even though his words were soft, there was a command in them. Sheriff Drew wasn't used to being told no. Who was I to turn down a second date with the sexy cop? "We could do that. I'm not a morning person, so don't come over before ten."

His eyes sparkled like he'd won a prize. "I'll bring brunch and coffee."

"Then it's a date," I said as I wrapped my arms around Drew's neck, smiling. "Where were we before Larry freaked you out?"

Drew chuckled and pressed his lips to mine just as a whizzing sound passed right by my ear, followed by the thud of something hitting the wall.

Jerking back, I looked around and spotted the offending sound. "What now?" I growled and walked over an arrow sticking out of the wall, pinning a note in place.

HAD a wonderful evening with you both. The four of us simply must do this again. Name the place and time.

Smooches,
Luci

I LOOKED UP AT DREW, who had read the note over my shoulder. "I'm going to pretend that the note never made it here. And I'll be needing your help to research how to send the devil back to Hell."

"I'll make a few calls to some old contacts." He circled his arms around my waist and pulled me closer. Then he kissed me, slow and exploring.

Much too soon, he pulled back. "I'll see you next weekend, if not sooner."

He walked to the door, and I hugged my waist so I wouldn't reach out and grab him and drag him up to my room. That would be a mistake. No matter how my body responded to him,

I wasn't ready to take it to the bedroom yet. I opened the door for him. "See you Saturday, or sooner," I said softly.

He gave me one more soft, quick kiss, then exited the house. I watched him get into his SUV and drive off.

Closing the door, I pressed my back against it and sighed.

Happy Valentine's Day.

SNEAK PEEK INTO A NEW SERIES COMING SOON

A bunny bit me on the finger and everything went sideways after that.

That's just the beginning of my insane life. The Fascinators, the local ladies' club, suddenly are incredibly interested in having me join their next Bunco night, which is a thinly veiled excuse to drink and gossip.

I've been dying to get into that group for years; why now? I'm over forty, my daughter is grown, and all I do is temp work. What's so special about me?

After I shift into a dragon, things become clearer. They're not a Bunco group. The Fascinators are a pack of shifters. Yes, shifters. Like werewolves, except in this case it's weresquirrels and a wereskunk, among others.

And my daughter? She wants to move home, suddenly and

suspiciously. As excited as I am to have her home, why? She loves being on her own. It's got something to do with a rough pack of predators, shifters who want to watch the world burn. I hope she's not mixed up with the wrong crowd.

There's also a mysterious mountain man hanging around out of the blue. Where was he before the strange bunny bite? Nowhere near me, that's for sure.

Life is anything but boring. At this point, I'm just hoping that I'll survive it all with my tail—literally—intact.

Preorder your copy today

A CURSED MIDLIFE

WITCHING AFTER FORTY, BOOK 4

CHAPTER ONE

"Coming!" I called.

The persistent knocking on the door roused me from a dead sleep. I'd just settled into the deep bliss of dreamland. And my crazy house didn't help. Every time whoever-was-about-to-get-an-earful-from-me-for-waking-me knocked on the door, the house echoed the sound upstairs, and I would've sworn it was doing it on purpose. Right outside my bedroom door. The last double tap was so loud I jumped out of bed. Literally landing on my buttocks on the hardwood floor, and then I understood why they were called *hard*wood.

Rubbing my behind, I stomped down the stairs, paying back the house for waking me. Whoever it was could have left a message and gone away. I'd call them back, maybe. Eventually.

The last time someone woke me up this persistently, a skeleton stood on the other side of the door.

"Where is everyone?" I mumbled loudly. I'd told Alfred not to answer the door unless he knew who it was, but my son was here for the weekend, and Owen, my friend, roommate, and teacher, was hanging around somewhere. Apparently, neither of them was home.

As long as our new houseguest, the fully defleshed skeleton, Larry, didn't answer, we'd be okay. It was way too fudging early to deal with the aftermath of anyone seeing him.

Alfred stood beside the door, dry-washing his hands. He shrugged at me, his eyes somehow looking worried even though he couldn't move the skin on his face to convey that emotion. "It's okay," I said softly. "Just stand behind the door."

As my ghoul, Alfred had become a beloved member of our family, even if he wouldn't let me take out the strings tying his lips together. His vocal cords definitely worked, because he made grunting noises all the time. I've even caught him mumbling to Snooze once. So he *could* talk. I wasn't sure why he didn't *want* to. But I filed it under one of the many mysteries of life I didn't have time to solve at the moment. There was something about him he wanted to keep hidden. But, hey, who was I to judge? I'd kept my necromancer side hidden for over twenty years.

Sometimes we suppressed part of who we were, and that was okay. So I wasn't about to push him to share his secrets.

Peeking out the peephole, I frowned. Nobody out there. "Probably some town kid playing a prank," I muttered. We had the spooky old house on the hill. Well, spooky with fresh paint and newly renovated insides.

I'd been thinking about doing some major upgrades, but at the last minute decided to restore the old house and keep the historical value of it. Although the value may have been zero since the house was basically alive. It wasn't possessed or anything, it was just... animated. My theory was the house had absorbed so much magic through the centuries that it formed its own spirit along the way.

I opened the door cautiously in case there really was someone out there. Couldn't be too careful after the winter we'd had. Murders and Satanic Christmas parties and all that. It had been chaos. The neighborhood was going to Hell.

Or was that just my new devilish neighbor? Definitely was Luci because I was going to send him there. Hopefully soon.

Casting thoughts of the devil aside, for now, I frowned at the absence of a warm body—or cold body, with my luck— standing on my porch. But instead of being greeted by a person, I stepped back when an envelope fluttered into the house and hung suspended in my entryway.

"Er, okay." The envelope turned toward me when I spoke and froze in midair, leaving the front so I could clearly read my name written in a bold red calligraphy. Ava Calliope Howe Harper. Wow. They'd middle named me. I hadn't been middle named since I was a teenager living here with Yaya and Aunt Winnie.

What the heck was I supposed to do now?

I plucked the envelope from the air as Alfred shut the door behind us. He moved closer as if curious to what it was. That made two of us.

"What've you got?" Owen walked down the stairs smoothing back his long black hair. He looked freshly show- ered, which explained why he hadn't answered the door.

I lifted one brow, at least I thought I did. Usually I ended up moving them in all directions while trying to lift only one. "Where were you? Did you not hear the door?" He was a morning person. I wasn't. This was his time to be adulty.

"I was in the shower." He studied me for a moment. "What's wrong with your eyebrows?"

"Nothing." I waved him off and focused on the envelope, then answered his question. "This floated into the house when I opened the door. I'm hoping it's not cursed." I laughed even though I was being serious.

We all walked into the large kitchen and sat at the table. I spied my son, Wallie, on the porch drinking coffee. We'd opened up the back wall of the kitchen to let in more light. Half of the back of the kitchen led into a large conservatory where we grew herbs and plants mostly for use in spells. The space was big enough, I could put in a small antique wood burning stove and a workstation for me to do my potions and spell casting. The ritual room in the attic was used for bigger magical things. Like accidentally conjuring Satan last Christmas.

Before we'd knocked down the wall, we had to go through the conservatory to reach the back deck, but thanks to a little elbow grease and a lot of magic, big French doors now also led to the porch from the kitchen.

I didn't blame Wallie for having his coffee out there. We'd recently learned how to create heat bubbles around ourselves, something among the *many* things Owen had taught us. Since I'd rejected my necromancer side and strongly suppressed even my elemental magic all my life, I'd had to relearn all the things my mother, aunt, and grandmother had taught me as a child and teen.

Plus, there was a whole world of magic I'd never given them the chance to share with me. One of my biggest regrets now that they were all gone.

"Alfred, will you get Wallie?" I said studying the envelope. A hum of magic flowed from it, telling me another witch had sent it.

Alfie grunted and tapped on the glass in the door, making Wallie jump and turn with wide eyes. Then he laughed when he realized he'd been startled by the house ghoul. I chuckled softly.

Larry and our big, fat, Maine coon cat Snoozle walked in behind Alfred. Mr. Snoozleton, to be precise, but he was called all sorts of things.

"Good morning," Larry said. "I hope you're all well on this lovely winter morn."

Good grief, the skeleton was a morning undead person. I

didn't do morning or morning people, undead or alive. Flesh or no flesh.

I had to force myself not to roll my eyes at the skeleton's turn of phrase. Or the fact that it still creeped me out that he could speak so eloquently without the aid of any *vocal cords.* Or tongue, for that matter.

"The doorbell rang," I explained. "Then someone knocked until I answered, but nobody was there. Just this envelope."

Larry leaned close and his head pulled back as the sound of sniffing filled the air. "Smells like magic," he whispered.

How...? Nope. No, I wasn't going to ask how the skeleton could smell. Nope, not asking. *Just go with the crazy.*

"Hello?" A voice from the front door made me turn my head, but I didn't get up. I knew who it was before she spoke.

"Come in, Olivia!" I yelled. She came over all the time, but I didn't mind. She'd quickly become my best friend and partner in crime, even though we'd been enemies in high school.

Times changed us all. Life changed us. "Get in here," I called. "I got a mysterious letter."

She hurried in the kitchen with her arms full. Of course, she'd cooked. I looked up at her and spied a big pink box. Nope, she brought donuts this time.

Her son, Sammie, scurried in the room, arms held out toward Snoozle. Nice to see how I ranked with the kid. Did he not know I was the closest thing to an aunt he'd ever have?

Snooze hunkered down, but he let Sammie pick him up and hug him. "Hello Mr. Snoozer," Sammie said. "I missed you."

The look Snooze shot me made me snort. There was real panic in his eyes.

"Okay, he loves you, too," Olivia told Sammie. "Put him down."

Alfred grunted and Sammie launched himself into Alfie's arms. "Hey, Alf!" he cried. "I missed you, too."

Alfred grunted a few more times, which Sammie apparently understood, because they ran out of the room and thundered up the stairs as Olivia's husband and my lifetime best friend, Sam, walked in.

"You shouldn't have given Alfred an iPad," Sam said. "Now Sammie wants one. He's been driving us nuts about it."

I blanched and shrugged while hiding my smile. "Sorry, friend. I had to have a way to communicate with Alfred. I don't speak grunts."

"What is that?" Olivia asked, setting the donuts on the table.

"A magical envelope." I smiled at her.

"Will you open that thing already?" Owen asked. "I'm dying to know what it is."

"As am I," Larry said pompously as he sat in one of the kitchen chairs. His pelvic bones clacked against the wood of the chair.

I closed my eyes briefly, hoping no parts fell off him.

Tearing my gaze away from the still-shocking sight of a skeleton at my kitchen table, I ripped the back of the envelope open.

The parchment inside was the thickest I've seen and probably expensive. I unfolded it and read the contents to the room.

Dear Ms. Howe-Harper,

The Shipton Harbor Coven cordially invites Ava Howe-Harper, Wallace Harper, and Owen Daniels to the monthly coven meeting on this Saturday at 8 pm. It will be held at the home of the Coven Master. Repeat the spell on the bottom of this paper when you are ready to travel, and the direction will be made clear to you.

With Respect,

Bevan Magnus

Recruiter

Princeps invenire pythonissam

. . .

"IS THAT THE SPELL?" Olivia whispered. Her eyes were wide and excited as she bent over my shoulder. "Can I go?"

"Yes. It means something along the lines of *Find the High Witch.* And no," I said evenly. "Because I'm not going. These people ostracized Aunt Winnie and Yaya because of my dad. No way."

I crumpled the parchment and tossed it on the table. As soon as it landed, it started opening up from its ball. Within seconds it was smooth as when I pulled it out of the envelope. I pointed and said, "See? Cursed."

Owen stared at it. "It's not cursed."

Yet he eyed it like it was going to attack him. *Ha, not so sure, are we?*

"I thought they invited your mom," Sam said. "But I don't remember the details."

I sighed and looked around the table at my new family. "They invited Mom, but Winnie and Yaya always said it was because they wanted an in with a powerful necromancer. Which never made sense to me since they once hated my dad for that same reason. Back then, I wasn't suppressing my power, and they sensed how strong I would be. When Mom died, Winnie withdrew from the coven, and I began to suppress my powers. Yaya and Winnie wouldn't force me to use them, so the coven sort of shunned them. Yaya stayed in because of, as she said it, keeping her enemies close, but she was basically trolling them."

They'd treated her like crap. We never got invitations to the witch parties, I was never invited to play with the other children of the coven, and once Winnie had pulled away and stopped being social after Mom died, her invitations dried up as well.

"I loved my coven in Nebraska," Owen said. "It was like a

big family. Maybe this one has changed." He raised his eyebrows. "What would it hurt to go see?"

I tapped the parchment that wouldn't die. "Bevan Magnus was one of the ones that could've made us feel welcome after Mom died, and could've tried to get us back in the fold. But no, he did nothing but stick his nose up at us. I'm telling you, they're not good people."

"I'd like to go, too," Wallie said. "I'd like to meet other witches. This Magnus might be a jerk, but they can't all be. And it's hard to meet our kind without the coven network." He grinned. "Michelle took me to meet her coven. It was awesome."

Michelle, his witch girlfriend, had come home with him for Christmas. Some big exam had kept her on campus this past weekend, but she was a sweet girl.

I sighed and stared at Owen and Wallie's hopeful expressions. "Fine," I growled. "We'll go. But mark my words. These witches are bitches."

CHAPTER TWO

With a sigh, I stood and grabbed a donut from the box. Then I pointed to Sam and Wallie. "What are you two doing here on a Tuesday morning, anyway?"

Sam grinned. "I'm off. I came to take Wallie and Sammie ice fishing."

Wallie grinned from ear to ear. "I've been dying to go."

"Aren't you due in class?" I asked.

He shook his head. "My classes on Mondays and Tuesdays are online, and I worked ahead. I'll drive back to campus in the morning."

I walked around the table and grabbed Sam's hair, yanking his head back to pop a rough kiss on his forehead. "Love you." He knew the kiss was a thanks for taking Wallie along.

He beamed up at me. "Love you, too. I'm leaving Olivia with you for the day."

His wife and my newest friend snorted. "I'm a frikkin' delight," she said dryly.

Sam including Wallie in ice fishing with Sammie made me love my best friend all that much more. Sam and I grew up

277

together. His parents owned the house just down the road, and he'd been the closest child to me. We'd never had the first inkling of a romantic feeling for one another. So much so that Olivia, while she'd been somewhat jealous at first of our unique sibling-like relationship, had soon seen that was all it was.

Sam was my brother from another mother... and father.

I refilled my coffee cup and bit into the donut with a moan. "Well, I'm going to the grocery store, then when you master fishermen get back, Livvie and I will have a nice warm stew ready for all three of you. Sound good?"

I looked back at the table to see everyone nodding eagerly, even Larry the skeleton. "Larry, you don't eat," I reminded him.

"I can pretend," he said, staring at me with sightless eye sockets. "Pretending is almost as good."

Alrighty then. Not for the first time, I found myself wishing I'd raised him when he was... more a person and less a skeleton, like Alfred.

But I was pretty sure the circumstances around Alfie's death had somewhat mummified him, rather than leading to his decomposition. He looked like he fell straight out of a movie about ancient Egypt, without the white wrappings.

Then again, I didn't know anything about Alfred's death or his raising since the necromancer who animated him was dead. Only Alfred knew and he wasn't talking. Literally.

Larry had been buried out in the woods, straight in the dirt. He'd decomposed quickly and easily. We still had to get his whole story, but I'd been waiting until Drew or Sam could be around to get the full statement. They'd have to be creative in their reporting, but they could still officially investigate the death.

"Larry, we'll talk about your death tonight over dinner, okay?" I asked. "Sam will be here."

The skeleton nodded once. "Thank you."

He'd turned up Sunday, on Valentine's Day, just before my

first date with the only man I'd been attracted to in the five years since my husband, and Wallie's father, died.

No way I was able to deal with a walking, talking skeleton then, so I'd allowed him to stay with us until we could figure out how to help him. Hey, what was one more undead under the roof? I was starting a collection.

Tonight, we'd get his full story and see what we could do to get him back in the ground and at peace.

"Well, we better get going," Sam said.

Wallie jumped up and nodded eagerly. "Back later, Mom. We'll have fresh fish for dinner!"

My heart swelled at the excitement in Wallie. Both of us had been just moving through the motions of everyday life. Who knew moving back to my hometown and relearning my powers would help us live again? There was the murder of a family friend, William Combs, whom I inherited Alfred from, then I accidently summoned Lucifer a few days before Christmas, who pretended to be Santa at the party and moved in next door. Life had been one crazy right after another.

Waving at the guys, I didn't say anything about the stew. I'd have it ready in case they didn't catch anything. And if they did, well, they'd be cleaning it, and I'd fry it up. I'd cook it, but no way I was pulling out all the guts and stuff. No, thanks.

I shuddered at the thought.

"Come on, Olivia," I said, wiping the donut film off my hands with the kitchen towel. "Let's hit the store."

She poured our coffees into two of my travel mugs, then handed me one. "Gimme your keys." She grinned. "I'll drive while you tell me about your date."

I pulled on my jacket and gave her a confused look. "I already told you."

"Yes," she said with a gleam in her eyes. "But I want to hear it again."

"I'll stay here," Owen called. "Don't worry about me."

We waved as we walked out the front door. "Okay!"

Once we pulled out of the driveway, I tried to think of a way to tell the story differently. "I should have known the date was going to be derailed when we almost hit a ferret and the little shit flipped us the bird."

Olivia burst out laughing. "Are you serious?"

"As much as I am about sending Luci back to Hell."

She nodded, knowing that was serious business. "How could a ferret flip you the bird?"

"My guess is it was a shifter. But he looked rough and wild. I don't know anything about shifters or any other paranormal beings except witches and necromancers. And I even avoided them for most of my life." I looked out the window, knowing that was a mistake. Now that I was open to learning and controlling the growing magic inside me, I wished I had done it years ago.

Clay hadn't cared that I was a necromancer. It was his family who had looked down at me, and they didn't even realize I was more than a little *off* as his mother said once upon a time.

So, to keep the peace, I always kept my powers suppressed. I loved my husband and would've done anything to keep him happy. He'd felt the same way and had done everything in his power to make me and Wallie happy.

Shaking out of thoughts of my deceased husband, I went back to my recap of the big Valentine's Date with Sheriff Drew. "The restaurant was great; the food was great. We were alone in a public place, perfect for a first date. Then Luci showed with Carrie."

Olivia giggled. "Then everything got derailed."

"Yep. With a snap of Luci's fingers we were in Paris, Tennessee. Then he snapped again, and we were in France." I laughed telling her how Lucifer twisted the history of the museum pieces at the Louvre and Carrie had corrected him each time.

We parked in the little grocery store's parking lot, and Olivia swooned. "That's amazing. Next time Lucifer decides to take you to France, stop in and get us! I could've dropped Sammie at Sam's parents' house."

I snorted. "It went so fast I didn't even think. I just tried to stay ahead of the whirlwind."

She sighed as we pulled out a buggy. "I can't believe sweet little Carrie."

"I know." I giggled. "She's got a hidden wildcat, I swear."

"She's not the only one."

Olivia and I jumped and whirled to find Sheriff Andrew Walker standing behind us in uniform. I let my eyes roam over him, drinking in his broad shoulders, thick muscled arms and trim waist. His uniform fit him a little snug and left nothing to the imagination. In short, the man was hot. Also, he was the object of our conversation and had been my date on Valentine's Day.

In times like this moment, I forgot why I wanted to take things slow with him. Then I started overthinking and came back to reality. I still didn't know much about the sheriff.

"Hey, Drew," I whispered, meeting his teal eyes.

His dimple deepened as his smile did. "Hey, Ava."

A shudder went through me at the sound of his husky tone, and my insides melted.

"Well," Olivia said loudly. "I'm going to go pick out a big roast. We'd love to have you join us at Ava's for dinner, Drew," she said pointedly with a big smile plastered on her face.

"Be a little more obvious," I hissed, then turned back to Drew. "Yes, we would."

He ducked his head but waited until Olivia scurried away with the shopping cart before he replied. "I'd love to come for dinner," Drew said in a low voice. "But only if you're sure it'll be at your house. Our date Saturday was literally magical, and I had a wonderful time. And don't get me wrong, I don't regret going, but..." He looked around surreptitiously. "I threw up all day Sunday."

Gaping at him, I put my hand on his arm. "Oh, no. Are you okay?"

He nodded. "Yeah, I think so. It felt just like when I get motion sickness on a boat."

I poked out my bottom lip at the news he was sick, while inside I smiled a little. He'd shared something that most men wouldn't admit to. Now I knew he got motion sickness. That little peek into the mysterious Sheriff Drew made me want to know more.

"I did wonder why I hadn't heard from you," I murmured. "I'm sorry it was for such a bad reason."

He shrugged. "It was worth it. But maybe next time we just say no."

I snorted. "I'm not sure I know how to say no to Luci. But I'm going to be putting some effort in figuring out how to send him home, that's for sure."

Luci had been the unfortunate mishap of trying to summon Santa for a Christmas party. Instead of Santa, I'd gotten Satan.

Whoops.

But now I had to figure out how to send him back, because he kept causing all kinds of chaos and had *no* desire to go back to his Kingdom.

"Would you like to go out again?" Drew asked. "Hopefully just the two of us this time."

I'd had a really good time with him, after all. "Sure," I said softly. "Dinner and bowling?" I asked, to take the stress off of him having to plan.

He grinned. "It's a plan. But I have to warn you. I'm going to kick your ass at bowling."

I snorted. "You only think so, Walker. I'm the bowling champion of Philadelphia, Pennsylvania."

We'd made it around the produce section by now and were fairly close to the meat department.

He turned and took my hand, then looked deep in my eyes. "If you use magic to win, I'll lock you up."

I laughed so loud Olivia jumped and whirled around, knocking against the big meat case she'd been peering into. Ignoring my new best friend, I fingered a button on Drew's shirt and batted my lashes at him. "Darling, I don't need magic to outbowl you."

He took my hand and moved closer until our bodies almost touched. My blood boiled and my legs began to shake. Not to mention my girly parts were chanting a victory song. He kissed my palm and flashed me a dimple-filled smile. "We'll see."

Then he left.

Damn, that man was hot.

"Oh geez, you have it bad." Olivia sneaked up behind me and sighed.

I waved her off as I moved back to the produce to get potatoes and carrots for the stew. "I have no idea what you're talking about."

I didn't have it bad. I had urges and some of them were a little wicked leaning on the naughty side. *Okay, so maybe I did have it bad.*

CHAPTER THREE

Olivia had the carrots chopped, and I'd just thrown the meat cubes into the big stockpot when the front door opened.

"Hello?" Wallie called from the foyer. "We come bearing fishes!"

When he walked in the kitchen, followed by Sammie and Sam, he held up a string of the saddest, smallest fish I'd ever seen.

I arched an eyebrow and looked at Sam, who shrugged. "It wasn't a biting day."

With a snort, I pointed to the back porch. "Owen, will you show Wallie how to clean them with magic?" He nodded and rose from the table where he'd been reading an ancient-looking book.

I waved my hand and focused on the water Wallie had let drip from the little fishtails and it disappeared without a sound. Moving to the hall that led out to the front door, I did the same there.

Sam crossed to the sink and washed his hands while Sammie followed Wallie to the back porch.

Thirty minutes later, we had fish frying merrily in the skillet while the stew bubbled and cooked. It would take a while for the beef to be done, so the fish would make a nice appetizer while we waited. They weren't big enough for much else.

But my boy was proud of those little fish, and I was happy that he had a great time.

"Excuse me," Larry said as he wandered into the room. "Would now be a good time to talk about my murder?"

I sighed and sat at the table. "Yes, but the sheriff is on his way to eat with us. Let's wait until he gets here." No sense in going through it all twice.

The doorbell rang just seconds later. Alfred grunted and shuffled out of the room, followed closely by Sammie and Snooze.

My stomach clenched with nerves, even though I'd just seen Drew a few hours before at the store. "Do I look okay?" I whispered as I flipped the fish.

Olivia fluffed my hair. "You look great," she said, then raised her voice. "Hey, Drew. Come on in."

She acted like my house was hers, but that was how she was. A natural-born hostess. I didn't mind. Olivia and I were growing closer the more time we spent together.

"Great," Larry said. "Thanks for coming."

Drew jumped a little and his hand flew to his side where his gun was probably hiding under his jacket. "Oh, hey, Larry," he said. He'd met the skeleton after our date Sunday night.

And had shot him.

Larry gave Drew a dark look. "Hey," he muttered.

How had I known Larry had given Drew a dark look? Larry didn't have any skin! It was like a feeling I had that was most likely tied to my necromancer powers.

I was going to have to stop questioning this stuff. It just was what it was.

"So, everyone here? Can we do this?" Larry was starting to get a little testy.

"Yes," I said. I could listen just fine as I cooked. "Go ahead."

But Alfred shuffled over and took the spatula from my hands and grunted, giving me a little push toward the table.

"Thanks, Alfie," I said. I didn't like automatically expecting him to cook or clean for me, but that seemed to be what he preferred to do.

I joined my friends at the table as Wallie came back downstairs. He'd gone up to shower and change after cleaning the fish. "Sammie is playing with Snooze and Alfred's iPad."

"Tell us what happened," I told Larry. "As best you remember it."

"Well, it was in the eighties. Eighty-nine." Larry clacked his fingers on the table.

The year after my mother died, I realized. She'd died in eighty-eight. Sam, who remembered it vividly, glanced at me out of the corner of his eye. I nodded once to acknowledge that we were both thinking the same thing.

"And were you a human or a witch?" Drew asked. He'd pulled out a little notebook.

"Witch," Larry replied. "Elemental. Air."

Drew's pencil scratched on the paper. "And how did you die?"

"I was sucked into a patch of quicksand," Larry said matter of factly.

"Where?" I asked. Maybe he'd been killed elsewhere and moved here.

"About a mile away, I'm guessing. It was hard to tell how far I walked to get here." He shrugged one bony shoulder. "I can show you."

"Um, Larry?" Sam said. "There's no quicksand in Maine."

He nodded. "Exactly. I believe I was murdered by a witch."

"If you really sank in quicksand, it would've had to have been magical," Olivia said. "You can't actually *sink* in quicksand. The density isn't right. You'd go to your waist, maybe."

The skeleton spread his hands, palm up, as if to say, *see?*

"What was going on in your life at that time?" Drew asked.

"Well, I'd just joined the local coven. The same one you're going to go to a meeting with." He nodded toward me.

Drew looked at me with one eyebrow up, but I just shrugged. "Hey, I didn't want to go."

"Everything seemed perfect. But then I was walking in the woods, in the summer. I can't remember the month now. But I stumbled across someone deep in the trees. He was slitting the throat of a deer. It really freaked me out, because I felt the magic in the air, and the sense of perversion. He was doing some intensely dark blood magic. I took off running, and the next thing I knew, I sank."

"What's the other side like?" Sam looked awestruck and his voice came out a whisper.

Larry sighed. "I don't remember. The last thing I remember is sinking. And then waking up and being pulled to Ava. Owen told me how long it's been."

Owen nodded. "Yes, Larry told me his story on Valentine's night while you two were off in Paris."

I couldn't stop the flush rising up my cheeks. "Is there anything else you remember about your death?" I asked, drawing the conversation back around to the skeleton and not my date.

"He slipped a coin in my pocket," he said. "At least, I think it was a coin. I was running, and he almost caught me. I kept running, but he stuffed something in my pocket. I figured I'd see what it was later, and it didn't occur to me it was causing

288

me to sink. But in retrospect, I think it could've been a cursed coin. I remember a flash of silver."

"For it to be a cursed coin, it would've had to have been silver. Modern coins don't have enough precious metals in them to contain a curse. Nickel, zinc, copper, those metals won't hold a curse. It takes gold, platinum, but the most common is silver," Owen said.

I nodded in agreement. I'd actually known that, some left-over knowledge from my witch studies as a child.

"Actually, there are a number of coins made up until 1964 that are ninety percent silver," Olivia said.

"How do you know this random stuff?" Owen asked.

Sam patted Olivia's hand. "This woman is a trivia queen. Always try to be on her team in a trivia contest."

She blushed and nudged him with her shoulder.

I sighed and sat back in my chair. "Did you see the witch?" I asked.

Larry shook his head. "No, he wore a hood."

"So, it could've been a woman?" Sam asked.

"I suppose." Larry looked off in the distance as if thinking. "But the presence felt masculine. I don't know how to describe it." He blinked rapidly.

Wait. He couldn't have blinked! He didn't have eyes! Ugh, damn necromancer powers were making me crazy. Or I was just going insane.

"Your cat is chasing an animal in the backyard," Larry said and pointed out the door.

Alfred grunted and walked toward the door. At some point, he'd put on an apron that said *Kiss the Cook*. That silly ghoul.

A brief memory from my childhood flashed in my mind. It was of my dad cooking with a similar apron. Frowning, I shook off the memory as Alfred grunted again and opened the back door, scurrying out with a big wooden spoon in his hand.

Leaving the back door standing open, he hurried out into

the yard. I scraped my chair back and followed quickly to see what in the world Snooze had gotten into. There was no telling with that crazy fat cat.

I stood on the patio, surrounded by Drew, Sam, Wallie, and Olivia. Larry and Owen stepped down the porch steps.

"Is that a ferret?" Olivia asked.

Alfred stood by and waited for the mystery animal and Snooze to streak by, then at just the right moment he reached out and thwacked Snooze on the rump with his wooden spoon.

Snoozle stopped short and turned around toward Alfred with a yowl that sounded suspiciously like he was saying, "Ow!"

Alfred put both hands on his hips, glaring at the cat. Then he pointed to the back door with a stiff arm.

"What kind of relationship do these two have?" Olivia whispered.

Snooze hunched down and stalked toward the house. He stopped at the stairs and turned to growl at Alfred.

Alfred stopped walking and put his hands on his hips again. He grunted once, and Snoozle walked past us and into the house.

Alfred waited for us to all follow Snooze back into the kitchen.

With a loud click, Alfred closed the front door and locked it. He nodded once at the lot of us, still close to the door with our heads turned toward the cat, staring at the spectacle, then went back to the stove to finish dinner.

"Ohh-kay. Anybody hungry?" I asked.

CHAPTER FOUR

S am's work phone squawked halfway through dinner. I internally groaned at the interruption. If Sam left, there was a good chance Drew would too.

Before we started eating, Alfred had urged Larry to go upstairs with him to do who knew what dead things did. I shuddered to think.

Honestly, they were probably just playing with furious birds on the tablet. Of course, Larry had to use a stylus. No skin.

I bit into the fish, which was surprisingly tender and flaky, as Sam answered. "This is Thompson."

I couldn't hear whatever came over the line, but Sam's face darkened. That wasn't good. "Yeah, the sheriff is here with me."

Sam covered the mouthpiece. "We gotta go."

Drew's forehead creased and he pursed his lips.

"Okay, text me the address." He paused. "Oh, I know where that is." Another long pause. "Seriously? Okay, we're on our way."

"What is it?" Drew asked, scooting out his chair. "Why didn't they call me?"

Sam jumped up and shoveled several more bites in his mouth. "Said they did. Old Miss Miriam was killed at her shop," he mumbled around a potato.

Drew pulled out his phone. "Shit. It's on silent."

Larry and Alfred peeked down from the top of the stairs as we followed Sam and Drew to the door. "Sam, your uniform," Olivia said. Drew was still in his.

He shrugged. "It's okay. I can work a case in plain clothes. It's better that we get there fast."

As she pressed a kiss to Sam's cheek, I considered doing the same to Drew, but that felt *way* too intimate after we'd only had one date... And whatever dinner tonight could be considered. Not a date.

Even though we've kissed before, a couple of times, I didn't think we were at the point of the quick goodbye kisses.

"Should..." I looked around at my friends. "Maybe we should come."

Sam furrowed his brow. "Wasn't old Miss Miriam a friend of your Yaya's?"

I nodded. "Yeah. Which means she might be a witch."

Drew shook his head. "I don't think it's a good idea."

He and Sam exchanged a long look. "Maybe once we've assessed the situation, we'll have you come to the morgue, look for one of those witch's marks," Sam said.

I nodded. "Okay. Call us if you need us."

Drew glanced back, looking like he was considering the same kiss I had. He dipped his head and touched my hand briefly. "Good night."

Okay. Definitely too soon for the *have a good day at work, sweetie* kiss.

I watched them, Drew specifically, rush to Drew's patrol car as I slowly closed the door. Olivia tugged at my arm. When

I glanced at her she giggled, which made me roll my eyes. I did not have it bad for the sheriff.

I had something, but it wasn't bad.

As a group, we shuffled back to the kitchen, with Alfred and Larry joining us. "Remind them to look for a coin," Larry said.

"Oh, good idea." Olivia pulled out her phone and sent a text to Sam.

When we entered the kitchen, I gasped and threw up my hands, ready to shoot a beam of... Hell, I didn't even know what I would've shot. It was instinct and my magic was ready to blast the intruder on my command.

Well, that was new. Maybe opening my senses to my power made it easier to access. Of course it did. That meant I had to be careful and not be so impulsive. I didn't want to blow up my house or anyone.

I stared as Luci stood at the stove, dishing himself up a bowl of stew as Sammie kicked his legs at the table, eating and wearing most of his dinner. "This smells amazing," Luci said. "Sammie here tells me he caught this delectable fish. Good man, Sammie-boy."

Olivia rushed to sit beside her son. Her face was as white as, well, a ghost, which was one damn dead thing I'd yet to deal with—and had no desire to.

It was one thing for me to go on a date and end up double dating with Luci and Carrie. It was another thing to walk into the kitchen and find little Sammie happily eating with the devil himself.

"What are you doing here?" I scowled at him, crossing my arms.

He turned and winked at me. "I hear you've got a corpse problem." Pausing with the ladle in one hand, he gaped at Larry. "Larry Parks? I wondered where you'd got off to."

Larry froze. "You know me?"

Luci nodded. "Of course! There's not many souls that escape Hell."

We all slowly turned to stare at Luci. "Larry was in Hell?"

"I mean, he was a witch. What do you think happens?" Luci shrugged and looked at all of us. "But don't worry. It's not all as bad as it's cracked up to be. I mean, sure, we torture evil souls for eternity, that much is right. But not everyone that comes to my domain is evil."

He walked to the table with his bowl of stew. "Even Hell needs bureaucrats."

"How'd you recognize me?" Larry asked.

"I never forget a face," Luci said. I wasn't touching that comment. "How are you? What are you doing here?"

Never forget a face. I studied the skeleton for a long moment, trying to find the face Lucifer mentioned. Nope, just a skull.

Larry glanced at me. Like turned his eyeless, fleshless face toward me. Then he directed his attention back to Luci. "Man, do you know who murdered me?"

Luci sighed and sat down while the rest of us stood in a huddle and gaped at him. All but Olivia, who had her arm around Sammie, glaring. "I'm sorry, Larry, I don't. I'm not privy to most things that happen up here. Unless Larry knew and told me himself, I wouldn't have that 411. Or maybe when his murderer dies, I'll find out then. But in the meantime? Zip. That's why this time here with you all is so fun." He grinned and took a big bite. "Oh, heaven. Absolute heaven. Nothing like a good winter stew." He seemed to realize for the first time we weren't all terribly comfortable with him there. "What?" he asked. "Sit. Eat."

I would figure out a way to get this—erm, man?—back to Hell. In the meantime, I surely didn't want to piss him off.

"Thank you," I said. "Alfred and I made it."

Luci narrowed his eyes at Alfred, and to my shock, Alfred

was glaring right back. "I'm afraid I don't know your Alfred. Either he looked different from his persona in my realm, or he'd been in Heaven before he was resurrected." Luci shrugged. "Either way, I get the feeling he's not a big fan."

"Alfred is just ornery," I said. "That's all. He means no offense, do you Alfie?"

Shaking his head and looking away, Alfred shuffled over to the stove and began rinsing out dishes, preparing them for the dishwasher.

"What was all the kerfuffle about?" Luci asked. "Where'd the handsome Sheriff and Deputy go?"

"There was a death in town," I said as I tried to relax and act normal. I didn't think he meant us any harm, but he was volatile and unpredictable at best.

"Oh?" Luci's eyes flashed and he leaned forward conspiratorially. "I thought I heard something about you wanting to go. Is that true?"

Nosey much? I nodded. "We'd like to know if this murder relates to Larry's." Or my mother's, but we had no proof that her death was the fault of anything but a freak lightning storm. But two murders so close to each other over thirty years ago raised a buttload of suspicion inside me. Especially when the two who died were witches.

Then it dawned on me that Larry might have known Aunt Winnie.

Luci tapped his nose. "I've just the thing. Come here."

Larry, Alfred, and Sammie jumped up as the rest of us did, but Luci winked at them. "Alfie, be a good man and take the children out to play, would you?"

Snoozle growled from the corner. I hadn't even realized he was in the room. "Shoo," I said.

"Cute cat," Luci drolled. "Okay, now if I can draw everyone's attention to the pot of soup."

"Stew," I muttered, then glanced up to see Luci arching an

eyebrow at me. "Sorry," I whispered.

He winked at me again and waved his hand over the pot. I leaned in closer and Olivia did the same on the other side of Luci. We watched as the dark liquid began to swirl as if it was being stirred by an invisible spoon.

The stew stirred faster until an image formed in the center of the whirlpool in the pot. I'd seen Yaya and Winnie do this type of scrying before. I've even attempted it a few times but never mastered it. Maybe since I was all open to my full powers, I could.

Focusing on the image in the stew, I scrunched up my nose and tilted my head to the side. "Is she wrapped in yarn?"

Luci nodded. "It appears her auto-knitting machine went on the fritz and trapped her in a skein of yarn."

"That's crazy," I said in disbelief.

"A freak accident," Olivia added.

Larry leaned over my shoulder, resting his skull on it. I tried not to jerk away from him. I didn't want his head falling into the stew pot. "Magical accident."

Luci eyed the scene with a raised brow. "I'd have to agree with Larry. But what a way to go. Death by a yarn cocoon."

"Lucifer! That's not funny." I pushed him, but the demon didn't move. He just laughed.

Poor Miss Miriam.

Just then Drew and Sam came into view. Drew directed another officer to cut her out of the yarn.

We watched in fascination as she was cut out. Sam put on a latex glove, knelt down, and searched her pockets. After reaching in the second pocket of her long coat, he pulled out a coin.

The coin was nothing like I'd seen before. It was silver and looked to be as big as a silver dollar. Then again it was hard to tell from a vision in a pot of stew. It had a bird that was surrounded by flames.

"That's it!" Larry jumped with excitement. "That's the coin the witch put in my pocket."

CHAPTER FIVE

"Not like that!" Owen called. "You've got to *mean* it. If anything is buried nearby, you'll raise it."

I sighed and sat back down. We'd been at it for hours, practicing while everyone else was busy with their lives. Wallie was back at college, Olivia was doing her turn as room mother for Sammie's kindergarten class, and Sam and Drew were working the murder case. Not that there'd been any leads. A big crock of nothing. I would've much rather worked the murder case with them, but I really did need to learn to work my powers more effectively.

Snooze was on his back all stretched out in a patch of sunlight. Snoozing, of all things. Did I tell you that's how he got his name? That lazy cat was a master of naptime.

Larry and Alfred had opted to stay back at the house. Wallie had left some game system for them, something he said he never played anymore, and they were hooked. They'd been in my living room all week learning how to use the controls.

Owen's words brought me back to what I was supposed to

be paying attention to. "Focus on just this clearing. I sense several small critters that have died and been interred to the ground within the clearing. You should be able to find them and raise them, even if it's for a brief time."

"I'll end up with another skeleton in my guest room," I grumbled. At this rate, I was going to run out of rooms soon. But then I sucked in a deep breath and tried again. I'd never get better at this or be able to use it for good if I didn't practice. I was supposed to be super powerful, but I couldn't even sense all the bodies that Owen could.

Closing my eyes, I cleared out all my thoughts and imagined I was in a pitch-black room of nothingness. Thoughts of Drew tried to enter my dark space, but I pushed him out. Not the time to think about the sexy sheriff. I had dead things to find.

Once I chased Sheriff Hottie out of my head, I got down to business. A calm washed over me as I stretched out my senses. The ground under me warmed and an energy drifted up and circled me. The low pulse of earth magic reached out to me. I opened to it, and let it direct me to what I was searching for.

The half of me that was witch was elemental. But all witches used nature and the earth to draw power from. I used that natural energy to search for the dead animals buried in the small clearing.

Finally, I felt one. A few feet to my left, something small rested there, and recently dead. I turned to find it, but the ground looked undisturbed. Odd. A body that fresh should've had some sort of sign. The freshly dug dirt or something. An animal dying of natural causes in the woods should've been just laying on the ground, come to think of it. Not buried.

Focusing on the small animal, I breathed deeply and pushed my magic into it.

Without warning, Snooze sat up and yowled at me, making

me start and breaking my concentration. At almost the same time, dirt exploded from the ground and an animal streaked across the clearing, straight for me.

I screeched and held up my hands, reacting without thinking, blasting the little guy with whatever magic chose to come out of me.

The animal flew to the side and Snooze pounced, growling, tail swinging wildly.

Seconds later, the small animal, which I was pretty sure was another ferret—what the heck was going on with ferrets lately?—morphed into a naked, dead young man.

Mr. Snoozerton, the big, strong kitty cat, who had been so vicious moments before with the little ferret, squealed like a stuck pig and streaked off in the direction of the house, yowling at the top of his voice.

"Coward," I whispered.

"What the shit?" Owen gasped. We both scrambled to our feet as the boy rolled over.

Owen yanked off his jacket and threw it over the teen to give him some modesty. "Who are you?" I asked.

He opened his eyes and they were filmy and cloudy. "Who's there?" he whispered.

"My name is Ava," I said. "I was trying to raise an animal, but I didn't know you were a shifter."

The teen struggled to sit up. Owen put his arm around the boy, and I grabbed his hand. "What happened to you, son?"

When I got close, the smell hit me. Necromancy was not a glamorous branch of witchcraft. Not by a longshot. This poor kid smelled like he'd been dead a while. Looked it, too. His skin was mottled and rotting away in some places. "What happened?" I asked.

"I was killed in a shifter fighting ring," he whispered. "But I don't know where it was. I was forced to shift with magic and put in a dark box until it was time to fight. I think I was used as bait." He looked around, but I had no idea how much he could actually see with his milky eyes.

Then again, Larry saw fine with *no* eyes, so who knew?

My stomach twisted while anger made my blood run hot as I processed the boy's words. A shifter fighting ring? Of all the horrible news! "Sweetie, did you recognize anyone? Or hear any names?"

The boy closed his eyes and let his head relax against Owen's chest. "No," he whispered. "They were really careful, and I wasn't there all that long."

He continued trying to look around. "Can you take me back to my parents?"

"Of course, sweetie." I put my hand on his arm. "What's your name and your parents' names?"

He blinked rapidly. "I'm Ricky Johnson, and my mom is Dana and my daddy is also Ricky."

Owen gave me a significant look. "Let him go," he said. "Release the magic animating him."

Focusing on the boy's mottled forehead, I imagined cutting the magic source from him.

It worked. He slumped in Owen's arms, then as quickly as he'd shifted into a person, he shifted back to a ferret. "Why did he shift back?" I asked.

"Shifters die in whatever form they're in. His body is at peace as a ferret, and his soul is at peace. I don't know if you could feel it, but he didn't want to be here."

I nodded rapidly. "I did feel that!" There had been a resistance I never got from the ghoul or skeleton currently in my home. Or Snoozer. "Is that why Larry and Alfred are so difficult to let go?"

Owen nodded as he wrapped the little furry body in his jacket. "They cling to life. Those at peace fight it."

That made sense, at least. And it meant I'd know, if ever I

tried to bring someone back, if they had found paradise. That might be why I hadn't been able to heal or bring back my mom when she died.

I gathered the little guy up, already in Owen's jacket. "Let's get him to his parents."

∾

A SIMPLE INTERNET search gave us the info we needed. Rick and Dana lived two towns over, about a forty-five-minute drive. I grabbed a small box and wrapped little Ricky up in my prettiest kitchen towel, then filled Alfie and Larry in on where we were headed. This boy's parents deserved to have their son back.

We pulled up to the address an hour later, after stopping along the way for a pee break. Neither Owen or I were any sort of spring chicken, and a bathroom pit stop had been required.

Sucking in a deep breath, I climbed the steps of the small, rundown bungalow, and rapped on the screen door with my knuckles.

A small woman with wide hips and curly dark hair answered. "Yes?" she asked guardedly. "Can I help you?"

"Ma'am, my name is Ava, and this is my friend, Owen. Are you Dana Johnson?" My heart ached for this poor woman and what I was going to have to tell her shortly.

She nodded with a stricken look on her face. She knew what I was going to be telling her. A mother always knows.

"Is your husband home?" I asked.

She nodded. "Yes. What's this about?"

"I'm sorry, ma'am, but we have news about your son, Ricky." I pursed my lips. "Can we come in?"

Tears filled Ms. Johnson's eyes as she unlocked the screen door. "Yes, come in."

"Rick!" she yelled. "Get in here!"

Rick walked in, tall and lanky, reminiscent of the boy who had died in Owen's arms. Re-died. Ugh.

Damn. I didn't want to do this. I should have called Sam to do it while I hung out with the scaredy-cat, Snooze. Sam was a cop, surely he had experience with telling loved ones bad news.

"Please, sit," Ms. Johnson said. "I'm sorry, your names again?"

"Mr. Johnson," I nodded at the man as he put his arm around his wife and introduced Owen and myself again. "We're here about your son."

I leaned forward and put the shoebox on the coffee table. A sob caught in Ms. Johnson's throat. "What is that?"

"Ma'am, I'm a necromancer," I whispered. I cringed because I hadn't said that out loud to strangers before. "I was out in the woods near to my home in Shipton Harbor this morning, practicing my craft. I raised a small animal, and when he came above ground, he shifted into your son."

Dana sucked in a breath and covered her mouth with her hands. Tears filled her eyes. Rick stared at the box for a long time before he finally picked it up. His hands shook as he took off the lid.

Sobs came from Dana and she reached inside to touch little Ricky. "He's so cold. Rick, he's cold."

Mr. Johnson curled an arm around his wife and held her to him. "I know baby. But he's home now."

The couple held each other with their son in a box in their lap. It was all I could do to keep my own waterworks from breaking the dam holding them back.

When they'd calmed down, they clutched the box between them and glared at Owen and me. The father asked, "What did he say?"

"He said that he'd died as the result of being..." I sucked in my breath and searched myself for strength. "He was a bait animal in a shifter fighting ring."

This so sucked. I hated every part of it. My heart ached for the couple. But what else could I do? They had to know.

Dana cried harder while Rick worked his jaw. His anger was outweighing his sorrow. I wasn't sure if that was good or not. I would've been angry in his place, for sure. Hell, little Ricky wasn't my kid, and I was angry.

"If you want us to take this to the police," I said. "I can call in the sheriff of Shipton Harbor. He knows about the supernatural world."

They shook their heads quickly and vehemently. "No. We'll handle this among the pack. Shifters..." Rick squeezed his wife. "We're private. We don't generally like interference from humans."

Owen nodded. "I figured as much. That's why we didn't do it to begin with."

"Is there anything we can do?" I was growing a little antsy, wanting to call Wallie, and tell him I loved him. Plus, I didn't want to start crying in front of these poor people. "I can help with any funeral costs."

If I didn't have the money, Olivia and I could start a fundraiser for the family.

The couple stood. They shook their heads but didn't refuse or accept any funeral help. I'd check on them in a few days and offer again. Owen and I stood as well, then Dana rushed at me and hugged me. "Thank you for bringing my baby home."

"It was the least I could do. I have a son. I can't imagine..." I let the statement drift off. When Dana released me, I conjured my notepad and pen from the phone table in my hallway at home. After writing my name and number down, I tore off the page and handed it to Dana. "If there is anything you need, just call. I'm usually up late and sleep in, but Owen is an early bird."

"Thank you," Dana said, walking us to the door.

I handed the keys to Owen and climbed into the passenger

seat. First, on the drive home, I called my son and thanked him for not being a shifter and for still being alive. He was confused but played along, promising he had no plans on dying.

After I hung up, I cried the rest of the way home.

CHAPTER SIX

E ven though we said we wouldn't, I ended up filling Drew in on what had happened with poor little Ricky. In my defense, the sheriff called me not long after Owen and I got home and my emotions were still raw. By that time fury at what the boy must have gone through had mixed with my sorrow for his parents.

I tried to play it off as allergies and a scratchy throat, but no, Drew was too intuitive to fall for my lies. He came over and I spilled everything. Even a few more tears. He knew how shifters were and promised to keep the information unofficial, even though I knew he'd be investigating the best he could off the records.

And so would I.

The shifters would be trying to track this fighting ring and deal with it their own way if they found them before we did.

I didn't really care who found Ricky's murderers, as long as they were found and punished.

But I had to put that in the back of my mind, because Owen, Wallie, and I were ready to go to the Coven meeting. I hadn't been able to talk them out of it. That meant I had to go. Double ugh.

Wallie had driven home as soon as he finished his afternoon class last night. I pulled the mom card and told him he didn't need to be driving back and forth so much. It was a four-hour drive one way. A lot could happen.

He'd just stared at me with a raised brow, reminding me so much of his father.

So here we were, standing in my living room ready to go face the witches.

"*Princeps invenire pythonissam.*"

We waited for the spell to reveal the who and where and nothing happened. "Well, we must have been uninvited." I started to walk off but Wallie grabbed my hand.

"We can try it in the car. Maybe it'll work when it knows you are making an effort."

I huffed. "I *am* making an effort." To not go. Didn't say that last part though...

Owen and Wallie didn't buy it. They stared until I gave in.

"Okay." I rolled my eyes and stomped out of the door and to my car. You know, for effect.

Once in the car and the engine started, I repeated the spell. Owen drove, I navigated. "Let's do this."

And my too-smart-for-his-own-good son was right. Darn it. The spell worked.

"Mom," Wallie said as we drove down a long stretch of road by the coast. "What are we doing about our house in Philly?"

I sighed and turned in my seat to face my son. "That is a conversation we need to have. It's the home you grew up in, yet it isn't *my* home. Not really, and not anymore." As hard as it would be to say goodbye to the house I'd lived in with my Clay, I knew my place was in Shipton Harbor. I wasn't meant to live in Pennsylvania anymore. "Do you want to move back there after college?" I asked.

Wallie shook his head. "No. I know I should, since it's technically my hometown. But I want to come to Shipton. I feel like I belong here as much as you do."

I smiled and reached back to pat his leg. "Then we'll sell the house. We should get a nice bit of profit for what we've already paid off on the loan. We'll put that aside and you can use it for starting out in life. I think your father would love knowing he helped you get your start with the home he worked hard to pay for."

Wallie nodded and squeezed my hand. "Thanks, Mom."

I hummed, thinking how nice it would be to have Wallie so close all the time. "We have plenty of land. You could build a house and not even be all that close to me." On one side, our property ended near Lucifer's brand new house.

But on the other side and back to the ocean, we had about ten acres. Most of it was woods or wild, untouched by any development. It would make for a gorgeous, secluded spot for Wallie's home.

Suddenly, the spell telling me where to go shifted direction. "Turn!" I squawked.

Owen slammed on the brakes and stopped in the middle of the road. "Left or right?"

I looked back and forth. "Oh, sorry. Left." I probably should've specified that when I yelled.

"I think we're close." Leaning forward, I squinted out of the windshield and tried to see past the illumination of the car's headlights.

As we turned a corner, an enormous house came into view, suddenly visible once the car cleared the trees. The mansion was at least three stories of gothic perfection. It even had a few gargoyles perched on the roof. Dark grey stone covered the exterior and red shutters that accented the windows only added to the witchey look of the building.

On either side of the front of the home, two round, tower-like structures melted in with the rest of the structure. My Victorian would be so jealous if he saw this. So I wouldn't be telling him. Wait, he might already know. This mansion in front of me had been the meeting place for the coven for as long as my family had owned my house. Maybe it had taken on a bit of personality as well.

We pulled right up to the front door and a teenager in a suit ran down the stairs. "Let me park your car for you, sir," he said as he rounded the car to Owen.

Since it was my vehicle, Owen raised his eyebrows at me. I nodded once, so he handed the keys to the young man while Wallie and I got out and shut our car doors.

When we reached the front door of the mansion, it opened without warning. We stepped inside to find nobody holding it. "Ohh," I whispered in a sing-song voice. "Magic."

A thrill went through me. It felt good to be around others that were open with their magic. Even though I still didn't trust most the members of the coven or their intentions for wanting me—a necromancer—to be inducted into their inner circle.

Owen and Wallie chuckled as we moved farther into the entryway. The interior was a mix of contemporary and gothic style. A black, cast iron, spiral staircase sat to our left that was wide enough for two people to walk up, side by side. The floors were white and black marble. I wasn't sure if it was real marble or just ceramic flooring made to look like it. But with how elegant the house was, I was going with the former.

The white walls had dark grey trim, while the doors were all black, sticking with the gothic theme.

"This place is amazing." I'd have to seriously talk with Winston—my house—about some upgrades. That would mean he'd have to let strangers inside to make said changes. I couldn't do all of it with magic, and he was still mad at me for wanting to sell him.

Soft footsteps brought my attention to another teenager, a

girl this time, exiting a doorway to our right. "Please, allow me to take your coats."

She smiled eagerly, her blonde hair in a long braid down one side of her head. I had no trouble imaging her in a bouncy cheerleader uniform.

"Friends," a rich female voice drifted across the large entryway. "Thank you so much for coming." We turned to find a woman walking serenely out of a large double door to an impressive library.

"Cynthia," I said. "How nice to see you." Ugh. I hated putting on this face, this fakeness. But that's what it took to be in a coven. *This* coven, at least.

Cynthia was beautiful and youthful. Her blond hair was gathered in a neat bun at the base of her neck. A few curly strands hung loose to frame her pale, heart shaped face. She had brown eyes that had flecks of silver through them. It was an odd mix of color but worked on her.

"Please, call me CeCe. And come in. We were just about to get started." She stepped to the side and held out her arm for us to enter the library.

We walked in to find eight or nine witches sitting in a circle. Men and women I'd known off and on all my life, mostly. There were a few faces I didn't recognize.

"Please, sit," a man said. He stood and smiled, but the distaste rolled off of him like a stinky cologne. I had to stop myself from curling my lip at him. For whatever reason, he didn't like me or maybe Owen. Maybe both since we were necromancers. He'd have no reason to dislike Wallie. Nobody here knew him. I doubted these people even knew he was my son. Except the invitation had included his name. Maybe they did.

"We were just about to have a drink to the memory of our beloved lost coven member, Miriam Buckner." A tray floated toward us with three champagne flutes resting on it. I took one, pretending the act of magic was no big deal. Even though I'd begun doing much more with magic myself, now that I'd fully embraced my magical side, I still felt like a fish at a bird convention with all these lifelong practitioners around me.

The man, the one who didn't seem to like us, spoke first. "To Miriam. A blessed friend and sister to us all. She will be missed. May her next journey be all she wants it to be."

CeCe raised her glass and looked around the room. "Now, we will continue to honor our fallen sister in our actions and deeds." She sighed and looked at the man who had given the toast. "Bevan," she paused and looked at me. "Bevan Magnus, our recruiter, secretary, pretty much a jack of all trades, eh, Magnus?"

Magnus nodded his head once at her as more disapproval flowed off of him. Surely I wasn't the only one who could feel it?

"Bevan will update us on the reunion at the Witch Academy," CeCe said, then gave Bevan her full attention.

Well, heck. I hadn't even attended the witch academy. Once I'd told Yaya and Aunt Winnie I didn't want anything to do with it, they'd left me alone about witch stuff. Part of me wished now I hadn't done it, but it was what it was.

"The reunion planning is moving along smoothly. All invitations have been sent out. Catering selections were finalized." Bevan smiled at everyone in the room except for me.

Yeah, the feeling's mutual, buddy. Something about him didn't sit right with me.

CeCe took the floor with the last few items on an agenda that I hadn't seen. I guessed I had to be a member to see the meeting's to-do list. "And the final current business is the New Moon Ritual. This month it will be held at Bevan's house. Don't forget to sign up to bring a treat or drink."

Oh, the New Moon Ritual sounded nice. I bet Olivia would love to see it.

"It's a real shame that your mom and grandmother aren't with us to attend the reunion," a woman said as she walked up to us. "Hi, I'm Lorelai."

She smiled, and her apple cheeks and red lips dazzled under kind blue eyes and perfectly coiffed honey-blonde hair. She looked like she could step into any boardroom and take complete charge. At the same time, I had no trouble picturing her in jeans and a sweater, teaching kindergarteners.

"Ava. But I guess you know that." I laughed softly, completely out of my element. There were too many mixed energies here that made me a little uneasy.

Lorelai smiled at me and it felt genuine. I liked her. "I was friends with your Aunt Winnie at the Witch Academy," she said. "And our Bevan went through with your mother."

I raised my eyebrows. "Oh, really?" I hadn't realized he knew my mom.

Lorelai nodded. "Indeed. They invited your mother and Winnie to join the coven, but both declined at first. Of course, you know your mother was in the process of joining when she died." She sniffed and dabbed at her eyes. "A tragedy."

The older woman seemed sincere, but who could truly tell with these people? "That's when Bevan moved here," she continued. "I suppose word got around the Academy that your mother was not able to join us after all, due to her dying, and there was an opening. Bevan moved to Shipton Harbor then."

Interesting. He'd only gotten in because my mother had died.

Lorelai sighed again. "Of course, now, we hold to the traditional thirteen. If all three of you wanted to join, we'd be in a pickle. Times change, you know, but a coven must have thirteen."

They'd invited me before Miriam died. "So, you're down two now? With the loss of Miriam?" I asked.

Lorelai started. "Well, dear, I suppose we're down three. I

hadn't thought of that. We just now got organized after losing poor Doras Miller just after the New Year. She had a heart attack and passed away in her sleep. And Bill... Well, you know what happened with him, as you helped to uncover his killer."

I frowned and averted my eyes, hoping she wouldn't bring up the army of skeletons I'd raised in the cemetery. Those skeletons dragged the witch hunter, Carmen Moonflower, underground. I didn't know where they took her, but I had a feeling I was better off not knowing.

Lorelai added, "Penny isn't here tonight. She's not feeling well."

I raised my eyebrows. "I didn't even know Bill and Penny were a part of the coven."

"Oh, yes. Beloved, both of them. Of course, we invited Bill after your mother passed and you declined to join. We were trying to open ourselves to being more inclusive, and a necromancer certainly did that." She tittered behind her handkerchief before catching the eye of a woman across the room I vaguely remembered from visiting Yaya. "Excuse me, dear." She started to move away, then turned back to me, touching my hand. "Don't leave without saying goodbye."

Then in my head, she said, "*I need to discuss an urgent matter with you.*"

My eyes rounded, but I quickly schooled my reaction, because I got the feeling she didn't want anyone else to hear. She wouldn't have spoken directly in my head if she wanted the whole room to know. That didn't make me feel anymore comfortable being there.

"How convenient they have three openings," I whispered to Owen as he and Wallie closed in on me.

He shrugged. "Probably a coincidence."

Maybe. But someone killed Miriam and Larry and possibly my mom. I wasn't sure how her death fit into it all, but I was going to find out.

We mingled for a few more minutes. I found everyone pleasant except for a set of twins, Brandon and Ben Stamp. They were a quiet pair and mostly stayed to themselves. Whenever I glanced their way one of them, Brandon, I believed, glared at me. He didn't want me there. I didn't blame him, I didn't want me there either.

I found Wallie at the refreshment table with Owen. "Hey, I'm ready to roll but I have to say goodbye to Lorelai, so I'll meet you two in the car."

They nodded and headed out the door after a lot of goodbyes.

I turned just as Lorelai exited the library. I took that as my cue, so I followed her while trying not to be obvious about it.

Once in the foyer, she and CeCe moved toward me. CeCe smiled wide. "It was so good to see you. Thank you for coming." She looped an arm with mine and walked me outside as if seeing me off.

Lorelai stood on my other side. Once we descended the steps, a warmth of magic surrounded us. I swallowed my panic. "What's going on?"

"I put a privacy circle around us so no one can hear what we are about to say." Lorelai glanced at CeCe.

The coven leader took my hands and spoke while smiling. I was betting she was doing it in case anyone was watching us. How did I know that? "We don't think Miriam's death was an accident."

Lorelai looked a little scared. "We can't trust anyone else in the coven with our speculations because there are too many things that don't add up."

Did they know about the coin in Mariam's pocket? I didn't think so because it wasn't in the news reports. Plus Drew wouldn't make something like that public. Especially since Larry had confirmed it was the same one his murderer had used.

So, I didn't mention the coin to Lorelai or Cynthia. "What makes you think it wasn't an accident?"

Voices coming out from the foyer drew our attention to the twins. CeCe quickly said, "We can't talk here."

The circle of magic dropped from around us and Lorelai drew me into a hug. "We have to get together for tea or wine sometime."

"That would be great." I had to find out what they knew. I glanced at the twins in the doorway and waved at them before getting into my car.

CHAPTER SEVEN

I didn't feel like shopping for dinner or cooking or anything. And I couldn't ask Alfred to cook every meal I didn't feel like preparing. Plus, he didn't even eat! Why on earth he insisted on preparing my meals was beyond me. Huh. Maybe he was poisoning me slowly.

I chuckled. Nah.

The weather didn't help to bring me out of my lazy mood. Rain had poured down all day, creating a miserable, soggy mess. Not to mention making it feel colder than it already was.

On the way home from my shift at the bookstore, I popped into the Mexican restaurant at the edge of town and put in an order for a veritable smorgasbord of food. It was just me and Owen tonight, but Olivia was supposed to come over and help me go through my grimoires, looking for anything that might help us send Luci back to Hell.

That was something I was betting wasn't going to be easy. I wasn't the type to give up on things once determination set in. And it has set. The devil needed to return to his kingdom.

I had called in the order right before I left work. It was a good thing, because it seemed like I wasn't the only one who wanted take out. As I sat on a bench near the front, humming to myself and looking around at the artwork—and pretending not to smell the delicious aromas coming from the kitchen as my stomach growled like an angry creature, the front door opened. I turned to see who had come in and my heart stopped for a few beats and the pit of my stomach burned.

Drew walked in with a gorgeous woman on his arm.

She was younger than me. Thinner than me. And looked up at him like he'd hung the moon. My chest tightened while jealousy churned within.

"*Corium*," I whispered, waving my hand in front of my face, hoping Drew didn't sense the magic. If he did, would he know it was me? Crap on a cracker. I did the spell so that anyone who looked at me would find their eyes slipping past where I sat without noticing me there at all. It was like an invisibility spell, only I wasn't really invisible, just easy to forget if someone looked hard enough.

"Two?" the hostess asked, and Drew nodded, the svelte woman still hanging onto his arm.

Shit. I couldn't be sure. It could've been someone from the police department. It could be an old girlfriend whom he wasn't involved with anymore. Hell, it could've been his cousin or something. Plus, neither. of us had said anything about exclusivity.

Then why in the seven Hades was my pulse hammering so fast?

We weren't like... engaged or anything! So we'd had one great date in Paris. So, we'd sat on the top of the Eiffel Tower together. That didn't mean he couldn't date other people.

So why was my blood boiling? And I wanted to yank all the hair out of her head? Whoa, I needed a drink and to chill. I picked up my phone and texted Olivia.

Don't forget the wine.

She texted back instantly. **Already in my bag**.

The server came out of the kitchen with two big bags. "Harper?" He looked around, then set the bags down on the counter and went back to the kitchen.

My pulse quickened again, and I searched the restaurant for Drew and his *date*. To my relief, they were seated far enough away that he couldn't have heard my name.

I'd already paid when I placed the order, so I snatched the bags up and ran out the door, nearly bowling right into a young couple as they reached for the door.

"What the hell?" the guy exclaimed. "I didn't feel any wind that would jerk the door open like that."

"Me, either," the girl said. "Creepy. Let's go somewhere else to eat."

Crap. Crap. I scurried to my car and bent down behind it, getting soaked by the heavy rain. "*Revelare.*" Visible again, I straightened up and put the food on the back floorboard. It wouldn't be good if someone saw my car driving itself down the road. Although that would be a good reason to have a dashcam. Playback people's reaction to a driverless car. Might make some good money if it went viral. I snorted at my thoughts. I really have lost it.

Olivia was already there when I got home. She rushed out to grab one of the bags from me while holding a large umbrella. It was impressive. Like family size. "That's a big umbrella."

She grinned. "I know, right? I found it at a craft fair my mom and I went to a few years ago." She watched me from the corner of her eye as we hustled inside my house and put the food on the coffee table. "What's wrong?

I straightened and pretended to play dumb. "Besides that I'm soaked? Nothing. I'm going to get out of these wet clothes. Can you get some plates and glasses? I'll let Owen know to come down and get food."

I rushed up the stairs, sloshing away before she could call

me out on the nothing comment. I planned to tell her, just not until I was in dry, comfy clothes. And with an enormous glass of wine.

Sporting my neon pink flannel sleep pants and a black tee that said, "What's up, Witches," I headed down the hall. I yelled to Owen when I got to the top of the stairs. "Dinner is on the coffee table."

By the time I got downstairs, Owen was fixing a plate. Wow, that was impressive. "Did you learn to teleport? Because that would be cool."

Owen straightened and frown lines formed on his forehead. After a few moments, he laughed. "No. I was already down here when you yelled for me."

Oh, that made more sense. But I was a little disappointed that necromancers couldn't teleport. Imagine the gas you'd save.

He'd recently started working at the bookstore, too. I'd been writing more since moving here, and my book sales were picking up, meaning I didn't have to take on as many shifts. The house was paid for, so all I had was electricity, water, and the internet. I didn't watch much TV, so didn't bother with cable. I did have a few streaming subscriptions from when Wallie lived at home in Philly. Alfred and Larry had been enjoying them.

"Are you hanging out with us tonight? We're going to start the search for a way to send Luci back." Olivia asked.

He held up his plate. "After I eat, I might."

When he walked off, I grabbed a plate and loaded it up.

With a snap of his fingers, Owen whirled to face me. "That's what I meant to tell you. I convinced Cliff to let me put in an occult section so we can order books that are relevant to the witches in the area. Real, good books. Not Paranormal fiction."

That was a great idea. "Spot on, Owen, wonderful. He was cool with it?"

He shrugged. "Well, he thinks it's for Wiccans, which some of them will be. But I don't think he knows there are more than that sort of spiritual witch around."

"Good." I threw out our trash. "Let's keep it that way."

Once we were alone, I tried to ignore Olivia as she stared at me. It was difficult because she was worse than Snooze when he wanted something.

I had a fork full of rice halfway to my mouth when she said, "Come on, spill it."

I locked gazes with her and shoved the rice in my mouth. Then chewed very slowly. That only earned me a throw pillow upside the head. I started laughing, which made me choke on the rice.

Alfred rushed down the stairs, and I waved him off. "I'm fine."

Larry stuck his head over the railing. Thanks to the gods, it stayed attached to his body. "You're choking. Do you need the Heimlich?"

"No!" My voice squeaked as I yelled the word. Then I calmed and said softer, "No, thank you for your concern."

The thought of Larry's boney fist on my chest sent a shiver through me. Not in this lifetime. Or the next.

"What is it?" Olivia insisted again.

"Could you imagine the skeleton giving you the Heimlich? No way will his boney hands be anywhere near the girls." I made a circular motion over my breasts as I shuddered.

Olivia giggled, which turned into a full laugh as she fell to her side on the couch and rolled to the floor.

It took her a good ten minutes to recover. She sat up and remained on the floor but still didn't let me off the hook. "What is bothering you?"

"What makes you think anything is bothering me?" I took another big bite.

"Because your eyes are greener than normal. That means your magic is close to the surface, right?"

Well, look who'd been doing some witchy homework. "It does," I mumbled around my food.

Damn, most witches' magic was tied closely to their emotions. Now that mine ran free inside me because I was no longer suppressing either side of my powers, my emotions at seeing Drew with that woman had struck all of my nerves. And my magic.

After taking a drink of my wine, I told her about Drew. "...So, anyway, I have no proof that it was any sort of date. But Liv, you should've seen the way she looked at him."

Olivia took a bite of refried beans and then pointed her fork at me. "I'm going to string him up by his balls."

"Olivia! You'll do no such thing. Especially before we figure out who she was." If anyone was going to be stringing up balls, it would be me. But I wouldn't.

She scowled at me. "You're no fun."

I snorted and took a big bite of burrito. "I'm a blast. But I'm not going to castrate Drew because he knows another woman." Or had dinner with her. It was just food. I'd keep telling myself that until I got a chance to ask him about her.

She sniffed but didn't press it. "I'm sure you're right," she said. "She's probably his therapist or something. She helps him suppress his violent urge to murder his new girlfriend for being a witch."

"That's totally it." I let sarcasm leak into the words. Then added an eye roll for visual effect.

Olivia and I finished our dinner and cleaned up our mess in the living room, which we'd converted to a sort-of library. All the books that had been scattered on shelves all over the house now resided on the built-ins here in the living room where previously they'd been full of knick-knacks that were boxed in the attic. Most of them had been precious to Yaya or Winnie but didn't mean a lot to me. I hadn't been able to get rid of them, but didn't need them displayed, either.

"Okay, so we're basically going through all these old books, looking for any hint of a spell that could be used or adapted to help us send Luci back," I said. "Just grab a grimoire and start reading."

Owen was still eating in the kitchen. But Alfred wandered in with Larry in tow. "We can help," Larry said. "I can't turn pages well, but Alfred can, and we can both read."

I handed them a book. "We'll take all the help we can get, but why don't you two stick to the newer books that aren't as valuable, just in case?"

I had really ancient ones in the attic somewhere. We'd have to search for them if none of the ones down here panned out.

Alfred nodded once and took the book to the desk in the corner where he and Larry got to work. Snooze wandered in and stretched out across the desk a few minutes later, forcing them to pull the book back and give him room.

"Bad kitty," I whispered as Snooze's tail twitched and he opened one eye to stare at me. "Yeah, I'm talking to you." Crazy cat.

About an hour after we dug into searching the grimoires, Oliva squeaked and yelled, "I found something!"

I jerked my gaze to her and waited while she read over the page. She sagged back into the oversized chair she'd moved to a few minutes ago and her face scrunched up. "Never mind. That's not it."

I sighed and went back to my own search. We had a few more false hope outbursts over the next few hours. I tossed my head back against the sofa and groaned. "There has to be a spell for finding a spell. Like a magical internet search for grimoires."

Owen chuckled. "There might be. It just comes down to finding the right spell to suit your purpose."

"That doesn't help." I laughed, then let out a dramatic breath and focused on the book in my lap.

Wallie nudged me while placing his grimoire on top of mine. He pointed to the page. "Will this work?"

The title of the spell was "Get rid of unwanted evil," and I snorted.

"That is exactly what I want to do." I studied the incantation and ingredients. It was more of an evil-spirit banishing spell, but I bet I could tweak it to include a demon. Demons were kind of like spirits. And my new neighbor was the king of evil.

"Nope. That won't work."

The sound of a male's low whisper in my ear made me jump a foot off the couch, spilling the books on the floor. I whirled around with my hand raised. My magic instantly flowed into my palms, ready to blast the man at my command.

I narrowed my eyes and called the magic back. "You need to learn to knock."

Luci straightened from where he leaned against the back of the sofa. How long had he been there reading over my shoulder? *Without* me sensing him?

He waved his hand and the book with the evil spirit banishing spell floated over to him. Opening to the page with the spell, he shook his head. "This won't work."

Stepping forward, I snatched the book from him. "Not the way it's written. I'll modify it and make it work."

He disappeared and reappeared directly in front of me. I gasped and fought the urge to run. I could talk the crap, but when it came to backing up my sass with the devil, I was chicken.

Pathetic.

A slow, wicked smile formed, and he leaned closer. "You

could just accept the fact that I like your little town, and I'm here to stay."

"Not today, Satan." I pushed past him to put some space between us. "You are a menace and don't belong here."

That reminded me, I also needed to make anti-compulsion charms for my family and friends. Myself included.

When I got a few feet from him, I turned and asked, "If you're so smart, how do we get rid of you?"

He laughed. Out loud. "My dear, Ava. If I told you that, I wouldn't have any fun watching you try to find out."

Then he dematerialized.

Damn demon.

CHAPTER EIGHT

Dancing around the book stacks, I dusted and bopped to the tune blaring from the radio up front. I was the only one that didn't mind dusting; Owen and Clint hated it. Plus, I'd honed my cleaning spell, so the dust danced in front of me at ground level, as we worked our way toward the back door. I just had to make sure to do it when Clint wasn't here.

My boss didn't know about magic. At least I didn't think he did. I wasn't going to be the one to tell him either.

"Love me all niiiiiii—" I cut off abruptly as my alarm went off, the magic from the spell nipping at my skin.

Magic was a handy thing. Owen and I had rigged an alarm that beeped loudly whenever anyone entered the store. The catch was that only he and I could hear it.

As I said. Handy.

Sure, there was a bell on the door that Clint could hear, but Owen and I had wanted something that went off the moment someone touched the door. It gave us that second or two to check out the energy of the person coming in and hide our spells and magic if we needed to.

We couldn't be too careful since Owen had been kidnapped and almost killed last October by a crazy witch hunter. We weren't taking any chances. Necromancers had a bad rep, plus I was supposed to be this all powerful necro-witch hybrid. So far, I wasn't all *that* powerful. The jury was still out on whether or not I was special at all.

At the sound of the magical alarm, the dust dropped to the floor, scattering under the stacks as it had been instructed to do.

The dust could hear the alarm too, because why not?

"Hey," Clint said. "Was that you caterwauling?"

Clint was thin and about four inches taller than me with tanned skin that I didn't know was real or from a can. His gray eyes twinkled, telling he was teasing me with his comment.

I put one hand on my hips and shook the feather duster at him. "Hey, now. I can't be good at everything."

He chuckled, but something told me he was questioning my sanity. There were days that I questioned it too.

I had to be careful around him and probably warn Owen to be. Clint was a good guy, but I didn't need to deal with explaining all this mess to him. He was, as far as I knew, fully human. It would be tricky.

"How goes it?" I asked. "Oh, did you approve the occult section?" I glanced his way, trying to sound casual as I kept dusting without the aid of the spell.

"Yes, I did. I need to order the books," he called.

Since his voice drifted out from the back room, I twirled my finger and grabbed up all the dust I'd been accumulating, coaxing it out from under the stacks. "Come on," I muttered. "Quickly." Scurrying backward, I snatched up the small trash bin and hid myself between the stacks, still swirling my finger. The dust rose in a tornado.

"Do you know anything about this stuff?"

This time, Clint's voice came from much closer. Crap.

I pointed into the bin and cut off the spell. The dust fell, most of it hitting the trash can liner. Stepping forward, I shook the can a bit to get the dust to settle. "Sure," I said. "I'd be happy to put in the order for you."

Walking out of the stacks, I nearly stepped right into Clint. I jumped and swallowed a scream. He furrowed his brow at the trash can. "I thought you were dusting?"

"There was a lot of dust on one of those shelves." I laughed nervously and changed the subject. "Show me the ordering system?"

He looked skeptical but turned toward the front counter with the laptop in his hands. He must've brought it out of his office before scaring me to death.

A few minutes after I sat down and started browsing the options, Clint got bored and left me to it. Good.

I was anything but bored and had to make myself stop browsing and shopping before I spent all of the bookstore's money. "Okay, Clint I made a big order, but I'm going to buy several of these as soon as you get them in," I called. "And it's time for me to go!"

He sauntered out of his office with a smile on his face. "So, you're into these occult books, huh?"

"Yeah." I nodded, hoping to look innocent. "They're great research for my novels."

With my bag on my shoulder, I started toward the door, but as soon as I looked at the glass, I stopped. "I forgot about all this rain," I said with a sigh. "I love rain, but enough is enough."

It'd been pouring off and on for the last several days. I was so over it.

Clint chuckled. "Here." He handed me my umbrella, which I'd almost forgotten. "Have fun swimming home!"

"It would be a lot more fun if it wasn't so cold." I waved and opened the umbrella, needing it even though my car was only like ten feet away.

As soon as I shook it off and managed to shut my car door, I sighed. The act of closing it and shaking it off had me nearly as dang wet as I would've been if I'd just rushed to the car without the stupid thing.

Shivering, I cranked up the heat just as my phone blared the ringtone that Olivia had set for her contact when I wasn't paying attention. *Witchy Woman* blared from the device and it had me cracking up. So forever now, when Olivia called, it was with that song, plus a picture I'd sneakily taken of her when she wasn't looking. She'd been picking something out of her teeth.

She'd also set my home phone line to ring on my cell as *Monster Mash*, which with the menagerie at my place, I'd also left that one on there. It fit our lives at the moment.

"What's up, frand?" I answered.

"Another death," she replied in a hushed tone and my heart sank. "And Sam said if we hurry, we can check out the scene so you can do your thing."

"No way," I replied, also whispering. "I mean yes to doing my thing. No way in that I can't believe there's been another death." I paused, then asked, "Why am I whispering?"

"I don't know," she hissed, then laughed although it didn't sound as happy as her normal laugh did. "I don't know why I am either!"

"Okay, where is it? Who was it? I just left the bookstore." I didn't pull out until she told me where I should go.

"I don't know this person," she said. "It was at her house on Beaver Drive."

I snickered. "I love that street name."

"Me too." She chuckled along with me. "Beaver."

"Okay, okay. What was the person's name?" I asked. We were too giggly when there'd been a murder.

"Um, Lorelai Fontinell."

My heart sank to my feet while sadness churned in the pit of my soul. "No," I began whispering again. "She's a member of the coven."

"You're joking."

"I'm not."

With a heavy heart, I put the phone on speaker and the car in reverse. "Are you on your way?"

"Almost there," she replied.

"I'll meet you there." I hung up and swiped tears away as I headed to the other side of town.

Lorelai had been so nice to me at the Coven meeting. She'd made me want to consider joining. She also had information about Mariam's so-called accident. Something nagged at me, confirming for me the accidents weren't accidents. Meaning someone was causing them. But why and how?

I pulled up behind Olivia's 4-Runner and brushed the tears from my cheeks. I was getting really sick and tired of finding dead witches.

Olivia jumped out of her car and hurried to open my car door. "Come on and leave the umbrella."

"Why?" I asked as I burrowed my face into my jacket to avoid the freezing rain.

"You'll see."

Uh oh. I didn't like the sound of that. Or the look of horror and disgust that briefly flashed across Olivia's face.

Sam stood in the front doorway. Luckily for us, Lorelai's house had a nice, deep porch to shield us from the rain. He put one hand on my arm and one on Olivia's. "Brace yourselves," he said. "It's bad."

I sucked in a deep breath and closed my eyes, opening them when I felt Sam move out of the way.

Olivia gasped and I wanted to, but the shock was too much. It hurt my heart.

Gore and gross things were quickly becoming a way of life, considering I was a necromancer.

"Is anyone here?" I whispered.

"No," Sam said. "The coroner just left. We're alone for now but he'll be back in an hour for the body."

"Did you find anything on her?" I asked.

He nodded and checked his notes. "Yep. A coin."

The same one that was left on Miriam and Larry, I bet.

I walked carefully around the body of what might have become my friend. "Can you remove the umbrella yet?" I asked as I stared down at what I could see of Lorelai.

A small, black umbrella covered most of her. Squatting down, I looked underneath to see if what I suspected was what happened.

Yep.

The pointy end of the umbrella protruded from Lorelai's eye.

Damn it.

I tried not to breathe. Not sure why because she didn't stink yet. One would think that as a necromancer, I'd be used to seeing the dead.

I was not. I'd avoided it at all costs until a few months ago.

"I guess," Sam said. "We're ruling it an accident, so there won't be much in the way of forensics."

I glanced up at him. "The coin is a link to Miriam's 'accident'." I used air quotes to make my point.

He shrugged. "If that truly is the case then it is a supernatural cause of death that the humans don't need to know about. So it's still ruled accidental, for now."

I nodded. That made sense, sort of. For now. "Okay. Remove it."

He put on gloves and reached for the handle. It came out of her eye socket with a sickening squelch sound.

Olivia gasped and covered her face, then turned her back.

"Time of death?" I asked.

"Sometime yesterday between noon and two," he said.

"Okay. I think I can get her to talk without too much magic or disturbing things too much."

I studied Lorelai for a long while, noticing her blackened witch's mark shining from her chest, just visible inside the collar of her shirt.

Sucking in a deep breath, I closed my eyes and called on the magic Owen and I had been working on. To animate a corpse partially and not have them jumping up and running around town. I just wanted Lorelai to tell me how this happened.

I sent barely a sliver of magic toward her while concentrating on Lorelai's brain and vocal cords, trying to animate just her head and upper chest area.

"Lorelai, how did you die?" I whispered, leaning close. If I did this right, she wouldn't speak loudly, and I'd have to strain to hear.

Scaring the crap out of me, Lorelai sat up suddenly, her blonde hair matted with the blood that had drained from her eye socket. I scrambled backward, deeper into the house as Sam and Olivia retreated onto the porch to watch in horror. "This isn't me. That's not my magic," I squeaked as I jerked the small bit of my magic away from the corpse.

"Keep your magic away from the witch, necromancer," Lorelai's pale lips said as her head turned all the way around to stare at me with one milky eye. "Let the dead lie."

Her body relaxed and fell back on the ground, landing in the exact same spot it had been in before I tried to raise her.

"Shit," I whispered, rapidly shaking my hands as if to shake off the bad juju. "Shit, *shit*."

"What the hell was that?" Olivia screeched from the front porch.

Sam peered around the corner with his gun pointed at Lorelai's body and Olivia peeked around the other side of the door. "Is it safe?" she asked.

"It's safe," I said. "Sometimes witches put spells on themselves so that when they die, they'll stay dead. They don't want their bodies used by dark necromancers." Not that I'd ever use that kind of magic. It took a real sicko for that. That's how Alfreds were created, but ghouls didn't normally end up benevolent chefs like mine. "But that also means we can't use her body to get answers about her death."

Feeling like a failure for not being able to get a lead on how the two accidents could happen and why, I moved to the front door where Sam and Olivia still waited, eyeing Lorelai's body as if it was going to jump up again. "Can I see the coin?"

Without looking away from the body, Sam pulled a small bag from his pocket with the coin inside. I took it and studied it. "It's the same one found on Mariam. Larry says it's also the same as the one was placed in his pocket moments before he died."

"Yeah. But we don't have Larry's." Sam frowned. "And we can't use him as a source."

I knew that. No one would believe that a skeleton claimed to die in an accident while having a coin in his pocket.

When I started to open the baggie, Sam covered my hand. "Don't touch it. We need to take prints...you know, off the record."

Nodding, I said, "I wasn't going to touch it. I'm checking for magic." But there wasn't anything lingering. This was the freshest coin I'd been able to examine.

He took it from me after putting on a glove and then dumped the coin out of the bag into his palm. Ah, that was better. I hovered my hand over it, feeling the charge of dark power. Just as we feared, the coin was cursed. I just didn't know how or by whom. Without that information, I didn't know how to uncurse it. Or protect other witches from suffering the same fate.

"After you check it for prints off the record, can I have it? I might be able to do a locator spell or some other kind to find who the owner is."

Sam nodded. "Yeah, sure."

And I was out. I couldn't take being in the same room with Lorelai's corpse any longer. The whole anti-necromancer spell was a shock, and it had freaked me the heck out.

CHAPTER NINE

"Snooze, stop it."

Mr. Snoozerton lay behind me, randomly scratching my butt with his back feet. He wanted my attention, or he wanted food. It was hard to tell with him at times. I'd swat him off, then a few minutes later, he'd do it again.

"I'm not playing right now, Snooze!" I turned and laughed when I found him splayed out on his back, showing his big, fluffy belly for pets. "I love petting your super curly belly hair, Snoozer, but I'm busy." I gave him a quick pat on the tummy then turned back to the trunk.

Alfred shuffled over and glared down at the big, rotten cat.

"I swear, the only thing we're going to find up here is a bunch of dust," Olivia said as Alfred and Snooze had a staring contest. She glanced at the two, frowned, then shook her head.

Alfred grunted and Snooze rolled over the other way, taking his claws with him. "Thanks, Alfie," I said, still marveling at the power the ghoul had over that insane cat. "I can fix that," I replied to Olivia about the dust, not the attention-whore of a cat. There was no help for him.

Actually, I had already fixed him when he died as a kitten. I ended up turning him immortal somehow. That crazy cat was going to outlive us all. I shot Olivia an alarming look that made her sit up straight. "What's wrong?"

"I just realized that Snooze will outlive me."

Her eyes got big. "You need to find him a god-parent or something just in case."

Yeah, but who could I trust with my big furry baby? "Wallie can take him and then pass him down the family."

Olivia snorted. "He's not a family heirloom."

I gasped in mock surprise that she would say such a thing. "He is too! A precious heirloom."

"Precious is right." Olivia giggled and then motioned to all the dust.

Oh, yeah. I was supposed to fix it.

Doing my finger twirl, I gathered up the dust and sent it out the small vent in the corner of the attic. "There. Better?"

Olivia nodded and opened another box. "Perfect, thanks. How much would you charge to come do that to my entire house once a week?"

"Remind me, and I'll do it every time I come over, free of charge." I was supposed to be super powerful, yet I used my magic to clean house more than anything.

Sam and Olivia tended to come here more than I went there, though. With all the myriad of creatures living here, I liked to be around as much as possible to supervise things. Alfred was a pretty stern babysitter, but still, he was a ghoul.

"Nothing in this box either." Olivia sighed and rocked back on her heels. "Are you sure there's more grimoires up here?"

"I thought there were," I said. "The really old ones that we had copied into new books and didn't want to disturb anymore."

"If you copied them, why are we looking for them?" Larry asked.

"Because I'm desperate," I snapped. With a sigh, I relaxed and closed the trunk. "I'm sorry. I didn't mean to bite your head off."

Olivia snorted, then quickly covered her mouth, and looked at the skeleton in horror.

His head had an unfortunate tendency to fall off.

I bit back my own laughter and avoided looking at Olivia at all costs. The last thing I needed was to get a glimpse of her laugh-strangled face and burst out giggling myself.

We were no closer to finding Larry's killer than we'd been the day he'd turned up on my porch. I didn't want to make him think we weren't taking this seriously.

The truth was, we'd been doing spells and the police department was doing everything it could as well. Sam and Drew had even snuck one of the coins to us to spell. Nothing Owen or I had tried gave any results. Whoever was using these coins was covering their tracks too well with their own spell work.

It was going to take some old-fashioned sleuthing to get to the bottom of this mystery.

And in the meantime, I had to figure out how to get Lucifer to go back to Hell without taking all of us with him. Some of the books I'd ordered for Clint had descriptions that had made me hopeful that they'd have something helpful inside. We'd find out when they arrived.

Olivia had scoured the online book world for occult books, but apparently witches hadn't gone electronic yet. There was a stunning shortage of authentic occult eBooks.

As I opened another trunk, I considered the possibility of turning some of my family's grimoires and books electronic. But I'd have to figure out a way to make them seem like fiction to the humans.

Could I put a spell on the internet?

This was the sort of thing I'd like to discuss with a coven, but they had to be total assholes. I supposed I could call Cynthia. We hadn't yet had our talk about Mariam's accident. And now Lorelai's.

"Here's something," Larry said. "This box has books."

I hurried over to the corner to peer down into the crate Larry had just opened. "This is it," I said excitedly. "Thank you."

Turning, I carried it to the small table against the wall to go through it. If I sat one more minute on the hard attic floor, my back would revolt on me. It was already trying to.

I stepped over Snoozle, who was sniffing around the floor. "There's nothing there, Snoozer."

He chuffed at me, looking up with his little tongue barely sticking out.

"You've got a blep," I told him. "In case you didn't know."

The old meanie shot me a glare, then delicately licked his front paw, as if he'd meant to have his tongue sticking out the whole time.

I shook my head and went back to inspecting the contents of the box. As I pulled out the first book, carefully opening it, Snoozer walked toward the back of the attic.

Olivia sat in the other chair and grabbed a book, too.

When Alfred and Larry came closer, I held up my hand. "Olivia and I will handle these. Thanks, guys." I appreciated their help, but we didn't need their dry and bony fingers ripping pages.

Snooze meowed a couple of times from the corner as Olivia and I slowly read through each of the grimoires. I had no idea what the cat was doing, so I ignored him. He sometimes meowed at Winston, the house. At least I hoped Winston was the house itself and not a ghost. I wasn't ready for them yet.

I'd gotten to the third book when a racket scared me to death. I jumped in my seat, almost dropping the grimoire.

340

Snoozle was howling something fierce, but when I rushed over to the back of the attic, he was nowhere to be found.

"Snoozer!" I yelled.

He went silent for a second, then yowled again, and I could've sworn it sounded like the word help.

"Where are you?" Olivia called from right behind me.

Snooze yowled again, and Alfred dropped to his knees beside me, scrabbling at the wooden planks of the floor.

I ran to the corner, to an old box of tools, looking for a hammer. There wasn't a hammer in the box, but there was a crowbar. It would do!

Returning to the other side of the attic and my pitiful cat who was still crying and howling at the top of his lungs, I wedged the crowbar between the planks of wood and pressed down on the end to try to loosen them.

Snoozer went quiet, then yowled again, and I paused, looking at Olivia. "Did he just tell me to hurry?"

"It sure sounded like it," she muttered. "That cat is something else."

I heaved against the crowbar, and the plank came up on one end with an awful squeal.

Snooze's head wedged out of the small space I'd created with the crowbar. "Snooze, wait," I cried. "I don't have it fully up yet!"

Leaning against the crowbar, I held the plank up as long as I could while Snooze wiggled his way out of the hole. "How did you get in there?" I yelled when he finally got free, then shot across the attic. I turned my head to see his tail disappear out the door.

"Wait," Olivia said. She reached carefully into the hole while I tried to use the crowbar to hold the plank steady. "There's something here."

She pulled out something wrapped in an old, ratty towel, then peered down in the hole again. "Hang on."

Reaching into her back pocket, she pulled out her phone, then turned on the flashlight on it. After a careful examination, she shook her head. "That's all. Let it go."

"How in the world did he get under there?" I asked, letting the plank fall back into place.

I stood and stepped on the floor. Nothing. No sound and no movement. None of the planks nearby were loose either. Olivia knocked on walls and the floor around the area. We didn't find anything that told us how the fat cat got under the floor.

"Was it the house?" Olivia asked as she wiped a bead of sweat from her forehead. We'd looked everywhere. There was no way we could find that Snooze could've gotten under the floorboards.

"I don't see what else it could've been. Winston up to mischief again."

As if agreeing with me, the shutters on the front of the house rattled in the wind. "Yep, it was him."

I returned to the table and took the towel-wrapped mystery from Alfred. "Let's see what Snoozer accidentally found. Whatever it is, Winston really wanted us to have it."

CHAPTER TEN

"I t's a mirror," I whispered. Why in the heck would a mirror be hiding in the floor of the attic? Apparently, Winston knew or the dang house wouldn't have trapped poor Snooze in the hollow spot with the mirror.

Winston and I were going to have a serious talk about his attitude.

"Hey, what are you guys up to?" Owen said. "I heard a racket." He stuck his head in the attic door and looked around. "Everything okay?"

I shook my head. "We think the house is acting up again. Snooze got caught under the floorboards and we had to fight to get him out." I sat back and looked at Owen. "And now that I think about it, I'm wondering if the house wasn't fighting me a little."

Definitely having a talk with Winston. His behavior was unacceptable.

"Why would it trap the silly cat, then fight you to get him out?" Olivia asked. "I think the house wanted you to find whatever's in that towel."

I shrugged and picked up the mirror. "Let's see." A beautiful, antique hand mirror. The silver handle and frame holding in the mirror looked to be hand carved with floral-like designs. Going by the weight and the magic that kissed at my fingers and hand, it was cast from real silver. Would have to be to have a spell on it.

"I don't remember ever seeing this before," I said. "Why was it hidden?"

Owen held out his hand. "May I?"

I nodded and handed the mirror over. Owen closed his eyes and held it, then smelled it, then peered closely at the reflective surface before turning it over and licking it.

Ew! "Why'd you do that?"

He wiped off the back with his sleeve and gave it back. "Some magic tastes bitter. Try touching it with the tiniest bit of magic," he suggested.

I eyed him suspiciously. He knew something, but like the good teacher he was, he wanted me to discover the secret on my own. Fine. Whatever. With a shrug, I took it and did as he said, drawing out my magic and picturing it as a single strand of hair glancing up against the mirror's surface.

To my shock, the mirror blazed to life, light coming out of the glass like it had a freaking hundred-watt bulb behind it.

"What the frack?" Olivia squawked.

We all peered into the glass. "If we get sucked into this mirror," I whispered. "I swear..."

I had too much stuff to do to be lost inside a magical mirror. I had a killer to find and a sheriff to seduce. Wait... I had no idea where that last thought came from. But it sounded fun. It's been a *long* time since I wasn't responsible for my own orgasm.

Filing the seduction of the sheriff away for later, I studied the mirror again.

A voice came from the glass, which no longer held my reflection, I belatedly realized. "Who's there?"

344

I gasped and my heart jumped in my chest. I knew that voice. "Yaya?" I whispered as tears filled my eyes. "Is that you?"

My sweet Yaya's face appeared in the reflection of the mirror. Her olive toned skin was as flawless as it had been before she died. There were only a few fine lines around her eyes, mouth, and forehead. Yaya had been the master of looking young. She'd always told me it was good genes. I had told her it was that *and* a little magic.

Yaya's bright green eyes lit up. "Oh, my goodness. Ava. You're all grown up."

"How are you in this mirror?" I cried. "Are you real?"

My chest tightened and my heart ached to hug her.

She shook her head. "In a way. I'm an imprint."

I'd read somewhere about imprints. "So you have the knowledge and personality of Yaya up until the moment she put you in this mirror."

She nodded. "Exactly." Her gaze shifted behind me. "Who are your friends?"

"This is Olivia," I said. "She's my best friend."

Olivia stuck her head over my shoulder. "It's a pleasure to meet you, ma'am. I've heard so much about you."

"And this is Owen, he's been teaching me necromancy." I twisted the mirror so Owen could wave.

He smiled nervously. "It's a real honor to meet even the imprint of the famous Yaya."

My grandmother tittered. "I'm happy to meet you all, but Ava, honey, we don't have much time. An imprint only lasts so long. When you pull back your magic, the mirror will go dark. You'll be able to see the imprint again as long as the magic I imbibed in it lasts, but I can't tell when it will fade until it happens."

"How long do they usually last?" I asked.

Owen answered. "It varies and depends on the strength of the witch that cast the imprint. Generally several hours."

"Okay," I said. "You won't be like... lonely or anything when I'm not talking to you, right?"

"No, sweet girl. It's sort of like I sleep. When I made this mirror, you were just a teenager. And now look at you." Her eyes softened. "You're just beautiful."

My bottom lip trembled slightly. "Not as beautiful as you."

As much as I wanted to spend hours catching up with Yaya, I didn't have that much time. But I did spare a few minutes to tell her the short version of my life. "Clay and I ran off to Philly after our wedding. We had a beautiful baby boy, Wallace Clayton. We call him Wallie, who is not a baby anymore. He's going to Harvard to be a doctor. My Clay...he died in a car crash a little over five years ago."

"Oh, sweetheart, I'm so sorry. I know how much you loved that boy."

We were silent for a few seconds, just staring at one another before Yaya asked, "Darling, is there anything you need to ask me? I have all the memories and knowledge up until this point in my life."

I shook my head and smiled. "No, Yaya, I'm just so glad to see you."

"Yes," Olivia said. "We do!"

I looked over my shoulder at her, frowning. "What?"

"Ask her about your mom's death," she said.

Well, duh. I wanted to slap my forehead. "Oh, Yaya, yes. Was there any suspicion that my mother could've been murdered?" I asked.

Yaya winced. "I always had a feeling of it. But I never had anything more than that. No proof, not even a hint of a spell."

"What about a coin?" I asked. "Was there a strange coin in her pocket?"

Yaya's eyes widened. "As a matter of fact, there was. It's in my jewelry box, dear one. I kept it."

I nodded. Feelings of dread, sorrow, and hope for being

closer to finding the killer swirled inside me. "Okay, Yaya. Thank you. I'll check for it. If I have more questions, I'll contact you again, but I'm going to let you go for now so that there will be plenty of time for Wallie to meet you, okay?"

She smiled and leaned closer to her side of the mirror. "I love you, my Ava girl. I'm so proud of the woman you've become."

With a sniffle, I pulled the thread of magic back into me and collapsed against Olivia as I cried. My Yaya.

"She had to have made this not long before she died," I whispered. "She died when I was nineteen." It was the year before Clay and I got married.

Once the mirror went dark, I wrapped it back in the cloth we found it in. Glancing to Owen, I asked, "Can you grab that box of grimoires and take them to the living room? I'm going to find a safe place for the mirror and search for that coin in Yaya's jewelry box."

I kept that jewelry box in my room on the top shelf of my bookcase. I never opened it because I didn't want to grieve anymore loved ones at the moment.

"Sure." Owen picked up the books on the table and added them to the box before lifting it in his arms.

Olivia and I followed him down with Alfred and Larry right behind us. The attic stairs ended on the second floor at the end of the hall on the side where my room was, so I darted inside while the guys continued on to the first floor. It was close to dinner time, so I figured Alfred and Larry would be starting dinner. I'd told them I could call for delivery, but they'd argued with me.

I opened the top drawer of my dresser and set the mirror inside. Olivia came in and sat on my bed. "Are you okay?"

I glanced at her and nodded. "It was great seeing her, even though it wasn't really her."

Moving to my bookcase, I lifted my hands and pushed out

magic to lift the jewelry box from its high perch and bring it down to me. I moved to the bed and sat with one leg bent in front of me and the other draped over the side. Olivia turned to face me, mirroring my pose.

Neither one of us spoke as I searched each drawer of the box until I found the coin. My heart beat crazy loud in my ears and my hands shook as I pulled out the coin. If this matched the one found on Mariam and Lorelai, it would confirm my mother had been killed by the same curse placed on each of the coins.

My heartbeat froze as I stared at it. "It's the same," I breathed, holding out the coin for Olivia to see.

"I'm so sorry." Olivia placed her hand on my arm. "We'll find out who did this."

Damn straight we would.

"Is that coin going to kill us?"

I snapped my gaze to Olivia's very worried look. "No. There is no magic left in this coin. If Yaya didn't feel any in it when *she* found it, then I'm guessing the curse is a one-time use deal. Once it did what it was intended, then the coin is just a coin."

"That makes sense." She hesitated. "How'd you feel magic on the one at Lorelai's then?"

"I'm guessing Yaya didn't get this one until a while after Mom died. Probably the hospital or funeral home returned it to us. But to be safe, I'll take this downstairs to the conservatory to douse it in saltwater. Neutralize any magic left in the silver." I waved my hand and the box floated back to its home on the top shelf of the bookcase.

When we reached the bottom floor, a knock sounded on the door. Olivia and I glanced at each other, and I stuffed the coin in my pocket and answered the door. No one was there, and I got a feeling of deja vu. Then, an envelope floated inside and stopped inches from my face. Yep, definitely been here before.

I plucked the coven letter out of the air and closed the door, then went through the kitchen to the conservatory. Setting the letter on my workstation while I filled a glass bowl with water and dumped salt into it. Once the bowl was full and salt mixed in, I dropped the coin inside. A puff of dark grey smoke shot up from the water.

"What was that? Please tell me it's not Satan's evil twin or anyone else." Olivia backed toward the door.

I snorted. "No. That was the last tiny bit of magic that was hidden inside the coin."

"Ah. Freaky."

Picking up the letter, I turned to press my back against the counter. I *so* didn't want to go to another meeting. But I had to play nice with the coven if I wanted to figure out who was behind the cursed coins.

"Are you going to open it or stare at it?"

"I don't know, I thought I could try to read it while still in the envelope." I tore the seal and pulled out the letter. My frown deepened as I read.

"Well?" Olivia prompted.

"Wallie, Owen, and I have been invited to a coven party. The dress is formal." I tossed the letter on the counter and sighed. "I don't want to go."

"But you have to for the sole reason that I *can't* go. You need to live the experience for me, then give me a play by play of the night." She grinned and batted her lashes. "Oh, are you taking Drew?"

"What? No."

"Why?"

I stared at her for a moment. "Because he's a born hunter. I'm pretty sure that would be frowned upon."

Olivia laughed. "It would be funny to see their faces if he showed."

The thought *was* tempting but I couldn't put Drew through

the torture of mingling with witches. Heck, I didn't even want to mingle with witches.

However, I couldn't turn down the invite because I had info to fish for.

CHAPTER ELEVEN

"Hey, thanks for coming!" I opened the door wide and stepped back so CeCe could come in. "I really appreciate it."

"No problem. I don't mind helping a new witch with her protection spells." CeCe walked in with a big smile on her face. "Even if you're not a totally new witch, I know you're learning a lot right now."

I twisted my hands together after I closed the door. "Actually, hang on."

Gathering my power, I spread it over the house, creating a barrier. Not a ward, anyone could come through it. But as long as the person wasn't under the barrier they couldn't hear anything that went on in the house. "There. Nobody can hear us now."

CeCe's eyebrows flew up. "Is this not a bit of training?"

I shook my head and smiled ruefully at her. "I need some help with something kind of major that I'd rather not have the whole town knowing."

She nodded as we walked into the living room. We sat and

Alfred walked in with a tray and tea. He grunted as he sat it down. CeCe's eyes twinkled. "Thank you, sir."

Alfred nodded his stiff neck and backed out of the room. Was he a bit smitten? It was hard to tell.

"I told you on the phone I needed help doing some mixing, but in reality..." I sucked in a deep breath before admitting the truth. "Do you know that I accidentally summoned Satan at Christmas?"

CeCe's teacup froze halfway to her waiting lips. Amusement lit up her eyes. "No?"

"Okay, so, yeah. I tried to summon Santa, and Satan is who came. He likes it here, and he's moved in next door." I pointed in the direction of his house.

"Oh-kay." The saucer tinkled as she set her cup back in it. "That can't be good."

I shrugged. "It's not been *bad* exactly, but Luci comes with a certain amount of, shall I say, *influence*. He can compel people to do as he wants, sort of enchant them."

CeCe whistled through her bottom teeth. "A rare ability."

"Right. So, I found an anti-compulsion spell, but I need juice to make it stick. Owen and I tried, but he's a full necromancer. He can do spells, but he doesn't generally have a lot of power behind them. Not like a witch does. And though I'm half necromancer, I need some help doing this."

CeCe rolled up her sleeves. "Let me at it. What are we charming?"

Jumping to my feet, I walked around the chairs toward the kitchen. "I have all my potion ingredients and stuff in here."

At the back of the kitchen, I opened the doors to the conservatory with a flourish, letting CeCe go in ahead of me. "Ohh," she said. "Black Oleander. That's a rare poison."

I let her admire my plants for a few moments before opening the grimoire to the appropriate charm.

"Are you trying to get rid of me again?" Luci asked,

appearing out of the blue at the end of the conservatory, right in front of CeCe. We both jumped and I screamed.

She stepped back with her hand at her throat. "My goodness," she said. "You're the devil."

He tipped an invisible hat as he gave a slight bow. "At your service."

CeCe turned to me with an eyebrow up. "Well, they do say the devil is handsome."

Luci preened as CeCe walked to the table and inspected the objects I had laid out there. I'd gone into town and purchased several necklaces, bracelets, and rings from a local craft shop. "I was hoping we could charm these so I could let my loved ones wear them. I'd rather they not be able to be compelled."

Luci scoffed. "Hey," he said in indignation. "I'm standing right here."

I arched my eyebrow at CeCe but ignored the devil. "Are you up for the charm?" I asked.

CeCe clasped her hands together, then pulled off a pretty diamond ring from her right hand. "Only if I get one, too."

"Deal," I said, and turned the book so she could read it, too. "Now, according to this, we brew a potion and until it comes to a boil, we have to say this incantation over and over. That part will be dull, but once it's boiled, we just dip the objects in the potion and we're done."

CeCe nodded and squinted down at the ingredient list. "Seems simple enough."

Luci pulled the book toward him. "Yeah, if you have enough juice. If you're not strong enough, the incantations won't take hold and the potion won't do anything but taste bad." He smacked his lips and grimaced. "Trust me."

"We'll take your word for it." I gave him a dry smile and started gathering ingredients.

"You know," Luci said. "Black jade holds hexes, curses, and charms better than other stones."

I looked at the jewelry. None of it was black jade. "How do I even know you're telling the truth?"

CeCe winced. "He is. I actually knew that."

Pursing my lips, I narrowed my eyes at Luci. "Conjur us a bunch, please."

He mouthed at me for a moment before snapping his teeth together, then waved his hand over the table. A handful of black jade stones appeared beside the jewelry. "I can't believe I'm helping you make sure I can't influence people."

"If you're as charming as they say you are, you don't need compulsion to get people to do as you'd like." CeCe fluttered her eyelashes at the devil. I wasn't sure if she was teasing him or maybe she liked flirting with danger.

Either way. I didn't think he'd hurt her, at least.

When it was time to turn the heat on the potion, we joined hands around the table as Luci poked around in my plants. I tried my best to ignore him as we chanted, but it was difficult. "*Et perspicuitati conducit*," we repeated over and over.

I focused as hard as I could, but when Luci snapped off a piece of black oleander, then sniffed it, my attention wavered.

Then the fool popped it into his mouth and started chewing. "Luci!" I exclaimed. "That's highly poisonous."

Luci grinned and chewed. "And absolutely delicious."

"Focus," CeCe hissed, then went back to chanting. I joined her.

Thirty minutes later, we had several pieces of jewelry as well as a handful of black jade stones, all covered in anti-compulsion charms. All in all, it had been a successful day, even with Luci looking constantly over our shoulders. And apparently immune to black oleander.

"Well, this was fun," CeCe said. She pocketed one of the jade stones and put on the ring we'd charmed. "I want us to get together again soon, okay? We can play with some powerful spells, see if we can't irritate the devil."

Luci sniffed. "We'll see." He winked. "It was a pleasure doing business with you, ladies." He tipped his imaginary hat again and disappeared.

Once Luci was gone, I turned to CeCe. "You and Lorelai said you wanted to talk to me about the accidents."

She leaned in and whispered, "Be careful. I don't think they were accidents. Someone is using dark magic."

"Do you have any guesses on who?"

CeCe frowned. "No. It's more intuition. But it's too much of a coincidence that it's only coven members dying." Her phone beeped and after she checked it, she said, "I have to go. We do have to get together again soon."

I walked CeCe out. Stepping out on the porch I saw Luci watering his roses. In the dark. Creepy, nosey neighbor. I waved and went back inside, shaking my head. Whatever was going on, at least Shipton Harbor was never boring.

CHAPTER TWELVE

"So, I have to ask..." I peeked at Drew out of the corner of my eye as my stomach rolled with anxiety. He slowed, approaching the stop sign at the end of my street. Taking a deep breath, I tried to will away the dread burning my insides. "I don't have any right to ask. We haven't said anything to each other about exclusivity or anything like that."

After glancing in the rearview mirror, he turned his head and waited at the stop sign, his features a mask of confusion. "What is it?" His voice was full of concern, not a note of suspicion. "I don't mind you asking me anything."

"I went in to pick up dinner at Guac On! the other night on my way home from the bookstore," I said carefully.

He looked in the mirror again but must've seen no cars coming, because he returned his attention to me instead of going. "Yeah?"

"And I saw you there with a woman." I threw up my hands, waving them between us. "Now, we've made no claims on one another, and in fact, I'm not actually wanting to nail this down as something super exclusive or like a—a commitment or something." My words came out rushed and in a bit of a panic. I had no idea what I was saying. I was just a rambling mess.

The corners of Drew's lips tipped up. Great, he thought I was nuts. I tried to explain and pull myself out of this mess. "I just think that if we *are* going to date other people, we should maybe make some ground rules." I sucked in a deep breath. "Like, maybe giving the other person a heads up when we might be dating in town. I'd rather not *actually* run into you on another date if possible."

Especially when it was likely that I'd get jealous and hex his date, which I had no right to do. Or claim him as mine. Did I?

Did I want to?

"Ava," Drew said gently, drawing my attention back to him. "It's not what it looked like."

Oh, I hated that line. That was always the first thing they said when caught cheating. I couldn't stand the thought that Drew might turn out to be one of *those* guys.

"No, you don't have to make an excuse or anything." I turned straight in my seat and clutched my knees, wishing I had something to do with my hands. "I'm not old fashioned or anything. This is all fine." Fine. It was *fine*.

"Ava." We both jumped when a horn tooted behind us, a short sound that made me think the driver wasn't mad, just letting us know they were back there. Drew cranked down the window on his old truck and waved out the window. "Sorry!"

He turned onto Main Street toward the town's only bowling alley. "That was my sister."

Sister? Now it made sense. The younger woman. The way she looked at him. It was love for a big brother. I sighed in relief before I could stop myself.

"Oh," I said in a small voice and scooted down in my seat. I really wanted to crawl under the seat. Damn it. Why had I let my mouth run away from me? I knew darn well that it could've been his sister or cousin or something. I'd even told myself that repeatedly.

"She was in town but just passing through. We had dinner and she went on her way, traveling south to see her grandkids." He winked at me. "And I *want* to be exclusive. I take it you don't?"

Great. My verbal diarrhea had really put me in the middle of it this time. "Well, I do, actually. But I still want to take it super slow." Shoot! Admitting that was scary. I'd rather have faced something undead.

He nodded and covered my hand with his, giving a small squeeze. His touch made me relax a little. "I'm okay with that. I know it's got to be incredibly difficult dating again after losing your husband."

The silence stretched between us. "It is," I said finally. "But a large part of me is ready. A smaller part feels incredibly guilty for moving on at all. He was the great love of my life. Am I allowed to have that *possibly* happen again?"

Heavy talk, mentioning love, but I wanted to be honest with Drew. He was a good man, and these were my true feelings. Plus, there'd definitely been sparks in the kisses we'd shared on a few occasions. Sparks I hadn't felt in five years. I wanted to see if they would catch and cause a wildfire.

He parked at the bowling alley, then turned in his seat. "I'm not sure if you've bowled here before?" His words held sarcasm.

With a laugh, I patted his knee. "Honey, you forget I grew up here. I remember when they opened this place."

He nodded and sighed. "Well, I hope you don't mind, but they have the best onion rings on the planet in there, and their salads are delicious if you don't want something heavy. I recommend the burger, though, if you don't mind the grease."

"I remember," I whispered. "And I love the grease. Salads are for non-date nights."

We decided to sit in the dining area and load up on calorie-laden yumminess before I kicked his firm behind in bowling.

So much had happened in the few days since we last spoke. More since we'd last *seen* each other, though we texted each other at least once a day. Usually just a brief check in about the case. But he hadn't checked in with me yesterday, so I hadn't had the chance to tell him what I found out from CeCe, which wasn't a whole lot more than we already knew. "Oh, I almost forgot."

I reached into my pocket and pulled out a silver men's ring with a black jade setting that was infused with the anti-compulsion potion CeCe and I cooked up a couple of nights ago.

Drew lifted a brow. "What's that?"

"A gift." I smiled and slid it across the table. "It's infused with magic. A charm to protect against Luci's compulsion and other evil things."

He picked it up and placed it on the middle finger of his right hand. "Thank you."

A warmth settled inside me. "CeCe helped me with the spell. Plus it gave us a chance to talk about the *accidents*."

I told him about Yaya's imprint and finding the coin that was on my mother when she died. "It's the same as the others: blackened, which means some sort of magical death, most often means murder."

I didn't need to say that my *mother* was murdered out loud. Drew connected the dots quickly and covered my hand. I rolled mine over and held his.

"How was the coven meeting?"

I shrugged, easing my hand from his to pick up an onion ring. "I'd say boring. But it was also interesting. I knew they were snotty before, but they don't get involved with the community at all. It's like they live separate from humans or try to as much as possible."

I told him about the twins, how odd they seemed. Also

Bevan, how it seemed like he didn't like anyone. "I didn't sense strong enough emotions from any of them that would warrant them killing their own."

"Yet, it is a witch who is cursing the coins?"

I nodded. "I think so, unless there is a powerful demon running around." I snorted as Lucifer popped into my mind. "Besides my new neighbor. But Luci wouldn't let one of his Hell buddies run rogue, would he?"

"I agree with you. I think he enjoys it here too much to let a demon spoil it for him." Drew took a bite of an onion ring and chewed before speaking again. "My hunch is this is a witch with a grudge."

That was my thought too. But we'd talked shop long enough. Wanting to change the subject to something more date related, I asked, "Where are you from?"

One corner of his mouth dipped, making a sexy half frown. "Asheville, North Carolina. My family has an obscene amount of property in the mountains. They use it for hunter central and HQ. Training and so on."

Something dark passed through his irises.

"You didn't like it there?" I chewed, giving him time to answer but he replied immediately. No hesitation.

"Hated it." He took a drink of his beer. "I never understood the purpose of killing and torturing beings only because they were different or not human. Especially when those beings were innocent of crimes. Most were just trying to live a normal life and wanted to be left alone."

"So you moved to Shipton Harbor where there is a really old family line of witches?" I was sure the hunters knew of my family bloodline. It went back hundreds of years. At least my mother's side did.

He smiled. "I moved here about ten years ago, joined the police force and was voted Sheriff two years ago. I like it here. And my family knows not to come here hunting. This is my domain. If they come to visit, they aren't to stay more than a few days."

Wow. That was interesting. I knew he had a good relationship with his mom and apparently his sister. He'd told me he and his dad didn't always see eye to eye. I didn't know he could just tell them not to hunt in the area he lived in and they would actually respect his wishes. "So we can rule out hunters for cursing the witches?"

"At least hunts from my family. But don't worry, I would know the moment another hunter came into the area. No one but Lily has been nearby since my parents visited last summer." He finished off his last onion ring.

"Does your no hunting in Shipton rule extend outside the family?"

"Hunters don't follow a single ruling body. They pretty much govern themselves. That's why it's easy for those like Carmen to get away with killing senselessly for so long." He watched me for a few moments, which made me a little uncomfortable.

Don't get me wrong, I could've stared at him all day, every day for the rest of my life just as long as he didn't stare back.

Um, did I just say every day for the rest of my life? Well, don't tell Drew. I didn't need him getting pushy and demanding on me.

CHAPTER THIRTEEN

Owen and Wallie both were going straight onto my crap-list. I'd given them an entire week's notice to be ready for this party. But, no, they had other, more important things to do besides being by my side like the supportive family they were supposed to be.

I didn't want to be rude and cancel altogether, but going by myself had caused my nerves to go haywire on me. Taking a deep breath and releasing it, I tried to exhale all of the frustration that had built up inside me since Miriam died in a yarn cocoon. I had to find out who killed her and Lorelai. Because that killer was most likely—I was a hundred percent sure—the same one who killed my mother and Larry.

What better way to start looking than with the coven? So I had to go to the fancy party.

Alone. Darn them!

Wallie, I understood. It was March, almost spring break, and he had big tests to study for. But Owen could've rescheduled his date.

He'd taken a shine to Kelly, the owner of the bakery beside

the bookstore. Apparently, when he worked shifts for Clint, he liked to stop in and sample Kelly's eclairs. And had plans to sample other things.

I shook out of that thought with a shudder. I was not thinking about what he could possibly be sampling. Kelly was beautiful and one of the nicest people I'd met in a long time. Owen deserved to have a real life and spend it with someone. I just didn't need any visuals that I couldn't unsee.

And they could've rescheduled their date.

I pulled up to the valet, and as I slowed the car, I stared at the entrance of CeCe's house. Well, mansion. Light, new age music drifted from the open door.

A tingle of magic caressed my skin as Luci appeared in my passenger seat in an all-black tux. I jumped and swallowed a scream. After my heart started working again, I glared at him.

Darn him. He looked amazing. Devilishly amazing.

"Hello, darling," he said smoothly, a wicked smile spreading across his face. "Fancy a date for the soirée?"

A date? With the devil? Uh, *no*!

Movement behind Lucifer, outside the car, caught my attention. Great. The valet walked forward, one of the coven member's teenage sons again, and waited with his hands crossed while I turned to glare at Luci. "What are you doing here?" I hissed.

"I stay apprised of the local coven's goings on, and imagine my dismay when I learned you had no date to tonight's festivities. I had to come to my new friend's rescue." He winked at me. "Where is the beau anyway?"

Friend? I wasn't sure I'd call us that. Not even close. And as for *beau*... "I'll have you know, he is working. Not that it is any of your business. Besides, I don't need a date," I said, glancing out at the kid. "And this isn't the sort of function I could just bring anyone to."

Could Luci disappear without the guy knowing he'd ever

been in the car? I didn't think so. "Shoot," I muttered. "You're going to have to go with me. He's seen you."

Luci's face brightened in a wide grin. "Fantastic." He threw open the passenger door and launched himself out of the car. "I've got her door," he called and hurried around the car. Oh, great.

The boy stepped back and Luci opened my door with a flourish, our clothing and his behavior so out of place for my Hyundai, Dia.

But then, I didn't really fit in at this fancy house, anyway. Mansions weren't exactly my style. If one of my books took off and started making tons of money, I still wouldn't want to buy another home. Not only because my coastal house seemed to have its own personality, but because fancy-schmancy wasn't really in my repertoire.

The dress I'd chosen was long and black, and I had on enough girdles and shapewear under it to keep me from eating or breathing all night. At least it had lace sleeves. They made me feel pretty sexy. Especially in the heels.

But as I started up the stairs to the front door, the heels began to pinch.

Damn. It was going to be a long night.

The door opened on its own and Luci and I stepped inside. "Wait," I hissed. "Who are we going to say you are?"

He grinned wickedly and waved his hand over his face. He'd done the spell so I could sort of see the glamour and his true face at the same time, though I suspected I was the only one. "Cousin Bertrand, visiting from out of town."

I studied him, and I had to admit it was impressive. To a stranger no one would think twice if we said we were related. But someone who knew my family would be a little harder to convince. However, Lucifer had transformed into a handsome, older man with grey in his temples and a streak in his bangs that were swept to the side. His skin was a little paler and his jawbone squarer. He'd even changed his eyes green to match mine. Well, not an exact copy. Luci's new eyes were lighter, less dark-magic. I wasn't even sure how he'd pulled that off. The eyes were the portals to our soul. At least that was what I'd always heard.

The click of heels against marble tile brought me out of admiring my new cousin.

I turned and smiled as CeCe walked out of the library. "Ava," she cried. "You came." She hurried out down the hall in a gorgeous crimson gown that hugged her modest curves and flared out about mid-thigh. She looked like a gothic queen with her black hair and pale skin. Bevan Magnus followed her out.

CeCe grabbed my shoulders and pulled me close, pressing a kiss to each cheek. "And who is this handsome fellow?"

"CeCe, this is my cousin. He's from..." Shit. We hadn't said where he was from.

"Florida," Luci said. "I'm Bertrand." He offered CeCe his hand and simpered. "So sorry for the intrusion, but I begged dear cousin Ava to bring me. I adore my coven at home and couldn't wait to meet the people inviting Ava to join their ranks."

"It's no intrusion," CeCe said graciously. "Though I did hope your son and," her voice rose questioningly, "*friend,* Owen, would've been able to come?"

"I'm so sorry, Wallie couldn't get away from his upcoming tests, and Owen had a prior engagement."

Bevan pushed himself closer. "Pleasure." He held his hand out and looked at Luci with more respect in his eyes than he'd shown me. Of course. "I'm Bevan."

"Bertrand." Luci held out his hand to Magnus. "Call me Bertie."

Now it made more sense. Bevan didn't like women. Or at least, didn't like women in positions of power. Great.

"Please, come in," Bevan said, holding his hand out. As

Bertie walked forward, Bevan put his hand at the small of his back.

Maybe it was less about not liking women and more about Bevan liking Bertie. Interesting.

The crowd was small, and CeCe held up her hand. When she started to speak, the room fell silent. "Friends, we're all eager to celebrate the inclusion of Ava in our midst but let us take a moment of quiet for our dear departed witch, Lorelai. A horrible, tragic accident. I propose at the end of our night, we participate in a protection charm together. Our coven has endured an awful coincidence of tragedy lately. Perhaps we can do a bit to turn Lady Luck around."

The small group clapped quietly.

"To Lorelai," Bevan said, holding his champagne glass up. Someone appeared at my elbow with a tray. I took a glass and raised it.

After a few seconds, Bevan drank, then raised his glass again. "And to Ava, the newest member of our great coven."

Erm, what? I stumbled while leaning toward CeCe, then quickly righted myself. Bertie-Luci grabbed my elbow for a little added support.

His hand was really warm.

"I'm sorry," I said softly. "But I haven't accepted entry yet, have I?"

Cece turned to me with wide eyes and a face full of surprise. "We just assumed," she hissed. "We never thought you'd say no after what a wonderful time we all had the other night."

"I mean, it was nice, sure, but I'm not sure I'm the coven type," I said. "I've done things on my own for such a long time."

She stepped back and her face closed down. "Of course. However you wish to proceed is fine."

Well, shit. I'd offended her. "How about we take it slow?" I asked, feeling like I was talking to Drew again. "And go from there?"

With a sniff, CeCe nodded her head. "That's fine."

She went to leave, but I stopped her with a hand on her arm. "This is sudden. No one mentioned that I'd be inducted tonight. You must understand that the history my family had with the coven isn't puppies and rainbows."

CeCe relaxed and she took my hand in hers. "That was before I took over as coven leader. Your mother's death was a huge hit to all of us. She was loved among all the coven members as were Winnie and Esme."

I hadn't heard anyone say Yaya's first name in a long time. It sent a pulse of sadness through me.

"Did you know your mother was set to be voted as coven leader a few weeks before she died?" CeCe swiped a finger under one of her eyes. "We've all lost too many friends and family." That was odd. She'd not even fully joined and they'd planned to make her coven leader? How was that?

I stilled and studied CeCe. I hadn't known Mom was to be the coven leader. "No, I didn't know that. Then again, after she died, I withdrew from magic. Especially my necromancer powers. Yaya and Winnie pulled away from the coven then."

CeCe nodded. "I stepped in after that. We gave your family the space they needed to grieve. But we had hoped that you would rejoin. I don't tolerate prejudice against others and have opened membership to all magic born."

But they kept the coven to thirteen members. No more, no less. Apparently, there were some traditions that didn't go away. And there were only witches. *All* didn't mean the same thing to both of us.

At the sound of her name, CeCe glanced up to see Bevan calling her. She sighed. Before she let go of my hand, she sent a thought to me. "*The High Witch position is yours as it was your mother's. Just say the word, and I'll step down and pass on the torch. Ah, it's a potion, actually."*

While I processed her words, she drew me into a hug and said out loud, "Welcome to the coven, Ava." A potion? Why a potion?

Then she darted off to tend to Bevan. I watched her leave, stunned. Why did she tell me that telepathically? Was it not public knowledge? Then again, she believed there was a killer inside the coven and maybe didn't want him or her knowing I was next in line to lead the coven.

How in the Hell did she send me her thoughts? That was a trick I needed to learn. I wonder if Yaya's imprint knew how.

I caught Bevan's stare... more like glare. For a brief moment his aura shifted to a darker grey, then was back to its usual blue. Interesting.

A laugh drew my attention to the other side of the room where Luci...er *Bertie* was entertaining a couple of female witches. Leena and Mai, I believed were their names.

Frowning, I made a mental note to make more charms for the coven. When I stepped forward, one of the twins appeared in front of me. I jumped and moved back a few steps.

He didn't materialize or anything. I just hadn't seen him approach. Damn it. I really needed to pay attention.

"Welcome to the coven."

I forced a smile. "Thank you."

He stared at me, so I stared back, lifting both brows, because I wasn't talented enough to do the one brow lift. Dark magic flowed from him, tingling my skin. It surrounded me, teasing my own dark powers. I didn't like it. But I couldn't run out the door because that would make me look weak. A weak prey was dead prey.

"Can I help you with something?" I asked, amping up my own dark magic.

One side on his mouth lifted in a smirk. "Do be careful. Coven members haven't had much good luck lately."

Once again, I was left standing in the center of the room with my mouth open in shock as I watched him walk out.

This was definitely going to be a long night.

After the twin, whom I never got to ask which one he was, the evening was pleasant. My guess the twin was Brandon, because he was the creepier of the two. But I could have been wrong.

The other coven members were nice, and I didn't get bad vibes from anyone else besides the twins and Bevan.

Luci came up to me a while later, after I'd talked to everyone at least once. Some twice. "You look ready to go."

"I am. These shoes are killing me. Plus I've had enough playing nicey nice to the witches." I laughed at my own joke and quickly realized that I was starting to like some of these witches.

Well, that was a twist I hadn't seen coming.

Luci took my arm and curled it in his. "Come, Ava, dear, let's go home."

"Thank you. You know, for crashing the party and pretending to be my cousin."

"Any time, dear." Luci really came through tonight and almost seemed normal.

I had to remember. No matter how nice he was, I was still finding out a way to send him back to Hell.

CHAPTER FOURTEEN

My sofa had never been so comfortable. After drinking entirely too much champagne last night and letting Luci drive me home, I didn't want to be anywhere but right here, bundled up in my fluffiest robe, watching bad reality TV.

Just a lazy, relaxing day.

So—of course!—my doorbell rang.

Great. I hoped it wasn't anything that would involve me leaving the house.

"I got it," Larry called from the kitchen. Or preferably the couch.

"Don't answer it if it's someone that will freak out," I replied, frowning.

He stopped in the living room doorway. "Give me a little credit, Ava."

I would not. The darn skeleton kept forgetting he was all bones. He liked to hang out with the flesh-wearing people too often. I even caught him meditating in the middle of the backyard the other day. It was a good thing my only neighbor close enough to see him was a demon. *The* demon.

"Hello, Officer," Larry said. I sat bolt upright. Please tell me this was not Drew.

"Uh, hello?" Drew replied.

Crap!

Waving my hand over my face, I glamoured myself just enough to not look quite so crazy. Or homeless. I hadn't taken my makeup off before collapsing in bed the night before, so I removed my dark circles and tamed my hair. I didn't mind Drew seeing me without makeup or in my robe, but he didn't need to see the blotchy leftover foundation or my racoon eyes.

Too bad I couldn't get rid of this hangover so easily. There was a potion cure for a hangover, but it was so disgusting I wouldn't use it. Drinking raw eggs and frog toes wasn't on my list of things to do the day after too much champagne.

"Hello," I said softly as I muted the TV and scooted over on the couch to make room for Drew to sit next to me.

"Hey, there," he said, studying me for a long few seconds. Did he know I was glamouring myself? Probably, since he was a born hunter and was sensitive to magic. "Late night?" He looked at his watch and raised his eyebrows.

I moaned and let my head hang back. "Yeah. There was a coven meeting. The invitation said fancy dress, and when I got there, it turned out it was a party to celebrate me accepting their invitation."

Drew furrowed his brow. "But at our date last weekend, you said you weren't sure if you'd join. I got the impression you were leaning toward not."

I snorted. "Apparently they couldn't conceive of the possibility that I might refuse them."

He nodded. "I see."

"That's not the best part. Although, this ended up being a big help to me. As I pulled up to the party, Lucifer appeared in the car beside me."

Drew's jaw dropped. "What happened?"

I sucked in a deep breath and thought about how Luci had captivated the coven. "Actually, having him there took the heat off of me a bit. He was charming and made the rounds, so I wasn't the only new person in the room. He introduced himself as my distant cousin, in for a visit." I imitated his British accent when I spoke the last sentence.

With a chuckle, Drew shook his head. "Didn't they recognize him? He was at the Christmas party, and I imagine several of the coven came to that. Plus, he's not exactly been hiding from the town. He goes out and about often."

"No, he glamoured his appearance so he looked different." I shrugged. "I'm not saying I want him to stick around, but it was nice having him on my side last night. Plus, I was able to observe everyone better."

Drew pursed his lips. "Well, at least he did something nice."

"Hey," I said. "Paris was nice."

We both dissolved into laughter. However nice it was, it had also been freaky and had given Drew some insane motion sickness. "What brings you here this morning?" I asked.

"Well," he said and pulled a folded piece of paper out of his jacket pocket. "I've been doing some research."

The white paper crinkled as he unfolded it and handed it to me. "I've been searching all cases of accidental deaths in the county, looking for patterns, and there's a big one."

"Oh?" I asked as I took the paper from him. He explained the names and dates listed on the paper.

"Yeah. These are all people that died with an odd coin in their pockets. Most of the coins were given back to the families, but in one case, there was no next of kin. The body was cremated, and the ashes buried cheaply in the town cemetery. I have the coin here." He pulled a small baggie from his pocket and handed it over.

Sure enough, it looked exactly like the ones we'd found so far. "No," I breathed.

"Yes and get this. That death was in the seventies." He stared at me with his eyebrows up and nostrils flared.

"You guys keep records and personal effects that long?" I asked.

He nodded. "Forever, really. If we run out of room, we'll rent a storage place or build a shed, but you never know what might come up that you need evidence like this for." He pointed to the paper. "Case in point."

Reaching over, Drew took the paper and shuffled it. I hadn't even realized there was a second page. "This is a list of all deaths that weren't attributed to natural causes in the county going back to the sixties, no matter if coins were noted or not. Accidents and murders."

I browsed the list. Most of them were car wrecks. But there were more that were freakish, out of the norm like the umbrella thing or a freak lightning storm. Some of the others included smothered by a pile of winter coats, drowned in a vat of molasses, slipped on a banana peel and broke neck, a firework blew up in one person's face.

"Holy crap," I whispered. "This is terrible." So many people and they all had a coin found on them.

I lifted the bag with the coin up. "Can I take this out? The coin my Yaya found on Mom still had a little of the curse left over. I want to put it in saltwater just to be sure."

He stared at the coin and nodded. "Yeah, do that."

Setting the papers on the coffee table I stood and waved Drew to follow. "Step into my magical office."

He chuckled, but I caught a spark of concern light up his teal eyes for a second. It occurred to me in that moment that he wasn't used to magic and all the craziness that had happened over the last several months.

I turned to face him, and he stopped short, his hands resting

374

on my hips. My breath caught as heat filled every part of me. "You don't have to come into the conservatory if it makes you uncomfortable."

He lifted one hand and ran his knuckles down my cheek. A soft sigh slipped from my lips as I leaned into his touch. It'd been too long since I gave myself over to a man. Clay had been my only lover.

"Magic is a big part of you. Dark, light, and everything in between." He slid his hand around to cup the back of my head. Then his lips pressed against mine and my world exploded in a rush of power and desire.

He ended the kiss and rested his forehead to mine. "I want all of you, Ava. You never have to hide who you are from me."

Something bloomed in my heart. Most of my life, I hid what I was, my power. I did it with Clay to keep the peace with his family. Recently, I caught myself doing it with Drew because he was a born hunter. Even though he swore he denied that half of him.

I placed my hand over his heart. "You don't have to hide who you are either." I pressed a finger from my other hand to his lips. "Hunters are born with magic and other abilities. I've done some research. You don't have to hunt down innocent people just because you're a hunter. Use your gifts for good."

A seductive smile formed on his handsome face. "I will if you will."

"Deal!" I linked my fingers with his and pulled him toward the kitchen. That was when I noticed Alfred standing in the archway to the kitchen, watching us.

Maybe I was crazy, but I sensed emotions coming from him. Concern and protectiveness were the strongest, but there was also caution and dislike. Did Alfred not like Drew?

I stopped in front him and his gaze softened as he looked at me. Then he handed his tablet to me. On the screen he'd typed, **"What would you like for lunch? Dinner?"**

"You don't have to cook all the time. We can order out. Or Drew and I..." I turned to Drew, noticing for the first that he was dressed in plain clothes. A pair of dark blue jeans and a charcoal grey t-shirt. "I guess you aren't working today. Did you have other plans?"

"I was going to ask you the same thing."

"Looks like we're spending the day together." I tugged him through the kitchen to the conservatory. I heard Alfred grunt as he took steaks out of the freezer, making an executive decision about dinner. That was fine with me. I wasn't picky.

I went straight to the sink and filled a glass bowl with water while pulling out the salt from the shelf over it. From the corner of my eye I watched Drew drift over to the plants lined up on shelves along the far wall. "Don't touch the ones on the top shelf. They're poison."

He looked at me with a raised brow. "Should I ask why you have poisonous plants?"

I shrugged. "You never know when you need them." Then I started laughing. "They were Aunt Winnie's and for some reason lived through the last year without anyone tending to them. So I take it as a sign that they need to stay where they are."

I sure hoped I'd never have to use them in a spell or on anyone. Killing people by poison was not on my to-do list. Ever. But there were still some nonlethal spells that required them. Until I learned how to use them properly, they would stay on that shelf like little creepers, watching over the others.

Once the saltwater was ready, I took the coin out of the bag and dropped it in the water. The same grey smoke puffed out of the water as soon as the coin went under.

"Was that...?"

"The curse, yes. What was left of it." I faced him, and he moved closer. His clean cedar scent enveloped me, making me want things I hadn't had in *so* long.

"What did you want to do today?"

A few naughty thoughts flashed in my mind. But I said, "I'm open to whatever."

Desire flashed in his gaze, making my flesh hot. "There is the Founders' Party going on downtown."

"That sounds great." It was the perfect thing I needed to keep my mind off the accidents-slash-murders and the fact that I hadn't a clue who was doing it. "I just need to clean up and change."

Clint had wrangled Owen into helping with it, to my delight and his disgruntlement.

I took the coin out of the water, dried it off and placed it back into the bag. Drew stuffed it back into his pocket. "I'll need to return it to evidence."

Rushing upstairs and to my room, I heard water running in the upstairs bathroom. When I passed it, I stopped and stared with my mouth open, truly shocked. After the things I'd seen over the last few months, I hadn't expected to be shocked again. Ever.

Larry stood in front of the sink, water running, with a washcloth in his hand. And he was cleaning out his eye sockets.

Eww. It was disturbing, yet I couldn't look away. How the hell could he see to know he was cleaning them thoroughly?

Owen stopped next to me. "That is not right."

"Tell me about it." We stared in silence as he finished with his eye sockets and wiped down all of his... uh, *face*, and even his teeth.

Just then Larry turned to us and we jumped. "Morning... well afternoon, guys." Then he turned off the water, draped the washcloth over the faucet, and then left the bathroom, walking past us like it was totally normal for a skeleton to clean his eyes sockets.

When did my life take a turn to crazytown?

CHAPTER FIFTEEN

"I'm more excited than I thought I'd be." I had butterflies in my stomach, but I was thrilled to be doing something other than reading grimoires and raising the dead.

We walked down the sidewalk from the spot we had to park in. It was a good thing my date was the town sheriff, otherwise, we'd have been just as likely to find a parking spot in my yard, way outside of town.

Everyone in the county had turned up for this shindig. I hadn't remembered it being this busy when I was a kid.

"You know," Drew said as his knuckles brushed mine, sending a jolt of pleasure through me. "Your family were founders."

I glanced at him out of the corner of my eye as we stepped onto the sidewalk lining Main Street, leaving his SUV in the police department parking lot. "I do know that. How do you?"

He shrugged. "I read the founders' book." For some reason, he didn't quite meet my eyes.

Tipping my voice up into an innocent lilt, I gave him a megawatt smile. "You did?" I asked. "Whatever for?"

He snickered. "Don't act like that. I can't be interested in what's going on in my town?"

We crossed the street at the town's only stoplight, heading for the big gazebo in the park in the middle of town. All of the shops were designed in a square around it with the police station and fire station just down the road.

"Hey!" Carrie called. She had a bean bag toss game set up. "Play? Proceeds go toward getting new desks in the Kindergarten classrooms."

"Sure," Drew said, pulling out his wallet. "How much?"

"A dollar gets you three throws. If you win, you get to pick a prize from the prize bucket."

I peered into the bucket and clasped my hands together. "Please, win me a prize," I said. "I *need* this tiara." There was a silver, plastic tiara in the bucket that would look amazing on me.

Drew grinned and tossed the little bean bag in the air a few times before turning to the table.

"Stand there." Carrie pointed to a piece of tape on the grass. "The blue tape is for adults. Green is for kids. Pink is for toddlers."

"Whoops," Drew said. He was standing on the green and backed up. "Here we go. A tiara for my lady."

I clapped as he threw and missed completely. "Aw, that's okay." I tried to give him a supportive and encouraging look, but it really came across as me just laughing at him.

"Uh-huh," he said. "I'm just getting warmed up."

He threw again and tipped the top bottle on the triangle. "See?" he said. "Third time's a charm."

"Right." I squinted at the last beanbag in his hand. As he threw it, and while it sailed through the air, I twitched my finger and set it on more of a straight and true course.

Unfortunately, Drew had thrown it very wide, so when I corrected it, there was a noticeable curve. As the bottles clattered to the ground, both Drew and Carrie eyed me suspiciously.

I looked around the square, pretending they weren't staring at me and trying to figure out if I'd helped him. With a small jump, I faked noticing they were staring at me. "What? Oh! You won! Yay!" I hurried forward and grabbed the cheap tiara from the prize bucket. "Awesome."

Drew took it and carefully positioned it on my head, shaking his own as he did. "Cheater," he said quietly.

"I don't know what you're talking about, but I want to go over there next." I pointed toward the next booth. "I think we're expected there."

"What do you mean?" Drew eyed the dunking booth suspiciously. "Why would we be expected?"

Luci walked around the large booth and clapped when he saw us. "Oh, lovely. Our first volunteer. Come around here and get changed, please."

Drew turned to me with wide, panicked eyes. "What is happening?"

"Well," I said carefully. "Luci here, asked me yesterday if you'd be game to take a turn in the dunking booth, and I said sure, why not?"

His face went from shocked to scrunched up and suspicious. "Are you trying to get me to get you back?"

I shrugged. "Perhaps. Maybe I find it interesting to see what you think you can come up with to pay me back."

He laughed low in his throat. Not quite amusement, more of a promise of retribution. "Oh, I look forward to coming up with something."

"Come along," Luci called. "I've got a little changing tent back here."

Drew walked around the tank, but kept his narrowed gaze on me, his eyes promising I was going to regret this.

Whatever he came up with would be totally worth it.

Two minutes later, he climbed into the tank and sat on the little pedestal in a pair of swim trunks. He shivered and crossed his arms around his wide chest.

He had a dusting of hair on his chest, not much, but what I could see of it was just beginning to go gray. Like the hair at his temples.

His stomach hadn't begun to paunch, even though he was certainly old enough for it. Instead, he sat there, shivering, with the body of an older man who took care of himself. Thick, firm muscles. Broad shoulders.

Oh, geez. Now I was nervous about the fact that we might, in the near future, see one another totally naked. My insecurities about my body flashed through my mind, but I shoved them to the side as I fished five dollars out of my purse.

"Come one and come all!" Luci said in a booming voice. "Dunk the sheriff for a mere five dollars! All proceeds go to helping the firehouse get new hoses!"

I chuckled and Luci gave me a dirty look. Not many of us even knew he was the actual devil, but at least a handful of townspeople would likely get a snicker out of the fact that the devil was raising money to help put out fires. Irony.

"I'll go!" I called. Unbeknownst to either Luci or Drew, I sent a small spell to the water. Drew was cold now, and he'd be cold when he emerged from the water, but I made sure the water would be warm and comfortable. He'd want to get dunked to warm up. It was the least I could do after volun-telling him that he was dunking.

Luci took my money and handed me three balls. Stepping back to the line in the grass, I squinted at the bullseye and pulled my arm back.

"No cheating!" Drew called.

"How could she cheat?" Clint asked from behind me. "She either hits it or she doesn't."

I turned and winked at my part-time boss. Owen and I had

managed to keep our supernatural side from him thus far. Hopefully, it stayed that way.

"You ready to get wet?" I asked Drew.

He rolled his eyes. "Sure."

"What you probably don't know about me was that I played softball all through high school and could've had a partial scholarship to college playing softball."

I didn't need magic to do this. Poor Drew. His face darkened as he glared at me.

Aiming carefully, I put just enough spin on the ball and let it fly.

Straight into the bullseye. And not even a drop of magic.

Drew yelped and his arms flew up as the podium fell, and he slipped off and into the water. Hey, it could've been a lot worse. I could've left the water cold.

A small crowd had gathered, including Olivia and Sam. They cheered the hardest as Drew climbed back onto the seat again. "Okay," he called. "You got me. Let someone else go."

He wiped the water from his eyes as I held out the next ball. Olivia darted forward. "I believe I will!" she chirped.

As I handed her the ball, I winked at Drew. "Don't worry!" I called. "She wasn't on the school softball team!"

"That's right!" Olivia agreed. "I played on my *church* softball team." She flung the ball at the bullseye and nailed it, sending Drew splashing back into the water.

He came up sputtering. "Okay, the next person isn't allowed to have been on any softball team."

When he climbed up and looked back out at us, it was just in time for me to hand the last ball I'd paid for to Sam.

Drew's face pinched as he glared. "Deputy, kindly remember I'm your boss."

Sam's face split into a broad grin. "I know. And you're off duty." He pulled his arm back, then addressed Drew again.

"Have we ever talked about my favorite weekend passtime in college?"

Drew shook his head slowly.

"Darts." Sam threw the ball and rocked on his heels as it hit its target. "Not quite the same as being good at softball, but it gets the job done," he said as Drew splashed around in the tank.

After another round of dunking Drew, we let the kids that had lined up to sink the sheriff have their turn.

Drew was relieved. I knew my payback was going to be wicked by the playful glares he sent me. It would all be worth it.

Hell, it was already worth it to see him without his shirt.

Half an hour later, one of the firefighters replaced Drew in the dunk tank. Once he was in dry clothes, I used magic to dry his hair. He was all smiles and admitted he had fun. But still said he would get me back.

By the end of the day we were walking hand in hand. I really didn't realize it when it happened, but I liked it. I liked him. One thing I learned about Drew was underneath that alpha male, sheriff façade, he knew how to have fun. And he was so easy to talk to.

I looked forward to more dates with him.

CHAPTER SIXTEEN

"Uno!" Sammie yelled, doing a little dance in his chair. "I beat you again!"

Alfred grunted and threw his cards down on the table, then he wagged his finger at Sammie while the child giggled mercilessly. "You can never beat me, Alfie!" he crowed.

"Don't be a sore winner," Olivia called.

I chuckled as I walked back toward the living room with mugs of tea. The ghoul, the skeleton, and the kid had set up a card game in the dining room, within eyesight of us in the living room.

She'd come over since I didn't have a shift at the bookstore, and I'd just finished writing the first draft of my latest manuscript. I liked to give my books a week to breathe before going back in and starting my second run through.

We'd been going through the occult books that had finally come in at Clint's shop, looking for a way to *un*summon the devil.

There were shockingly few spells to undo a summons, and

the only ones we'd found had failed. The devil was not an average, garden-variety demon, apparently. Just our luck.

No, he was a fallen angel tasked with the job of ruling Hell. And there was nothing about vanquishing an angel.

Olivia's phone rang as she sighed and leaned back, rubbing her eyes. "Hey, honey," she chirped when she picked up. Must've been Sam.

Her face fell as she listened. "Oh, no. I'm sorry to hear that." She listened for a few more seconds. "Yes, we'll be right there."

"What is it?" I asked as soon as she hung up.

"We've got another accidental death. Drew wants us to come down and see if we can see anything or sense anything that he can't. They found a coin."

I heaved a big sigh. "Leave Sammie here?" I asked as I jumped up and headed for the foyer and my sneakers. "Owen is here."

"That would be great." She grabbed her jacket. "Owen, Sammie," she called up the stairs.

Sammie came out of the kitchen as Owen stuck his head into the stairwell. "Yes?"

"We've got to run an errand. Alfred is entertaining Sammie, but could you keep an eye on them?"

He nodded. "Sure, no problem. I was about to come down for some lunch, anyway. Has he eaten?"

They arranged for Owen to make a round of PBJs, and we hit the road.

"Have you warned Sammie about Alfred?" I asked. "I mean, he's great with him, but he's still a ghoul."

She nodded as we got into my car. "I did. I told him to keep at arm's reach and always be aware that Alfred is undead. Can't be too careful. I'm glad Owen is there with them."

I'd done a spell on the house a few weeks before. Olivia and I had found it in one of the old grimoires. No harm could come to the innocent in that house now. Nobody could hurt Sammie, though I didn't know if it applied to stuff like accidents or if the little guy fooled around and hurt himself somehow. Still, we both had peace of mind leaving him like this.

"Did Sam say what happened?" I asked. "Or where we're going?"

She gave me a dark look as I pulled to the end of my driveway, waiting on a direction and wondering whether I should go to the left or right. "It's the leader of the coven," she said. "CeCe."

"No." I gasped. "How?"

She knew CeCe from living in town all her life. Plus, I'd told her all about both coven meetings and when CeCe came over to help with the charms. "He didn't say. But if they found a coin, I'd be willing to bet it's something weird."

That much was true. My chest tightened at the thought of CeCe dying. I was starting to like her. Then another thought hit me. With CeCe dead, I was next in line to lead the coven. Crap.

"So, to the mansion?" I asked.

"Yep." She sighed. "He did say it's not pretty, so brace yourself."

Ugh. I knew what that meant. It was probably bloody or particularly gory. Not what I wanted to see after just having been there the weekend before.

Sam and Drew met us outside. "Our guys have been over the scene already," Sam said.

Drew put his arm around me, and I sank into him, loving his warmth. "We're officially calling this a string of murders," he said. "The coins are too much of a coincidence."

"Okay, so you just want me to confirm her witch's mark?" I asked. "I already know she's a witch."

Sam and Drew exchanged a glance. Drew cleared his throat. "Er, actually, I can see the marks. We thought you could try to get her to talk like you tried before. See if she saw anything or knows anything."

"Sure," I said. "I can try. Are we alone here?"

Drew nodded and pulled me closer to him. "Her husband is human, right?"

"I have no idea. She never introduced me to a husband, and the only people here when I was were the coven members and a few of their older children."

Drew sighed. "Okay. The husband is probably human if he wasn't at the coven meetings. We sent him to the station to fill out paperwork. And their children live out of state. They're flying in. We're alone here for the moment."

They led Olivia and me into the house that had magically welcomed me in just a few days before.

CeCe laid in a pool of blood in the doorway of the big entrance hall and her enormous dining room. "What happened?" I asked, moving closer.

Sam said, "She fell."

I peered at the body. "Is that...?" I wasn't sure if what I was seeing was really what I was seeing. "A casserole?"

"Yes," Sam said. "She was on her way into the dining room with a casserole for her and her husband. She tripped and the glass broke, cutting her carotid."

"It's not the blood loss that often kills the person when they cut the carotid," Olivia chirped.

We all turned to stare at her. "What?" she sniffed and tossed her hair back. "I know stuff."

"Well, what is it then?" Drew asked.

"Blood pressure loss to the brain. Eventually, blood loss would do it, sure, but the loss of blood to the brain is the main culprit."

I wasn't sure she was right about that. I'd done a bit of research myself, being an author. I was pretty sure I'd read that a fully cut carotid would cause death by blood loss in five minutes or so.

Not that I was about to contradict Olivia. At least not at the moment. Besides, It didn't matter to me how CeCe died. I was just sorry she was gone.

I knelt down beside CeCe and tried to ignore the casserole. Focusing on my would-should have been friend, I called to my magic. "CeCe, who did this to you?"

Her eyes flashed open and my heart dropped to my feet. I would never get used to that. At least CeCe hadn't put a spell on herself so I couldn't raise her. I was about to ask my question again when she started to speak. "Coin is cursed. Don't let him put the coin in your pocket."

"Who?"

"Don't take the coin. He isn't sane." Then her eyes closed and my magic broke off suddenly.

I pushed magic into her only to have it snap back at me like a rubber band, hitting me in the chest and knocking me on my ass. A groan escaped me as something wet seeped through my jeans. Nice. All I needed was to sit in CeCe's blood.

Drew was at my side in an instant, helping me up. "Thanks," I said resisting the urge to wipe at my blood-soaked ass. "You don't happen to have a change of pants or shorts?"

I was joking, but Drew nodded and led me out to his patrol car. Opening the trunk, he pulled out a pair of sweats and handed them to me. "They're clean. I didn't make it to the gym today."

He worked out? Olivia was slipping. She was supposed to tell me all the scoop on everyone in town whether I asked for it or not. That included Drew. Yet, she hadn't told me he had a gym membership. I was going to have to tell her about her failures as the town's busy-body.

Now I'd have to check to see which of the two town gyms

he used. You know, so I could get a membership and watch him work out.

"Thank you." I waved a hand and said the incantation for the invisibility spell, then changed out of my soiled jeans and panties. Drew started and turned in a circle. "Ava?"

I giggled and pulled up the pants. Drew's sweats were huge on me and rested on my hips even with the drawstrings tied as tight as they'd go.

Once I released the spell, Drew blinked and frowned. "Where did you go?"

"I was here. I did a spell to take the attention away from me while I changed. It's like being invisible." I moved to Olivia's 4-Runner.

She was waiting for me, looking a little paler than I've ever seen her. Handing me a plastic grocery bag, she said, "You okay? How did your power bounce back like that?"

"I'm not sure. I guess that she was ready to move on. Or it could have been the curse keeping her from giving a necromancer too much information." I was betting on the latter. "And nothing she said helped us get any closer to figuring out who did this.

Fatigue started to set in, and I yawned. Drew massaged my neck, and I almost told him he'd have to follow me home and give me a full body massage. But I needed sleep.

I turned to him. "Olivia and I are looking through the occult books that I ordered through the bookstore tomorrow. I'll also look through some of the grimoires and see what I can find on this curse."

There had to be a way to track the magic back to the witch who cast it.

Drew kissed my forehead. "I'll call if I find out anything new."

I nodded and climbed into Olivia's SUV and fastened my seat belt.

When we got home, Olivia collected a sleeping Sammie and left with promises of coming back. Or were those threats? I still wasn't sure.

After my new BFF and the cutest kid on earth—besides Wallie, of course—left, I went straight to my bedroom and showered. When I exited my own personal bathroom, thankfully wearing my robe, I jumped seeing Alfred sitting on my bed. "Alfie, is something wrong?"

He shook his head and stood, then motioned to the teacup on the nightstand. I walked over and picked up the cup and inhaled. Chamomile and mint. It was what I needed to relax. "Thank you."

I stared at him for a few seconds before reaching out to touch the string hanging from his mouth. He knocked my hand away while shaking his head and moving to the door. "Alfred, I know you can talk. Why don't you want me to take the string out?"

The ghoul was weird about the string. He didn't want it removed. He lifted the tablet I hadn't noticed until then and typed. When he turned it around to show me, the words didn't make sense.

Too soon. Not the right time.

Then Alfred disappeared out of my room.

Why in the world was everyone being so cryptic today?

CHAPTER SEVENTEEN

Bright and early the next morning...Okay it was 9:00 a.m. but that was still too early for me. Olivia came over with warm, fresh donuts and caramel mocha lattes. The woman was spoiling me with her early morning delivery service.

Sammie was with his grandparents, so we were on our own for the afternoon. The possibilities were endless.

Yet, instead of actual fun, we were hunting for clues and trying, *again*, to trace the magic behind the curse on the coins. Drew was able to steal the coin found on CeCe and had dropped it by the house last night. I'd been asleep so Alfred answered the door. I hoped he didn't answer the door that often. Eventually we were going to scare a human to death.

When I came downstairs minutes ago, Alfred pointed to the coin on the table. The one Olivia was staring at like it was going to jump up and choke her. Stranger things had happened recently.

"Is that...?"

I nodded. "Yep. The coin they found on CeCe. There is

enough of the curse still in the silver that I may be able to trace it this time. So don't touch it."

"Hadn't planned on it. But wouldn't having it in the house, this close to us, kill us?" She stared at me with wide eyes.

"No." At least I didn't think so. But, just in case, I had called in backup.

Right on cue, Owen entered the dining room. He eyed the coin suspiciously as he moved to the coffee pot.

Olivia picked up the latte she got for him and handed it to him. "Kelly made this for you."

At the mention of Kelly, the sweet baker and owner of Peachy Sweets, Owen's cheeks colored. He took the cup from Olivia,gave a short, shy nod and took the seat across from me. "The curse is still in there. Not strong, but I can feel it."

"Yeah, I was hoping that we can trace the magical signature of who created the curse." Using my own magic, I called to the glass bowl in the conservatory and filled it with water, then directed it to float into the dining room. The salt followed it. Both settled on the center of the table.

Owen sipped his latte and pointed at me. "You know that telekinesis is a rare power for witches."

I stared at him for a moment and said, "So is having three necromancers in the same town."

Olivia perked up. "Three?"

"There were three before William was killed." I dumped salt into the water and twirled my finger over the bowl. The water swirled on its own, mixing the salt.

"Why is it rare? I thought they would network like witches do with their covens." Olivia looked from me to Owen, waiting for an explanation.

Owen answered her, because I didn't actually know why. "Necromancers don't work well with others, generally. Ava's not like any other necromancer that I've met. Anyway, it's a bad omen to have too many necromancers in one area."

"What kind of bad omen?" I asked while stopping the water in the bowl from swirling.

He shrugged. "I think it's myths passed down. It might have been started by witches not wanting groups of necromancers hanging around. Our powers are dark and go against the natural order, according to witches."

"Like the dead should remain dead," Olivia added. Owen and I nodded.

Owen continued. "There are different stories that tell why. One is that witches cursed necromancers. Others say that it's the combined power of too many in one area. But all the stories say that chaos follows the dark ones. The more there are in one place, the stronger the chaos." Well, that did fit my life lately.

"Wow." Olivia cradled the latte in her hands. "How many is too many?"

I lifted my brows at Owen. I also wanted to know this.

"More than three." Owen picked up a donut from the box.

Note to self–get the coven to check the town for more necromancers.

Speaking of the coven... "CeCe told me that I was next in line to be the high witch."

Owen and Olivia stilled and stared at me for a few seconds. Then Olivia smiled. "That's great. You are the new leader. I mean it's sad that CeCe died, but you're the boss now."

I didn't want to be the boss. Ever. "I have no clue how to run a coven. And I don't want to talk about it right now." I pointed to the coin and wished I hadn't mentioned it. "We need to do the trace before the curse weakens more."

My theory on the cursed coin was that each one was spelled for a certain person and once the deed was done, the curse faded.

Owen nodded and shoved the donut in his mouth, then wiped his hands with a napkin. After he chewed and swallowed, he held his hands out to me, over the coin. I took them and opened up my magic.

We chanted the simple tracing spell, and the coin began to rattle against the table. Larry came sliding into the room and stopped a few feet from the table. Did he feel our power or the curse from the coin? I didn't have time to ask.

A cloud of smoke rose from the coin and a blurred image formed. But before it cleared, the cloud exploded. Running on instinct, I threw up a bubble around the table at the same time, containing the curse inside it.

"Crap. That backfired." I checked on Olivia. "You okay?"

Her wide eyes met mine. "Yeah. That was...unexpected."

"Definitely," Owen agreed.

Larry moved forward. "You need to neutralize it before it escapes that bubble."

Great. I didn't need more complications. I definitely didn't need to be cursed to die by a freak accident. Taking a deep breath, I focused on the bowl of saltwater. Using my telekinesis —as Owen called it—I pushed the bowl over, spilling the contents on the table and the coin.

The curse dissipated with a hiss. Of course the donuts and coffees were ruined. "Sorry about breakfast."

Olivia shrugged. "But what happened? The tracer was working then it exploded."

"I think there was an anti-tracker spell mixed in with the curse. Whoever did this is covering his or her butt." I wanted to scream in frustration.

Please, Universe give me a sign. Anything to point me in the right direction to stop the evil witch.

Just then the doorbell rang, sounding like a scream. Olivia and I both jumped. Olivia asked, "What the Hades is that?"

"Doorbell, I think. Winston thinks he's funny." It wasn't the first time the house had slipped in a random doorbell sound.

I stood up and moved toward the door, motioning for Larry

and Alfred to hide. With everything that had been happening, I was leery about answering the door at all. Every time I opened it, something else crazy happened. And I had just asked the Universe for a sign. So I was betting on the weird.

I couldn't have been more right.

I opened the door to find Rick and Dana Johnson, the ferret shifter parents. "Hello," I said in shock. "What—are you doing here?" I didn't say it unkindly, but I couldn't imagine why they were back. "How did you find my home?" I stepped back, giving them room to come in.

"Everyone knows where your home is," Dana said. "All the local supernatural folk are plenty familiar with the old white house on the cliffs by the ocean."

I gaped at her as they walked in. "Oh," I whispered. I'd known that most of the Shipton Harbor residents knew the house, but these people lived a few towns over. "What's going on?"

"Our other son wasn't in his bed this morning," Rick said. "And the rest of the pack is getting scared. After we got Ricky's body back, they all started withdrawing, staying home a lot and keeping to themselves."

"Not that we blame them," Dana added. "But now Ricky's brother, Zane, is missing. We have to find him."

"Come in," I said, gesturing toward the living room. "How long do you think he's been gone?"

They moved into the living room. Owen sat beside Olivia on the sofa, giving our guests the chairs to sit in. I joined my friends.

"I go to bed late," Rick said. "And I always check on him before I lie down. He was there around three."

"And I get up early," Dana continued. "But I didn't check on him, then when he didn't come down for school, I went up. Around seven-thirty. And he was gone. We've contacted anyone in our pack that could help, and only the alpha stepped up. He's tracking Zane with his nose, being a wolf shifter. But we thought maybe you could do a spell or something?"

I met Owen's gaze and he shrugged. "We could certainly try. Did you bring something that belongs to your son?"

Dana nodded and pulled a jacket out of her bag. "He left without a coat." Tears filled her eyes. As I took the cloth from her and opened it up, I realized how small it was. "Wait a minute, how old is Zane?"

"Six," she said softly.

Olivia gasped. "Oh, honey. Did you call the police?"

Rick shook his head. "No. This wasn't a human. No human could sneak into a shifter's home, even a shifter such as us, ferrets."

"This was the same people that took Ricky." Dana sobbed quietly into a handkerchief. "There's no way it's anyone else."

I stood. "Okay," I said. "Let's do this."

CHAPTER EIGHTEEN

We put little Zane's coat on the middle of the coffee table. "Locator spells are simpler than anyone thinks," I said. "It's really just a matter of putting magic into an object that belongs to the person." I'd known how to do a locator spell since I was a kid and used to mess with Sam by appearing at all sorts of places when he hadn't told me where he'd be.

As long as it didn't explode, we were good.

"*Quaerere dominum.*" I spoke in a commanding, no-nonsense voice and sent magic into the jacket as I said the words.

Seconds later, a light appeared in midair. A line, sort of like it was made from a neon sign. Only I could see it. "Let's go. Wherever he is, he's not somewhere guarded." Magic could be done to make a location unsearchable. My home had been protected that way probably since the day it was originally built. That reminded me, I needed to refresh that spell.

Spells didn't last forever, though I suspected the house wouldn't let its inhabitants be found... or messed with.

"Come on," I said urgently, walking toward the front door

and grabbing my coat on the way. The line of light preceded me, directing me to Zane.

I stepped out to see the Johnsons had a SUV. "Oh, good, can you drive?" I asked. We'd all fit in it.

They ran out ahead of me, and Olivia and Owen followed. I ran back inside and yelled up the stairs. "Back in a while!"

"Okay," Larry called down. "Be careful."

Seconds later, I was in the passenger seat, giving directions to Rick. "I have no idea how far it will take us," I said. "This sort of locator spell isn't like when you do a scry over a map." I described the light I saw and how we were following it. We drove down the coast road for a good ten minutes before anything changed. "Hang on," I barked. "Turn here." The light veered off to the right.

"There's no road," Rick said. "Just a field."

"Well, go as far as you can in the vehicle, then we'll walk."

Olivia leaned forward. "There's not a road nearby that I know of. This is a bunch of woods, owned by the government if I'm not mistaken."

"Text Sam," I said. "Let him know what we're doing."

Rick pulled off the road and drove carefully across the field, getting close to the copse of trees. "Now what?"

"Let's go." I unbuckled my seatbelt. "We might be walking a while. I can't tell."

We didn't end up having to walk far before the light blinked and faded. "It's gone," I whispered.

"What does that mean?" Rick spoke in a hushed voice. Something about the woods made us all feel like someone was looking over our shoulders.

"Either someone intercepted our spell," Owen said. "Or Zane crossed onto spelled land where he can't be tracked. Given where the spell took us, I'm guessing he's on spelled land now."

"Let's keep going forward," I said. "Maybe we'll get lucky."

As we walked, hope began to wane.

And then, a noise. I held up my hand and everyone froze. "I heard something," I said in a hushed voice.

Very carefully, we tiptoed forward until a clearing came into view behind the trees. There was an old horse paddock, what looked like pig pens, and a barn. Farther back, near the other side of the clearing, was a small shed.

A small service road led off into the forest on the opposite side. As we stood looking around, the sound of a vehicle starting made us all duck, but it was parked out of sight down that road, because we never saw it leave as the sound of the engine faded.

After another several minutes, when nobody came out of the barn and nothing seemed to move, we tiptoed out of the woods and toward the big, faded red structure.

We circled the barn, but the only door was inside the horse paddock. Pushing open the gate, I tiptoed into the big circle and moved quickly toward the barn door.

"I smell him!" Rick rushed around me and pulled the door open, despite my hurried whisper for him to wait. Dana followed quickly behind.

We followed on their heels, not that I could've stopped Dana from going to her son once they had a line on him.

The interior of the barn was dim; the only light was from the a few missing boards over the windows in the loft area. The ground was dirt and hay. There were three stalls on each side.

We found the poor shifter kids in one of the horse stalls, huddled in the corner. "Mama," one little boy cried and ran forward. "Papa!"

I smiled as Dana and Rick got their son back, exclaiming in relief to see him, then we entered the stall, and my smile faded. These kids had gone through hell. It made my heart ache to think about it. Well, we were here now, and they'd never have to fight again.

Olivia and I crouched down. "Hi," I said softly. "Are you guys okay?"

A teenage girl stepped forward. "We're hungry, but everyone here healed from the last fight." A tear tracked down her face. "We don't know where the shifters who lost the fights went."

My chest tightened even more while my magic roared to life deep inside me. I was going to make whoever was responsible for this to pay. Long and painful.

"Well, we'll figure all that out," Olivia said. "Let's get you out of here."

"The bad man just left," Zane said as we helped kids of various ages off the dirty ground.

While I took calming breaths, I ran around to inspect the rest of the barn and make sure nobody else was hiding anywhere. "Is there anyone else we need to look for?"

"No, they usually had us fight other real animals like dogs or roosters," the teen girl said.

"What's your name, honey?" Olivia asked.

"Jennifer-Nicole," she said. "I'm a wolf shifter"

"Adams?" Rick asked.

Jennifer-Nicole nodded, her eyes brightening a little with hope that someone knew her. "Yeah."

"I know your parents." He held one arm out, and she gratefully cradled herself under in his arms as tears fell. "Let's get you home to them, okay?"

Sniffling, we led the kids out of the pen. Well, Olivia was sniffling, I was blinking back tears while counting all the ways to make everyone involved in this pay. Both alive and dead. I wasn't the type to wish ill on anyone, but what I saw and heard since raising little Ricky made me rethink some of my morals. Some people just plain sucked and needed to be introduced to Luci.

"We're going to have to get creative to fit all six of these kids in that SUV," I whispered to Olivia.

"We'll call Sam to come help as soon as we get far enough away," Olivia said. "We've got to get them out of here."

I picked up a little girl who was sniffling and shaking, then set her back down. After wrapping her in my jacket, I pulled her back into my arms and cradled her close. "Hey, sweet girl. How old are you?"

"Seven," she whispered.

Holy crap. She was so small, about the size of Sammie, who was five. "How long have you been there?"

She shrugged and burrowed into my coat. The poor girl stunk to the high heavens, but I'd never tell her that. "I think two years."

My throat squeezed. "Have you fought all that time?"

She nodded. "I'm a panther. I have very sharp claws."

Oh, no. This poor child. I closed my eyes and prayed to the goddess to give me the strength to get through this.

Warmth enveloped us, and I turned my head to smile at Owen. He'd given us a spell to keep all of us warm as we walked. The kids certainly needed it.

He had a little boy in his arms, too.

"Clear," Dana whispered after she and Zane peered out of the barn.

We rushed across the field the way we came, not going as fast as I liked, but there were more kids than adults. Many of the kids were weak from lack of food and fighting for their life.

When we reached the trees, Owen moved closer to me. "Do you feel that?"

"Yeah. Can you tell what it is?" A low pulse of magic nipped at my skin but I couldn't tell what it was or where it was coming from.

"You're the witch." He flashed me a grin even though there wasn't much humor in it.

"Half witch." I sat the little girl down on her feet and tugged my jacket tight around her, buttoning the top button. "Why don't you run up ahead and see if there is anything in the forest. I'll scan the area with my *witchy* powers."

Owen eyed me and handed the little boy over to Olivia. "If I die, I'll come back to haunt you."

I flashed him a smile. "Only if I don't heal you first or turn you into a ghoul. Whatever works."

He grumbled something as he walked forward holding out his hands like he's walking in the dark. Olivia snickered beside me. "What is he doing?"

"Feeling around in the dark, what else?"

Dana moved into the spot Owen just vacated. "What's going on?"

"We sense magic but don't know where it's coming from." Which was odd. I should have been able to pinpoint the source.

Opening my senses, I searched the area for the strangemagic, stretching my magic out. It didn't go far before it bounced back to me, catching me off guard. I gasped and cut my flow of energy.

Olivia placed a hand on my arm. "What's wrong."

Owen yelled back at us at the same time I answered her question. "There is a magic barrier." I sighed and added, "We're trapped unless we can figure out how to get out."

"Can we just run through it?" Olivia asked. "Maybe with all of us rushing at it at the same time will weaken it or break it all together."

I glanced at Owen, who had returned from his short walk. He shrugged. "We could try. I hit it with my fist a few times and it rippled."

"Okay." I met Dana's and Rick's gazes then the kids. "I think the kids should move back a little."

Zane and Jennifer-Nicole gathered the kids in a group and

directed them back a few feet. Then they returned to our side. Zane lifted his head high. "We will help."

I was about to say no way, but Zane's dad studied the two of them. "Are you sure? It'll hurt a lot if the barrier holds."

Jennifer-Nicole shrugged. "I've felt worse."

I locked my jaw and turned away from her. The grand-master of the fighting ring was going to suffer.

"Okay let's do this." Olivia bounced on her feet, making me snicker.

"On the count of three," I said.

Owen started the countdown. "One."

"Two."

We all said three at the same and ran right into the barrier a few feet ahead. We didn't actually bounce off the magic wall as much as we were thrown a few yards back. My body seized as an electrical current shot through me. When we landed, I was sure we were all going to die.

CHAPTER NINETEEN

A jangling sound brought me to my feet and put me on alert. We'd been sitting in the shade of the barn for a while, comfortable, at least, thanks to Owen's warmth bubble. He and I had been steadily shooting magic at the barrier, trying to weaken it or, ideally, bring it down.

Nothing worked.

But now, someone was here. And I had to prepare to defend myself and the kids against whomever or whatever might be coming our way.

We'd talked about using our necromancer powers to try to raise something nearby, but we'd decided against it for a couple of reasons, one of which being what if we raised one of the poor kids who had already died?

What these poor littles had been through was bad enough. They didn't need to see the reanimated corpses of their friends.

Though, that would be a chore for me and Owen later down the road. Any shifter child still missing would have to be found. How we'd do it without bringing up every legitimate dead person, I had no idea.

We'd figure it out. Because their families needed closure.

A person stepped around the barn, and I squinted against the sunlight at their back.

"Howdy, pardner," the man drawled.

I gasped and dropped the hand shielding my eyes. "Luci?"

He walked forward so the sun no longer blinded me and grinned broadly. "Heard you needed a rescue."

Turning in a slow circle, he allowed us to take in his getup. He'd dressed like a stereotypical cowboy, from the pristine white ten-gallon hat to the spurs. He even had a six shooter on his hip.

"Luci, my friend," I said. "I'm beyond glad to see you, but you look absolutely ridiculous."

He chuckled and snapped his fingers, his normal suit and tie returning. "Better?" He'd kept the hat.

"Much. Can you get us out of here?" I threw a rock toward the barrier to show how it rippled with magic, only visible for a brief few seconds.

"I intercepted your attempts to get in touch with your fellow humans," he said. "Good thing, too."

Bending over, he peered through the paddock slats at the children. "What have we here? Kiddos? I love the young!" He beamed at the huddling shifters behind us. "I'm Luci, my little appetizers. How are you?"

Jennifer-Nicole stepped forward. "Scared. Can you get us out of here?" Brave girl. She tossed her red hair over her shoulder and stared at Luci.

The grin on Luci's face faltered. "My, my. You've been through quite the ordeal, haven't you?" He squinted at Jennifer-Nicole. "You have my solemn vow, my little snack-sized human. Your tormentors will suffer."

She cocked her head as she studied him. "You have a lot of power?"

Luci spread his arms and straightened up. "The most."

"Please, take me home to my mother," she whispered.

Luci winked at us, then spread his hand out in midair. He stroked the air, as if caressing a lover, but I knew he was getting the makeup of the ward to bring it down. "Clever," he whispered. "This ward is specially made to make sure nobody outside it could sense the torment inside. It wasn't, however, made to contain a full blooded witch, which is why you were able to signal me."

I hadn't even thought of signaling him. Not that I would've anyway. He was still too much of an anomaly. And not on my hero call list.

"It was also not made to withstand me." He grinned again, straightened his tie, then snapped his finger once. "All clear. Let's go find our bad guys."

"Now hang on," I cried, rushing toward the paddock gate on the other side of the barn. "You can't go rushing off to attack whoever did this. We don't have enough information."

"Silly woman," Luci thundered. "I am the de—"

"Dear friend of the coven, I know," I said hastily. These kids had no idea Luci was the devil. And no way did I want them to find out.

"And the best *witch* in town," he said darkly, then turned to the kids. "Come on out of there."

I wasn't sure I liked the way he looked at the kids, like he couldn't decide if he wanted to make them soldiers in his Hell army or cook them for dinner. Over my dead body *and* my ghost once he killed me for protecting the little angel warriors.

Turning to the adults, I said, "Get the kids out of here. It might be easier to take them to my house and have the parents come there." My house was warded to protect the innocent. Plus it would save us a bit of gas and time. "Plus they can shower or bathe while waiting for their parents."

Olivia nodded. "I'll call Carrie to see if she could bring some clothes over for them. There should be some in the school lost and found."

Rick said, "We can take those who are close to our pack."

"I can run out to the second-hand shop in town and pick up some things, too." Dana added, in full momma shifter mode.

It was great to know they had everything under control.

"Carrie is at my house," Luci offered with a sly grin.

I opened my mouth, then closed it. I wasn't going to ask. None of my business. Plus, I was sure Olivia would ask Carrie a buttload of questions when she got there.

As the kids disappeared through the trees, I turned and glared at Luci. "Now listen," I said, wagging my finger at him. "No charging off without me. We need to do this right, so we get to the bottom of the whole mess. This is no one-man operation."

Luci glowered. "This isn't my first investigation, Ava. I am the devil, after all."

"Yes, and as such, you're used to getting your way and going in guns blazing. We do this my way."

He twinkled his eyes at me, as if tolerating my insubordination. My stomach churned, knowing I was out here in the middle of nowhere alone with him. As attractive as he was, knowing what he was made of, made it impossible for me to be anything but nervous. But I damn sure wasn't going to show it.

"Let's check out the barn with a better light source," I said. "Then that shed."

He led the way and created a glaring ball of light, throwing it up to hang in the eaves of the barn. "I'll go left, you go right."

With a sharp nod, I inspected each stall on the right. They stunk, and both animal and human feces were piled in the corner of each. Wishing I knew a spell to remove the sense of smell, I burrowed my nose in my shirt and moved quickly, scanning the dirt floor for any sign of any clue.

There was nothing. And as disappointed as I was that we still had no idea who had done this, I was more than ready to get out of the barn.

We exited the back of the barn, that door opening easily now that the ward was down, and walked around the outside, Luci again going left while I went right. The ground was clean, the dirt smooth and trackless. My own shoes left footprints, so whoever had driven away just before we got here must've done something to remove their tracks.

"Shed?" I asked when Luci and I met around the paddock.

He looked around. "Unless there are more buildings in the woods, it seems the shed is our only other recourse."

We fanned out and walked across a small dirt clearing to the woodshed. Something glinted in the sunlight near the door. "Hang on," I said, hurrying forward.

I bent and picked up the object, gasping as I wiped off the metal. "I don't believe it."

The circular item was a coin, and it had been stamped similarly to the coins found on all the murder victims. "We've got to get Drew out here," I murmured. "I think this is going to be bigger than shifter kids."

"Don't shifters avoid human police interaction?" Luci asked. "They keep to themselves."

"They do, but this looks like a half-stamped coin just like the ones we've been finding in pockets of murder victims." Including my mother.

"Then, by all means, let's get into this shed," Luci said.

We hurried toward the door, but about the time Luci reached out for the padlock, the sound of a vehicle on the road reached my ears. Luci heard it a split second before I did, because his head swung around toward the lane, and he froze.

"Out of sight," Luci hissed before grabbing my arm and pulling me around the back of the shed. "Let's see who I get to kill today."

"Stop," I whispered, slapping his arm. "You're not killing anyone. We might need whoever it is to give us information about the murderers."

"You're no fun," he whispered in my ear, making me shiver.

We stood behind the shed and peered around the corner, covered by a large bush, as a small silver sedan parked behind the barn.

"No way." To my complete, utter, devastating shock, Penny stepped out of the car.

Penny! The woman whose husband had died just before Halloween, killed by Carmen Moonflower. Her husband, William—Bill—had been a necromancer and the original owner of Alfred.

What in the world was she doing here?

"Stop, foul beast!" Luci yelled as he ran out from around the shed.

Oh, damn it. Why'd he have to be so dramatic? I hurried after him. "Don't hurt her," I called. "I know her."

Catching up, I yanked on his arm. He was pointing a potent finger at my Yaya's lifelong friend as I felt his power increasing. I stepped in front of him, drawing his attention to me. "Hang on, Luci. Let her explain."

Penny stared at us with her jaw hinged open. "Ava." Her voice squeaked and her eyes rounded as she stared at me and then Luci. "What are you doing here?"

"Looking for the missing shifters," I said with the calm I definitely didn't feel. "How can you be involved in something like this?" *Please have a reasonable excuse.*

Penny was the sweetest person I'd ever met. Or at least I'd thought she was. It broke my heart that she would have anything to do with the cruelty that had gone on here.

"I'm not," she stuttered. "I'm doing the same thing."

I gave her a flat look and Luci scoffed. "A likely excuse. Care to elaborate?"

"I know a shifter family and they asked me to find their daughter," she said. "I did a locator spell that led me here."

I knew she was lying as much as I knew my own name. But I had no proof. "I'm sorry, Penny, but we can't let you walk away from here on just that information."

But what to do with her? "Luci, can you put her in the barn and put up a ward so she can't get out?" I asked.

He gave me a low bow. "I live to serve her majesty necromancer."

But I didn't miss the scathing look that accompanied that bow. He didn't like me taking charge. He'd tolerated it for a while, but his patience was waning.

Well, that was too dang bad. We were here on my dime right now. As appreciative as I was that he'd rescued us, I had to do this right or the people behind the fighting ring might get away.

"Thank you," I said stiffly.

I searched through Penny's car, but didn't find anything. With no way of knowing if Olivia and Owen had made it back to the car yet to call Sam and Drew, I had to decide if we should wait here for them or take Penny's car back to my house and wait.

If nothing else, I wanted to see what was in that shed. With the half-pressed coin outside it, surely there was something good inside.

Luci walked out of the barn and straightened his suit. "Well, as you seem to have things in order, and a vehicle to get yourself back to your home, I'm going to leave you to it."

"Hang on," I said, but he held up a hand.

"No, you're obviously doing so well on your own that you don't need me." He sniffed. "The ward on the barn will disintegrate if you walk through it. Only you. So *don't* do that unless you're ready for Miss Penny to leave with you."

Crap. I'd offended him by taking the lead. "No, I'm sorry."

Luci grinned at me with that familiar mischievous glint in his eyes. "Don't be sorry. But I'll see you later."

With a snap, he disappeared, leaving me with Penny locked in the barn and no clue what to do next.

I pulled out my phone and realized it had no service. Ugh. I walked away from the barn hoping to get a signal, but with no luck. They must have had a spell for that, too.

The rumbling of a car engine made my pulse increase. I whirled around and blew out a breath in relief to see Drew's cruiser driving down the service road.

When I reached the barn, he and Sam stepped out of the police car. I wasn't sure how much Olivia had told them, so I recapped and filled them in about Penny. "I can't believe she's involved with something like this."

"You'd be surprised what people are capable of." Drew reached out for me, and I took his hand and allowed him to pull me into a hug. "How are you?"

"Sad and disgusted." I breathed him in and instantly relaxed. I enjoyed the feeling of being wrapped in his warmth a little longer, then stepped back. "I have the kids at my house. Or did I say that already?"

I was so tired I was repeating myself.

Drew touched my cheek. When I raised my gaze to his, he said, "Let Penny out so we can take her in, then go take care of the kids."

Nodding, I pressed a kiss to his cheek before leading them inside the barn. Just as Luci said, the ward holding Penny broke as soon as I walked through it. Not able to look at the older woman, I left her in Drew and Sam's care.

When I drove onto the main road, my cell worked, so I texted Olivia to pick me up at Penny's house. I had to take her car back anyway so the neighbors wouldn't ask too many questions.

414

On the way to my house, I was having Olivia stop off at the liquor store so I could grab a bottle of wine. I was going to need it after this day was through.

CHAPTER TWENTY

Owen picked me up from Penny's. "Olivia is holding down the fort. Alfred didn't know what to do with all those kids so he took Larry upstairs. So, I think we are on our own for dinner. Also, I think Snooze packed up and left."

A laugh burst from my lips. "Did you actually see Snooze pack up?"

He chuckled. "No, but he had his favorite toy in his mouth as he ran out the back door."

"He'll be back." I was still smiling at the thought of my fat, immortal cat running away from home— just because of a bunch of kids —when we pulled into my driveway. There were a few cars I didn't recognize parked out front. Must be parents picking up kids.

Before getting out of the car, I said, "I want to go back to see if we can get into that shed. Lucifer and I didn't get a chance to check it out before Penny showed."

"I'll go with you."

I was hoping he would offer. Sam was going too. He just

didn't know it yet. I wanted a bit of police presence at the scene.

Inside my old, cranky house was a form of organized chaos I wouldn't have believed if I hadn't seen it. The coffee table had been loaded down with snacks, both junk food and healthy fruit. There was even a veggie tray and cheese platter. A few of the younger kids were on the sofa watching a cartoon on TV, while a couple of kids at the dining table sat with a plate of food. One, a little girl, was on the phone most likely talking to her parents from the way tears filled her eyes as she smiled.

It'd been a long time since these kids smiled.

And I wasn't going to think about that. They were free from evil and going home to their parents.

Carrie emerged from the hallway carrying a clean and adorable little boy. His name was Sammie and looked just like my childhood BFF. Carrie smiled at me. "Welcome to Ava's shifter day camp."

"It sure looks like one. Where did the food come from?" I loved junk food as much as a college student, but I didn't remember half the stuff in the coffee table spread.

"I picked it up on my way over." Carrie walked to the sofa and sat down while drying off Sammie. Owen had gone up to his room to get out of everyone's hair, his words. I had a suspicion he wasn't comfortable around so many kids. Although he'd been great with them at the barn.

"Thanks for coming to help out." Voices in the kitchen drew my curiosity so I thought I'd check it out.

Olivia was in there with someone's parents, talking privately, out of earshot of little ears. She looked over and introduced me to the parents. "This is Ava Harper. She discovered the...where the kids were."

The last part of the statement held sadness and anger. I've never heard outright anger come from Olivia. Not even when we didn't like each other in high school. Holding out my hand, I shook the mother's then the father's. "I'm a mom, too, but I could only imagine what you and the other parents went through."

That was when I noticed more parents out on the back porch.

"I'm Nick and this is my mate, Ashley," The father said as he took my hand and held it a little longer than I expected. "We're Jennifer-Nicole's parents. We had to come and thank you in person. If you ever need anything, just call."

"I was just doing what I felt was the right thing. I do have to tell you that the police have one suspect in custody. The kids said she brought them food." I'd found dog food in the car. It turned my stomach to think the kids would eat that or starve.

"Why the police?" Nick's voice took on an alpha tone, which I ignored.

Locking gazes with him, I said, "The fighting ring is connected to a serial murder case. The sheriff and the deputy know about the paranormal world and are working on concealing the supernatural part of it from human notice." In fact, the paranormal aspects of the investigation were completely off record. As far as the record was concerned, all the deaths had been run of the mill human psychopath murders. But I didn't need to tell them that. There were too many holes that needed to be filled first.

The alpha wolf gave me a short nod, but I could tell he wasn't happy about it. Tough. This was my rodeo and I'd do what I want. Including using the help of the police.

Suddenly something hit my side and latched on. I wrapped an arm around the sweet teen and hugged her close. She smelled of apples and spring air and her hair was still damp. "How are you?"

Jennifer-Nicole flashed me a smile. "Much better. Thanks to you."

"Hey, I didn't work alone." I rubbed her shoulder and squeezed her tight.

"Well, thank you and everyone who helped save us." Then she darted out the back door, followed by her parents. My gaze moved to the conservatory, relieved it was closed off to the kids. I didn't need them getting into anything in there, especially the poisonous plants.

I spent the next few hours talking with parents as they collected their kiddos and took them home.

After my house was mine again, I sat on the sofa and took a piece of cheese from the platter. "Owen, Sam, and I are going back to check out the shed."

Olivia sat beside me. Carrie had left about thirty minutes ago. After a few seconds, Olivia said, "I'll need to take Sammie home to put him to bed. He has school tomorrow."

I glanced outside through the window and frowned. The sun had begun to set. "I hadn't realized it was so late."

Olivia's phone chimed. When she looked at it, she giggled. "Does Sam know he's going with you?"

"No." I grinned.

That made her laugh. "I'll inform him he's been volun-*told* that he's going."

"You do that. I'm going to shower and change."

Olivia stood and called to Sammie, telling him it was time to go home. Moments later Alfred descended the stairs with a sleeping little boy in his arms. Taking her son from Alfred, Olivia, said, "Thanks, Alfie."

The ghoul grunted and then handed me his tablet. One word was typed in. **Dinner.**

"No. Owen and I will be leaving when Sam gets here so we'll pick something up.

Alfred looked put out that he couldn't cook, which made me laugh. The ghoul didn't even eat. "Alfie, thank you for everything you do."

His features softened without actually softening, and he nodded before going back upstairs. I had a great group of friends and family. With all the twist and turns my life had, I needed these people to keep me semi-sane.

When Olivia went out the door, Drew came in. I frowned. "Why are you here?"

"To go back to the barn with you."

"Okay, great." I guessed Sam wanted to hold his son and be with Olivia. Who could blame him after seeing what we did today? "Owen, you ready?" I called up the stairs.

"I'm right here. You don't need to yell."

I jumped and whirled around. He stood in the archway to the kitchen with a half-eaten sandwich in his hand. "Geesh. I didn't even see you come down."

We piled into Dia, my Hyundai, and drove out to the site. This time I knew where the service road was, so we didn't have to walk through the woods.

It was a wasted trip. The darn shed was magically sealed. Nothing Owen or I tried worked to break the spell. Drew even tried old fashioned brute strength. He kicked the door, rammed into it with his shoulder, and even shot it. Nothing worked.

I needed witches for this. After all, it had been a witch who'd cursed the coins. With Penny involved, it made more sense it was a *local* witch. I just had to come up with a plan to fish the murderer out.

After returned to my house, I called Sam and Olivia and put them on speaker. Owen, Drew and I were in the conservatory because I'd found a truth serum recipe. I was cooking up the serum while we planned our next move.

"We are sure the murderer is a witch," Sam said.

I nodded, agreeing with him. "It has to be. It doesn't take a lot of power to curse something, but whoever was doing it would have to know how to create a curse and it takes magic that only a born witch has. Humans who study witchcraft don't have the natural magic in their blood to activate the curse."

I stood a little straighter because I'd actually known that one. Mainly because I read it in one of the grimoires the other day, but I didn't have to tell them.

"Right. The only way to activate a curse is with witch blood," Owen added.

"So it has to be someone in the coven," Olivia said. "That would make sense because only coven members were killed."

My thoughts exactly. "So we need to set a trap. What better way than a coven field trip?"

I poured the serum into an amber-colored jar and sat it in the window where it would get the morning sun. Unfortunately, as tended to be with these things, it took a week to mature. We were on our own until then. If I found myself in any real danger, as long as I was close enough to a cemetery, I could defend me and mine, but out in the woods like that? I wasn't sure if my witch side could step up to the occasion. Even though I was supposed to be all powerful, I didn't feel like it. I wasn't ready to test the theory either.

CHAPTER TWENTY-ONE

B right and early the next afternoon, I drafted a letter and sent it to every member of the coven I knew. Owen helped me use their names and the internet to find addresses for each of them. If we did our spell right, they'd get the letter and come to my home this evening for an emergency coven meeting.

As the unofficial leader of the coven, I had every right to call such a meeting, but to them I was a newbie among their ranks. CeCe had told me I would be the new leader in secret, so I assumed none of the other members knew. I wasn't really sure how any of that worked.

Someone was bound to know now that CeCe was dead. Either way, the members would definitely be too intrigued to pass up the invite. At least I hoped so.

Since we had hours before the coven would arrive, if they did, Owen and I traipsed out into the woods past Luci's house.

I'd wanted to go straight back to the barn where we'd found the children and start looking for buried bodies, but Owen and

Drew and Sam *and* Olivia had all advised against it until we had a better idea of who was doing this.

Although, I wasn't against seeing the corpse of a big bear or mountain lion go after whoever had done this to these poor shifter babies, I couldn't be sure there'd be enough for me to raise way out there. The bones had to be close enough to the surface.

So, Owen and I were going to practice near my house and see if I could bring up any more animals here. One shifter had already been found buried in these woods. Why not more?

We returned to the same clearing we'd found Ricky in, and I began. For hours, I expanded my reach, raising anything I found and drawing them to me.

I got a lot more than I bargained for.

"Whoa," Owen said when I stopped to rest. All around us, animal carcasses lay, at rest once more, in circles going across the field. "We're going to have to rebury all these animals."

We hadn't come across any more shifters. Just more bunnies, birds, and squirrels. A few skunks, a fox, and three deer. "I'm going to try one more time," I said. "I'm getting miles out now."

Owen shook his head. "I've never seen anything like this, Ava. You're more powerful than we ever knew. I don't think we ever really tried to test you like this."

I opened one eye and squinted at him. "Now we know."

I was just as shocked as he was.

What we'd do with it after this? I had no idea. What good was a necromancer, really? I had no plans to use my powers for evil. What could I do with them?

After my brief break, I closed my eyes and searched farther out. "Oh," I gasped. "I can feel the difference. There's a human."

"Can you go over it?" he asked.

I shook my head. "No. If I'm right about its location, it's not buried in a cemetery."

He sighed. "Make him hide himself on his way," he urged. "We don't want anyone seeing a dead body walking around. The animals are bad enough."

I chuckled and did as he asked. It took nearly an hour for the skeleton to get to us. As she neared, I felt her, knew she was female, and when she was very close, I could tell stuff like the age of the body. "No," I said. "She's too old."

A skeleton walked into the clearing. If I hadn't been able to feel the difference, I would've thought it was Larry just by looking at her. I couldn't tell the difference in bones from a male or a female. I wasn't a doctor, after all. Or bone scientist. Who knew about bones? Anthropologist, probably.

"Hello," I said.

The skeleton walked closer. "Hello," she whispered. "How am I here?"

"I'm trying to find anyone who was killed, murdered," I said. "Were you?"

She sighed and looked up at the trees. "When is this?"

I didn't want to freak her out. "When did you die?"

Her white head, smudged with dirt, moved around as she took in our surroundings. "I believe it was 1966."

Owen and I exchanged a glance. That was when our witchy serial killer was getting started. "Do you know how you died?" I asked.

"It was an accident," she said. "But then, after I died, someone in a hood came and buried me in the woods. Why would he do that if it was an accident?" Her wispy voice sounded far away. Nowhere near as strong as Larry. I wondered if it was the twenty years that made a difference.

"Are you at peace?" I asked.

She nodded. "I was. My parents came to me recently. We moved on together."

"Can you tell me anything about how you died?" I asked. "Or your name?"

"My name was Megan Frey," she said. "And I died cutting through a big field, going to school. I was bitten by a snake, but I'd left late for school and nobody heard me yelling."

"A snake," I gasped. "That's horrible."

She nodded. "Yes. I'd like to go back to my parents now, please."

"Of course, dear." I gestured to an empty spot on the grass. "Please, lie down."

Pulling my magic back the way Owen had taught me, I let sweet Megan go back to her peace.

"Well," Owen said. "We don't know if she was killed by our serial killer, but it's apparent we have a lot of work to do. I think it's time I helped instead of trying to teach you."

I squinted up at the sky. "Yes, but for now we have to get back."

We rushed back to the house, leaving all the bones in the clearing for now. We had to get Sam and Drew in on the skeleton mess. I was fairly sure I could lead them to her grave site, which might pick up more clues for us.

I hoped.

"We took longer than I thought," I said, breathless from running back home. I needed to start working out. I laughed at that thought. Yeah, right. That would be the day.

"We'll barely have time to clean up," Owen said. "But I think we'll make it."

Before we left, we'd asked Alfred to make finger foods for our guests, and Larry had been excited to help.

Once we had the murderer, I was going to be sad to see Larry go. He was a sweet house guest, if odd at times.

As it turned out, we didn't have time to clean up at all. As we rounded the house, Bevan Magnus stood from my porch swing. Figures that weasel would be the first one there.

"There you are," he called, holding up the letter I'd sent to him. His expression told me he resented that I'd summoned him and the rest of the coven. "How dare you call an emergency coven meeting?"

Yep, he was pissy about it. And he'd have to get over it.

I almost apologized as I walked up my porch steps. Almost. Luckily, I came to my senses. He didn't deserve my apology after turning his nose up at me the two previous times we'd met. I plastered a fake smile on and said, "Please, come in."

Hopefully, I'd sent enough invitations to other coven members that he wouldn't be the only one to show up.

He gave me the willies.

Bevan followed me in the door. I wasn't sure if he'd been at the Christmas party or not. There'd been so many people in and out of the house then, there was no telling. But the way he looked around in interest made me think he hadn't come.

Alfred shuffled out of the kitchen holding a tray with lemonade.

"Please," I said again, a fake smile still intact. "Sit in the living room and enjoy a drink. Owen and I will be right back down. I just want to wash this dirt off."

"Of course," Bevan said, staring at Alfred with wide eyes.

I started up the stairs, but when I heard the telltale clack of Larry's bony feet on the hardwood floor, I stopped and turned. Pressing my lips into a thin line, I tried to keep in the giggle that bubbled up.

The skeleton walked into the living room carrying a tray as Owen and I watched on. "Hello, I'm Larry."

Bevan, just in my line of sight in one of the high-back chairs, paled considerably. "He-hello."

Owen started to chuckle, and I elbowed him. If he started laughing, there was no stopping me.

"Can I interest you in a finger sandwich?" Larry asked and bent over.

"Sure," Bevan whispered and took one. I couldn't tell for sure from this far away, but I thought his hand trembled. "Larry, you say?"

"Yes. I was murdered in the eighties," he said matter of factly, studying Bevan with interest. "You seem familiar. Perhaps we knew one another."

"I don't think so." Bevan took a bite, but his gaze kept darting up at Alfred and Larry, bouncing between them like he was watching a tennis match. He swallowed hard, but then I tiptoed on up the stairs, followed by Owen.

As soon as we hit the upstairs landing, we fell all over each other in laughter.

And the doorbell rang. Crap. "Don't get that," I called to Alfred. Just in case it wasn't a witch. "Glamour?" I asked Owen.

He shrugged. We certainly didn't have time to shower now. We both ran our hands over our faces, hiding the dirt. Seconds later, Owen's black hair was shiny and clean, and his face looked like it had been scrubbed pink.

"Perfect," I whispered. "Let's go."

When I opened the door, all of the rest of the coven stood on my porch. "Oh," I whispered. "Hi."

I shook each of their hands as they walked in. "Please," I called before they started in. "Go into the living room. We've got refreshments and I've had my house ghoul bring plenty of seats in."

"Hello, Melody, Cade." I shook Melody's hand as she walked past.

"Leena, Mai." Nodding at them, I smiled encouragingly.

"Thank you for coming, Joely." She beamed at me, her rosy cheeks always cheerful-looking.

"Alissa, you look nice." I smiled at one of the younger members of the coven, then turned to the last two. "Brandon, Ben, thanks for coming."

The nearly-elderly twins came through last, and I shut the door behind them. Ben hung back. "You have a house ghoul?" he whispered.

"Oh, yes, Alfred. I inherited him from Billy Combs when he died."

Ben's eyes widened. "Impressive."

"Hello, everyone, and thank you for coming. Please, have lemonade, or," I gestured toward Alfred. "Alfie here will be coming around with plain iced water if you prefer."

Alfred nodded once. I noticed he'd come up with a rather lumpy-looking brown suit from somewhere. How sweet. He wanted to look nice for our company.

"I brought you all here today because a great tragedy has occurred in our community." I met their eyes one by one. "Someone has been running a shifter fighting ring right in our backyard."

Ben and Brandon's faces registered pure shock, as did Leena and Melody. Bevan's eyes darkened and his mouth thinned into a line.

Interesting. He'd creeped me out all along. Maybe he was involved.

Mai raised her hand. "That's horrible, but what does it have to do with us?"

"The police are working with the shifter community to find the people responsible for this travesty," I said. "But there is a shed on the property that has been magically locked. I can't get it open on my own. I need your help."

"Absolutely not," Ben said. "This is shifter business. Shifters do not like interference."

I raised my eyebrow at him. Why such a strong opposing opinion? "This is far beyond a shifter problem," I said. I didn't want to tell them yet we suspected the murderer in our town was related to the shifter ring.

Ben harrumphed as Brandon shook his head. "The shifters become hostile when we interfere. We've tried it before."

"Not this time," I said. "This time, they need our help." Plus, I guessed by finding the kids, I'd made some kind of alliance with the shifters. Again, though, that was not information I was ready to share with the coven. Not until I weeded out the killer.

CHAPTER TWENTY-TWO

We piled into three cars, with me driving one, Bevan driving his monstrous SUV, and Alissa driving her minivan. She looked like a soccer mom, so it made sense.

Drew had been on standby to meet us out there, so I texted him when we left my house.

The sun had begun its late afternoon descent by the time we pulled in, but we still had a couple of hours of light left before it was totally dark.

I smiled when I saw Drew leaning against his patrol car. His ankles were crossed, and he looked hot. Sexy, not temperature. My heart did its little rapid beats as we locked gazes.

Once everyone was out of the cars, I introduced the sheriff. "Everyone, this is Drew."

He stepped around his cruiser and joined me by my car as everyone gathered around. Olivia was going to plotz when I told her about all this. She'd be so mad she wasn't here.

"And this is Sam," Olivia's voice chirped. She and Sam came walking out of the barn. That little turd. She'd convinced them to let her come. I couldn't help but grin at my best friend.

Sneaky little she-devil. At some point, she'd taken Sam's place as confidante numero uno in my life. And I was okay with that.

"What is the meaning of this?" Bevan hissed.

"It's okay, everyone. Sam has known about witchcraft since we were kids. We grew up together. And Olivia also knows. They're not going to blow our cover." I rolled my eyes. I was pretty sure the whole town knew I was a witch. It was partly why I loved Shipton Harbor so much.

The coven studied them with guarded, suspicious eyes, then as one unit, turned their attention to Drew. I caught a few reactions that were covered up. They suspected he was a hunter.

I'd felt it when we first met, too. Something about him wasn't quite human and I'd recognized it. Of course, I hadn't known about hunters at the time and didn't know what he was from the magical energy surrounding him. But the coven members *would* know about hunters.

"And Drew..." I waited a brief few seconds. "Drew comes from a long line of hunters." They'd figure it out anyway. Might as well be honest.

Drew grimaced as the witches gasped and backed away. "No," he said swiftly. "It's okay. I rejected that part of my life. I can't say I wouldn't take down an *evil* supernatural creature, but I'm not hunting innocent witches or shifters or anyone. Most of us just want to live our lives."

Everyone stopped moving backward, at least. Nobody was overly excited to have Drew, Olivia, or Sam here, but at least they'd stopped looking terrified.

"Anyway," I said. "This is the shed we need opened. I was thinking if everyone touched it and said the same spell, maybe we could get it open."

Bevan sighed. "It might work."

I arched an eyebrow at him. "Do you mind helping?"

He dipped his head toward me. "Not a'tall."

Creepy little effer.

We walked to the shed, and the coven lined up alongside it, each of them placing two hands on it. "Okay, everyone, just use a simple unlocking incantation," I said.

"*Intrabit* should do the trick," Owen called down the side of the shed. Everyone nodded, most of us being familiar with the simple spell. It wasn't the spell itself that would do the trick, it was our combined power.

But no matter how hard or how much power I sent into the shed, it wouldn't open. "It feels like someone is working against us," I muttered low enough only Owen heard me.

He nodded. "Let's take a break," he called. "Could half of you come with me?" He pointed to a few of the coven, including Bevan and the twins. "I need help with something in the barn.

I wiped imaginary sweat off my brow. "I'm going to rest a minute and we'll try again when you get back."

Relief flowed in my veins when no one in the group complained, much. Bevan did glare at me as he walked away.

When they disappeared into the barn, I sighed and looked at the shed. "Come on, let's give it a shot," I said. "Maybe we loosened it the first time."

Olivia, standing behind me, snorted. "It's not a jar of pickles."

I shot her a quieting glare and put my hands on the door. "Come on, give it your all," I called.

Almost as soon as we began, the padlock sprang open, then hit the dirt with a thud. The door creaked open, the shadowy interior of the shed too dark for me to tell what was inside. "Holy freaking crap," Olivia muttered.

"Find a way to tell Owen that one of the witches in the barn was trying to stop us from opening this shed," I said.

She nodded and hurried away.

"Ava, wait," Drew said when I went to open the door the rest of the way. "Let me."

I hid my amusement and stood back. Sure, he was *the law*, but he was also not magical. "If you get caught in any magical booby traps, I don't want to hear it," I teased.

He chuckled and switched on his flashlight before he leaned into me until our faces were inches apart. "Hunter, remember?" I shivered and it wasn't from the fact he was a hunter, but from the seductive edge in his voice. He put some space between us and said louder, "Wait here."

Seconds after disappearing inside, he called for me. "You need to see this. Don't touch anything."

I hurried in and gasped when I saw what his flashlight illuminated. "Is that a coin press?"

Indeed, it was. "Is it possible to melt down silver with magic?" he asked.

"Absolutely." There was nothing in the shed to indicate they'd been melting it here the human way, anyway. "It's more than possible."

"Then whoever has been leading this ring is likely also our murderer," he said darkly. "And it could be any of the people out there."

"Drew," I hissed. "It's one of the people in the barn with Owen. Only when they left were we able to open this shed."

He nodded. "Any way to tell?"

I shook my head. "No, and we're still days away from having a truth serum."

"Okay. Get everyone out of here. We'll comb the place for fingerprints. I'll call you in the morning." As I turned to step outside, He grabbed my hand and pulled me to him. I stumbled then gasped as he claimed my mouth. When he broke the kiss, much too soon for my liking, he said, "Be careful."

"I will." I stood on my toes and gave him another quick kiss on the lips, then darted out of the shed.

Outside, I met Olivia's stare. She pinched the sleeve of my shirt and tugged. "Did you two make out in the shed?"

"What? No!" My cheeks colored and I struggled to not giggle like a third-grader. "Who do you think I am?

She opened her mouth, and I held up my hand. "Don't answer that." Sucking in a deep breath, I calmed myself. Even though I was so nervous I was giggly, this wasn't a happy chore.

Turning to the witches, I lied. "It was empty except for a few old tools. If there was once something here, it's gone. Sorry, I wasted your time."

A few of them muttered as they got back in the vehicle they'd ridden in on the way out here. Bevan glared as he walked to his SUV. I glared back and added a smirk for good measure.

I was sure someone would mention that we got the shed open. In fact, I was counting on it. It'd make the killer nervous knowing that I knew the fighting ring and the murders were connected. Nervous criminals made mistakes.

So, I'd let whoever it was sweat it out until the truth serum was ready. Then we could have a little show and tell party.

After the coven left, Drew replaced the padlock with one of his own and Owen spelled it surreptitiously while I announced, "I'm coming back here tomorrow to work on bringing the dead shifters to me and then getting them to their families."

Drew walked me to my car and opened the door for me. Then he caged me in with his arms against the hood. "Should I come over?"

The corners of my lips lifted. "Should you?"

Wickedness flashed in his eyes. Even though we weren't at the point in our relationship to have sex, I wasn't totally against the thought. But I did want to take it slow. Something was still holding me back.

He cupped my chin and lifted it. "What are you thinking?"

I crinkled my nose. "Overthinking. Again. Are we moving too fast?"

"I don't think so. Do you?"

I shook my head but said, "Yes...I don't know."

"I told you I want exclusive, and since we've been on three dates, it's time to make it public that we're dating." There was that seductive edginess I'd caught before. I knew from the first time I met Drew he was the alpha male type. I guessed he'd been giving me some time. And my time to decide was up.

"We're a couple, huh?"

He pressed his body into mine and dipped his head until his lips brushed my ear. "Definitely. I don't want any other man thinking you're available or anything."

Yep, the alpha male had woken. And I liked it.

I threw my arms around his neck. "I might embarrass you from time to time. Like going up to the station and staking my claim on you." I nipped at his ear. "I don't want any other woman thinking you're available."

He chuckled and pulled back a little. "I look forward to it."

CHAPTER TWENTY-THREE

A s promised, *way too early* the next morning, Owen and I
began our work. I was working on my third cup of coffee
as Olivia had shown up before it was even light outside with a
large thermos of coffee and a sleepy Sam in tow.

"Come on," she said. "We can't help with the kids, but we
can help keep you hydrated. I've got a cooler in the car."

Alfred ran out as we exited the house with a big plastic bag.
I peeked inside. "Sandwiches?"

Grunt.

"Thank you, Alfie. You take good care of me." I touched his
hand and instantly had a flash of a familiar scent. But it was
gone as fast as it appeared.

I shook off the feeling, the memory, or whatever it was,
stirred deep in my core. Waving at Alfred, I climbed in one of
the county's police SUVs with Drew. Olivia and Sam took her
4-Runner and we were off.

Drew and I rode to the cursed site in solemn silence. Today
was going to be somber work and neither of us looked forward

to it. When we pulled up beside the barn, Drew reached over and held my hand and gave it a little squeeze.

I smiled at him. "I'm dreading this, but the families need to put their kids to rest properly."

He kissed my forehead. "You got this."

His faith in me touched a deep place in my soul that I didn't think anyone, except for Clay ever had. Maybe it was time to move on. Keep my promise to Clay that I'd live and find love again.

I'd think harder about that subject another time. Today, I needed to raise the dead and send them home.

I had Dana and Rick along with Jennifer-Nicole's parents put the word out to any shifters who had a child go missing to meet us out here. But not until after I raised the kids from the ground. I didn't want any parent to see their kids as an animated corpse.

"Okay," Owen said as he sat down in the folding chair Sam pulled out of the back of the SUV. "I'm not as strong as you are, so I'm going to go in the direction of town. It seems less likely there would be any bodies out that way, or at least not as many."

"Good thinking," I said sitting in another chair a few feet from him. "I'll go toward the coast and then along the woods that stretch away from town." There was a large span of forest and mountains surrounding Shipton Harbor.

We sat and focused. Almost immediately, I began to feel them. Now that I'd done so many animals back near my house, I could tell the difference right away. I left the pure animals to their rest and only called to the shifters.

"They're coming," I whispered. A mountain of emotions swirled inside me.

Not long after the first bodies walked or crawled to us, Alissa turned up in her minivan. Several of the coven members poured out, including Bevan. "We're here to help," she said.

I'd called the coven too, and asked them to come, but I wasn't hopeful they'd show. Of course the killer would be curious, but the whole coven?

"Thank you," Olivia replied. I was too deeply focused on finding bodies to even welcome them. "I think the plan is once they get all the bodies here, we'll get them to shift and tell us who their families are. So if you could grab a notebook and pen and help me write down their information, that would be great. Once they're all raised, I'll send a text to our shifter connection."

"Where is the hunter sheriff?" someone asked. I almost laughed and broke my focus.

"He left so that he doesn't have to feel obligated to report the murders. The shifters wouldn't want their children listed in some human database, and in fact, many of these children likely don't exist on paper," Sam said then added, "For the record, I'm not here as a cop, so I don't count." I tried to tune them out as they kept talking and finally succeeded.

I stretched my net far and wide and found shifted animal after shifted animal.

Some were old. Very old. My stomach churned and my heart broke. So many kids.

Eventually, as my net widened nearly to the next town down the coast, I ran out of dead shifters to call. And as we waited on them all to come, we began the heartbreaking work of cataloging the names of the dead.

The witches quickly learned how to have the children shift from animal to human form as Owen and I animated them. Olivia and several of the coven members wrote their information down on a piece of paper and pinned it to their little bodies when they told us their details.

A couple of them looked twice at Magnus, but not enough for me to try to blame anything on him.

As they shifted back into their little bodies, Sam carefully and reverently put them in black canvas bags, then moved the location information to the outside.

I sent a text to Dana to let her know it was okay for the shifter families to come. I knew they were close by, waiting for the word.

Finally, well into the evening, all the bodies had been claimed by their parents or friend of the family. The sense of closure was there, but there was also a lot of sadness and anger. I couldn't feel any more bodies coming our way, and none of the children had been able to identify anyone other than Penny.

"It certainly seems like Penny was a major factor in all of this," I said with a sigh once all the shifters had left. I turned my gaze onto Bevan. "What do you think, Magnus?"

He looked from me to Sam and back. "How would I know?"

I shrugged. "You seem shrewd. I thought you might've drawn some conclusions."

He gasped, then snapped his mouth shut. "I haven't."

Guilty much? But the sucky part about the whole thing was we couldn't hold Bevan or anyone without proof they were involved. The truth would soon be revealed. There wasn't much we could do but wait until the serum had the time to mature.

Just as Drew pulled back up next to the barn in the same SUV he'd dropped me off in, I heard sobbing. Soft, female cries. I glanced at Olivia, who obviously heard it too. Had we missed one?

I followed the sound behind the shed where I stopped dead in my tracks. Sitting against the shed with her legs pulled to her chest and her head rested on the tops of her knees, was a small person. She looked to be around fifteen to sixteen years old, but my magic and intuition said she was older than that.

Glancing over my shoulder, I noticed that Olivia, Drew,

Owen, and Sam had followed me. Dana and Rick stood back a little further. Olivia motioned for me to talk to the girl. I rolled my eyes and knelt down in front of her, leaving a few feet of space between us. I needed reaction time in case she attacked me. She didn't look like she'd been dead long, but ghouls could be extremely unpredictable.

"Hello," I said softly.

She sniffed and lifted her head. Yellow cat eyes searched me. It took me off guard at first, but I managed to not gasp or jerk back. I was just too tired to freak out. Plus, enough crazy crap had happened in the last several months that I was over being shocked that another undead thing had entered my life.

She glanced behind me and shrank away. "Don't send me back."

Oh, no. "You mean back to the dead?"

She nodded. "I want to stay."

I caught Owen's attention and he shrugged. "It's up to you." Then to the girl he said, "You do understand that you would be under Ava's protection and control. If you go rogue or turn on anyone, she will send you back with a single thought."

Wow, I could do that? Owen would know since he was my necromancer trainer. I was more powerful, but he was more knowledgeable.

The girl sat up a little straighter. "I understand. She is my Alpha. Got it. And I'll be good."

I sat on my ass in the grass next to her because my legs were starting to go numb from squatting. "What's your name?"

"Zoey."

"No last name? Do you have family we can contact?"

Her bottom lips trembled, and she shook her head. "No. My parents died when I was young, and I've been on my own since. I didn't know where to go. I'm a tiger shifter so my cat helped me survive on my own." She ducked her head. "Or, it did, I mean."

441

Olivia moved closer and knelt down, then fell on her butt and rolled to her side. I laughed at her. "Graceful much?"

Zoey snickered as Olivia threw a handful of grass at me, then studied the girl. "She looks human. I mean of course she does, but she doesn't look like Alfred at all. Zoey could go out in public with a little makeup, and no one would be the wiser."

My bestie was right. The girl's skin was smooth and pale, not at all like the leathery zombie-like texture of Alfred's skin. Except for the yellow cat eyes, Zoey looked like any other young adult in Shipton.

I rolled to the side and stood, then offered my hand to Zoey. "You'll be staying with me. I'll have to move Wallie into my office so you can have your own room. And we need to give you a last name." I thought about it for a few and said, "Lowe. That is my maiden name. My dad was a necromancer and it would be easy enough to say you're a long-lost cousin."

Sam snorted. "A cousin who can shift into a tiger."

I waved him off and pulled the girl to a stand. She was only a couple of inches shorter than me. "Semantics." We started walking to Drew's SUV, but I stopped and turned to Zoey. "How old are you?"

"Eighteen, I think. I might be off a year or two, but I'm pretty sure it's eighteen." She glanced from me to the others as if unsure.

I started walking again. "Sounds good to me. let's go home. I'm exhausted."

CHAPTER TWENTY-FOUR

Saturday night, the truth serum was ready. We would finally be able to find out who cursed their fellow witches into accidental deaths. So I stayed up late sending letters to all the coven members to invite them over to my house for an informal meet and greet the following afternoon.

Sunday morning Drew, Sam, Olivia, Owen, and I sat down and made a plan and got everything prepared for the guests to arrive.

The coven arrived at noon. Owen and I made sure to be late. Around five after twelve, we came hurrying out of the woods. "I'm so sorry," I called, scanning the people on my porch and thrilled to find every living coven member had arrived.

Nobody wanted to miss the news about the shifters, which was my little hook to get them there. Especially the killer, who would come if it was just a social gathering. Besides, the guilty party likely figured we'd gotten it wrong since we hadn't arrested anyone or accused anyone thus far.

And thus the desperate need for information.

"Please, come in." I opened the door to find Alfred and Larry waiting expectantly, each holding a tray of drinks. Zoey sat in an oversized bean bag close to the fireplace reading a book. I motioned to her. "This is Zoey, my cousin on my dad's side of the family."

She gave them a small wave as Snooze stalked into the room and climbed on the bean bag with her, flopping down in her lap.

Several of the members nodded to her. She was good at keeping her gaze down enough to seem like she was looking at you without you noticing her cat eyes unless you stared at her long enough. Which Bevan did.

I stepped in front of Bevan, cutting off his line of sight. "Sit, drink, and give us just a minute to freshen up and we'll be right down." It was the same thing we'd done last time, but this time we'd carefully planned it.

We rushed upstairs and peeked down at the crowd as they settled into chairs, taking sandwiches and glasses of tea, water, or lemonade from Alfred. "We have to give them time to drink," I whispered.

A few minutes later, Owen nodded. "I think they've all had at least a sip," he said. "One drop is all it takes."

"Let's go."

We headed downstairs and stood in the living room door. "Thanks again for coming. I thought you all deserved to be apprised of the situation."

Everyone's attention was on me, all of them quiet, all of them expectant.

"Now," I said and clapped my hands together. It was Drew and Sam's signal to bring Penny out.

Everyone gasped as they walked from the kitchen, where they'd been waiting just out of sight, with the spelled Penny between them. We'd put a bubble around her before we left so that nobody outside the ward could hear her at all.

"Penny, please, sit." I motioned for the only remaining chair in the room. "Have a glass of tea."

I'd warned Drew not to let her have anything to eat or drink this morning. So she was thirsty.

She gulped down a glass of tea as she perched nervously on the end of the chair.

"Lovely," I said. The coven stared at Penny with mixed reactions of horror, suspicion, and sympathy. "Everyone, your attention here, please. Would anyone that had anything at all to do with the shifter fighting ring please stand?"

Most of the coven just looked startled, but immediately, Penny and Bevan Magnus rose to their feet. As did Melody Gonzales and Cade Duran, two of the quieter, more reserved coven members. I hadn't gotten a read on them either way before now.

Owen and I activated the ward waiting for us. Anyone who had guilt in their heart and had drunk our potion, which had combined truth serum with the guilt potion wouldn't be able to leave.

"If anyone else has any knowledge at all of the shifter fighting ring, something you knew before we broke this open, please stand."

Joely Travis stood.

"Wow," Olivia whispered. "That's insane."

"Indeed," Drew said. "Everyone else, please head to your homes. Thank you for your help."

"It's all her fault," Bevan cried, pointing to Penny. "She's a psychopath!"

"Which of you is the murderer?" I asked.

Bevan slammed his lips shut and his face began to turn colors. First pink, then red, then a purple. Sinking into his chair, he began to sob. "She's my sister," he gasped. "She's been running the shifter ring. She ran it with her husband."

I gasped, staring at Penny. "Is this true?" I couldn't imagine her and Billy being this devious.

She hung her head but didn't answer.

"What about the murders?" I asked. I had to be the one to ask the questions since I'd brewed the potion.

Bevan moaned, ran his chubby hand through his brown hair, and finally he spoke again. "It's me," he whispered. "Billy figured it out. I was getting rid of anyone who crossed me, and he bound my ability to take a life for years... decades. I don't know where he got a spell like that, but I couldn't kill anyone. But when he died, it all came back to me." He grunted, trying hard to fight the compulsion to tell the truth. "All my power, unrestricted."

I moved back a few steps as his face twisted in perverse pleasure. His brown eyes darkened.

"My mother?" I whispered.

He stopped grinning and looked me in the eye. The room went quiet as Bevan sucked in a deep breath. "Your mother found out I was Penny's brother. She kept sticking her damn nose in where it wasn't wanted." A little piece of spittle flew from his mouth.

Fury raced through my blood, hot and ready to zap the snot out him. Magic I didn't know I possessed pooled in the palms of my hand. Drew stepped up behind me, placed his hands on my shoulders, and whispered, "He's not worth wasting your magic on."

He was right. Leaning back against him, I calmed my emotions as the truth settled in.

Bevan killed my mom. Stole her from me. The magic tingled in my fingers, ready to unleash. Just then, Drew kissed my temple and the raging current settled down. A little.

"The coin was all too easy to slip into her pocket. After that, I just had to wait for the curse to do its job. A lightning strike?" He laughed, the deep sound pounding against my eardrums, freaking me out since he didn't actually smile or look away from me. "Hers was a particularly..." he paused and sucked in a deep breath. *"Delicious* kill."

Drew stepped around me, but I held my hand up to stop him. I had a grip on my magic now. Walking toward the man who killed my mother, I bent in front of him and leaned forward, not at all scared he might hurt me. I whispered, words only for the murderer. "I hope you live a *long* time in prison, Magnus. Because the moment you die, you will belong to me."

As I pulled back, I finally saw a glimpse of fear in the psychopath's eyes. "Burn his witch's mark before you take him to jail," I said. "He won't be able to practice magic with a scar over it."

As a hunter, Drew knew all too well what I meant and probably already knew how to do it.

I put my hand on Drew's arm. "Burn it deep."

"I know," Drew murmured. "I will."

Walking out of the living room, I headed straight for the back door, went down the patio steps, and kept walking until I couldn't go any farther.

I sat down at the edge of the cliff, looking out over the ocean. Tears rolled down my cheeks and my chest tightened. Memories of the day she died filled my mind. The lightning, her falling. Me desperately trying to heal her with my magic. Instead, I sort of halfway raised her, but she wasn't herself. At least not the mother I knew.

I now realized it hadn't been my failure as a necromancer or my inexperience. It was the curse that had kept me from healing or raising her properly. Magnus must have added that into her curse so she couldn't be brought back.

"Mom." My voice broke. I didn't know what to say. I wasn't sure if she could even hear me.

"Ava?"

The familiar voice startled me. I turned to see my mom standing a few feet behind me. "Mom? How are you here?"

Her sea green eyes, just like mine, twinkled. "You called me." She tossed her blonde hair, unlike mine, over her shoulder. I'd forgotten how svelte she was. I didn't get that from her either. I was curvy, to say the least.

I'd called her? I had no clue I could talk to a ghost. Wait. "Are you a ghoul?"

She laughed and shook her head. "No, I'm a ghost."

There was something in her voice that set off warning bells. "Mom, are you okay?"

She looked around like she wasn't sure where she was then focused on me. "Thank you for setting the children free." She looked around. "I have to go." Then she vanished.

I ran forward. "Mom!"

But she was gone. I dropped to sit on the ground, feeling defeated and inspired at the same time. I'd talked to a ghost. My mom's ghost. I could do it again. And I would figure it out one way or another.

"Ava!" Drew yelled. "I need you to come in here!"

I turned from the cliff, wiping my eyes. Drew stood on the porch frantically gesturing. "Now!"

Okay, Mr. Bossy Alpha Man.

Running as fast as I could, I crossed grass-covered ground, watching where I was going so I didn't face plant. I wasn't as coordinated as I once was. Not that I was ever terribly coordinated.

I hadn't really learned any defensive magic yet, outside of calling for dead things to aide me. I gathered my power as I vaulted up the porch steps. There was a field full of dead animals that I could call to help us if Bevan had managed to do something Owen and the non-witches couldn't handle.

But when I thundered into the living room, prepared to release a huge burst of necromancy magic, Luci sat on my couch with his feet propped up. "Lovely of you to join us," he said as he bit into a shiny red apple.

Gasping, I let the power go and leaned forward with my hands on my knees. Bevan and Penny had been bound by magical ropes, by the feel of it.

Relief spread all through me, and my adrenaline dropped. Heaving, I hung my head and stood bent over in the middle of my living room, desperately trying to catch my breath.

Mortified that Drew was seeing me so out of breath after one small sprint, I righted myself and bit back my heaving breaths.

But that made black spots appear in my eyes. I gulped in a deep breath as slowly as I could, praying it wouldn't look like I was still winded from that small bit of exertion.

Damn it. I was getting a treadmill desk, pronto.

"What are you doing here?" I asked. "I thought I'd made you mad so you'd abandoned me."

Lucifer waved his hand. "Don't be silly. I've never abandoned you. It was apparent you wanted to do things your way, so I let you. I've been watching, don't worry."

Crossing my arms, I glared at the devil. "If you've been aware of all this, why did you allow these people to be killed?" I asked in a near-yell. My emotions went back to running rogue from everything that had happened.

Luci stood and sucked in a deep breath. "Oh, yeah, see there are rules. Strict edicts I must obey. But if you'll notice, since the moment I began to suspect who our culprit was, there haven't been any more murders." He winked at me.

Bevan's head swung around. "You? You were the one who kept me from getting a coin into Ava's pocket?"

Me? I glared at Bevan. "I can't wait for you to die," I whispered, and this time, everyone heard me.

"Well, my dear, I watched you, all right." Luci tapped my

nose. "I'm very impressed. Whenever you're ready, I've got a few managerial positions I desperately need to fill in Hell."

I gulped and looked around for any of my friends to help.

The cowards. They all stood back and blanched when I turned to them for help. "Thanks," I said shakily. Then I held up my hand to him. "Not today, Satan. Or, you know, ever."

"If all the fun is over, I'll just..." He turned to Penny and Bevan, then snapped his fingers.

With a sound like a roaring campfire, they disappeared, leaving a black scorch mark on my floor. "Perfect," Luci said. He turned and clasped his hands. "You don't have any more of that stew do you?"

Alfred grunted behind me, and I slowly turned my head, then my body, as I watched Lucifer follow the ghoul into the kitchen.

When I fully turned, I caught sight of all the shocked expressions behind me.

"Well," Drew said. "That's one way to do it."

CHAPTER TWENTY-FIVE

T*wo weeks later*

"THANK you all for coming to our new and improved coven meeting." I stood in my living room and beamed at the full house.

After a huge debate and a lot of begging—mostly me pleading with the coven that I really wasn't leader material—I caved and drank the High Witch potion. I was their leader now, and as such, I made a few changes. Which explained my full house.

Olivia had to bring chairs from her house, and Drew had even dropped off a few camp chairs. But we had enough. Alfred had been cooking all week. Larry was thrilled he didn't have to hide from the guests. He'd decided he wanted to stay with me because I kept things interesting. His words.

And my *cousin*, Zoey, was thrilled to meet so many magical people her own age. But we kept the little fact that she was undead to our small inner circle and the magical dozen, the natural-born witches who were honest and strong enough to pass my tests.

Owen had helped me figure out what to look for when selecting the twelve witches who would back me when high magic and planning was needed. I considered them to be my board of advisers.

"Our new coven is all-inclusive. We welcome all walks of witches as well as the humans who know about us and might need some witchy support. Sitting on either side of me are my magical dozen, the officers and board members of the coven. If you have an issue or questions you can go to any of them."

Olivia stood and held up a hand. "Please, humans, fill out the sign-up sheet for the Not a Sup Support Group, or NAS for short." She pointed toward the foyer where we had a table set up with reading material and the NAS sign-up sheet. "We're going to meet once a month at my place."

She was in her element, absolutely thrilled to be a part of this. Sam stood back, a little overwhelmed as he looked at his life-long neighbors that he'd never known were magical.

"Now, for our first coven meeting, we have very special guests." I clasped my hands in front of me. "Please welcome Ricky and Dana Johnson."

Everyone knew what they'd been through, losing a son and then almost losing another. When they stood and waved, the entire group clapped, and slowly, everyone got to their feet as Dana buried her face in Ricky's chest and sobbed.

I held one hand up and everyone sat back down. "Ricky and Dana have graciously agreed to be our liaison with the shifters, which is something we've needed for a very long time." I addressed the couple directly. "You're always welcome in this coven, and if you ever have a need for a friend, you know where to find a bunch."

"Thank you," Dana mouthed as they took their seats.

Alfred grunted in the doorway, and I looked over to see he had his tuxedo apron on and he nodded sharply at me when he caught my eye. "I'm being told dinner is ready. Please, enjoy."

I stepped back as everyone got to their feet, nodding at my coven. All the witches who hadn't been involved with the shifters and the murders had readily agreed to join the new, improved coven.

Alfred stood back with Larry, who had flat refused to be laid to rest. The ghoul grunted something to the skeleton and Larry ran over to the counter, grabbed a stack of napkins, and wedged himself between the people lined up on either side of my table to make a plate of the bountiful feast.

Larry brushed up against the twins, having darted between them, and they both jerked back with mirroring faces of horror at having a skeleton touching them.

I put my hand on my mouth and bit back a giggle. I had warned everyone about my menagerie beforehand.

"Now."

Jerking around, I looked behind me for the person who dared speak to me like that. But nobody was behind me.

"Now."

What the fudge? I looked in a circle, then Snoozer rubbed against my legs. When I looked down at him, he looked up at me with his big smoochy face. "Meow."

"Geez, Snoozle," I said, bending to scoop him up into my arms. "I thought you said now."

As if on cue, his stomach gurgled. "Oh, it's your dinner time, isn't it?"

"Now."

I stopped and stared into his too-intelligent eyes. "If you're going to start talking, I'm packing up and moving back to Philadelphia, cause that's the straw that broke the camel's back.

"Meow."

"That's better."

I handed him off to Alfred. "He's hungry."

Alfie grunted, then glared at Snoozle. "Now," Snooze said.

"And demanding," I added.

A couple of the coven members' kids ran by, closely pursued by Sammie, who was having the time of his life.

"Uncle Drew is here!" he screeched as he ran onto the back porch.

Owen and I had made a big bubble for the backyard so that we could all go out back and enjoy the weather without being cold. I laughed at the kids and moved toward the front door to greet Drew.

But when I opened it, he was quickly walking back down my front walk. "Drew?" I asked.

We'd had one more date since the day Luci took the murdering Bevan and Penny to Hell. In fact, we'd been spending a lot of time together since we spent the entire day at the festival, just the two of us laughing and goofing off.

And it had gone very, very well.

He turned slowly and squinted at me. "I forgot."

Cocking my head, I walked down the porch steps and met him halfway up my walk. "Forgot what?"

"That you were having your big meeting tonight. I'm sorry."

"Why are you sorry?"

"It's one thing to give up a life of hunting, but that?" He shook his head rapidly. "I can't be closed up in a house with that many witches. It makes my skin tingle." He gestured to all the cars parked along my yard and driveway. "As soon as I pulled in, I figured out what was going on, but I wanted to come say hi anyway."

"And then?"

"When I got close, I got itchy. I had to back away from the house quickly."

I laughed and grabbed his hand. "How about a kiss for the road and you come to dinner tomorrow night?"

A sexy smile lifted the corners of his mouth and he wrapped his arms around my waist, jerking me close. I sighed as he claimed my lips like he was starving. Pressing into him, I deepened the kiss. My body tingled all over and ached in all the right places.

The chime of my phone broke us apart. I pulled it out of my pocket and drew my brows together as I read the text.

"What is it?" Drew leaned over to read my text.

"That's Uncle Wade, Clay's uncle. He said the realtor has a buyer for the house and she wants to meet with me next weekend." While I was thrilled that the house sold, it also meant one more thing to let go of. My entire life with Clay had been in the house.

Drew cupped my chin and lifted. "Are you okay?"

I nodded and pocketed my phone. "Yeah. I am." He raised his brows. "Honestly, I'll be fine. It'll be rough letting go of the last thing I have of Clay's, but it'll be okay."

Drew kissed me softly on the lips. "Not the last thing. You have Wallie and your memories and your love. Clay will always be in your heart."

How did I luck out with such a compassionate, understanding man? Twice.

"I'll be going with you."

"What? No. You can't—"

He kissed me again to cut off my words, then said, "I'm going and Wallie will go. You're not doing this alone."

The man I was lucky to find was also bossy and completely wonderful. "Thank you."

"No need to thank me." He gave me one more kiss before stepping back. "You better get back to your party."

"See you tomorrow."

He gave me a wicked grin and turned toward his car. I took

a few minutes to enjoy the view. After he drove off, I sent Wallie a text.

House has a buyer. You need to come with me to meet them next weekend.

His reply was instant. **Sure meet you there?**

Yep.

Another chapter in my life was about to end. When I looked at my new family, the coven I was rebuilding, and the new beau in my life, I knew everything was going to be okay.

Clay would be proud of me.

A GIRLFRIEND FOR MR. SNOOZERTON

WITCHING AFTER FORTY BOOK 5

CHAPTER ONE

E very time I looked at it, I saw something different. The first time I thought it was demons in a multi-colored ink cloud, screaming as they tried to escape and take over the world. Now that I looked at it closer, I saw puppies and wild-flowers.

I wondered if it was enchanted.

Fear made me somewhat cautious of the thing. If it was enchanted, what would my magic do to it? Especially since my magic was going through some kind of tantrum at the moment. Like a two-year-old who wanted something but when they got the thing, they screamed that they didn't want it.

I was so glad I didn't have to go through that anymore. Wallie had been the worst at wishy-washy tantrums.

Placing the abstract painting on the wall over the fireplace, I looked at Larry with my eyebrows up. "Better?"

It was the millionth time I'd moved the weird piece of art today. Larry wasn't happy with it in the hallway, where I didn't have to see it.

Hey, I tried.

The skeleton nodded once, and as usual, my throat clenched for a split second while he moved. *Please stay on.* I breathed a short sigh of relief when his head didn't fall off of his neckbones.

Don't judge me. My fear was warranted. It had fallen off more times than I could count on one hand. I'd tried to stop counting altogether, but it was seven.

At this point, it was too comical, and I wasn't quite as horrified as I had been the first time it happened.

"Thanks, Ava," Larry said, seeming to be happy with the painting's new home. Finally.

He'd become a part of the family since showing up on my doorstep Valentine's Day morning. Without realizing it, I had raised him from his grave days before while training with Owen, my friend, and necromancer mentor. Larry was sure I could find his killer and wouldn't leave until the mystery was solved.

I, with the help of my growing group of extended family, had found Larry's killer, who had also turned out to be killing local witches with a nasty curse. My mom had been one of those murdered by the coven member, Bevan Magnus.

He and his sister, Penny Combs, had also run an illegal shifter fighting ring. We'd put a stop to that as well. Then Luci —Lucifer. Yes, *the* Lucifer—teleported them to Hell for their sins.

The fall-out of the whole ordeal had put me in charge of the coven. Yep, little ol' me—half necromancer, half witch, was now the High Witch of the Shipton Harbor Coven. Yay me!

In the end, Larry had decided to stay with us. I liked having him around, even if he was a walking, talking skeleton with no eyes but seemed to see just fine.

Another mystery that I wasn't about to attempt to figure out. Some things were better off not being solved.

"I think it's perfect there."

"Yeah, perfect," I said absently as I returned to the kitchen and smiled at Zoey, the tiger that I'd somewhat adopted. She wasn't a tiger, exactly.

She was a tiger shifter whom I'd accidentally raised from the dead when we'd returned all the poor shifter kids to their families after discovering the location of the fighting ring. For some reason that I hadn't yet figured out, Zoey was more like Snooze than Alfred. Snoozer was a ghoul, but he was more alive and looked completely normal, like other cats. Alfred— also a ghoul—had a more undead, zombified look. Then again, I hadn't raised Alfred as a ghoul myself. A family friend had and then I'd inherited him when Bill Combs was killed by a crazy witch hunter with a vendetta against necromancers.

Maybe that was the difference. My magic was supposedly more powerful than any necromancer alive. Owen reminded me of that often. I didn't understand any of it, mostly because I had refused to learn that side of myself and lived as a low-grade witchy human all my adult life.

The other difference between Zoey and Alfred was Zoey was also a shifter and only eighteen. The latter broke my heart. She'd been forced to fight her own kind and had died in the process. *Way* too young.

So, I didn't feel bad that Bevan and Penny were spending eternity in Hell.

Meeting Zoey's gaze, which was her tiger's golden eyes, I grinned. "You ready to practice?"

Zoey nodded eagerly, her little, pointy tiger ear twitching on top of her head. Only one ear this time, so that was an improvement. I hoped.

Something about the spell I'd performed to raise her, and the other shifter kids had enabled her to still shift from human to tiger—ghoul, technically—but she had the hardest time fully shifting *back*.

"Okay, let's hit the backyard." I opened the door to the

patio and smiled at her as she walked past with her long, thick tiger tail swinging back and forth out of the bottom of her skirt.

She pretty much had to wear all skirts now. Unless we could get her used to shifting fully back, her tail was very uncomfortable in pants. She never knew when it would suddenly appear. Poor thing couldn't go out in public without me or an illusion charm.

Owen and I had worked on a dress for her. It had a charm that meant it hung neatly in her closet when she was a tiger, but if any part of her was human, it appeared and covered her while hiding the non-human parts.

It hadn't been easy. But Owen had gotten the spell from the local shifters.

We had a liaison to the shifters, a ferret shifter couple. We'd saved Rick and Dana's son from the same ring of animal fighters Zoey had been in and the couple had been friends ever since. Even though it'd only been a couple of weeks, they were happy to be the bridge between the witches and the shifters.

Apparently, spells like the one we got from the shifters had been around for a long time. The problem with getting it to work was to find a witch willing to perform it. Witches and shifters hadn't always gotten along. Hence the liaison.

And it was a good thing I was the High Witch—leader—of the local coven. A title I was still getting used to, along with the extra magic running in my veins.

My fellow witches had each taken a garment of clothing to work on the spell, which was incredibly difficult. The potion had to be brewed just so, then the garments sometimes just disappeared after they were dipped. We had no idea where they'd gone, but they weren't here, being useful to us or the shifters.

"Okay. Let's focus on your ear." We sat in the middle of the yard in the bright, early March sunshine, which was deceptive. From indoors, the ocean view past my backyard made it look like it was warm enough to run down to the beach and have a swim.

It was *not*. I put a bubble of magic around us, warming the air in our vicinity so we'd be comfortable.

Zoey bobbed her head and closed her eyes, which would not shift back to human no matter what we tried. She suspected they'd been shifted when she'd died and also when I brought her back to life because she'd used her tiger's sight to fight in the fighting ring. She said it wasn't uncommon for them to half shift to get an advantage.

The thought of her and the other children being put through that made me want to go to Hell and join in on Bevan and Penny's punishment.

But that wasn't who I was.

Not most days, anyway.

Besides, I could easily hide Zoey's tiger eyes with a glamour spell.

"Breathe," I whispered. I'd spoken to Dana, our shifter liaison, about Zoey's inability to fully shift to human. She'd given me some pointers but seemed as baffled as I was. Then again, Dana admittedly knew nothing about necromancer magic. That made two of us.

Magic was a fickle, mischievous friend. Especially mine.

"Now, envision yourself without the ear," I said in a soothing, calm voice. "See yourself as fully human."

Zoey's breathing slowed, and I felt her shifter magic flow around her. She swayed slightly, her face looking calm and worry-free. At peace. I hoped I could keep her that way as long as possible. She didn't have parents or family to speak of.

Well, she did now. Me and mine.

In the very short time of having her with me, I was beginning to think of her as a daughter I never had.

Without warning, she flung her eyes open and gasped. The gold in her irises glowed and she jumped to her feet as her lower body shifted into the back end of a tiger, throwing her top half to the ground so she was forced to use her human arms and hands to hold her upper body upright. Well, crap on a cracker.

Larry's snicker from the back porch drew my attention as I fought not to laugh at the comical sight of poor Zoey half-shifted. It wasn't funny, not really, but yet... it was.

Larry bent over as he laughed, shoulders shaking, one hand on Alfred, my ghoul and the first of my adopted mystical family, who didn't look amused at all. Alfred glared at Larry as the skeleton's head began to topple. As Larry righted himself, his head disconnected, bounced on the wooden deck, and rolled straight to the stairs.

A giggle escaped me, and I threw my hand over my mouth.

Larry dropped to his knees as Zoey turned her half-tiger body around to look in time to see the skull bounce down the four stairs and land in the grass a few feet away from us.

Zoey burst out laughing and rolled onto her back, back feet waving, as Alfred sighed, long-suffering and irritated at Larry.

I didn't know where to look or who to laugh at, honestly. Zoey, rolling around on her back with two muscular back legs tipped in razor-sharp claws and two human arms wrapped around her stomach.

At least her charmed dress had stayed on. That was progress, right?

Larry moved along the grass on his bony hands and knees, feeling his way around, looking for his head.

Alfred edged past him and picked up the skull, holding it in his hand in front of his face. He glared at Larry's face...facial bones...and grunted several times. As if scolding the skeleton for his shenanigans.

The skull in Alfred's hands sighed. "I know, Alfie, I know. I should be more careful."

Larry's body grabbed Alfred's pants and used them to help

him stand up so Alfred could settle the skull back on the neck bones.

"Well," I whispered. "This isn't going well."

The dynamic duo had left the back door open, which was fine. My fat, immortal Maine Coone cat, Mr. Snoozerton, was allowed to come and go as he pleased. He wandered out to see what all the commotion was about, but then spied Zoey's tail twitching on the grass. His eyes zeroed in on that tail and he crouched low on the deck, butt wiggling.

It was more temptation than he could resist. And this wasn't going to end well.

Before I could tell him it wasn't a good idea, Snoozer took a flying leap off of the deck and landed squarely on the middle of Zoey's twitching tail.

Zoey shifted to a full tiger with a ferocious roar. Snooze took the time she shifted to streak around the front of the house.

As Zoey took off in pursuit, I jumped to my feet. "Stay to the safe places!" I yelled at the top of my lungs, hoping they heard me. I knew Zoey's tiger wouldn't hurt Snooze. Those two had become close and played like this all the time.

Part of the yard and a huge chunk of the forest had a ward over it. Humans would be repelled by it. Suddenly, they'd find themselves heading back home with no idea why they'd decided it was a good idea to alter their course.

That gave my menagerie the freedom to wander outside the house without humans seeing them.

Back inside the house, I went to my office where I'd left my cell phone. Picking it up, I scrolled through the notifications. Olivia had texted me a few times with pictures of Sammie feeding a goat. His kindergarten class had gone to a petting zoo for a field trip and Olivia went along as a chaperone.

Smiling at the cutie pie, I sent Olivia a text. **Watch out, Mama. He'll want to bring one home.**

Olivia: **Ha! Not happening. Unless he keeps it over at your house.**

I snorted and replied, **Not happening. My zoo is full at the moment.**

Olivia: **LOL. True**

Though, it might be good for lawn care... But no.

I closed the messaging app and dialed Uncle Wade's number. He wasn't my blood uncle. He was Clay's, my deceased husband. Wade had claimed me as family when he first met me, many years ago. I was grateful because Clay's parents hadn't cared for me much. It was because I was a witch, totally evil in their eyes. I hadn't dared to let them know I was also a necromancer.

Wade knew all my dark secrets and loved me anyway.

"Hey, sweetie," he answered on the second ring.

"Hi, Wade. How are things there?"

I heard a rustling sound before he answered. "Good. I went over to the house today and dropped off some boxes, tape, and bubble wrap, and also turned on the air so it won't be so musty in there. Will you need help packing?"

"Thanks and no, Wallie and Zoey will be with me."

"Who's Zoey?" I laughed, forgetting I hadn't had time to sit down and tell Wade all about my new crazy and adventurous life. I gave him the short story, ending with how Zoey became my new daughter. Because that was what I was calling her from now on, my daughter. "It's been a wild ride for sure."

"I'd say," he said with a chuckle.

I sighed and thought about what we'd have to do in Pennsylvania. Wade had been an enormous help getting the house sold. "Was the buyer okay with moving the meet and greet out another week? What's her name again?"

He paused for a few moments. "Haley Whitfield. She's a nurse relocating. Nice woman. It was a quick sale because she is best friends with the neighbor on the right."

"Then why does she need to meet with me?" I knew the neighbor he was talking about. Kendra was also a witch and a good person. Plus, she was the only neighbor I had ever talked to much. The house across the street seemed to have a new tenant all the time, so I'd never gotten close to anyone. My other neighbor had been an elderly couple who had always seemed to be on vacation most of the year. Florida, usually.

Besides, I'd stayed to myself. I'd been busy with writing and being a wife and a mother. And I'd loved every minute of it.

"She just wants to talk with you about the house and neighborhood, I guess. The realtor said it would be good. I didn't ask." Wade paused then said, "If you want, I can show her around or have the realtor do it."

"No, I have to pack up the house anyway." And I needed to say my final goodbye to Clay and my life in Philly. It was time to move on.

Technically, the house was in Chestnut Hill, a suburb of Philly, but it was easier to say the name of the closest big city. "So, I'll see you next week."

"Yep. What time will you get in on Wednesday?"

"Late afternoon. At least that's what I'm aiming for. It all depends on how many times I have to go to the bathroom." I laughed. It seemed the older I got the more visits to the loo I made.

"See you when you get here."

"Thanks, Wade." I paused. "For everything." He had no idea how much I appreciated him.

"Anything for you, dear."

I hung up the phone and sat at my desk. Staring at my closed laptop, I sighed while my chest tightened. Selling the house hadn't been on my priority list. I wasn't expecting it to sell so quickly, which meant I'd have to say goodbye.

It was time to close that chapter in my life, but not forget it.

Never forget my Clay.

CHAPTER TWO

That damn doorbell. Groaning, I rolled over in bed and threw my pillow off of my head. Why did she have to come over so dang early? "Someone let Olivia in!" I screeched, hoping any member of my family would hear me so I wouldn't have to get out of bed.

My house, aka Winston, wouldn't let me sleep too late anymore. The doorbell dinged again, and Winston echoed the sound, much louder than it needed to be, through the upstairs. Ugh.

Olivia was always showing up here at the ass crack of dawn. I forgave her because she was my best friend and because she usually brought something yummy like donuts. But why was she using the doorbell? She usually just walked in, which was okay with me. Especially this early in the morning.

"Hello?" My son's voice carried up the stairs. "Mom?"

"Wallie!" I cried as I rolled out of bed and fell straight onto the floor. When I stood, the sheet wrapped around my foot, making me fall again with a big thump. After cursing the kitty pawprint cotton sheets that apparently didn't want me out of bed any more than I did, I finally unwrapped my foot and stood.

My son was waiting on me. I hadn't known he was coming home this weekend. Throwing on my robe, I hurried toward the stairs as Alfred and Owen poked sleepy heads out of their bedrooms. "Wallie's home," I cried as I passed by.

Hurrying downstairs, I stepped over a big pillowcase full of his dirty laundry—no surprise there, he was a college student, after all—and held open my arms for my taller-than-me son to give me a big hug. "What are you doing here?"

"Michelle has a big test Monday, but I already took mine. She says I distract her from studying, so I thought I'd come down a few days early." That explained why he'd come without his sweet little girlfriend. Wallie squeezed my shoulders before heading toward the kitchen. "Anything to eat? I'm starving."

I snorted. Of course, he was starving. College student and still a growing boy. At least he would be still growing for another year or so.

"What made you drive in so early?" I asked as I shuffled after him, eyeing the clock on the wall that said eight in the morning. That was too early to be coherent.

"Couldn't sleep. I've been up all night." He opened the fridge and began rustling around. "Good old Alfred," he said as he pulled out a plate full of fried chicken. "He's like a grannie."

I sighed and lamented the two extra hours I could've slept, then helped him unload the leftovers from last night's dinner and heat them up for breakfast. "He is. It's crazy."

Zoey wandered downstairs as we pulled the chicken out of the microwave, yawning. "Morning."

She stopped short and stared at Wallie. They'd only been around each other a couple of times. But as a predatory shifter, Zoey would be leery of new people in her space. At least until she got used to them or considered them nonthreatening.

"Hi," Wallie said and held out the plate of chicken. "Hungry?"

Zoey nodded mutely and her ears popped up on top of her head. Wallie grinned. "Cool." He grabbed the bowl of potato salad and went to the table as Zoey's cheeks reddened. And just like that, she accepted the new person—even though they had met before.

"Thanks." She fingered the tip of one ear and nibbled the chicken.

As I walked to the table, I pointed to his bag of laundry still in the middle of the foyer. "Wallie, you know where the washing machine is." He nodded and moved to the stairs.

I loved the kid, but I wasn't doing his nasty laundry for him. "Good, I'm going to go shower." I took my time and did my full skincare routine, which, thanks to online videos, had never been fancier. Self-care was important. Just as I finished dressing, I heard Olivia's voice.

She usually came over on the weekends... or any day, really. Her son loved playing with my house full of creatures.

Sure enough, as I walked down the stairs, little Sammie streaked by, screaming at the top of his lungs, with a giant tiger hot on his tail. "Outside!" I yelled. We'd learned the hard way that Zoey inside shifted as a tiger equaled broken, well, everything.

Wallie was still munching on chicken at the kitchen table, but Alfred had come down and begun cooking more, his favorite pastime. A big pink box on the table caught my eye. "Yum," I said in way of greeting Olivia. "Sam here?"

"No, he's doing some firearms training with a recruit." She handed me a napkin as I took a bite of the big, chocolate donut from the pink box. "He'll be here later."

"Cool." I sank into the seat across from her. I wanted to know if Drew would be coming over, but I wasn't comfortable with the whole girlfriend thing yet. Plus, I didn't want to sound needy. But hey, the sheriff was hot, and I liked having him around.

Sammie ran in the back door off the kitchen. "Where's Snoozer? I can't find him."

"I'm sure he's around here somewhere," Wallie said, then stood. "Come on, I'll help you look. He likes to hide in the attic."

"Make sure the house didn't trap him in the floorboards again," Olivia called as her son dragged mine up the stairs. Sammie was more comfortable in this house than Wallie at this point.

"Gods, I hope not," I muttered. It had taken everything we had to get Snooze out of the attic floor. That was when we'd found an old hand mirror that had my Yaya inside it. Not really her, but an imprint of her. A spell used for giving loved ones messages or enabling them to say goodbye after they passed away.

I wasn't sure how much time Yaya's imprint had left. Wallie and I talked to her for a long time last weekend before he went back to school.

"When do you leave?" Olivia plucked a donut out of the box.

I shrugged, thinking of the trip to Pennsylvania. "Wednesday, bright and early."

She snickered. "Bright and early means any time before noon to you."

I sniffed defensively. "Because it is."

We laughed, then fell silent. I stared out the window, watching the waves crash in the distance.

"You really don't have to do it alone," she said. "I can come."

"No, I want you here in case anything crazy happens. Owen is staying but this house is nuts."

She snorted. "This house doesn't like me being here alone. Drew's birthday party?"

It was my turn to snort. "Winston had better behave himself."

If I'd thought for one moment that the crazy house would've given Olivia a bunch of crap for being in my house without me, I would've had Sam keep Drew busy while the house was being prepared for Drew's surprise birthday party.

Winston had made sure to make it difficult for Olivia, that was for sure. He'd locked down the cabinets, broke the eggs, but before all that, wouldn't let her inside at all. I had a good talking to him, not that it did any good. The house had a mind of his own.

Times like that made me wish Yaya was still here. Winston had always behaved when she was around.

A few minutes later, as Alfred put a big platter of sandwiches on the table, Wallie and Sammie returned. "Still no Snoozer." Wallie shrugged. "He wasn't in his usual spots."

"Hmm." I stood and grabbed his treats out of the cabinet where we kept his food. "This is a surefire way to get him to come." I shook the treat bag and waited for the thumps of the big cat jumping off of one bed or another.

But none came. "Okay, let me do a locator spell," I said. "Where is Zoey?" It was silly to do one. He disappeared all the time. But Sammie looked so worried. So I'd play along. I mean, the cat was immortal. He couldn't die unless I did. And I had no plans of leaving this earth any time soon.

"Right here," Zoey called. "And I couldn't find him either. My nose isn't as powerful as it used to be, plus, Snoozer doesn't really have a scent." She walked into the room. "Neither does Alfred, so it must be a ghoul thing."

She was right. It was something I hadn't thought of before. Alfred looked undead and one would think he had an odor. But he didn't. Thankfully.

473

"Hand me one of his toys." I held out my hand and Sammie climbed under the kitchen table to grab it. He came back with a little stuffed bag of catnip that looked like a bag of seeds. "He loves this one," Sammie said.

I smiled at the sweet boy. "It came from that monthly subscription box you got him."

I was paying for the subscription box, but it was Sammie's idea, so I gave him credit for getting it for the nutty, fat cat.

Sam and Drew walked in just as I gripped the toy and started to focus on finding Snooze. Just before I spoke the incantation, they grabbed sandwiches and smiled at me. I gave them a nod in greeting and carried on. They could help us look once the spell found him. "*Quaerere dominum.*"

Nothing happened. "Odd," I said. "For it to not work, he has to be somewhere enchanted."

Olivia met my gaze and we spoke at the same time in matching flat voices. "Luci's."

"You two can go fetch him alone," Drew said with a grimace. "Luci gives me a stomachache."

I held in my smile as I crossed the room to him, then kissed him on the cheek. Drew was a born witch hunter, meaning he had low-level magic that gave him the ability to see the paranormal for who they were. It was more of a knowing when he was around a shifter or a witch or whatever else was out there. He'd told me that being around Luci, aka Lucifer Morningstar, aka Satan, aka King of Hell, aka...you get the picture. Anyway, Drew said his senses went haywire when Luci was around, and he preferred to avoid the devil if he could.

It was similar when I was holding coven meetings at the house. He said it was too many witches in one place, too much magic. It made his skin crawl. He couldn't help his lineage any more than I could. At least he wasn't still a witch hunter by trade.

"Me, too," Sam chimed in as he picked up another sandwich from the dining table then crammed it into his mouth. After chewing and swallowing, he added, "We'll start looking outside, walk around a bit. It won't hurt any of us to go for a walk, anyway."

I snickered and looked at Olivia, who rolled her eyes. "Let's get this over with."

CHAPTER THREE

Sucking in a deep breath, I pressed the doorbell beside Lucifer's front door. The enormous house was imposing, and I still wasn't sure it was even truly here on this plane. There was a weird ward around it that I couldn't figure out if it was there to keep people out or bring them into the devil's trap. Knowing Luci, it could go either way depending on his mood.

When I'd accidentally summoned the devil instead of Santa, he had enjoyed himself so much that he'd decided to stay awhile. And wham-bam, the house had appeared.

Before Christmas, the house hadn't been here at all. There was only an empty field where the gargantuan home now stood. The field, I believed, was part of my property, or at least partly so. I didn't have time to deal with it. Hopefully one day I'd find the spell or curse to send Luci back to where he came from. H-E-double hockey sticks.

The doorbell chimed with a long, intricate melody. "Is that Chopin?" Olivia whispered.

I shrugged. "I don't know but leave it to Luci to have such an ostentatious doorbell."

We giggled as the door opened mysteriously. Seriously, it opened on its own. It seemed Luci's magical house was well trained. Unlike Winston. How did one train a magical house to behave? I'd have to ask the devil for some pointers.

"Have you ever been here before?" Olivia asked.

I shook my head. "No, but I've been insanely curious."

She nodded eagerly. "Hello?" Olivia called into the massive foyer as we stepped inside. We shuffled forward together as we took in the décor. She lowered her voice. "It looks like the freaking Queen's palace."

The foyer was a mix of modern elegance and gothic romance. The black and white marble floor shone like glass. To the right, a huge spiral staircase had black metal railings that looked like a giant snake. The head of the serpent was at the bottom and its blue sapphire eyes appeared to be cracked.

To our left, a large open great room held antique furniture made from dark stained wood. The sofa was a deep red with ribbons of gold. The two armchairs on either side matched, as did the curtains.

"Luci?" I called, cringing when my voice carried through the house louder than I intended.

"Ladies." His voice came from above. I lifted my gaze to find him standing at the top of the stairs in a velvet dressing gown, tied at the waist, like some sort of playboy. "Please, come in." He descended the stairs in slippers that were probably more expensive than my whole house, Winston and all. "To what do I owe the pleasure?"

Olivia, who'd had far less exposure to Luci than I had, clutched my elbow. She trembled as she moved closer to me. By the smirk on Luci's face, he also sensed Olivia's uneasiness in his presence.

"We're looking for Snoozer," I said, drawing his attention to me. "We can't find him, and the locator spell didn't work."

Luci sucked in a deep breath and nodded. "Of course. He's

on magical land. I have caught that curious kitty in here many times. I've taken to leaving out a few treats for him." No surprise. Everyone loved Snoozles.

Luci spread his arms. "Well, ladies, I have a prior engagement, but you're welcome to peek into any part of my home. I have no secrets from the two most beautiful women in Shipton Harbor."

I couldn't help but blush a little as his eyes raked over me. I wasn't in the best shape of my life and had a few too many curves, but he looked at me as though he loved nothing more than curves. The compliment seemed to release Olivia from her nervous stupor. "Where are you—"

But with a wink, Luci disappeared.

"Maybe he's got a hot date with Carrie," Olivia said.

Carrie was our friend and Sammie's kindergarten teacher. She and Luci had been seeing each other ever since I'd summoned him in December. I checked in with her on occasion to make sure she was okay. But come to find out, she was part fae and knew exactly who and what Luci was. She said she'd have fun for however long it lasted. After all, we weren't getting any younger. Might as well join life.

I was all for that motto.

"Well, he said we're welcome to explore." I still spoke in a whisper, though I had no idea why. "I wonder if he has anyone here. Like a staff."

Olivia giggled. "Like on that TV show about the castle in England. Uptown Abbey or something."

I sniffed through my nose and held out my hand as if waiting for someone to kiss my ring. "Quite."

We wandered through the house, calling Snoozer's name. Though it was large and grand, it wasn't anything unusual. A den, formal living room, kitchen, dining room.

We ended up back in the foyer. "Upstairs or down?" I asked.

"I think downstairs will be more entertaining," she said with a mischievous look in her eyes.

"Let's go."

She was not wrong. The bottom of the stairs opened on a long hallway with doors lined down either side. "Are we underground?" I peered into the first room. It had no windows and was full of wrapping paper and ribbons. He actually had a gift-wrapping room. Wow.

"Looks like it. How far does this place go?" she squeaked. The hallway curved and ran out of sight.

We began peeking into rooms and calling Snoozer's name. Where the heck had that crazy fat cat gone?

"Ava," Olivia hissed. She'd gone about three doors down. "Look at this."

I followed her into the room and switched on the light. The entire room, which was easily as big as my bedroom, was full of jewelry. In glass cases, on little stands, busts, and hanging from the walls with elegant hangers. By the look of it, he had a collection of every type of gemstone on earth. There were a few I didn't recognize and wasn't even sure if they were from this realm. Most likely not. Given he was Lucifer and all.

"Think he'd notice if we took something?" she asked.

"Of course," I said with a laugh. "But I reckon he wouldn't mind us trying on a few things?"

Olivia's eyes lit up. "The tiara!" She squealed and headed for a sleek, black mannequin head. On it sat a tiara full of emeralds.

One wall was full of mirrors, and the lighting made the room bright and cheery. "Why else would he have mirrors if he didn't want things tried on?" she asked.

I carefully pulled a necklace full of the biggest diamonds I'd ever seen in real life off of a bust. "I know we keep comparing this place to the Queen of England, but seriously. I don't think even she has diamonds this big."

Olivia came over and took the necklace. "Here, let me." She clasped it around my neck, then we found a necklace, bracelet, and earring set that matched her tiara. I helped her get them on before picking out a diamond bracelet of my own.

Then, a diadem caught my eye. "Olivia," I breathed. It had a diamond in the center that was easily the size of a small lemon. Instead of being rigid, it was held together by a strand of diamonds that went around the circumference and diameter of the circle. When I nestled it on my head, the diamonds circled my head and went right down my center part, with the gigantic diamond taking up most of my forehead.

"It's so big it's not even attractive," Olivia said. We dissolved into giggles and danced around with one another, pretending to waltz in our fancy jewels.

After a few minutes, I sighed and gingerly took off the diadem, then we helped each other unclasp everything and replace it just so.

"Well, that was fun," she muttered as we left the jewelry room. "Worth the trip even if we don't find anything else."

"Agreed." We peeked into the next room, forgetting to even call for Snoozer as we stared at the contents. "Why?" I asked.

Olivia shrugged. "Have you ever seen him wearing makeup?"

I shook my head and looked at the labels. "This is some expensive crap."

As we looked closer, the room was organized with makeup and cosmetics from across the ages, perfectly preserved, though I couldn't see how. I didn't sense any preservation magic. Silver pots and soft brushes lined tables all around the room.

"Come on," I said after we'd had a good look. "Let's keep looking for Snooze."

We called for him a few more times and continued to the next door. The room was full of umbrellas. Open, closed, suspended from the ceiling. Umbrella after umbrella. "Snooze?" I called into the quiet room.

Olivia pulled back. "We'll leave the door open and keep on?"

After checking a few more rooms with more oddities like chessboard after chessboard, all set up to play, then a room full of spoon rests and... "Are those deviled egg plates?" I asked.

Olivia burst out laughing as we walked in and peered closer. "I gotta admit, the devil collecting deviled egg plates is pretty classic," she said as her phone chimed. She pulled it out of her back pocket. "Oh, I've got a text from Sam. They found that darn cat."

I was a bit reluctant to leave the exploration. We hadn't even gotten to the upstairs. "I suppose we should go."

Olivia giggled. "Yeah, but this was fun. Maybe we should lose him again so we can explore more."

"Or think of another excuse to come over." I sighed as I had an idea. "We could always break in. Have Carrie get him to leave the house."

"He would know. I bet he has the place magically rigged to let him know when intruders came in." Olivia frowned.

I frowned back at her. "He was probably watching us."

She shuddered. "We should go see what Snooze is up to."

CHAPTER FOUR

We hurried across the large expanse of yard separating my lawn from Luci's. Technically, it was all mine. I owned the land under Luci's house. Maybe I'd charge him rent. Yep, I was totally going to tell him the next time I saw him that he owed me rent.

When we reached my house, I spotted Snoozer in the front yard, circling the rest of the people and creatures that belonged with us. As soon as he realized I was heading toward them, he took off running in my direction, followed by Owen, who had been working a shift at the bookstore all day, then Zoey and Wallie, with Zoey constantly flitting little glances Wallie's way. I wasn't sure what that was all about. Then again, Zoey hadn't been around others her age. Alfred and Larry came next, both well within the boundaries of the ward we'd put up. Sammie and Sam brought up the rear.

"What's going on?" I asked. "Why is everyone out here if you found him?"

Snoozer yowled loudly and turned in a circle. What was wrong with him?

Wallie pointed to the crazy cat. "Because he's acting like that."

The big feline walked a few feet away, toward the big forest where I liked to practice my magic behind Luci's house. He yowled again as if he wanted us to follow.

As a group, we did just that. What an entourage. It was becoming ridiculous, yet I loved every moment of having my family around me. Even Larry had grown on me, becoming a part of my family, loose skull and all.

"Do you want us to follow you?" I asked.

Snoozer cried out again and went forward another few feet.

"I guess so," I muttered.

Sam moved around the crowd to walk beside me. "Drew had to go help with a call," he said. "He asked me to tell you goodbye."

"Thanks," I muttered as we followed my nutty cat.

"I told him I wouldn't kiss you for him, though, but Larry said he'd be happy to." Sam wiggled his eyebrows at me.

"Hey," Larry said. "I did not."

We all laughed until Snoozer stopped and turned to glare at us. "Whoa," Sam whispered. "He means business. I've never seen him so pissy."

"I have," I muttered. "He's a cranky ass."

Snooze growled low in his throat before turning and hurrying into the trees. He was in an extra cranky mood today. He really did mean business.

"Now, *that* I've never heard him do." He'd never growled at me a day in his long life.

Snooze stopped one more time and made a sound that I would've sworn was, "Help!"

We quieted down and followed him through the trees until we came to the clearing where I liked to go to draw dead things to me and practice my powers. In the middle of the clearing a small, white animal laid motionless. Snooze sprinted toward it, and we all hurried forward.

It was a cat, and from the looks of her, she'd been hit by a car or something equally traumatic. "Oh, no," I whispered. She was definitely dead. "Snoozer, is this a friend of yours?"

Snooze nudged her with his head and meowed. This time it sounded like he said, "Mine."

When did this cat learn to talk? I had no idea. We were all in trouble if his vocabulary increased any more.

"Snooze, do you want me to bring her back?" I asked and looked at Owen for his input.

He shrugged. "She doesn't look like she's been dead that long."

I nodded. "Yeah, but we've never even seen this cat before. Why does he want her?"

Snooze ran over to Alfred and stood up on his hind legs to claw at Alfred's leg, then yowled at the ghoul.

Alfie grunted back at Snooze. I knew those two seemed to have an understanding, but it looked like they were holding a full-blown conversation.

"Alfred says that Snooze is in love with the lady cat," Larry said.

We all swung our gaze to the skeleton. "What?" I gasped.

"I've become quite adept at translating Alfred's grunts." Larry's teeth clacked together a little as he spoke, his voice magically coming from vocal cords that were no longer there. "And he understands the cat. Snooze wants you to bring his girlfriend back."

Blinking rapidly, I processed this new development in my life, the fact that my cat talked to my ghoul, who was translated by my skeleton. "Why doesn't Alfred just take the string out of his mouth and tell me himself?" I asked, eyeing the ghoul. I was beginning to think he had secrets that he was keeping from me.

I wanted to know what. Especially if it was something like he'd been a serial killer when he was alive.

Alfred glared at me with angry, milky eyes.

I threw up my hands. "Fine."

Turning to the solid-white cat, I focused my power on her and easily raised her from the dead, healing her along the way so that by the time she woke and blinked her big blue eyes at us, her wounds were gone.

Snooze ran from Alfred over to the cat and purred so loud I heard him from several feet away.

"How did you do that?" Owen asked.

"Do what?" I asked.

"You healed her injuries." He pointed at the cat, which was grooming one paw as Snooze licked the back of her head. "That's not supposed to be possible."

I shrugged. "No idea, but I think it's going to rain." I squinted up at the clouds. "Let's get back."

I didn't want to answer a bunch of questions at the moment...or ever. It wasn't that I hadn't thought about it often. Although I was sure it had something to do with being able to make my own cat immortal and how Zoey was more alive than undead. I'd animated a skeleton who remembered who he was and his whole life before he died. That wasn't supposed to happen either.

I was starting to believe the rumors that I was the most powerful necromancer alive. Or maybe that was in history. The legend changed each time I heard it.

And it didn't fail my notice on how easy it was to raise the pretty white kitty and heal her at the same time. Like my magic was stronger.

How much? I wasn't sure.

Only time would tell.

CHAPTER FIVE

We headed back for the house. Owen walked beside me as we brought up the rear. "Healing and raising is a myth," he said.

"Obviously not. I just did it." I'd done it the day I healed Snoozer when he was a kitten. At the time I hadn't realized what I'd done. Now it was starting to seem that I had the ability to *actually* bring back the dead.

Snoozer yowled at Alfred, who grunted, then Larry turned. "Snoozer wants to know if she's like him, immortal."

I gasped dramatically. "So, then, he *is* immortal." We'd never known for sure if he would live forever or if I'd just given him a long life when I'd healed him as a child. We'd only supposed.

Larry shrugged one shoulder. "He thinks he is."

"I think it's much more likely he'll die when you do," Owen said. "I think you're connecting some part of your life force to the creatures you animate. That's how most ghouls work."

"So, why didn't Alfred die when William died?" I asked.

Owen stomped over a stray stick. "I'm not sure. But usually, there's enough magic in them that it has to wear off over time. Maybe when you accepted him as yours, it linked him as well. It's hard to tell. They'll die within days of you." We stepped over a log and exited the trees.

"Makes sense." Sort of. Then again, nothing in my midlife obeyed the laws of nature.

"The legends say that the necromancers of old could heal a body to the point it was at when it died before it was injured. And there were rumored to be a very few who could do better than that, healing the body to better than it had been while alive."

He pointed to Snoozer. "I think you might be one of those rare, mythical necromancers."

I leaned closer to Owen. "This is the same way I brought Zoey back. Does that mean if I die, so does she?"

He nodded. "Yes, within a few days. Unless you find another necromancer to take over her life force the way Alfred did you."

"Would you do it?" I asked as we neared my porch.

He nodded. "Yes, of course, but I've never heard of someone having this many strings. It's got to be a strain on your magic."

I shrugged. "I don't know. I feel fine."

In fact, I'd never felt better. It was like the more I raised—tying them to me-—the more powerful I felt.

"Could you do this to me?" Larry asked as we entered the living room.

I stopped and stared at him. Could I? He was nothing but bones. Yet, something in his makeup made him alive-ish. "I could try."

Zoey hadn't heard all of this conversation. At least she didn't seem to be paying attention. She and Sammie were chatting about a game or something. As soon as she went inside, she ran upstairs with the little boy. The rest of us went into the living room. "Alfred, do you want me to do that for you?" I asked.

Alfred shook his head rapidly and stepped back.

I rolled my eyes. "One of these days, Alfred. I'll have your secrets."

Focusing on Larry, I drew on the deep well of magic and focused it on him. I lifted my hands to him and tentatively, he placed his bony fingers in mine. And before my eyes, he changed. Muscles appeared and tendons. Internal organs. His head fleshed out, then skin covered the muscles. I kept pushing magic at him as eyes appeared in his sockets. He looked at his hands with his mouth wide open.

Then his features began forming. A chiseled jaw. His eyes took on color—brown. Hair sprouted from his head.

I'd been so engrossed on his head that I hadn't watched the rest of his body form.

Naked.

Zoey walked into the room. "Penis," she squeaked before whirling around.

Sam threw Larry a pillow off the couch, which Larry used to cover himself as the last of his body formed. "Wow," he whispered. "You can turn around, Zoey. I'm back to normal."

A handsome young man stood before us. "Larry?" I whispered.

He looked away from Zoey, who had turned to face him again with wide eyes, to me. "It's me." His voice was the same, but seeing his mouth actually move, and lips form words was completely wild. "Hey."

Alfred threw an apron at Larry. He covered himself and set the pillow back on the couch.

Olivia leaned toward me. "He's freaking gorgeous."

"I heard that," Sam said darkly.

Olivia snorted. "So? He is."

"Yeah," Zoey breathed.

I exchanged a glance with Olivia and Sam as Larry's gaze moved back to Zoey. They both looked like they'd been struck with cupid's arrow. "How old are you, Larry?" I asked.

It took him a second to answer. "Uh, I was nineteen when I died." He didn't look away from Zoey's face as he spoke.

Zoey sidestepped until she stood between the chairs Olivia and I sat in. She bent over to whisper in my ear while Olivia leaned close to listen. "I didn't know they could be that big," Zoey said in a very low, soft whisper.

That, nevertheless, was heard throughout the room.

Larry's face reddened. Alfred grunted at him. "Yes, right," Larry said. "I'm going to go find clothes." He backed out of the room, but when he turned to go up the stairs, we all got a good look at his firm rump. All the way up the stairs.

None of us knew what to say as we all looked at each other. Snooze and his little girlfriend had disappeared. Alfred grunted and walked out of the room.

"Well," I said. "That was..."

"Hot," Zoey said.

As we burst out laughing, the doorbell rang.

"Oh, what now?" I stood and went to the door.

When I opened it, two velvet jewelry boxes floated in midair in front of my face with a note.

I snatched them out of the air and hurried back into the living room to read it. "I would've noticed if you'd taken any. Please accept this reward for your honesty."

Olivia squealed and jumped up, scurrying over to me. I handed her one of the boxes with an enormous grin on my face. We opened them at the same time to find the necklaces we'd tried on. She held the one I'd had, and I had hers.

We switched and stared into the boxes at the massive jewels.

"Maybe Luci isn't quite so bad after all," she whispered.

Maybe, indeed.

Snooze and the little white kitty came back in as Olivia and I clasped the necklaces on each other and preened.

"Hey, sweetie," I crooned. She jumped into my lap and purred. "I wish I knew your name."

"She's got a tag," Olivia said.

"Oh, true." I pulled it closer and read. "Her name is Lucy-Fur."

Olivia snorted. "That's great. Luci will think we named her after him."

"I most certainly am not."

Olivia and I stared, slack-jawed, at Lucy-fur.

"Did she just speak?" Olivia whispered.

"I..."

"I did," Lucy said in a regal voice. "And I'd like to eat if you please. I'll be in the kitchen."

Snooze stared after the white cat as she walked smoothly from the room. He chuffed at us, then followed her.

"Well," Olivia said. "That puts us in our place."

MORE PARANORMAL WOMEN'S FICTION BY LIA DAVIS & L.A. BORUFF

Witching After Forty https://laboruff.com/books/witching-after-forty/

A Ghoulish Midlife

Cookies For Satan (A Christmas Story)

I'm With Cupid (A Valentine's Day Story)

A Cursed Midlife

Birthday Blunder

A Girlfriend For Mr. Snoozleton (A Girlfriend Story)

A Haunting Midlife

An Animated Midlife

A Killer Midlife

Faery Oddmother

A Grave Midlife

Shifting Into Midlife https://laboruff.com/books/shifting-into-midlife/

Pack Bunco Night

Prime Time of Life https://laboruff.com/books/primetime-of-life/

Borrowed Time

Stolen Time

Just in Time

Hidden Time

Nick of Time

Magical Midlife in Mystic Hollow https://laboruff.com/
books/mystic-hollow/

Karma's Spell

Karma's Shift

Karma's Spirit

Karma's Sense

Karma's Stake

An Unseen Midlife https://amzn.to/3cF3W54

Bloom in Blood

Dance in Night

Bask in Magic

Surrender in Dreams

Midlife Mage https://amzn.to/3oMFNH3

Unveiled

Unfettered

An Immortal Midlife https://amzn.to/3cC6BMP

Fatal Forty

Fighting Forty

Finishing Forty

ABOUT LIA DAVIS

Lia Davis is the USA Today bestselling author of more than forty books, including her fan favorite Shifter of Ashwood Falls Series.

A lifelong fan of magic, mystery, romance and adventure, Lia's novels feature compassionate alpha heroes and strong leading ladies, plenty of heat, and happily-ever-afters.

Lia makes her home in Northeast Florida where she battles hurricanes and humidity like one of her heroines.

When she's not writing, she loves to spend time with her family, travel, read, enjoy nature, and spoil her kitties.

She also loves to hear from her readers. Send her a note at lia@authorliadavis.com!

Follow Lia on Social Media

Website: http://www.authorliadavis.com/
Newsletter: http://www.subscribepage.com/authorliadavis.
newsletter
Facebook author fan page: https://www.facebook.com/
novelsbylia/
Facebook Fan Club: https://www.facebook.com/groups/
LiaDavisFanClub/
Twitter: https://twitter.com/novelsbylia

Instagram: https://www.instagram.com/authorliadavis/
BookBub: https://www.bookbub.com/authors/lia-davis
Pinterest: http://www.pinterest.com/liadavis35/
Goodreads: http://www.goodreads.com/author/show/
5829989.Lia_Davis

ABOUT L.A. BORUFF

L.A. (Lainie) Boruff lives in East Tennessee with her husband, three children, and an ever growing number of cats. She loves reading, watching TV, and procrastinating by browsing Facebook. L.A.'s passions include vampires, food, and listening to heavy metal music. She once won a Harry Potter trivia contest based on the books and lost one based on the movies. She has two bands on her bucket list that she still hasn't seen: AC/DC and Alice Cooper. Feel free to send tickets.

L.A.'s Facebook Group: https://www.facebook.com/groups/LABoruffCrew/
Follow L.A. on Bookbub if you like to know about new releases but don't like to be spammed: https://www.bookbub.com/profile/l-a-boruff

Made in the USA
Coppell, TX
20 September 2024

37529734R00282